FAIR FARE FROM FOUL FAITH

"You believe in the dragon, do you?" The Heinox head snarled.

The devotees turned on their knees to face him. "Oh, we do!"

"Then don't turn your backs on your god," the head that was Vicia said huffily. The entire group swiveled back toward him.

"One moment!" Heinox cried. "I'm also part of this dragon!"

The cultists were in a quandary. They huddled together. Then the priestess addressed the dragon, doing her best to make eye contact with both heads at once. "Lord, could both your heads stay on one side? I mean, Lord Dragon—"

"I am not your Lord!" Heinox snarled. "I'm not a god."

The worshipers reeled in disbelief. "Heresy! Heresy! The Divisionists must never know he's said this!"

"Your Divisionists won't hear of it," Heinox said. He was interrupted by amens and sighs of relief, but managed to finish: "Because I intend to eat all of you."

THE
Prophet
OF
Lamath

Robert Don Hughes

DEL REY

A Del Rey Book

BALLANTINE BOOKS • NEW YORK

A Del Rey Book
Published by Ballantine Books

Copyright © 1979 by Robert Don Hughes

Library of Congress Catalog Card Number: 79-63472

ISBN 0-345-28211-6

Manufactured in the United States of America

First Edition: October 1979

Cover art by Darrell K. Sweet

This was always Gail's book.

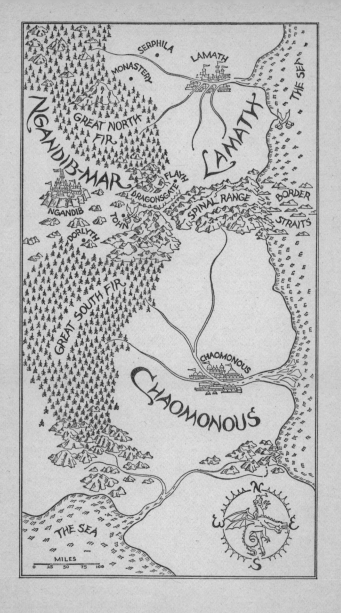

❧ Chapter One ❧

THERE WAS a saying in the land as old as the dust that stood ten inches deep in the back of his cavern, as old as the diamonds that he loved to toss from mouth to mouth. "Two heads are better than one," Vicia-Heinox would hear a passerby say, and he would nod with both of his in sage agreement, then eat the traveler whole. Vicia-Heinox was a two-headed dragon, the only one there had ever been—the only one which *has* ever been.

To say that Vicia-Heinox was the most powerful living creature anyone could remember is to understate the case. A one-headed dragon is a national emergency. A two-headed dragon, sitting astride the only truly usable pass on the north-south trade route, is a world problem. Vicia-Heinox was an environmental feature. He not only altered cultures, he was a factor in producing them. Three ancient nations feuded and skirmished around him, for he sat on the only frontier the three realms held in common. He had been actively involved in the history of each, and all held him in awe.

One could say that the dragon helped preserve the peace, for he refused to let armies march through his pass. On the other hand, one could say his presence constantly argued for war, for he strangled economic interchange between the giant powers. The only merchants he allowed to pass were very rich merchants. They had to be very rich, in order to pay his incredibly high toll in goods and slaves and still make a profit. They were also very wise merchants, who knew how to show honor and respect to the dragon who insured their financial well-being. No wisecracking merchant ever made his way through Dragonsgate. A misplaced remark about two heads, dropped thoughtlessly amid the

1

bargaining with the beast, had been the bane of many a
family fortune. Over a period of centuries this process
of unnatural selection resulted in a very small company
of sour, mean-tempered, closemouthed merchants controlling all of the interempire traffic.

This provided the primary cause of friction between
the nations. Everyone knew that it was the merchants
who controlled their economy. And because the merchants kept to themselves, each family holding a number
of private estates scattered through each one of the kingdoms, the people of every land viewed the merchant
families as foreigners. Because they hated merchants,
the public hated foreigners. Because they hated foreigners, they warred on their neighbors.

But Vicia-Heinox straddled Dragonsgate, and armies
couldn't march. The three lands waged no hot, quick
wars on sunny days, moving in colorful array across
great remembered battlefields. Instead, the three realms
wrestled in one slow, dark war, a night war, fought in
black and white. Skirmishes and raids replaced marches
and charges. Generals were made by intrigue, not ex-
cellence. Cruelty was valued over bravery. The great-
hearted leaders of memory had long since been replaced
by thieves. It was not a good world in which to live.

Except for Vicia-Heinox, who felt it couldn't be better. There were rulers of lands, but he ruled the rulers.
The merchants controlled the countryside, but he controlled the merchants. And he ate well.

Every week a caravan or two would labor up one of
the steep approaches to his pass. Some came up the
short, sharp northeastern defile, carrying farm goods,
rough textiles, and good sturdy tools from Lamath. Others toiled up the long, narrow southern route from
golden Chaomonous, patron of the arts. Finely crafted
luxury items and exotic objects from foreign lands came
with these southerly caravans, for the people of Chaomonous were seafaring men, who prided themselves on
their travels. But it was the western entrance to Dragonsgate that the beast watched most carefully, for two
reasons. Ngandib-Mar was a mountainous empire, and
caravans from this region did not have to climb so far to
reach the pass. One very tricky, very quick trading cap-

tain had managed to sneak in and past the dragon while he was napping once, but that had been many years before. Any captain so foolish as to try to repeat the trick Vicia-Heinox took great pleasure in charbroiling, for it was from the mines of Ngandib-Mar that the dragon obtained his wealth. Chaomonous was indeed called golden, but in fact most of its gold passed through Dragonsgate first—and the dragon always got his share. The jewels of Ngandib-Mar, though, were the objects of his passion. He demanded and received the finest Ngandib-Mar could send him: great, white gems the size of a giant's skull, and multifaceted, multicolored stones that dazzled even in the moonlight. These were the beast's playthings, in the idle hours between meals—caravans. Vicia, the dragon's left head, would grip a giant stone between his lips and toss it high into the air, then would move out of the way of Heinox, the right head, who would try to catch it. It pleased the dragon to watch the sparkling light dance through the gem as it twisted in the sky. The game was to see how many times a stone could be tossed and caught before one of the dragon's heads misjudged and it was swallowed instead. Vicia-Heinox swallowed a lot of diamonds this way. He was in constant need of a fresh supply.

And, naturally, he was also in constant need of food. Now, some dragons preferred to eat cattle. Others liked the sport of catching flocks of birds on the wing, though this was indeed a seasonal type of meal. Some dragons, mostly of the island-dweller varieties, really preferred seafood, and could move through the waterways as easily as they could soar through the air. But Vicia-Heinox was a perverse sort of dragon, the kind that gave all dragons a bad name. Vicia-Heinox took pleasure in talking to his dinner before he ate it. How the hideous beast came by this disgusting proclivity for dinner conversation cannot be dealt with here. It must simply be said that this was an old habit, one not easy for the dragon to break, even had he been so inclined. And this had resulted in a rebirth of the long-dead institution of slavery.

Before the dragon straddled Dragonsgate—before it

became Dragonsgate—slavery was viewed by civilized man as an aberration of primitives, to be stamped out wherever possible. But that was long ago. When the dragon first came, he didn't rest in the pass when he got hungry. He simply took to the wing, swallowing everything in his path. After the entire populations of several cities disappeared into the dragon's belly, the rulers of the world agreed that something had to be done. Royal armies, clothed in the brilliant livery of long-forgotten empires, marched on the beast from all fronts. It was the last great march for many storied kingdoms.

It wasn't that Vicia-Heinox breathed fire. That is a popular misconception. Though few lived who ever witnessed the beast's power displayed, those who did never mentioned any flames. Rather, the two-headed monster in some unknown way generated heat—waves of burning heat—and, focusing on an object with all four eyes, would char it out of existence. So went the combined arms of empires. So had gone every army raised against him since.

Now, Vicia-Heinox knew nothing about slavery. In fact, there were a great many things the dragon knew nothing about, for he was not a very curious beast, nor was he particularly bright. But the merchants knew of it, and to them it seemed the perfect solution to the otherwise insoluble problem of a dragon on their trade route. Hideous as he was, Vicia-Heinox did not bear full responsibility for the evil system that kept him fed. But it *did* keep him fed. He therefore preserved it.

On a day like most other days, the dragon lay on his back, playing with his baubles. He was not hungry, for only the day before a large caravan from Lamath had passed his home. The Lamathian warriors were generally not as cagey as the men of Chaomonous, but they were stalwart and level-headed. Some days before, a large troop of Lamathians had ambushed a Chaon slave-raiding party as it made its way toward the Spinal Range and safety. It was a truism known to all that "those who slave-raid are often slaves made," and most of the captured Chaons had served to subdue the dragon's appetite. He rested now, digesting, playing with his jewels and talking to himself.

"I think," said Vicia, "that I ought to learn how to count."

"Why should I?" Heinox replied, somewhat puzzled by the idea.

"In order to play the game better," Vicia answered himself. "I have played it so long, yet what have I to show for it?"

"Nothing," Heinox answered. "But then, I don't have anyone to show it to, either. Nor any reason to show it. Nor any reason to count—whatever counting is."

"Counting is what the merchants do when they try to bargain with me," Vicia observed.

"Which is foolishness," Heinox replied, "since I take what jewels I like and eat what food suits me."

"That's why I don't need to learn to count," Vicia nodded in agreement, and reached down to grasp a particularly large and beautiful stone between scaly lips. The jewel was gigantic by human estimation, but it was dwarfed by the dragon's gleaming teeth. With a mighty flip of his neck, the head known as Vicia launched it sparkling into the air. But Heinox heard a commotion from the southern approach to the pass, and the diamond bounced unnoticed off the dragon's hide.

"Why didn't I catch that?"

"Because I hear a noise in Chaomonous," Heinox growled, and the right-hand head craned over the left to peer deeply into the pass. Vicia dropped an ear to the ground, listening closely and hearing now the approach of a force of men.

"Of caravan size," Vicia murmured, "but coming much faster than a caravan would normally."

"Armed?" Heinox asked, rearing high into the sky, to the full extension of his mighty neck. There was a flash of reflected light far below him, like sunshine glistening off the golden armor of Chaomonous.

"Perhaps not the first party," Vicia advised, "but there is a second group of riders behind the first that may be. It moves much faster." Vicia-Heinox leapt into the sky, wings unfurling lazily. He soared upward, well above the lofty mountain cliffs surrounding his home, one head circling from south to west to north and back toward the south, the other head gazing intently at the column of armed warriors hesitating at the mouth of the southern entrance. The dragon screamed—a dreadful, piercing, full-throated duet of screeching sound—then flapped slowly toward the troop, both heads focusing carefully on it. The column broke immediately. Horses tossed riders, riders fought to turn their mounts from the dragon's gaze, and screams of terror echoed the dragon's screech back up at him. Within seconds the pass was clear of warriors. Those unfortunate enough to have been carried up the road by their panicked mounts, rather than down, died with their horses in an inglorious blaze. The dragon dropped down to investigate the remains, then jumped lightly over the caravan, now halfway up the incline. He settled slowly and gracefully onto the road thirty yards ahead of the struggling band, bringing it to an abrupt stop. Vicia glared straight down on the merchant captain, while Heinox cocked himself slightly to the side in a look of deep puzzlement.

"Merchant Pezi? And a week ahead of time?"

The merchant reined in his horse, which was well used to the sight of this particular dragon, and dismounted. He hitched his pants and started up toward the beast on foot. Pezi was fat and out of breath, and his pants immediately gave up and slipped back to their original position. He stopped to hitch them again, but couldn't find the strength. He looked up at Heinox and nodded. "Your Dragonship," Pezi acknowledged, puffing.

"Why so soon? And so hurried?" Heinox asked.

"And why do you bring soldiers to my nest?" added Vicia.

"I didn't bring them. They brought themselves."

"Against me?" Vicia growled.

"Against me," the fat man muttered. He pulled a handkerchief from his handbag and blew his nose. It was a purple and red handkerchief, the colors of the merchant house of Uda. Pezi's own colors were dark blue and lime, the colors of the house of Ognadzu. Perhaps Pezi became self-conscious, for he explained: "It's a Uda trade gimmick. Free hankies. Let me blow my nose on the opposition." The dragon didn't comment, and Pezi shoved the scarf back into his bag. "What is happening is this. I've got some valuable cargo, your Dragonship, and a certain ruler of Chaomonous—"

"Who?" asked Vicia.

"—who shall remain nameless, tried to steal it away."

The two heads rose into the air, and looked one another in the eye. Pezi took several steps backward and looked around for a good place to run. When the dragon looked at himself, that wasn't good. The great head named Vicia turned to stare at the fat merchant once more, and began slowly dropping out of the sky toward him. Closer and closer it came, until one eye gazed into Pezi's face from only a yard away. Pezi had backed into his animal, and now the horse, too, was spooked. The dragon rarely came this close to a living thing he did not intend to eat.

"I don't believe you," Vicia hissed. He spoke quietly, Vicia thought, but at this distance the noise rattled through Pezi's relatively empty skull, and the merchant slammed both hands over his ears. Heinox had by now surveyed the entire length of the caravan, eyeing everything carefully and throwing a terrible scare into all present. He investigated particularly a curtained litter that was being carried by a team of eight slaves, all Maris. It was a nobly carved carriage, from what he could see, but what most attracted his attention were the drapes. They shimmered as only fish-satin shimmered, and they were interlaced with threads of finely spun gold. Only a member of the royal house of Chaomonous would travel in such a booth as this, and the dragon knew it.

"Is this your cargo?" Heinox thundered from right above the litter. Pezi jerked around to look up at the head high above, but he quickly turned back to look at Vicia as the left-hand head snorted behind him:

"I was talking to you, merchant!"

"Oh, ah, yes, ah . . ."

"Is this the cargo, merchant?" Heinox roared behind him, and Pezi looked around again, but:

"Answer me, merchant!" Vicia snarled, and that was all for Pezi, at least for the moment. He fell into a dead faint beneath his trembling horse.

"Now what have I done?" Heinox murmured.

"I was only asking him a simple question," Vicia grumbled. Then he growled loudly, "Can't any of you answer me? You!" Vicia-Heinox zeroed in on a pale rider in blue and lime who held tightly to the pommel of his saddle to keep from shaking all the way out of it. As Heinox darted down from nowhere to look him in the face, the rider threw up his hands in dismay . . . and fell out of the saddle, flat on his back. Had he, too, passed out?

"You are faking. Get up!" Heinox ordered. The rider stayed put. "Get up or I'll eat you!" Still the rider lay in peaceful silence on his back, and Vicia-Heinox threw up his heads in disgust. He was focusing four eyes on the entire caravan, preparing to burn it all away, when someone spoke:

"Excuse me, your Dragonship, but perhaps I can shed some light on this situation." The dragon stopped in mid-burn and looked himself in the eyes. Vicia dropped down to look at the speaker, a ragtag character near the end of the line.

"Are you of the family of Ognadzu?" the dragon asked. "You are certainly not dressed for it . . ."

"I am not of the house of Ognadzu, nor of any of the trading houses. I am Pelmen, sometimes called Pelmen the player, lately of Chaomonous. I was enslaved by the King for making an allusion to one of his mistresses in an ill-received play."

"The Player? I've never heard of the family of Player," Vicia observed.

"But you can't be a slave," said Heinox. "You see, I've just eaten."

"Which I take as a stroke of great luck," Pelmen admitted.

"What is this caravan *for*, Player? It's too early, I'm still full!"

"I suppose it comes as no shock to a dragon of your experience that these merchants are not in business entirely for your benefit," Pelmen said quietly. Vicia shook his mighty head, and looked at Heinox.

"Did I understand that?"

"*I* didn't, did *I*?"

"I don't think so."

"There is a trade war going on right now, your Dragonship. Each house is striving to get the better of the other houses. In the struggle, one might say the ethics of the League of Trade have . . . slipped, somewhat."

"Ethics?" said both heads together. Vicia-Heinox was amazed at this little spokesman. Not only was Pelmen the player not trembling, he even took his eyes off of the dragon as he spoke. He behaved as if he conversed with a peer at the gaming tables.

"Now what is happening here is an indication of the kind of thing that has been taking place in Chaomonous for some time," Pelmen continued. He motioned the dragon to come closer. Both heads moved fluidly down to listen as he whispered conspiratorially: "You see, Pezi there has kidnapped the daughter of the royal house of Talith, and he carries her to Lamath to sell her for trading favors."

About this time, Pezi was regaining his consciousness, if not his composure. "Where am I?" the fat merchant groaned, and Heinox slipped to the front of the column to answer him.

"You are under your horse," the dragon said, which was true; and though Pezi's question had been rhetorical, the dragon's answer did bring back to him the realities of the situation. He jumped up. Rather, he tried to jump up, but bumped his head against his horse's underbelly and fell down again. He rolled over with great effort, and tottered slowly to his feet.

"What's going on?" he muttered.

"Quiet," hissed Heinox, "I'm talking to the man from the house of Player."

"Nonsense," snorted Pezi without thinking. "There is no house of Player. I know all of the royal and noble family names of all the districts, and the only Player I know is Pelmen the player, and he's—" It suddenly struck him. "You're not talking to Pelmen the player! Don't believe him! A pack of lies! The man's a public nuisance!"

Pezi forgot himself. He ran toward the rear of the caravan, so upset at this turn of events that he forgot who it was he was talking to. The dragon reminded him.

Quickly. Suddenly Pezi was running into the opened jaws of Vicia; when he managed to get his belly turned in the other direction and looked away from those gaping jaws behind him, he found himself looking down the throat of Heinox. He stopped dead in his tracks, and clapped both hands over his mouth. The two pairs of teeth snapped shut together, with an almost metallic click. Pezi swallowed with some difficulty. "Excuse me, your Dragonship." Four eyes focused intently on Pezi, and the fat man sank to his knees under the burden of that steel-hard double gaze.

Pelmen's rich, melodious voice broke the silence, filling the narrow canyon. "Of course, you really can't blame Pezi for his actions. Any of the trading families would do the same if they had the opportunity." Relief surged through Pezi as the giant heads lifted up and drifted back toward Pelmen. He fished his handkerchief out of his handbag and mopped his sweaty forehead. He was seriously considering retiring from the business.

"I have not seen a human of royal blood since I ate six of them during the last great rebellion. I want to see this girl." Vicia dropped down to look Pelmen in the eye. "You show her to me."

"I would rejoice in the pleasure of introducing the lady to you, your Dragonship, but—as you see—I am chained."

The dragon really hadn't noticed, but the fellow was indeed bound. Vicia-Heinox rarely observed such things, in any case. Only when he got pieces of chain caught between his teeth were they ever any problem to him. Heinox spoke to Pezi: "Release this man."

The chubby salesman waddled down to Pelmen as quickly as he could, fishing keys from his handbag. Once free, Pelmen walked to the beautiful golden litter with a style and grace that belied his rags. Here he paused dramatically.

"I am sure the lady would have spoken to you sooner, your Dragonship, but as you see—" He swept aside the drapes. "—she, too, is bound." Pelmen shot Pezi an accusing look. The merchant hung his head.

The dragon yawned. "So release her."

"With pleasure," Pelmen said, and he bent nobly to

his task. He was a spry and energetic figure, not an old man by any means, but neither was he young. He had expressive blue eyes, and shoulder-length brown hair, and a face that was ordinary enough to allow him to remain unnoticed if he chose to be. It was his voice that most impressed the dragon, for it climbed and dropped with such personality and dignity that Vicia-Heinox was nearly mesmerized. He could not recall hearing any man speak with such assurance.

And speak Pelmen did: "This lovely young lady, savagely ripped from the home of her father, will impress you, I think, with her gentleness. She has had the best of training in the art of being ladylike, for she's been surrounded since birth by the loveliest women of the realm. Now her father and I have not always seen eye to eye on every matter, I'll grant you, and the last time we spoke we did have a bit of trouble communicating, but I think he would agree with me that of all the ladies of his court, this one is the loveliest. I present to you the gentle Lady Bronwynn." At this Pelmen removed the scarf that had gagged the young woman's mouth.

Free from her bonds at last, she leapt to her feet on the satin and brocade pillows of the litter and, pointing a finger at Pezi, shouted, "You fat little Lamathian mudgecurdle! I'll have the royal chefs carve your belly and roast a hunk of it for—"

Pelmen clapped a hand over the girl's mouth and struggled to hold her quiet while saying, "Of course, the lady is a bit upset at the moment . . ."

"Quit that!" she managed to blurt out around his hand, and he let go of her as she fought her way out of the litter. She straightened her robes and lifted her chin, and muttered ":Where's the dragon?" to Pelmen. He pointed behind her, and she swept grandly around to get her first good look at this beast she had heard so much about.

Pelmen heard her sharp grunt, and he put his hands on her shoulders to steady her. She backed into the security of his arms, and gasped, "He's . . . big . . ."

"As I said," continued Pelmen, "a Princess of impeccable manners and great modesty. Try not to shake so much, will you?" he added quietly in the girl's ear.

"You think I'm doing this on purpose?" she whispered back.

Vicia-Heinox sat back on his hind legs, and raised his heads high into the air.

"What do I do now?" Vicia muttered.

"What do I mean, do now?" Heinox asked.

"With this caravan. I'm not hungry. I don't need any new jewels. What does this merchant have that I want?"

"I don't know, what *does* he have that I want?"

"The girl perhaps?" Vicia asked. "After all, she is a Princess, and there must be something important to that. Otherwise, why would they clothe her in such delicate wrappings?"

This statement was overheard by the little group below, and Bronwynn gathered her gown around her and shivered.

"Perhaps Princesses taste better than ordinary folk," Heinox suggested.

"Perhaps . . . perhaps I should . . ."

"If I might interrupt, I believe you would be wasting this Princess if you were to eat her. Consider keeping her, as a—a companion," said Pelmen.

"Thanks a lot!" the girl whispered fiercely. Pelmen squeezed her tight and leaned down to her ear. "Try to be quiet and I may be able to extract us from this." She stopped her struggling, and listened.

"A companion. I *could* do that," Heinox said.

"If I knew what a companion is," Vicia added.

"A companion is someone you spend your time with, talk to, learn from. A companion can be a friend." Pelmen noticed Bronwynn was gripping her ears and scowling at this.

"A friend?" Vicia said. "But I don't need a friend. I have . . . myself."

And that gave Pelmen an idea.

"Ah. I understand." He indicated Vicia. "You have him." He indicated Heinox. "And he has you. And you are friends."

Vicia-Heinox looked at himself, then both of his heads looked at Pelmen. "What?" the dragon asked. "I have myself and I have myself?"

"Not quite the idea," Pelmen went on quietly. "I mean you have each other."

"Each other?" Vicia asked. "He isn't another, he is I. I think," he added.

"He who?" Pelmen asked.

"Him," Vicia growled, growing irritated at the player's badgering tone. Then Vicia stopped. He looked at Heinox.

Heinox was already looking at Vicia. "Him?" Heinox muttered. The group of people below kept very quiet.

"I think I need to reason this out—" Vicia began, and Heinox said, "I think so too." The dragon looked at himself in great confusion.

Pelmen bent to whisper again in Bronwynn's ear. "You see the plateau at the high point of the pass?" She nodded. "When I shout, make for that plateau, and then run to your left."

"But that's Ngandib-Mar!" she protested. "Chaomonous is behind us—"

"When the confusion begins, make for Ngandib-Mar," he repeated strongly. He began to plot the quickest route to Pezi's horse.

"I just said I need to reason this out," Vicia repeated.

"I did too," said Heinox.

"Yes, but—"

"But what?"

"But I already said that!" Vicia growled.

"I know!" Heinox growled back.

"I know I know! I said I knew!" Vicia growled again, more loudly this time.

"I know I said I knew! I said I said I knew!" Heinox trumpeted back.

"I know!" screeched Vicia.

"Now!" grunted Pelmen, and Bronwynn scrambled up the divide as quickly as her legs and gowns would allow her. Pelmen drove toward Pezi's horse. The other slaves, still chained together, began to run this way and that, pulling each other backward and forward in a deadly serious game of whiplash, a centipede of people trying desperately to get coordinated. Pezi, seeing Pelmen grab the reins of his mount, hustled down the slope to jerk up the reins of the fallen rider's horse, which whinnied and backed away from this heavyweight who was trying to mount it. The fallen rider, who was just coming to, surveyed the chaos around him and decided he had been better off unconscious. He fainted once again.

And high in the sky, a curious thing was taking place. Vicia-Heinox, at an advanced age, had suddenly been confronted with a terrible identity crisis.

"I am trying to understand this, will I please cooperate?" Vicia bellowed.

"I *am* cooperating! I can't understand why *I'm* not cooperating!" Heinox screeched back.

Pelmen mounted Pezi's horse and kicked its sides. The beast sprang forward, puzzled but delighted at the lightness of this new rider. Bronwynn was about to reach the pass proper, and Pelmen urged the horse toward her at a trot.

"They're getting away!" Heinox shouted. "Can't I see they are getting away?"

"Of course I can see it!" Vicia rumbled. The sound echoed off the sides of the canyon with a presence numbing to the ears, like a thunderclap at close range.

"Focus! Focus!" Heinox cried, but it was no use. As Heinox focused on Pelmen, who was moving up the pass and bending down to sweep the golden Princess up onto the horse behind him, Vicia was focusing on Pezi, who was urging his reluctant animal into pursuit. Heinox shifted to focus on Pezi, but Vicia had turned to focus on Pelmen. The great dragon gave a headsplitting, blood-chilling, back-bending scream of utter frustration, and flew straight up into the sky.

Pelmen cast a glance over his shoulder at Pezi, and kicked his mount once again, driving it toward the west and the land of Ngandib-Mar. By the time Pezi reached the open clearing and looked after him, Pelmen and the girl were well on their way into the highland plain of that land. Though he could still see them, they were far away by now—too far and moving too fast to follow. He looked up and watched the dragon high above him, turning erratic circles in the sky. He pulled a sword from its scabbard on the horse's saddle and turned to ride back down into the gorge. The line of slaves still struggled to coordinate a run for safety, and Pezi leveled the tip of his weapon at the back of one slave's head. "Silence!" he roared, his confident manner restored by the change in the situation. The slaves stopped shoving, and all turned to look at him. "Now," he said when all was quiet, "we move on to Lamath. It's a long walk. I suggest you save your breath." The column turned and, under Pezi's watchful eye, began once more to ascend the slope. "Bring the litter! It's bound to be worth something," Pezi grumbled, but as they carried it past him he ground his teeth together in anxiety and disgust. He would have some explaining to do to his uncle Flayh. And who would believe the true story? As he reined his horse in behind the last walker, his mind was hard at work constructing a lie that would absolve him of guilt. Pezi wasn't good at many things, but he was an accomplished liar. "To the right!" he shouted when the first man reached the fork. It would indeed be a long way to Lamath.

The banquet hall of Chaomonous was built of yellow marble. When all the tapers were lit, the walls reflected the favorite color of the golden King; all were burning brightly tonight. But the dinner conversation was subdued this evening, and the occasional giggle seemed out of place in the near-funereal atmosphere. What conversation there was subsided when a golden-mailed warrior entered the hall. He walked hesitantly toward the elevated table of the King. All could tell by the expression on his face that the news he brought wasn't good. No one was surprised when the King's silver goblet streaked through the room like a meteor; Talith frequently threw things when he was angry. It was a shock, however, when the object bounced off the distant back wall. No one had seen him *that* angry before.

"Advisors! To me!" the King shouted, then turned on his heel and stomped off the dais. All over the hall there were muttered "Pardon's" and "Excuse me's" as the King's experts bade good-bye for the night to their ladies and trotted toward the doorway on the east side of the room. The King headed for the chamber of his council of war. Plans would be made tonight that would shape the destiny of the empire.

Ligne, the King's latest mistress, watched him out the door and then reached for his plate. The best piece of meat lay untouched there, and she took great pleasure in finishing it off. She wished she were privy to the words of the council—but she had her spies sprinkled through the experts, so she would hear soon enough. Thus far things were proceeding exactly according to her plan.

As she licked the grease from her delicate fingers she noticed the Queen eyeing her with suspicion. Latithia, the Queen and mother of the Princess, was out of favor with the King these days. Ligne licked the last of the juice from her hand, then smiled brightly at the Queen, her blue eyes twinkling. The Queen looked away, and Ligne was pleased to note the flush of Latithia's cheeks. Those seated near Ligne gave no thought to her smug smile. These days Ligne often smiled like that.

"They weren't even mounted!" the King was shouting. "A group of slaves on foot! Only two riders! And they escaped you?"

"It was a surprising move, my Lord," the exchequer said softly. "Pezi normally doesn't move his column until after he has a full complement of slaves. At this time of year he waits for the southern ships to dock, so he may add spices and fish-satin to his inventory. It will surely be two more weeks until the first of the fleet arrives—"

"General Joss!"

"My Lord?"

"What of your spies in the trading houses? Why wasn't I informed she was being held in the house of Ognadzu?" The King's face was very red.

Joss' eyes widened as the King grabbed his sleeve, but that was the only acknowledgment of his fear. He, too, spoke quietly. "It was a carefully guarded secret, my Lord. It must be admitted that when it comes to keeping secrets, we are no match for the merchants. Secrets are their stock-in-trade—"

"I don't need a lecture from my head of intelligence!" Talith bellowed. "And if you want to keep not only your headship but your head, General, you had best begin producing!"

The exchequer broke in again. "She wasn't being kept in the local house, my Lord, or we could have stopped them. The girl was being held at Pezi's own estate, on the edge of Dragonsgate."

"And how did she get there? Exchequer? General? I take it you don't know." The King's eyes narrowed dangerously.

"We know this," Joss began. "We know that when she was taken she was in the presence of your mistress—and that only a denizen of the palace could have spirited her past our watch." The General set his jaw and stared at his King. Though Joss was a cruel man, he did not lack for bravery.

"You are accusing Ligne?" Talith crooned menacingly.

"I accuse no one, my Lord," answered the General. "I share only what I know."

"Perhaps you should know, my Lord," the exchequer interrupted again, "that among those Pezi was carrying to Lamath was a certain Pelmen the player."

"Pelmen!" the King exploded. "Is he involved in this?"

"There could be no proof of that," Joss began, but the King cut him off.

"Pelmen! Of course. He's behind this. He has masterminded this whole scheme to get back at me!"

"I hardly think—" Joss began again.

Talith interrupted. "That's right, you hardly do!" He turned his back on his Chief of Security.

Joss closed his mouth and looked at the exchequer, who seemed even more nervous tonight than usual. The exchequer avoided his eyes, and spoke earnestly to the King. "He is a most clever adversary, my Lord. And you *did* deal rather brusquely with him when you sold him to Pezi. This stealth seems so unlike the fat merchant—could it be that Pezi and Pelmen plotted this together?"

"Of course," growled King Talith. "It must be."

Joss snorted, and the King turned to look angrily at him.

"Pardon, my Lord," Joss said. "I share your lack of affection for Pelmen. He shows by these plays of his that he is dangerously well informed. But Pezi would not collaborate with a traveling performer. If you wish to know who has masterminded this capture of our Princess, look to the elders of the house of Ognadzu."

"They're all in Lamath!" the King snapped.

"So, we believe, is Bronwynn," Joss said quietly, and then paused while the King mulled over his words.

The King did not think long, but his reaction was decisive. "Get me Jagd of the house of Uda. And arrest all who wear the blue and lime of Ognadzu."

For the first time since the interview began, Joss smiled. "Jagd is waiting outside, my Lord. I felt you might wish to see him, so I sent for him earlier. As for the arrests—they were all made this afternoon. The family of Ognadzu is having a reunion tonight in the dungeon."

"Send me Jagd!" the King bellowed, and a guard at the chamber door stamped the butt of his pike on the marble floor and announced as the double doors opened: "Jagd of Uda, to see the Golden King."

A wizened little man in rich robes of red and purple stepped briskly into the room, and he and the King were soon deep in a heated private discussion. As Joss stepped out of the way, he noticed once again Kherda, the exchequer. The man stood in a corner of the chamber, forgotten now, his face inscribed with anxiety and self-doubt. Joss watched him, and marked that expression well.

As soon as he cleared the west mouth of Dragonsgate, Pelmen turned south. To go straight meant to run directly into lands controlled by the trading houses. Though they would not be expecting him, the guards on those lands held by the Ognadzu family would surely be suspicious of a man in rags carrying a girl in golden robes, mounted on a horse that wore the blue and lime. Pelmen would take no chance. Instead he would travel along the high southwestern rim of the Spinal Range until he could turn west under the shelter of the Great South Fir.

Though he guessed that Pezi would not follow, he kept a cautious watch behind them as they rode through the green-cloaked foothills. He also watched the valley below, for any unusual troop movements across the lands of the merchant league. There was little danger yet, but Pelmen knew that certain of the larger houses had discovered ways of transmitting messages many miles without the use of a blue flyer. Pelmen assumed that in the next day or two, after Pezi reached Lamath, these hills would be covered with merchant riders. They would not allow so precious a prize as the Lady Bronwynn to be stolen away so easily.

Pelmen also glanced frequently to the sky, watching for the massive shadow of the dragon moving overhead. He urged the horse to move faster, and soon they were galloping full speed across the hillside. The more ground put between them and Dragonsgate, the safer Pelmen would feel.

Bronwynn, too, was watching, but with wonder rather than caution. Her homeland of Chaomonous was flat and fertile, a country of great rivers and vast fields. What few mountains she had seen were the short, round-top hills of the southern sector of that land. Never before had she seen mountains so tall and steep and of such stark beauty, nor valleys so wildly green. To her left, the sheer face of the Spinal Range climbed up and out of sight. To her right, the craggy highlands of fabled Ngandib-Mar unrolled as far as she could see. Every majestic mountain peak rose out of its own deliciously green little valley. It all seemed so close and immediate that Bronwynn felt she could reach out and touch it. Yet when she dropped her eyes to the vast plain below them, plaidlike from the crisscross pattern of furrowed fields and fences, she realized those hills and valleys that looked so near were really miles away. Still, somehow she had the sensation of being in an intimate land, a manageable land, a warm, familiar, close-knit land. Her feelings frightened her. To experience such exultation at the mere sight of this foreign place—this hereditary enemy of her homeland—seemed somehow treasonous. This was the homeplace of squat blond slaves, she reminded herself—a land of cannibals ·and witchcraft. But those craggy mountains across the valley stole her heart with their simple, powerful beauty. It was a jolting experience, one not entirely pleasant. Unexplained melancholy seized her; and though she had not cried once throughout the ordeal of her abduction, a stupid, senseless tear now trickled down her cheek. She brushed it away, and closed her eyes against the splendor of the world below her.

Their horse was tiring, but it proudly carried them on, up a small rise toward a grove of wild green apple trees. Here a stream found its way out of the mountains and dropped gaily toward the valley in a series of stepped waterfalls and rapids. Pelmen was sensitive to the horse's weariness and stopped. His own bottom felt weary as well. He reined in under an apple tree and hopped off, bending to stretch and relax his legs before reaching up to lift Bronwynn down from the saddle. They had said nothing to one another since they left the pass, and Pelmen was not really inclined toward conversation now. He pulled an apple from the tree and tossed it to her, then went to tend to the horse's needs.

As Pelmen stripped the horse of its saddle to get at the Ognadzu colors and remove them, Bronwynn wandered beneath the trees. She doffed her sandals, and tested the tall, moist grass with the soles of her feet. She was amazed at the greenness of the greens, and wondered idly if her father had ever seen anything so beautiful as this land.

Her father. He needed to know that she was safe. "How are you taking me home?" she called to Pelmen.

He put a finger to his lips to warn her to silence, then smiled. Pelmen had a toothy, attractive smile. It encouraged trust in the trusting, and suspicion in the suspicious. He walked toward her, pulling another apple from the tree. Then, dropping full length on the grassy rug beside her, he began to munch the fruit.

"Well?" she added, more softly, but with just a touch of royal impatience.

"How—meaning in what direction, or by what means?" he asked.

"Either," Bronwynn shrugged. "Both."

Pelmen took another bite, then rolled over onto his

back. He chewed for a moment, then spat out a seed. "The fact of the matter is, I don't know."

"You don't know! Then where are we going!"

Pelmen thought about that for a moment. "Away," he then said simply.

"That's no answer!" Bronwynn stamped.

"On the contrary, my Lady. In this case, it is the very best answer—for right now."

"I don't understand what you're talking about."

"Events have been put in motion, my Lady, events in which you play an important role. We must balance these actions with some unexpected reaction, or evil plans may succeed."

"What plans? What are you talking about?"

"I don't know myself, my Lady. But since these plans have already included your abduction and captivity, I would guess that you would prefer they be foiled."

"So take me home then."

"And let you be kidnapped again?"

"What difference does it make to you?"

"I don't know." Pelmen smiled. "Perhaps a great deal." He took another bite out of the apple, and Bronwynn began judging the distance between herself and the horse.

"My father always said you were crazy, Pelmen. He didn't know the half of it." She strolled casually toward the stream, watching out of the corner of her eye as the horse dropped his head down to drink.

"Your father and I have had our disagreements, it's true." Pelmen nodded, gazing at the blue sky between the leaves above him. "My major argument with Talith as an audience is that he always tends to believe he knows what you are going to say before you say it—and then replies to what he thinks you've said, rather than to what you've actually said. He takes it into his mind that he knows more about what's going on than anyone around him . . . which of course leaves all around him free to do anything they wish. He is suspicious of his friends, and trusting of his enemies."

"Mmm-hmmn," she agreed, bending down to the stream to take a cupped handful of the icy water. She judged herself to be twenty feet from the horse. Pelmen, behind her, was at least another twenty feet farther from the horse than she, and was lying on his back. Could she make it to the beast and onto it before Pelmen could react and catch her?

"Of course," Pelmen continued, "since he rarely listens to what others are saying, he's frequently surprised by what others do. He is chagrined when others seem to read his mind. But it is just that Talith is so obvious in what he thinks!"

"Yes, sometimes," Bronwynn said absently, moving a step closer to the horse.

"It appears perhaps you take after him."

"Why do you say that?" Bronwynn asked politely. She had decided that three more steps would put her close enough to make her dash.

"Because you're obviously planning to try to steal the horse, and don't realize that any fool could tell." Pelmen rolled onto his stomach and smiled at her shocked expression. "As I can," he concluded. She gave Pelmen her full attention now, and tensed her muscles, ready to make the attempt anyway. "Go ahead, my Lady, if you desire. But don't be surprised if the road back to your father proves difficult to find and dangerous to travel."

"There are paths through the mountains," she said defiantly. "Our slave raiders travel them regularly."

"So do raiders from Ngandib-Mar—or had you forgotten that slavery cuts both ways?"

"I could find the path and hide, until the golden warriors of Chaomonous approach, and then show myself!"

"I don't believe even you are that naïve, my Lady. The warriors of Chaomonous, while raiding for slaves, certainly don't advertise who they are by wearing golden mail. They disguise themselves. But assuming you should make contact with raiders from your own land—how do you think they would respond to you?"

"They would recognize me as their Princess!"

Pelmen chuckled.

"Why are you laughing? Are you laughing at me?" She stomped angrily.

"Bronwynn, can you imagine the reaction of a normal, sane warrior of Chaomonous to a dirty little girl he has captured in the mountains of Ngandib-Mar, when she claims to be his Princess? Few warriors have even seen you from a distance, my Lady. They wouldn't recognize you."

"But they will come looking for me! They know by now I've been kidnapped. My father will send his whole army after me!"

"I question that. He doesn't know you have escaped. I'm sure he will make some attempt to get you back, but most of his efforts will be aimed at the house of Ognadzu."

Bronwynn looked at him. "You mean he won't send soldiers after me?"

"He doesn't know you're here. How can he?"

"Well—where does he think I am then?"

"Surely he believes by this time you are being held captive at Flayh's mansion in Lamath. That's where we were headed, you know. He will probably attempt to work through the house of Uda to get you back, by force, or ransom, or—some way."

"But I'm not there! They'll tell him, won't they?"

"Why should they? And have all Ognadzu family members in Chaomonous slaughtered in retribution?"

"That *is* what my father would do." Bronwynn sat in the grass and tried to reason what course of action she should take. The sun was dropping behind the western mountains, and a cool breeze shook the leaves above them and caused several apples to drop. "I have it," she announced. "We go to Uda—here, in Ngandib-Mar. They do have a house here, don't they?"

"Many of them," Pelmen affirmed. "And that would be good thinking. Except . . ."

"Except what?"

"Why should you expect Uda to be any more trustworthy than Pezi's house of Ognadzu? Wouldn't it make more sense for the elders of Uda to play one side against the other while perhaps making their own deal for your sale to, say, the ruler of Ngandib?"

"This is all too complicated!" Bronwynn moaned.

"Not yet, my Lady," Pelmen said. "No, as yet it is relatively simple. You are free. Things would be far more complex at this point were that not the case. And,

while it might not be of great note to you, I, too, am
free—for which I am most thankful. And even if it
seems frightening to you at the moment that no one else
knows our whereabouts, I am delighted with the situation. I'd like to keep it that way as long as possible."

"But where will we go?" the girl pleaded with him,
and immediately wished she had said nothing. Bronwynn had heard herself speak, and felt she had sounded
like a frightened child. That was not at all the way the
Princess, daughter of Talith, should sound.

But Pelmen was kind, and he smiled a genuine,
cheery smile. "Away," he answered again. Seeing the
fear and concern dance across the girl's face, he went
on to add, "I am not without friends in this foreign
land, my Lady. In fact, it isn't foreign to me."

"You mean you've been here before? But you're not
a merchant, how could you—"

"The merchants and the raiders are not the only ones
who travel the world. In my profession, you either have
to change your act regularly or else change your location. I find it much easier to change location."

"Then you've performed here before?" she asked,
truly interested in him now as this new revelation sank
in.

Once again he smiled, but more to himself this time
than at her. Yes, he had "performed" here before. But
not as Bronwynn conceived it. He stood. "We need
something more than green apples to sustain us, I think.
I find it hard to believe that Pezi would travel anywhere
without a good healthy provision of food in his storage
bags. I'll check." Pelmen walked to the saddle which sat
now in the grass, and began to go through the sacks
attached to it.

Bronwynn wandered toward the west, listening to the
wind rock the branches. The sky turned pink behind the
mountains as the sun dropped swiftly behind them, and
once again she was stabbed by the strange desire to be
there, on one of those distant peaks, visible only in outline now.

"Will we be going there?" she asked, hiding her hope
behind an air of nonchalance. Pelmen glanced up to see
which way she was looking, then smiled to himself as he

gathered up the food he'd found and walked toward her.

"The mountains have witched you," he murmured as he came up behind her.

"No they haven't, what do you mean?" she said, but her protests were dreamy and vague, for her mind was far away.

"Yes they have." He sighed. "And you know what I mean." She didn't look at him, so he continued, looking now himself on the valley darkening below them and the outline of those far cliffs against the sunset. "Don't be too surprised, Bronwynn, at anything you see in Ngandib-Mar. It is a land of magic and witches, and powers ride on the winds, available for use by whomever can control them." She said nothing, but watched. He looked at her—her face was a golden-pink in the rays of the waning sun—and he could not bring himself to break that spell of wonder just yet. Instead he spoke quietly, soothingly. "Yes, we'll go there, my Lady. I have a friend who holds some lands on the far side of those hills. His keep will be open to us, as well as his heart. You may even find reason to remain there. You could do worse. Much worse," he muttered to himself, then he turned his back on the valley and sat in the grass. In a few moments the daylight was gone, and Bronwynn turned wistfully away.

The meadow was dark now, its mood of warm invitation having passed with the sunlight. "We're not staying here tonight, are we?" she asked in a voice tinged with fear.

"Amazing," Pelmen said to himself. "What a difference a little light can make. No, Bronwynn, we won't be staying here or anywhere else tonight. We've a long way to go, and before long merchant riders will be trailing us. You'll need all the strength you can muster. So eat, and thank Pezi for planning such a hog's feast. We have enough food here for forty—plenty to get us to the castle of Dorlyth without having to stop."

Bronwynn knelt in the grass beside him, and they ate in silence. As she chewed, she thought over his words regarding the powers on the winds. The people of Chaomonous laughed at such stories, and called them superstitions. Yet as Bronwynn watched the night bleed darkly through the meadow, she felt sure that a gay, bright power had left, and that a darker, sinister power had taken its place. She moved self-consciously closer to Pelmen, trying to gain strength and comfort from being near him. Pelmen, aware, ate leisurely. There would be plenty of time to rush, to act. Now it was time to ponder—and to plan well.

In the pitch blackness above the pass there was a mighty rush of massive reptilian wings thrashing the air, then the quiet plop of dragon feet touching softly down into the dusty ground. Vicia-Heinox had come home. Though no man had ever been fool enough to attempt the pass at night, the dragon made double sure he was alone. He did not rely solely on his keen sense of hearing, but vindictively shot great jets of heat in every direction, searing out any trace of greenery that might have taken root between the rocks. Though hardly in harmony, the two heads had concluded that the safety of each depended on some measure of cooperation. Having thoroughly torched the area, they turned back to the business of settling this insane dispute.

Vicia reared back and screamed at the brilliant stars in keen frustration. Heinox growled at him:

"Do I *have* to do that?" Heinox shook himself to clear his ears.

"Something must be done," Vicia snarled.

"About what?"

"I was talking to myself," Vicia muttered.

"I am myself," Heinox reminded Vicia, and Vicia lay down in the dirt and moaned.

"I must do something to make it clear when I mean *I*, and when I mean *I*. Ahhh!" Vicia groaned, "it's no use."

"Something must be done," Heinox agreed.

"I said that already."

"I know." Heinox, too, lay down on the ground. "This is why I ought to learn to count," Heinox sighed.

"Why?"

"So I could know which *I* was speaking."

"Why would that help?"

"I could number my heads. I could be one number, and I could be another number."

Excited, Vicia popped up into the sky. "That's it! I could be one number, and I could be another number!"

"Do I think it's a good idea?" Heinox asked, his own excitement growing.

"I think it's a wonderful idea!"

"Very well, I'll do it!" Heinox shouted. "The next caravan that passes, I'll force the captain to teach me how to count, and then I'll number me! I'll be one number, and I'll be the other number!" The two heads looked at each other, rejoicing, one might even say smiling if dragons could smile. But as they looked one another in the eye it dawned on them that they really hadn't settled anything at all. Both heads sank once again into the dust, exhausted by the day-long struggle.

"Heinox," said Vicia, "how am I ever going to be able to know which head is which?"

"I don't know, Vicia," Heinox answered in despair. "I don't know."

❧ Chapter Two ❧

PEZI BOUNCED from side to side, struggling to hold his seat as the little mare under him trotted up the cobblestones. He felt like a pullybone, being cut apart by the thinness of his horse and the weight of his own belly. Nor was he at all happy about the news he was about to deliver. He had already instructed his assistant to listen very closely to the details of the story as he presented them to his uncle. This the young merchant was only too happy to do, since he had missed most of the action in his unconscious state, and didn't want his fainting spells to become public knowledge. The young fellow was already terribly embarrassed, since he was walking into the compound rather than riding.

Pezi went over the story again in his mind, hoping only that his uncle Flayh would give him a chance to tell it. Flayh was an appropriate name for Pezi's uncle, for he was inclined to flay anyone who crossed him or cost him money. And Pezi knew Flayh would be most displeased.

The little mare smelled the barn; though Pezi had kicked her until he was out of breath just to make her walk faster in the earlier stages of the journey, it was now impossible to slow her from a trot. All too soon they were arriving at the inner gate of the Ognadzu compound in the land of Lamath—Flayh's mansion. The great wooden portals were opened before them, and the little mare pranced through the stucco archway as if she carried a conquering hero home from victory. What she carried was a fat, rather embarrassed merchant who was grimacing in pain. Pezi managed to stop her long enough to dismount in the courtyard; but even before he could stretch his legs, the little horse had found her way to the stable and food. Pezi muttered curses under his breath, and demanded of one of the court guards, "My uncle. Where is he?"

"He sits at dinner with guests," the guard replied, and Pezi pushed past him to walk toward the banquet veranda. "But where is the rest of your caravan? Your goods, your—"

"Mind your own business!" Pezi shouted at him, and threw open the front door of the house, banging it for the guard's benefit.

He did not, however, bang open the door out onto the eating porch. Rather, he cracked it slightly to peek out, established exactly where Uncle Flayh was seated and the quickest, most inconspicuous route to his chair, then crept through and quietly closed the door behind him.

It wasn't easy for a three-hundred-pound man to move inconspicuously. In fact, Pezi's ludicrous attempt called the attention of the whole gathering directly to him.

"Pezi! What are you skulking around for?" Flayh

bellowed. "Get over here and tell me how the captive made the journey!"

"Oh, hello, Uncle Flayh! Guests." Pezi nodded courteously, and approached the table. Flayh got up to meet him, and Pezi flinched instinctively.

"A problem, Pezi?" Flayh asked. His tone of menace did not go unnoticed by his rotund nephew. Pezi took a step back. When Flayh took a step toward him, Pezi took another step back; soon it became a question of whether his uncle would first reach Pezi or whether Pezi would make it to the door.

"A . . . slight . . . problem, uncle." Pezi was sweating profusely. He dipped into his handbag and pulled out his handkerchief to wipe his head. He noticed his uncle's eyes fix on the handkerchief, and remembered its purple and red color. He shoved it back into his bag and took another step backward.

"A . . . *slight* problem, you say. But our captive did make the journey, did she?"

"Ah, she . . . made . . . some journey, I'm sure, I mean—"

"Some journey? Speak up, man! Is she with you?"

"Well . . . ah . . . no—" Pezi stammered.

Whap! Pezi reeled back, his face stinging from his uncle's powerful slap. The second slap knocked him to the tile floor of the garden dining area. Flayh moved in as if to hit him again, then stopped himself. He gazed down with contempt on the cowering hulk he straddled, then jerked away.

"I knew it!" Flayh shouted, his face red with rage. "I knew there was no chance of Pezi doing anything right."

As Flayh spat out Pezi's name, the fat merchant cringed. He began to scoot backward on his sore bottom, still hoping to reach the door. His uncle spun around to look at him, the blood draining from his face. Flayh did not explode over trifles. Whenever he did find cause to erupt in anger, his first thinking reaction was inner-directed. He fought to control himself, to regain that calm, gentle assurance that was so threatening to all who knew him. Now he spoke quietly to Pezi, as if speaking to a child. The change in tone so frightened the fat merchant that he trembled visibly.

"How did it happen, Pezi?"

"I . . . it was . . . the dragon, sir, he—"

"What about the dragon, Pezi? Come now, relax. Stand up like a man, and tell me what happened." Flayh reached down to help Pezi up. His manner was kindly, but that only shook Pezi more. Had Pezi's knees not been padded with such a thick layer of flesh, they surely would have knocked together audibly.

"The dragon, he—he went crazy, he—"

"What?"

"He went crazy! Insane! I've never seen him so disturbed!"

"Start at the beginning."

"Well of course, it was an unusual caravan in the first place. Too early, he said. That roused his suspicions. Then, too, a troop of Chaons was chasing us into Dragonsgate just as we were reaching the pass! The dragon went down to frighten them off. I'm sure that made him more suspicious. He wanted to see my cargo. Of course I couldn't hide her, carrying her in the royal litter as we were, so—"

"You transported her in the royal litter?" Flayh interrupted.

"Of course—well, she wouldn't walk—"

"So you advertised her importance by carrying her in a golden litter!" Flayh roared.

"I—I thought it would be worth something—" Flayh stared at him. "It's outside if you want to see it—"

"Oh, is it?" Flayh smiled; then the smile decayed into a sneer. "And why should I want to see an empty royal litter of the house of Talith, hmmm?"

"Ah . . . it's . . . ah, pretty—" Pezi stammered. Then he gulped.

Flayh sighed. "All right," he said. "Leaving aside the fact that we possess illegally one of Talith's carved transport litters which is of absolutely no value to anyone *now*—leaving aside the fact that you advertised to that Chaon contingent exactly whom you were carrying away to Lamath—leaving all that aside, Pezi—go on."

Pezi scratched his head, then clasped his hammy

hands together and struggled hard to get his story straight in his head once more. Then taking a large breath, he began again. "I—I refused to let him see my cargo, so he threatened me. I mean, there he was, one head in front of me, one head in back of me, neither of them more than a foot from my body!"

"Get on!" Flayh roared.

"I—I refused to let him see my captive, whereupon he blew the curtains open and saw the Princess. I was afraid he was about to eat her! So I told him who she was, and that it was most important that I bring her here. He made me untie her, and of course she jumped out of the litter and began to run! I gave chase, but alas—" Pezi placed both hands on his stomach. "Alas, I could not catch her."

"Oh, really?" Flayh smiled coldly.

"Really! Then the strangest thing happened! The dragon became most confused, and began arguing with himself! Now I followed instructions to the letter; I mean I have *never* addressed the dragon as if it were two dragons rather than one—"

"Of course not. You're still here," Flayh muttered.

"But that's what happened! The beast screamed, and flew up into the air, and by that time the girl had taken my horse and ridden off!"

"Back to Chaomonous," Flayh observed to himself.

"No! To Ngandib-Mar!"

"What?" Flayh grunted in surprise. "Why?"

"I don't know," Pezi lied, "she just turned that way! Perhaps she felt she could best escape me there—"

"And she was right enough in that! You gave chase?"

"Of course," Pezi lied again. "But it was no use. She had too much of a start, and a far better mount."

"And then?"

"Then I got the column together, and marched all last night and all today to get here to tell you!"

Flayh nodded, thinking to himself. "A young girl alone in Ngandib-Mar, on a horse wearing Ognadzu colors. Shouldn't be too hard to find. Tohn mod Neelis may even have picked her up already." Flayh turned to spear Pezi with his eyes. "Assuming you are not lying."

Pezi managed a weak grin. "Oh, no, sir."

Flayh continued to gaze at his nephew for a long, tense moment—then smiled. "Of course not. You must be hungry—" He stepped to one side and motioned toward the table. Pezi wasted no time getting to it.

Flayh leaned back and peered up through the trellised vines shading this enclosed garden. The sun was passing midday. In a few hours he would talk to Jagd and Tohn mod Neelis. The plan could still succeed.

Assuming, he thought again, watching Pezi stuff himself with a roasted turkey leg—assuming Pezi wasn't lying.

Tohn mod Neelis was the elder of the house of Ognadzu in Ngandib-Mar. As such he ruled vast lands, much greater than those Flayh controlled in Lamath. For Ngandib-Mar was less an empire than a feudal confederacy, ruled in name alone by the King of the great city of Ngandib. Still, the Mar of Ngandib presented a united front to foes from beyond Dragonsgate. Though divided into small principalities and fiefdoms, the Maris, or men of the Mar, viewed themselves as one people, united against all other races.

Of course, that didn't stop them from fighting frequently among themselves. In the centuries of thrust and counterthrust on the part of scores of petty Princes, the trading houses had carved out their own fiefs. Between them they controlled most of the highlands near the west mouth of Dragonsgate, and lived in royal splendor as parties of two worlds: rich merchant traders, and recognized lords of the feudal confederacy.

It was a very good life, Tohn mod Neelis was thinking, as he walked the ramparts of his hold and gazed down at the green fields below him. The harvest would be good this year—if events allowed the harvest to come. He raised his head and inhaled deeply of the scent of spring, brought to him by a pleasant breeze that blew his stringy gray hair wildly. It was such a simple life—what need had he for more money, for more power? He had all the money and power he needed, plus he had this—a homeland.

It was the others who pressed the plan—always

pressing! Flayh and Jagd, those merchants dwelling in the flatlands, in the noise and confusion and the constant dust. They were the ones who pushed so hard for the changes—who connived to start the war. Well, Tohn thought to himself, let them have their war. But let it pass by the Mar of Ngandib. Let it waste the wheat of Lamath—but let it pass by these gentle hills.

He glanced at the sun. Soon it would be time to communicate with the others. Strange business, this, he thought as he left the parapet, walking the stone steps by memory. Strange to be planning in conjunction with the chief elder of Uda. The two powerful houses of Uda and Ognadzu had wrestled so long together for trading supremacy that they were in danger of becoming one house instead of two. There seemed to be much truth in the old saying that merchants were all of one clan, regardless of their colors. Was he of that clan anymore? Tohn wondered. Or had he been so long in the Mar that he thought more like a Mari than a merchant? He evoked the powers on the wind that they would not force him to make a choice between the two. The powers said nothing—he knew the truth already. Should the war by chance swing toward Ngandib-Mar he would be forced to choose, and choose quickly.

As he descended into the courtyard, the powers and the problems all receded. There was noise in his keep, much of it, with dogs barking, children running, mothers shouting and laughing. It was confusion, but not the confusion of masses of strangers in transit. This was the confusion of home. Each voice was recognizable individually, if one took the time to sort it out. If the changes came, this too would be lost—but how could he stop the changes, Tohn thought to himself, pushing past two nephews playing at swords with sticks in the main inner doorway. He stopped for a moment to regard their play. "No, too high, too high!" he heard himself instructing. "Thrust, don't hack. Let the enemy hack. He'll wear himself out—then you kill him." He acted this all out for the youngsters, who watched him carefully. "You see?" he asked. They both nodded wisely, then immediately went back to hacking at one another when Tohn turned away.

He chuckled as he entered the long dark hallway into the inner court. But his chuckle died in his throat as his mind swung back again to the plan, and the war, and the changes. These little boys—would they be carrying real swords by fall? Grown suddenly old by the whim of events? There was a heavy wooden door set in the stone wall to his left. This he opened after some fumbling in the dark for the key, then closed and locked it behind him. He turned to climb a dark stairway.

More steps, he thought to himself, and put his hand over his chest as if that would stop the pains that came now whenever he exerted himself. At the top of the stairs was another large wooden door, also locked, and Tohn struggled longer to find this key. When finally it was found and turned in the lock, Tohn opened the door with caution and a sense of awe. He was always in awe when he entered this room. This was a room full of powers.

The room was lit only by the bluish glow of an object sitting on a table. It was a triangular table, made of polished cedar wood for the express purpose of bearing the glowing object. Once again Tohn shook his gray head, amazed that he should be privileged to use it.

Jagd, in Chaomonous, had one just like it, but the chief elder of Uda did not treat it with such honor and respect. To him it was a device, nothing more—a communicator provided by science to be used as an effective tool for toppling governments. Flayh, in Lamath, felt the same way about his; though of course in the rarefied religious atmosphere of Lamath it would probably be referred to as a miracle. But to Tohn it was a magic thing, controlled by the powers, and belonging, really, to them.

Now it glowed with greater intensity, meaning the others were focusing upon it, forming the link. Tohn wasted no more time. He took his chair on one side of the triangular table and began to visualize the other two in the chairs to his left and right. As he did, he gazed into the pyramid—for that was the object's shape. It was a three-sided pyramid, tall and slender, formed of a crystal substance that burned with the blue-white light of a bolt of lightning. As Tohn focused his gaze on the side facing him, he began to see the face of Flayh on the inner plane to his left. Gradually the bluish clouds that normally kept the object opaque cleared from the right-hand plane as well, and there was the face of Jagd. The triangle was complete. The meeting began.

Jagd was smiling. Flayh was not.

In his excitement, Jagd spoke first. "It is working. It is working well."

"Don't be too certain," Flayh grumbled.

"Why? The plan is functioning perfectly. The girl is gone—carried off to Lamath by slavers. The people of Chaomonous will be in a frenzy by the end of the week!"

Tohn grunted. "I expected Talith to stifle that news."

"Of course he did," Jagd snapped, "but my people have spread the word in every tavern on the port. The story will be known, you may trust me for that."

"We shall, Jagd, we shall," Flayh growled, "but here is a part of the story you had best keep to yourself. My fool of a nephew has bungled it. The girl escaped while coming through the pass."

"What!" Jagd screamed, and Tohn covered his ears. It amazed him how well the crystal transmitted sound. He reacted with more subdued shock—this was a serious blow. He noticed that heavy feeling in his stomach again. He was dreading the rest of the news. "How did it happen?" Jagd yelled again.

"A long story," Flayh shot back, implying that he wasn't about to waste time retelling it. "My concern is that it did happen, and we need to move quickly if the plan is to succeed at all. Tohn."

"Yes," Tohn murmured.

"The girl rides toward you." The bottom seemed to drop out of Tohn's belly. He was involved after all. "Have you seen her? Have your guards picked her up?"

"I wasn't looking for her!" Tohn replied. "How would I know if I've seen her or not? I'll put my people on it right away."

"Wait!" Flayh called, for Tohn was about to break the link, and much remained to be said. All three of the pyramids needed to be in use for the link to be maintained. Tohn was obviously shaken by the news that these events were moving into his sector.

"I'm still here," Tohn grumbled.

"Unless my nephew is lying, she is alone, mounted on a horse wearing the blue-and-lime. She is still clothed in Chaon gold, unless she's been clever enough to filch a change somewhere. She should be no problem to find if your riders are competent."

"My riders are most competent," Tohn snapped.

"They had best be so. There is no way of manipulating the course of events if we do not recapture her."

"Not necessarily," Jagd broke in. "There's no reason for us to tell Talith that his daughter is no longer a captive. He trusts me implicitly, and expects me to deal with you as his agent. As long as we can maintain his belief that his daughter is in your hands in Lamath, we have his emotions in a vise."

"And the people will be aroused regardless."

"Right. But if she should somehow find her way back to Chaomonous—the lives and lands of all Ognadzu are forfeit in this golden empire."

"Why should you fret over us, Jagd?" Flayh sneered. "Won't Uda then reign supreme?"

"Of course. But to what effect, my friend Flayh? The plan will have failed. The changes will not occur. We will really have gained nothing for all our trouble except for a petty trading advantage."

"So you say," Flayh snorted. "As to the lives of my family members in Talith's dungeon, I care nothing. I made every effort to post all of my clan rivals—"

"Most of your clan rivals?" Tohn chuckled.

"All of my clan rivals who would go to Chaomonous before launching this plan." Flayh ignored Tohn's continuing chuckle. "But the Ognadzu holdings and lands in the Golden Kingdom are expansive—I should not like to lose those."

"Then Tohn had better look to his best, and find this Princess. That is, if you are still with us, Tohn mod Neelis?"

Tohn had been planning his search party, but he had been listening. One did not become an elder in Ognadzu by daydreaming. "I am still with you. We will find her."

Tohn sighed. "Can we get on with this? I'm tiring." It took a great deal of energy to maintain the ephemeral link, even with the aid of the pyramid.

Flayh rushed ahead. "There is more news, of a distinctly threatening nature. Something is bothering the dragon."

"What? Is he sick?" Jagd asked.

"Perhaps. Who could tell? But Pezi said the bargaining erupted in confusion the other day when the two heads began bickering with one another."

"Impossible!" Tohn shouted, surprising the other two. Tohn was an old hand at dealings with Vicia-Heinox. He had more caravans of experience than did any merchant living.

"I thought so too, but Pezi assures me it is so. Jagd, when does your next regular caravan pass Dragonsgate?"

"Two days."

"Have your trading captain carry a blue flyer with him. When the caravan is through, have him send the bird to me with the facts regarding the dragon's behavior. If the beast is behaving erratically, we will need to know soon."

Jagd chuckled. "Who can tell? This may be the perfect timing to insure our plan's success. If the dragon is divided, think of the disruption the news will cause in Lamath. That land will be ripe for political plucking." The three merchants pondered that for a moment, then suddenly Jagd spoke again, sharply. "Flayh, did Pelmen arrive there safely?"

"Pelmen? Dragon's-breath, no! I haven't seen that meddler in ages, and prefer things to remain that way."

Jagd spoke quickly then, with such intensity that he gripped the other two men as tightly as if he had seized them by their tunics. "We have a problem. Pelmen was with the group of slaves Pezi was taking to Lamath."

There was a long moment of silence. Then Flayh spoke. "I haven't looked at the new slaves . . ."

"Then look at them. If Pelmen is not there, we will need to assume that Pezi lied—and that Pelmen and the Princess may be traveling together through Ngandib-Mar!"

Tohn reeled with pain. Only a few moments before he had been hoping to keep the entire scheme out of his part of the world. Now, if Pelmen were involved, and if Pelmen were in his sector . . .

"Tohn! Tohn!" He heard Flayh calling him as if from a great distance; remembering where he was, Tohn fought to re-establish the link. The faces of the other two men shimmered before him, then once again grew solid. "There," Flayh grunted, as clarity came back into the vision. Flayh took a deep breath, then spoke quietly and calmly. The other two men knew this for a sign of his rage. "So Pelmen the player has crossed over again. I'll check my dungeons—but I'm skeptical. I have felt no emanations of his presence here."

"If Pelmen is free, he is probably in Ngandib-Mar. And if Pelmen is *there*," Jagd muttered the words that all three acknowledged as simple truth, "he is Pelmen the powershaper."

"And our plan," Tohn finished for him, "is in terrible jeopardy." Tohn was holding his head, for it was threatening to split in half from the inside. They had held the link too long. He knew that when they broke it, he would have to be sick.

"We shall see, then, what we shall see," Flayh muttered. "The link is breathing. We know our responsibilities. Until tomorrow at—"

Tohn broke the link, and rolled out of his seat to fall heavily onto the stone floor. It was several hours before he was able to stand. With what shallow breath remained to him, he committed every possible rider to the search, then lay back in his bed to await the news. That feeling of dread never left him. Indeed, it grew stronger by the hour.

It seemed to Bronwynn that the ride would never end. She clung to Pelmen, her arms locked around his chest, her head braced against his back, and fought to stay awake. It became more and more obvious to her that this man she rode behind was more than just a traveling player. But what? What was he, that he knew so well the valleys and forests of Ngandib-Mar? He seemed to be able to sense the presence of other riders,

for three different times during the night he had slowed
their horse and hidden them in the thickets or the rocks
or the fields as silent troops of grim-faced raiders
slipped stealthily through the darkness. He would turn
in the saddle to hold Bronwynn's head close to his
chest, gently covering her mouth and keeping her quiet
until the danger had passed. Each time, as they continued on, Bronwynn would wonder aloud of the race and
destination of the raiders, and Pelmen would cheerfully
tell her.

"How can you know so much about them?" she
asked, as the black sky behind them began to turn purple in preparation for the coming dawn.

"I have had my share of dealings with slave raiders,"
he answered. He seemed unwilling to go on.

Bronwynn leaned up to speak in his ear, to make herself heard above the noise of hoofs beating the ground.
"Are you one?" she asked. She felt Pelmen jerk in surprise at her question; then a chuckle rumbled through
him that she, clinging so closely, felt all the way through
her body too.

"No, my Lady. Not I. But I have traveled with
them—traded with them—been traded by them—"

"You'd been a slave before my father sold you to
Pezi?"

"Yes, my Lady," he rumbled, for she heard his words
less from his mouth than from the echo through his
chest. "Several times, in fact."

"What is it like?" She had often wondered, but had
never asked even one of the many women who attended
her. It was not proper for a Princess of Chaomonous to
concern herself with such trivia as the personal lives of
her slave women.

"It is like bondage of any sort," Pelmen said, turning
their horse in another of his sudden, mysterious changes
of direction that always seemed to help them avoid
meeting other riders. "It stops you from being yourself
and forces you to be something quite different."

"Sounds terrible."

"Not always," Pelmen continued, and that surprised
her. "Oh, the capture and enslavement is of course no
fun. A slave raider is a land pirate, with no regard for

the goals and sufferings of others. People aren't people to him, they are potential merchandise. It's hard to be friends with merchandise." Bronwynn thought of her own relationship to her servants, but said nothing. "As to the bondage itself, I discovered it can be instructive. Of this you may be sure, my Lady Bronwynn. The slaves know much more about the workings of the castle than the Lord and Lady do, for they give it their undivided attention."

"But to be caged, bound—" Bronwynn felt again those impossible ropes that just yesterday had gripped her wrists and ankles. "How can that ever be good?"

"It can make you appreciate freedom, Bronwynn. That's something that royalty sometimes is never able to do. Hush now." He guided the horse toward some large bushes. They ducked together as their mount moved into the cover, pushing branches aside, cracking some, others whooshing back into place as they passed. Pelmen stopped the horse, and they waited again.

The sky was a dark blue, but was growing lighter much more quickly now. Bronwynn listened intently, her eyes squeezed shut as if that would help her hearing. All she heard at first was the beating of Pelmen's heart, and the heavy breathing of the tired horse. But then the sound came. Riders, still some distance away but quickly coming toward them. She felt herself begin to tremble quite involuntarily, and Pelmen turned again to hold her head against him. The sound grew louder and then there they were—a troop of riders clothed in their nighttime camouflage uniforms of gray and brown. Their leader was the ugliest man Bronwynn had ever seen. His eyes were small slits, and his face was furrowed with a frown so chilling that it forced its reflection on the faces of all who beheld him. Though the early-morning air was cold, Bronwynn shivered not at the chill, but at the sight of that face. Then they were gone, moving swiftly to the south, riding hard into the cover of the Great South Fir.

"They're late," Pelmen observed quietly after they were well past.

"Who was that?" Bronwynn shuddered. Pelmen

craned around to look her in the face, a caustic smile
playing around the edges of his mouth.

"You don't know?" he asked. She looked back at him
blankly. "It's Admon Faye—your father's personal re-
cruiter of domestic talent." He spoke to the horse, and
they were once again on the way. It took a moment for
Bronwynn to make sense of his statement.

"That man is my father's slave master?"

"I'm not surprised that you've never seen him. He
and your father both make every effort to keep their
professional relationship secret."

They rode on some way before either spoke again.
Bronwynn imagined being captured by this frowning
slaver, and tried to relate that vision to the girls who
served her. Every one of her attendants had experienced *that*, she thought to herself. No wonder there was
such a bond of loyalty among them, a bond that sometimes made her feel shut out, even though she was the
Princess and they were her slaves.

"Remember," Pelmen said suddenly, "slaves aren't
the only people who are in bondage." Bronwynn sat up
in the saddle, surprised. She waited, but he said no
more.

They pressed on, as the dawn turned into morning.
They saw no more bands of raiders, but Pelmen warned
that their biggest danger now was a chance meeting
with riders of Ognadzu. Bronwynn dozed, and at one
point nearly fell from the horse. Pelmen stopped then,
and tied her to his back with strips of cloth from the
horse's silken colors. It was perhaps an undignified way
for a Princess to travel, but Bronwynn was too sleepy to
protest.

Between naps, the girl studied the passing countryside. Each hill they topped opened another valley to
view, and another hill beyond. It would have been
beautiful country in any other circumstance, but Bronwynn was tired of it. She longed for her own bed, and
dreamed of it, waking suddenly to find herself still tied
to the back of this curious stranger who seemed to know
so much about everything. She felt him bend forward,
and heard him talking; but though she strained to hear,

she couldn't make out any of his words. It puzzled her, until she felt the horse surge forward with renewed energy, and she realized he had been speaking to it. For the first time it occurred to her how far and how fast their mount had come with so little rest. She had often bragged to the children of other noble families that the stables of the King bred the finest horseflesh in the world. The suspicion grew in her that the merchants in fact bred the best. Certainly this horse of Pezi's was the most marvelous she had ever ridden. But was the incredible effort entirely due to the horse? Or was this Pelmen the player calling down the powers he said rode on the winds, and using them to buoy the horse up in its flight? When the beast began to flag, his energy fading, Pelmen would bend to speak a word in his ear. Just a word, and the great-hearted animal would leap forward again, goaded not by pain but by his pride. The rhythm of its hoofbeats hypnotized her. Bronwynn slept again.

When she woke this time her bottom was numb. She shifted position to get some feeling back into it, and wished immediately that she hadn't. "I'm so sore I may never walk again!" she moaned. "When are we going to get there?"

"So, you're awake again," Pelmen observed. He patted her hand, then leaned forward to dip his hand into the bag that hung from the saddle. He pulled out a piece of dried meat and passed it over his shoulder. She pulled her hand free from the wrappings that tied her to him, and took it.

"What's this?" she grumbled.

"Food. I thought you might be hungry."

She sniffed at it, and made a face he didn't see. "I'd rather die," she said crossly, and tossed it into the bushes.

"Your choice." Pelmen shrugged. Pulling more meat from the bag, he began to chew. An hour later, when she announced she had changed her mind, he wordlessly passed her another piece.

Long after Bronwynn had given up hope of ever seeing Dorlyth Castle, they crested a small hill and Pelmen pointed. It was not much of a keep, just two rather plain towers surrounded by a rough stone wall, standing

on an uninviting escarpment of rock. But Bronwynn
was exhausted. It didn't matter what the castle looked
like; to her it was beautiful. Pelmen rode slowly down
into the small field that stretched to its base, watching
with interest a tall young man who was chopping wood
nearby. Rather than using an axe, the lad chopped with
a greatsword, the heavy, five-foot-long blade that was
the favorite weapon of the Maris. It was so long and
hard to manage that most flat-landers had long since
moved to shorter swords, but in the hands of a large
man it could be a formidable weapon. And this man,
young as he was, was certainly large enough. He did not
look like most Maris—his hair was not blond, though it
was bushy, and his legs were long and straight rather
than squat. He was so intent on his work he didn't see
them until they were but twenty yards away. Startled by
their sudden appearance, he leapt atop the woodpile
and turned the sword into full wheel around his head.
Then his jaw dropped open and he stared in shock. He
had recognized the rider.

"P-p-pelmen! P-p-powershaper!" he stuttered. Without another word, he dropped the sword and vaulted up
the hill toward the gate of the keep and disappeared
inside.

"Some welcome," Bronwynn sniffed, and Pelmen
laughed. He patted the horse's side and untied the
cloths that had held the girl to him. "I hate this," she
murmured as he lowered her to the ground, and her
groan told him that she'd had good reason to dread. He
felt it too, as soon as he slung himself out of the broad
saddle and down. He walked a few tentative steps, then
came back to take the head of their stolen steed between his two hands.

"I don't know what Pezi called you, but to me you
are Minaliss, the steel-shouldered one—and a very fine
friend."

Bronwynn didn't hear him, for she was bending and
stretching and prancing around, doing all she could to
get life back into her legs. Pelmen took the horse by the
reins, offered his hand to the lady, and said grandly,
"Shall we walk the rest of the way?" She half smiled,
the best she could manage under the circumstances, and

took his hand. Arm in arm, they strolled together into Dorlyth Castle and safety.

Visitors to Flayh's mansion on the southern plain of Lamath often told him he lived like a King. This was a mistake, for Flayh considered that he lived better than a King. He lived like a *merchant*, thank you, and in Flayh's mind a merchant outranked a King by a large margin. Those who visited his main dining room could scarcely help being impressed. Great chandeliers hung the length of the hall, each one illuminated by a circle of twelve oil-burning lamps. The pieces of cut crystal that dangled below the lamps directed flashes of sparkling light to all corners of the room, and the gentle breeze that blew through open windows at either end of the hall kept them turning and shimmering throughout the course of the evening meal.

As always, the tables were heavily laden with fruits, nuts, vegetables of every kind, and exotic candies from faraway islands. There were colorful beverages in still more colorful decanters, and piles and piles of steaming meats of every sort, which filled the room with an aroma that was, to Pezi, quite heavenly. As he finished off the last of a venison steak, his belt unbuckled out of sight under the table, he was already dreaming of what culinary delights awaited him in his evening snack. Pezi felt the people of Lamath were the only people who truly recognized the finer things in life: beef, pork, venison, etc. He loved the time he spent at his uncle's—most of it, anyway. In fact, Pezi believed that except for one thing, Flayh's residence was the most wonderful place on earth. The exception, of course, was Flayh.

At this very moment Flayh was coming in the side door, and Pezi almost groaned aloud when he saw his uncle was headed straight for him. He dutifully pasted a smile across his broad, greasy face.

"Good evening, uncle—"

"I want to see your slaves," Flayh said flatly.

"But—you never inspect slaves—"

"I'm inspecting these," Flayh snapped.

"They're—they're in the dungeon, where I normally—"

"You're coming too."

"Why, yes sir, of course, sir—" Pezi began to send messages to his body to get up, but Pezi was bigger than most men and it took a little longer for his legs to get the word. "I—I wonder—do you not trust me?" he said.

Flayh sneered at him. "Trust you? Of course I trust you, nephew. I trust you as far as I could throw you." Since Flayh was only a little over five feet tall, and weighed only one hundred thirty, Pezi did not consider this testimonial particularly encouraging. "Get up!" Flayh demanded.

Pezi was trying, but halfway to his feet he had remembered his belt was unbuckled, and he was now trying to make some inconspicuous adjustments under the table. Some ladies on the far side of the room had noticed and were giggling and whispering together. He smiled wanly at them, and stood. His uncle was already almost out the door.

Below the dining hall was a gigantic kitchen. Below that was a dungeon. Flayh had felt this a very efficient arrangement. He had cut slits in the stone floor of the kitchen, and instructed his cooks not to pick up food scraps or take much concern for the appearance of their work place. At the end of the day they would simply sweep the scraps into the floor slits, and what fell through to the slaves below was what they ate. Some days some slaves were lucky, some days others were. But no one was lucky enough. Then the kitchen would be mopped down, and buckets of dirty water sloshed across the floor. The slave who knew enough to stand under a slit at the right moment got the only thing approaching a bath that was to be had in the slave quarters. Often new slaves, unlucky enough to fail in the scramble for scraps, would cry out through the floor for food. Or they would be too stupid or too proud to stand openmouthed below the floor slits while the floor was being washed, and would plead for a drink of water. Flayh had instructed his guards to beat these new slaves until they learned not to speak to the cooks. If a baker burned several loaves of bread, or a cook burned a roast, they would often blame it on a noisy slave, and that slave, guilty or not, would suffer for it. Most of the slaves learned quickly. Flayh's house might be a paradise for invited guests—for the slaves, it was little short of a hell.

To this dungeon Flayh now headed, keeping his own quiet counsel as his fat nephew struggled to keep up with him. It was as they were descending a spiraling stone staircase in the darkness that Pezi observed a curious thing—his uncle seemed to glow with a weird, blue phosphorescence, and he left a trail of glowing dust wherever he stepped. Though Pezi felt little rapport with his uncle, and no eagerness for conversation, his curiosity overcame him.

"Uncle, you're glowing!"

"I'd advise you to mind your own business." Then Flayh laughed bitterly. "Had you minded your business, the plan would not be in such jeopardy."

"What plan?"

"Mind your own business!" Flayh screamed, and Pezi jammed his jaws tight, resolving to say nothing save in answer to a question.

At the bottom of the staircase was a long dark corridor, low-ceilinged, lighted by flickering torches placed intermittently along the walls. "Guards!" Flayh called, and at the sound of that distinctive voice, completely unexpected in this dank, foul quarter, there was a great clatter of martial-sounding activity.

They turned a corner at the end of the hall, and a group of guards stood at attention. They were all unkempt, smelly denizens of the dungeon, made so by the cruel and callous nature of their assignment. Flayh looked with disgust at their blue-and-lime uniforms, caked with mud and the grease from a dozen dinners, and snorted. "Don't you ever clean yourselves?"

The leader of the detail cleared his throat and spoke nervously. "Had we known you were coming—I mean, we didn't expect—"

"Always expect me, keeper," Flayh said, yelling in the man's face. "This is my castle, my dungeon, and I expect my fighting men to reflect my personality! Always expect me, or you may expect to find yourself the slave rather than the slavekeeper. Understood?"

"Yes, sir!" the keeper snapped, and saluted.

"I may have need of you on the battlefield someday," Flayh continued more quietly. "I don't want you to smell so badly that other soldiers won't stand beside you in line! Open that door."

The keeper rushed to comply. The door flew open, and the stench flew out. Pezi gagged, but Flayh seemed almost pleased by it. He expected the guards to behave like soldiers. His slaves, however, ought by simple reason to smell like pigs. It helped to cement into their heads the true nature of their condition, and prepared them for sale.

He stalked to the middle of the large room, then put his hands on his hips and looked around. "Torch!" he called, and a guard raced in with a blazing torch that shed some light on these miserable subjects most unused to it. Flayh scanned the groups of slaves as they huddled in various corners. There was no feeling here of Pelmen's presence. "Take it around, put it in the face of each one." The guard did as he was instructed. The last slave was finally viewed, and Flayh slowly turned to look at Pezi. The fat merchant was sure he was shedding a pound every passing second. His fear was so great that he was sweating like a horse after a hard ride. "Bring the torch over here," Flayh murmured to the guard, "and hold it up to this fat fool's face."

The guard, puzzled but obedient, came quickly to Pezi's side. The fat merchant feared he was about to swallow his tongue whole. It felt like a dry wool sock rolled in the back of his throat.

Flayh gazed at him coldly, then spoke. "Where is he?" he asked.

"Where's who? Oooooff!" Pezi grunted, as Flayh buried a fist in his gut.

"Where, Pezi?"

"Where is who, tell me who you—" This time his uncle slapped him. The look on Flayh's face convinced Pezi that he had better start explaining. He began with a confession. "All right, you mean Pelmen."

"I'm glad to see you're not completely without sense. Tell me about Pelmen."

"He—he got away."

"Oh, really? Why, I never would have guessed. How on earth did he manage that?"

"He—it was he who confused the beast—convinced him to release the girl—started the riot in the pass that led to their escape."

"*Their* escape is it now? And did you follow them?"

"I—I had no chance! I was risking my life as it was, trying to save the caravan!"

"I would have given ten caravans joyfully to the dragon to have that girl and Pelmen here, in this dungeon! That was the purpose of this whole enterprise, you fat swine!" Flayh punctuated this last with another backhanded slap. Pezi rubbed his jaw reflectively, watching Flayh's hands, hoping to guess where and when they might strike again. "You've failed me, Pezi. Oh, you've done so before. But never like this. Never to this degree." Pezi's face grew very, very pale, though in the torchlight the change could not be seen. "Shall I just have these guards strip you, and toss you into the corner over there?"

"Oh, uncle, please—no—" Pezi found no difficulty in bending both knees and draping himself around his uncle's feet. "Please, don't do that!"

"I could have them cut your tongue out for lying to me. How would that be?"

"No. Oh, please—"

"It would be a fitting punishment, wouldn't it?"

"Oh, please—"

"Wouldn't it?"

"Yes, I guess. Oh, please—" Pezi babbled incoherently, the horror of his situation growing clearer with every sentence Flayh spoke.

"Yes, you say? Then I should do it? Guard, a poinard." Immediately Flayh had a knife in his hand; with the other hand gripping Pezi's hair, he pulled the fat man's head up to place the point on Pezi's lips.

"No! Please!"

That seemed to be enough. Flayh was a cruel man, a mean man. But he was not wasteful. He would misuse Pezi in whatever way necessary to insure his loyalty, but he needed Pezi's talents to accomplish his purpose, and that of the Council of Elders. "Get up," he growled. Pezi stood, trembling uncontrollably. "I want you to go to Lamath, Pezi. I want you to speak with the King of Lamath himself, and tell him that Talith of Chaomonous has accused him of stealing his daughter, and raises a great army against him. Tell him that the dragon is confused—and the pass is open. If he wishes to defend himself, he needs to make haste. Do you think that you can manage that, Pezi?"

"Yes. Oh, yes. Oh, thank you, sir—"

"Quiet." Pezi shut his mouth and waited, as Flayh went on. "Then you are to go to the High Priest of the Unified Dragonfaith. Tell him the King of Lamath has blasphemed the dragon and sets an army against the beast. The new High Priest is a young lad, and should be easy to manipulate. Tell him the King has moved at last to crush the Dragonfaith's power, and that he must do all he can to weaken the army's morale, or his position will be forfeit. Is *that* clear?"

"Yes, sir," Pezi sniveled.

"I want you on your way to Lamath tonight—*no* sleep, *no* midnight snack. *Now!* Take those lazy cousins of yours with you. Now!" He shouted again, and Pezi bolted from the room. Flayh looked around at the slaves who watched, amazed at this display, confused at the torrent of words completely unrelated to their situation. Flayh smiled at them humorlessly, and strode out of the room. Then the door clanked shut behind him, and they sat in darkness once again.

"I hate him," Vicia whispered ferociously. This audible hostility echoed down the canyon walls of the pass, bereft of vegetation from repeated displays of dragon temper.

"I hate the Player—I hate him!" Heinox said in unanimity with his twin. The dragon had slept only fitfully for two days. He had spent every waking moment since the encounter with Pelmen in chaotic dialogue between his two heads. Neither head could admit the possibility of its twin being a separate entity. Each head struggled vainly to re-establish that total rapport so lately taken for granted. But each sought to re-establish that state under its own control. Self-consciousness had robbed

Vicia-Heinox of his coordination, his personal unity, and his peace. It would seem only natural that in his frustration the dragon would come to hate that one who had driven a wedge between himselves. And the dragon was frustrated. As a unit or as a pair, Vicia-Heinox was the largest concentrated living mass of frustration in existence at that moment, and the inevitable explosion of that frustration into human injury and property damage only awaited some marginal agreement as to where he should begin.

"I'll destroy Chaomonous. Burn the city to cinders. Turn it into a wasteland."

"Why should I choose Chaomonous?"

"That's where the Player came from, isn't it?"

"I don't know where he came from. I only know he went to Ngandib-Mar, and I think I ought to lay waste to every castle and eat every villager in the whole of the highlands! Surely I would manage to come across that Player in the process!"

"And when I get him—oh, what I'll do to him!" Heinox rasped maliciously, his eyes glittering in evil anticipation.

"Yes—this is what I'll do!" said Vicia, and he began to catalogue once more all the terrible torments he would inflict on Pelmen, once he had the Player in delicious captivity.

"I already said what I would do to him," Heinox interrupted. He had no wish to precipitate another quarrel, but why did this other head take such delight in aggravating him?

"I know I have already said what I would do to the annoying human! I'm just reviewing it for my entertainment! Do I mind?"

"Yes I mind! I'm not entertained!"

"I *am*, I said!" Vicia spoke with great deliberation, exhibiting super-dragon patience with this vexatious appendage who seemed to consider himself the true seat of dragon control. He raised above Heinox and looked down at his rival threateningly. Then he shook with rage as he heard Heinox repeating yet another time the question that had for days been stealing every fragment of the dragon's once-fabled intrapersonal tranquility.

"Why is it that I can't just say a thing without my having to echo it? Why is it that I can't just agree to cooperate anymore? Why this constant internal bicking? Can't I see I am making myself very sick?" Heinox had risen to Vicia's level, and was now eyeball to eyeball with him. Vicia boiled.

"Am I implying that this is my fault?"

"I certainly am!"

Vicia roared. Surely no dragon, ever, anywhere, had been forced to take this kind of obnoxious nonsense from himself. It had gone beyond the limits of his endurance. With a scream so fierce that it would certainly have brought tears to the eyes of even the most insensitive of ogres, Vicia jetted to his fullest extension, then plummeted, jaws agape, to seize the armored neck of Heinox just behind the ears and shake it savagely. Of course, he immediately let go, for the pain registered throughout the whole dragon body. In short, Vicia-Heinox bit himself, and it hurt terribly. It even bled a gallon or two. The dragon left his feet, fluttering a few hundred yards above the ground, waiting for the pain to pass and howling pitifully. It was the first pain the dragon could remember feeling since—since he could remember feeling! No mere weapon could break through the mail-like armor of his reptilian skin. But dragonteeth! What substance could withstand the native keenness of such powerful incisors?

The dragon settled back to earth, and Heinox turned to his more reckless companion. "I hope I won't be so stupid as to try that again," he said acidly.

"I hope I won't either," agreed the chastened Vicia. "Why did I do it?"

"I suppose I just got sick of myself. I'm not really surprised, though I didn't think I was quite so stupid."

Vicia whipped angrily around and pushed himself into Heinox' pouting face. "And I never realized I was so obnoxious!" Heinox chose not to reply, fearing another attack from this lunatic who seemed to share his body. Though the pain was subsiding by this time, Vicia bent to lick the wound he had inflicted.

"I wish I wouldn't do that," Heinox complained. "That rough tongue is not the slightest bit soothing."

"Why don't I go stick myself in a hole in the ground?" Vicia shouted back. They glowered at one another for a full minute. Then, tiring, both sank down to rest in the dust, and to think bad thoughts about the other.

"I hate Pelmen," Vicia whispered. There was silence for half an hour or so.

"I feel a little sorry for the people in the next caravan," Heinox observed finally.

"Why?"

"Because I'm going to eat every last one of them just for spite."

The afternoon shadows lengthened, and the pass darkened as the line of the sun retreated up the face of the eastern cliff. But even when the sun was completely gone, the darkness at the bottom of that canyon was no match for the black bile in the depths of the angry dragon's seething soul.

❧ Chapter Three ❧

"I WISH I could read their minds," Pelmen sighed. He stood before a large window in the greater tower of Dorlyth Castle, gazing east across green fields wet with morning dew. Though it was nearing midmorning there was still little light; it was a gray day, and a chill hung in the air. A draft blew into the room, causing Dorlyth to shiver.

"You can't, though," he rumbled in his thick, hoarse bass. "So why don't you close that drape before I catch pneumonia?" Dorlyth took another sip of a steaming fruit drink that was his morning addiction and waved Pelmen toward a chair.

Pelmen smiled, shook his head, and let the heavy tapestry drapes fall shut to block the wind. The flames that struggled to bring light to this dark interior flickered, then burned up again brightly. Pelmen wrapped his purple robe around him and settled back into a feather-stuffed chair. If anyplace was home to the traveling player, this place was. He felt very content and relaxed, for he loved the company of this friend. At the same time he felt a keen responsibility to move swiftly on. He had no wish to involve Dorlyth in his problems. Certainly the merchant houses were trailing him by this time. When they arrived, he and the girl should be long gone. The question was, to where? What kind of plan had he upset by confusing the dragon? Who was behind it, and what did they intend to gain?

"You're thinking again," Dorlyth growled good-naturedly. "Haven't I told you I forbid that in my house?" Dorlyth took another long, hot sip. He was comfortably wrapped in a rug of thickest bear fur, and he lay stretched out on the padded couch he had slept on. He was a big man, much in character and appearance like that very bear whose skin now warmed him. His face was broad, his nose flat, his eyes very large and very brown. The rest of his face seemed shrouded in fur, for he was a very hairy man. His hair was bushy, almost kinky, of the shining honey-blond color so characteristic of Ngandib-Mar. His beard matched his hair in every detail but for a tuft of gray right under his lower lip. Pelmen enjoyed teasing him about that gray streak, but Dorlyth rather liked the distinctive little tuft. He said it lent some human dignity to his otherwise animal-like appearance.

He was smiling at Pelmen, but his eyebrows reflected the weight of his concern for his friend. Pelmen had entangled himself in another potentially catastrophic situation; as always, he seemed to be enjoying it a little too much. The man was a magnet of curious and fateful events. Long though he had tried, Dorlyth had never been able to convince Pelmen that his abilities were most needed here, in Ngandib-Mar. Instead, the man seemed to wander the earth, actively seeking new entanglements. Invariably he found them.

"If only I could find some key that would tie this all together. It makes no sense to see this as just an isolated incident in the ever-continuing struggle for control of the Chaon throne."

"What else could it be?" Dorlyth asked. "From what you've told me, this is how I figure it. The house of Ognadzu makes a deal with the King's mistress to kidnap the sole heir to the throne. The King rages, sends his soldiers to recapture her but fails, eventually losing track of the girl altogether. His dynasty threatened, his potency in question, he finally divorces his now barren Queen to marry the mistress, not realizing she laid the plot. The mistress favors Ognadzu, and eventually that house becomes more influential in Chaomonous than ever. It would then recoup any losses suffered as a result of participation in the kidnap, and with interest. It's simple. So forget it. Have a grape or something, stop making me think this early in the day."

"That just doesn't sound like Ognadzu. Far too risky for Flayh. What if the mistress, once on the throne, decided to burn the past, forgetting the deal with Ognadzu? What recourse would that family have?"

"I don't know. Maybe they have something over the mistress we don't know about. We don't know her loyalties."

"Yes we do," said Pelmen, raising his eyebrows knowingly. "Ligne has powerful loyalties, but they are extremely limited—they include only herself. Oh, I'm sure Ligne probably sees the plan just as you present it. But I can't believe that is the total picture. I think it's bigger than that."

"So it's bigger," Dorlyth frowned. "So what? Why can't you just let well enough alone?"

Pelmen stood, tenting his fingers before his face and plucking unconsciously at his lips. He began to walk around the room, his slippered feet whispering across the rich red carpet. "It may be the move. It may be their big move, Dorlyth."

"You're pacing again. You wear out that rug and you'll pay to replace it." He jerked his cup to his mouth a little too quickly, sloshing hot liquid onto his chin. He muttered something Pelmen didn't hear, which was really just as well.

"It would make sense," Pelmen said. "An incident,

arranged not just between one house and members of the court, but planned and executed by all the families in secrecy."

"Sounds like a lot of trouble to me. Meetings between the houses, deals, compromises—they'd never be able to agree. And what would they have to gain?"

"Power," Pelmen breathed.

"Dragon knows, friend, they have plenty of that already! Why should they need more?"

"Oh, they don't need it, Dorlyth. That fact doesn't stop their wanting more of it."

"But why should they want it? They've already got the world in their shoulder bag."

"Why do they want it? I'm a player, Dorlyth, not a philosopher. Don't ask me about why."

"You're a good deal more than just a player and you know it. If I could just get you to practice some—"

"Don't need any practice, friend. Once you learn . . ." Pelmen shrugged.

"You can still shape?" Dorlyth smiled, sitting up.

In answer Pelmen drew a tiny circle in the air with the thumb of his right hand, then cupped his hand under the circle. Gradually a glow began in that circle which spread and grew until Pelmen was holding a ball of lavender flame. He glanced over at Dorlyth, who was still smiling, then with a flick of his wrist tossed the fireball at him.

Dorlyth ducked beneath his bearskin, shouting. "You crazy—" Then he popped his head back out to see if the couch was on fire.

"Relax," Pelmen soothed, his mind already elsewhere. Dorlyth straightened his covers and glowered at his friend. The expression was wasted, for Pelmen had turned back to the window.

"Well, at least that's something," the hairy man said, after a moment of silence.

"A parlor trick," Pelmen snorted.

"Which very well could have burned my parlor if you hadn't snuffed it, which makes it a formidable weapon and a useful tool. Pelmen, why don't you leave the rest of the world alone and concentrate on this land? I'm sure the merchant houses would be happy to be rid of your annoying presence, and we need you! The Confederation of Lords is so weak the slightest breeze could topple it. I like King Pahd as much as the next man, but I fear he intends to sleep through his entire reign! If you must get involved in politics, get involved here!"

"I *am* involved here, Dorlyth. Can't you get that through your hairy hide? There are changes in the air, my friend, changes for everyone. You surely can't believe that Ngandib-Mar will be unaffected by the bickering between Lamath and Chaomonous—"

"We've avoided it before."

"We won't this time!" Pelmen was angry. Not at Dorlyth, but at the world, and what he saw taking place in it. The world was changing—it was always changing, naturally, but these changes were being accelerated by the plots and counterplots of nations and houses. And the chaos Pelmen saw looming on the horizon pleased him not one bit.

"A suggestion," Dorlyth said, and Pelmen looked at him. "Don't ask me how, or why, but I can get in contact with Admon Faye, Talith's slaver. Let's give him the girl to return to her father. May not stop your dread changes, but it could hold them off a little longer."

Pelmen's eyes were hard. Dorlyth wished he hadn't spoken. "Admon Faye? I can't believe you said that, Dorlyth. Not you."

Dorlyth shifted uncomfortably under that cold look. "Just a suggestion, that's all."

"I would not entrust anyone into the hands of Admon Faye. Not even Flayh himself." Pelmen jerked away, and walked to the window to sweep the curtains aside again. When he next spoke, his voice was soft once more. "Besides, my friend, the biggest change has already taken place—and for that I bear the responsibility myself."

"The dragon?" Dorlyth asked, and Pelmen nodded.

"The dragon is of a divided mind. The world we have always known is ending."

"How can you know that?"

"You believe in prophecy?" Pelmen inquired, raising his eyebrows.

Dorlyth snorted. "What do you think?"

"I do. This one, anyway."

Dorlyth chuckled derisively. "I guess you should, since you're the one who made it!"

Pelmen smiled sadly, then asked in a mocking voice, "Why do I waste my time with unbelievers?"

"That dragon has probably already forgotten that the whole thing even happened."

"I don't think so." Pelmen sighed, looking out across the land in the direction of Dragonsgate. "And when the word gets out in Lamath, the Dragonfaith will collapse."

"I wouldn't go so far as to say that." Dorlyth chuckled, standing to walk around the chair. He laid his large hand on Pelmen's shoulder. "From what you tell me, that's a mighty old religion. I wager it won't even be dented."

From the field below came the sound of chopping. Pelmen looked at Dorlyth, and the old warrior grunted. "The lad again, practicing with his greatsword. Says he wants to be a hero." Dorlyth shook his head, and now he took his own turn at pacing around the room. "I ask him if he knows what the life expectancy of a hero is—he won't listen to me."

"Why should he?" Pelmen grinned, folding his arms and leaning against the window ledge. "You're still here."

"Only because I had the good sense to run when I got into a scrap I couldn't win. I'm not sure he knows how to run."

"You never ran from any battle, Dorlyth."

"Oh yes I did! I ran from you, don't you remember?" They both laughed, minds replaying memories of long ago. These memories led them inevitably to thoughts of ageing, and each made his way back to a chair. "That was when you dug up that ancient book. Did you ever decipher that thing?"

"I did."

"What did it say?" This was an old question, one they always argued about. Dorlyth tossed it out casually as he drained the rest of his cup, now gone cold.

"It led me to Lamath," Pelmen said quietly, and Dorlyth bit his lip and examined the cup in his hands.

Finally he spoke. "What happens when you go there, Pelmen? You've never really explained it to me."

"I can't explain it to myself," Pelmen said. Propping his feet on Dorlyth's couch and lacing his hands behind his head, he leaned back and made an attempt. "You experience the powers?"

"Of course I do," Dorlyth grunted. "I just can't shape them as you can."

"It is a strange thing, my friend." Pelmen now held his hands together at his waist. Dorlyth jumped, for suddenly there was a little brown mouse in those cupped hands, then once again they were empty. He glanced up at Pelmen's face, but the man was looking elsewhere—at a place far away, perhaps in Lamath. "I shape the powers here as if they were extensions of my own mind. I think a thing a certain way, and the thing is there, in palpable form. I don't know why, I only know it is. But somewhere in the Great North Fir, as I near the Lamathian border, I stop shaping the powers—and the Power starts shaping me."

"Sounds unpleasant."

"Then you don't understand. Because it is the sweetest of pleasures—not less because it comes wholly unbidden, and is far beyond my control."

"The essence of the dragon gets you?" Dorlyth asked with a sneer.

Pelmen shook his head patiently. "Has nothing to do with the dragon, Dorlyth. Nothing at all."

"This ancient book explains the feeling to you?" Dorlyth asked, striving now to be fair to a thing he didn't understand.

"Partly. Partly the feeling explains itself."

"And that makes you want to go to Lamath—so you can get another charge?"

"No. I must go to Lamath someday in order to *be* who I *am* there. Whoever that is."

"You're Pelmen the powershaper, that's all I need to know," Dorlyth thundered, confused by all this and choosing to dismiss it from his mind. "That's good enough for me."

"But you see, my friend—that isn't good enough for me."

The huge oaken door at the far end of the room slammed open, and Rosha mod Dorlyth stalked in. He carried his scabbarded greatsword on his right shoulder, with his shirt slung over his left. His skin was smooth and slick with sweat, colored a gleaming, burnished brown, the hue of burned butter. He hung the sword on a wall hook and mopped his face with his shirt, then turned his head to grin at Pelmen over a sinewy shoulder.

"Y-you're up," he mumbled happily.

"Of course I'm up." Pelmen smiled back. "You expect me to sleep all day?"

Rosha jerked his head up, indicating the upper rooms in the tower. "G-g-girl is."

Pelmen raised his eyebrows, and looked at Dorlyth, who shrugged, his brown eyes sparkling merrily. "You have some interest in the lady?" Pelmen asked innocently. Rosha's face was dark, but even in the dim light of the flickering candles his blush was evident. His expression hardened, his jaws clenched together, and he shook his head. He found a seat at the far end of the roòm, retrieved the sword, and busied himself with sharpening its already razorlike edge. Pelmen looked at Dorlyth again.

"Pay him no mind, he won't talk to me, either," Dorlyth said.

Pelmen glanced again at the broad muscular back now turned to him and sighed. Then he chuckled quietly. "Looks like his mother, doesn't he?" Pelmen observed.

Dorlyth cocked his head, and regarded those gleaming shoulders skeptically. "That chunk of meat?" Dorlyth mused. Pelmen grinned at him. "Well, maybe in coloring." The hairy warrior's face expressed amusement mixed with fierce pride. It told Pelmen something he already knew—that Dorlyth loved this spirited young battler, above his land, above his castle, above his very life.

Dorlyth rejoiced at the rippling of the lad's muscles as he honed and polished the giant blade. He thrilled when he watched the lad whirl the heavy weapon around his head as if it were nothing more than a butcher's cleaver. He had trained Rosha in every battle art he'd learned himself through his long years of conflict, and had come finally to admit that the boy was a more natural fighter than he had ever been. In that admission his pride commingled with his fear, for he knew the lad was afraid of nothing that frightened other men, and Dorlyth knew how necessary fear was to self-preservation. How could he teach the boy his limits? Again and again Dorlyth had worked these worries through his mind, and again and again forced himself to acknowledge that Rosha was nearly grown and would need to find his own way through the world. Yet as he sat and watched the boy now, he wished that he could shape the powers as Pelmen did and force time to stand still.

"Not even I can stop time," Pelmen said, and Dorlyth jumped as if he'd been slapped.

"Have you taken up mind reading since your last visit?" Dorlyth asked indignantly.

"I could always read yours, my friend." Pelmen gestured toward Rosha. "He'll soon be ready to go."

"Let's not rush it, shall we?" Dorlyth snapped, standing. "He still has things to learn."

"Such as?"

"How to talk, for one."

"I t-talk all right," Rosha stammered fiercely, twisting around to look at his father.

"All right for a butterfly!" Dorlyth bellowed, then flapped his arms in the air. "Flit, flit, can't sit down on a word and make it stick!"

It was incredible to Pelmen how swiftly the boy was out of his chair, how gracefully he danced across the floor, and how effortlessly he brought the five-foot blade to his father's throat. His face was a violent red, and his mouth was screwed up as he fought to spew forth a stream of invective that just wouldn't come.

His father didn't flinch. He just glanced over at Pelmen and murmured, "You see? You tease him about his speech and he wants to chop your head off." His eyes shifted back to lock with his son's angry glare. "Even mine?" he asked quietly.

Rosha dropped his sword point to the stone floor,

and followed it down with his eyes. When he looked back up at his father, there was a trace of a grin on his severe lips. He shook his head.

Pelmen sighed deeply, and patted his chest. "That shocked me."

"That's what you get for throwing fireballs at unsuspecting warriors," Dorlyth grunted. He grabbed the drape and flung it shut. This time the candles blew out, and Dorlyth groaned at the nuisance. "Pelmen, would you mind . . ." he began, but already in the middle of the dark room there was the beginning of a turquoise glow that grew into a sphere of blue-green flame. The ball touched all the candles in turn, setting a blue flame on each. The three men became engrossed in the beauty of its dancing movement.

"How lovely!" Bronwynn exclaimed, her face alive with wonder, and immediately all eyes were fixed on her instead. Were he inclined toward speech, Rosha would have used those same words to describe his vision of her as she stepped through the doorway. She was not a tall girl, but short would not describe her either, for that has connotations of stubbiness about it, and there was nothing stubby about the Princess of Chaomonous. Except, perhaps, for her nose, which was turned up in a saucy peak, and covered with youthful freckles. The rest of her face was a lady's face. Her mouth was small and her lips full, and she pouted them together now for maximum effect. They glistened in the flickering candlelight, for she had licked them just prior to stepping into the room. Her eyes and chin were proud as she turned her head to survey the furnishings, and Rosha thought he'd never seen eyes so startlingly blue on anyone save his mother. She wore his mother's old robes—clothes treasured lovingly by his father in these long years since her passing—and in her regal bearing, Bronwynn did them justice. They were the orange-red color of a robin's breast, and the golden-brown hair awash on her shoulders in carefully cultivated disarray somehow made that color more vibrant and exciting than Rosha could recall it ever being before. One could say without exaggeration that he was taken with her. Nor was that fact lost on his father and on Pelmen.

"How did you do that?" she asked, her gaze of girlish admiration reserved for Pelmen alone, shutting the others out.

Pelmen cleared his throat, for the drama of her entrance had affected him as well. He felt the warmth of that look with some discomfort. "The—the powers I spoke of—"

"Then you are a sorcerer!" she squealed, clapping her hands in delight.

"I—shape the powers—sometimes. That's all."

"That's *all*? I would think that's quite enough, wouldn't you?" She aimed this at Dorlyth, who chuckled.

It struck him that the spell of enchantment she had so suddenly woven around the three of them showed that this girl had some magic of her own. "Surely." Dorlyth shrugged. "I've said it myself. But who can tell a sorcerer anything?"

"Do it again," Bronwynn pleaded, floating elegantly across the room to position herself in front of Pelmen.

"Later," he muttered, embarrassed. He took her by the hand and turned her around to introduce her to the others. "This is Dorlyth mod Karis, Lord of this castle and a member of the Federation of the Mar."

Dorlyth nodded his head graciously, and Bronwynn smiled. For the first time since she had been so rudely ripped from Ligne's chambers over a week ago, she felt some control over her own destiny. At least she controlled this situation.

"We welcome you to our humble keep, my Lady, and feel honored by the presence of such a renowned visitor." Dorlyth summoned all of his practiced charm. "It is our hope that you will find the same pleasure in the Mar of Ngandib that we find in looking on your radiant face."

Bronwynn's smile faltered, and she whispered to Pelmen, "Are all Maris this courteous?"

"Hardly." Pelmen smiled, winking over her head at his friend, who managed to stifle a grin. "And this—" Pelmen gestured to the young man hidden in the shadows at the far end of the room. "This is Rosha mod Dorlyth, son of Dorlyth mod Karis."

"Mod?" she asked.

"Loosely, it means 'son of.' "

"Very loosely, my lady," Dorlyth broke in grandly. "Mod means 'treasure of,' and the son of a Mari is his dearest treasure. This, my Lady, is my treasure, Rosha." It was an honest declaration, and true, but it trained those radiant eyes directly on the young man and stole away his tongue.

"Hello," she said, with just the right combination of shyness and flirtation to stun him further. He just gazed at her, his mind racing frantically through his vocabulary, looking for words he could say without stuttering. Bronwynn waited for a moment, then leaned toward him and cocked her head. "Hello?" she said again, a question this time, and Rosha found himself leaning toward her, too. He straightened up self-consciously, struggling to swallow, and managed a quick smile.

"My Lady, would you like a drink before—" Dorlyth began, but Bronwynn had already started toward Rosha and was speaking to him again.

"I suppose your father more than makes up for your lack of charm, but you could at least give me a greeting." Her tone was slightly taunting, but still quite flirtatious. That was the way the women of Talith's court related to men, especially to her father, and Bronwynn was pleased to find that it worked equally well in Ngandib-Mar. But she didn't realize just how powerfully her attention affected Rosha, as a cauldron mixed of frustration and pleasure bubbled within him, growing hotter with every step she took. Finally he could hold his tongue no longer, and he gave in to attempted speech. She was surprised when the torrent of fragmented words exploded from his lips.

"I-I-I am-m-m—you-y—glad t-t-to-to be N-n-ngandib-M-mar. Glad!"

"You're what?" she said flatly. He swallowed, and forced his lips by an act of sheer will to re-form the words he had tried to say.

"I-I am g-g-glad you ha-ha-have c-c-come—" Here he stopped for a breath, then: "to N-ngandib-M-mar."

It was not a pretty sight, this boy fighting to give this small greeting. But it certainly didn't warrant the cackle of derisive laughter that broke from Bronwynn's lips.

"Bronwynn!" Pelmen snapped, eyes flashing angrily as he crossed the room to her.

"But he talks so funny!" she giggled in response to Pelmen's scolding.

The player grabbed her by the arm and spun her around to face him. "Just because you are the daughter of the King, you feel you have the right to—"

"Please!" They both looked back at Rosha, surprised at the firmness and character he'd given to the word. He stood with both hands outstretched to her, indicating very eloquently to Pelmen that he wanted to deal with her himself. Bronwynn received a brief cold glance from Pelmen, before he turned and stalked away. She looked back at Rosha, who had forced his lips into a frozen smile.

"I—sometimes—have—a hard—time—s-s-saying— what—I feel," he gasped, mouthing each word slowly and punching it out in triumph over his halting lips. "I—can't—talk—very well."

"I—can tell," Bronwynn said nervously, wishing she could get this over with and get back to the two older men. She smiled faintly and began to turn away, but he stopped her.

"Wait." She hesitated, looking at him. "I—would— l-like to—t-talk—to you—better. I-I'm sorry." He shrugged, and grinned, then he picked up his shirt and strolled out of the room.

Pelmen and Dorlyth exchanged a look.

The young lady spun around and announced, "I'm hungry."

Dorlyth chuckled. "I'm not surprised. The kitchen is below us, my Lady. May I escort you to its table?" He extended his hand to her, and Bronwynn offered her own.

But before he led her from the room, she reached back to offer her other hand to Pelmen. "Aren't you coming, too?"

Pelmen took her hand, and the three of them walked together to dinner.

Much later in the day Pelmen wandered through a quiet glade near the castle, tracing the route of a small stream he had followed many times before. He had finally managed to get free from the little lady. She had shadowed him all day. She played now with the falcons in Dorlyth's aviary, finding in these savage, swooping birds of prey some strangely comforting feeling of communion. The way her gaze had followed him from place to place gave Pelmen the clear impression that she was the hunter and he the hunted. He thanked the powers for inspiring him to introduce her to her fellow predators. Dorlyth's bird handler had thrilled her by giving her a little falconet, and as Bronwynn had stroked the hooded bird and cooed to it softly, Pelmen had slipped out the cage door. He hoped he had covered his tracks well. He needed some time alone.

The stream turned into a heavily wooded area, and Pelmen waded in to follow it into the trees. Twenty feet farther on it twisted and turned through a series of large rocks. Pelmen pulled himself up onto one of these and stretched across it. The day had finally warmed up, but now in the late afternoon it was cooling off again, and Pelmen wrapped himself tightly in his robe and wished he'd not gotten his feet wet. "Still," he said to himself, "it's worth getting wet to have a little quiet."

"I'm here," someone said, and Pelmen jerked upright and looked around.

"Who's there?" he demanded, his hand raising slowly above his head, ready to call from the air some powerful defense if need be.

"What?" the voice said, and it was as if someone spoke inside his head.

Pelmen could see no one, and the voice came from no direction. Understanding suddenly slashed through him, and he fell on his knees on the rock and fought to clear his mind completely of any words.

"Yes, I'm back," the voice said. "I thought I heard someone at the door, and went to check it." There was silence for a moment. "No, there was no one there. But I had the clear impression someone was speaking to me—someone besides the two of you."

His eyes shut against the light, hands clasped tightly

over his ears to cut off the sound of the gaily trickling stream, Pelmen strained to hold all thought in check until the danger of discovery was past. Someone was using a tremendous coalition of the powers to communicate his thoughts to others. It was something Pelmen had never before experienced—unless . . . It seemed he had dreamed something of this feeling the night before. He had tumbled into bed as soon as they had arrived, even though the sun had not completely set. But for all of his exhaustion from the strain of the long ride from Dragonsgate, he had still slept fitfully.

Now as he squeezed his eyes shut, that field of vision behind his eyelids, normally black or dark red, turned a hot, bright blue. The energy coursed through him so powerfully that he feared some bodily harm, yet he still clung tightly to his thoughts and focused his mind on receiving more of the signal.

"I know you say that's impossible, Flayh, but you forget that I am in Ngandib-Mar. Things are possible here that aren't elsewhere." Pelmen realized there was another side to this conversation, possibly two, but he only heard the one. He held his mind in check still, waiting until the voice moved on to discuss something besides his uninvited presence. At last it did.

"I know I'm getting old," Tohn mod Neelis was saying, "but I'm not senile. Maybe I'm just more cautious than you two."

"I hear nothing other than you and Jagd," Flayh snarled. "Jagd? What of you?"

"I hear nothing either. Leave it, Tohn. It's your imagination."

"Perhaps so. I've been sick this whole day, ever since your announcement that I may have Pelmen to contend with."

"I take it you haven't seen Pelmen?" Flayh said coldly.

"Of course I haven't! This is a big country, dear cousin. You think I can search the breadth of it in a day?"

"You can attempt it," Flayh snapped.

"Gentlemen," said Jagd calmly, "is it wise to waste

our energies bickering when it is evident we have so much to discuss?"

Flayh sat back in his chair. This registered on the pyramids of the other two by his face growing smaller. "So report, Tohn," he grumbled, folding his arms across his chest.

"The search for Pelmen and the girl is continuing. It appears they moved south, following the foothills of the Spinal Range to the edge of the Great South Fir. There they *may* have turned west, or they may have moved south into the forest proper."

"They may have?" Flayh growled. "Don't you know?"

"Not yet, no!" Tohn thundered back, wishing the little man were really across the table from him so that he could wring his wrinkled neck. *Flayh feels free to say anything he chooses*, Tohn thought to himself. *This distance makes him feel secure. But let him bring himself to the Mar, and Flayh will see how Maris deal with obnoxious upstarts.*

"There was much traffic through the area night before last," Tohn continued, eyes boring down into Flayh's. "It appears every slaver along the Chaon-Mari border was in action. The paths crisscross one another in a matrix of confusion—"

"I thought your riders were competent," Flayh sneered.

"They are competent! And we *will* find them!"

"Please!" Jagd yelled, losing his temper. "I'm tired of this! If you two continue this family quarrel I intend to break the link!"

Flayh hid his frustration and asked coolly, "Do you think they are heading back to Chaomonous?"

"I hope so," Tohn breathed.

"As do I," Jagd smiled, "for I've laced those woods with red-and-purple riders. Pelmen will not expect trouble from the house of Uda—he may even seek help from us since he thinks his enemy is Ognadzu. Yes, I hope he is coming this direction."

"But I doubt he will," said Flayh. "After all, he is powerless in Chaomonous. In the Mar he's a power-shaper, with some leverage to make things happen. We are not dealing with a fool. He knows too much of us and of the workings of our council to be incautious."

"Supposing he were to remain in Ngandib-Mar," Jagd mused. "Where would he go? With whom would he stay?"

"Dorlyth mod Karis is his friend," Tohn offered quietly.

"Dorlyth the swordsman?" Flayh shot back.

"The same."

"How far is Dorlyth's castle from your estate?"

"A hard day and a half on horseback."

Flayh leaned forward now, his face the shape of a triangle from the view of the other two men. "Call in your riders, Tohn, and march for Dorlyth's castle with all the force you can muster. I'm guessing Pelmen is there and expects you to track him, but he won't be expecting an attack force so soon. Get him, Tohn, and kill him! He is far too dangerous to us to be allowed to live!"

Tohn mod Neelis replied quietly but with force. "I make the decision as to whom my force rides against. I follow no one's orders, Flayh. Especially not yours."

Flayh choked, and gritted his teeth. He replied through clamped jaws and a deadly smile, "Of course, my dear friend. It was only a suggestion, you understand."

"Very well. I will consider your suggestion, Flayh. But you recognize, I hope, that I would be breaking my bond to the Federation of the Mar by such action, and could be calling down the wrath of all the Maris on our house. Perhaps on all the houses." Tohn gazed down into Jagd's eyes.

Jagd shrugged. "If it is necessary to do a little cutting on the flesh of the merchant council in order to extract this damaging thorn—I say, do it." Jagd smiled.

And understandably so. Should the plan fail, Jagd stood in the best position to weather the consequences with a minimum of harm. He was in favor with the King of Chaomonous, and his Uda confederates in Lamath and the Mar, while not as strong as their Ognadzu counterparts, were still wealthy and powerful in their respective lands. He had been in touch with the Uda family in Ngandib-Mar, and already red-and-purple riders were combing the mountains beside the men in blue-and-lime, seeking Pelmen and the girl. It was anyone's guess what Jagd would do should Uda be the house to capture Pelmen. That would so alter the power balance as to demand a political realignment. All three men were aware of this—but these were, first and foremost, businessmen, and business was business, regardless of alliances. If the plan succeeded, Uda would rule the world alongside the other trading houses. If it failed—if Ognadzu, already out of favor with Chaomonous, should fall from grace in the eyes of the Maris as well—how could he lose? Jagd wore a well-deserved smile as he listened to these two cousins bicker over tactics. They could win or lose the battle. For Jagd's purposes, the war was already won.

Dorlyth grinned. He hadn't hunted in years—he was surprised he even remembered how. But it was all coming back to him as he traced his friend through the forest. Oh, Pelmen had done his best to hide his trail, but here a dried twig, freshly cracked, and there a bruised limb, lately bent to allow passage, told him exactly where Pelmen was going. Of course, Dorlyth chuckled to himself, the lady Pelmen hid from would never track him here, hunter though she was. She was more experienced in prowling carpeted halls than leaf-strewn woods.

Suddenly the track ran out by the edge of the stream, and Dorlyth listened for a moment. He heard nothing, and decided perhaps his friend had managed to lose himself. Then Dorlyth looked at the brook, murky in this waning light, and he chuckled again. He waded into it, just as Pelmen had done. Soon he too turned the little bend, and there he saw a curious sight. Pelmen was kneeling on a rock, his bottom in the air and his nose buried in the ground.

"Ho, Pelmen! Sniffing for buried bones?" he called, and threw back his head to let loose a hearty bellow of laughter. He cut it short, though, when he saw his friend's expression.

Pelmen pointed a hand at him and an aura of light encircled it for a moment, then was gone. Dorlyth felt a tingling sensation throughout his body. It was strangely soothing, and for some reason he felt no inclination to do anything but relax and remain silent. He stood rooted where he was in the water, like the stump of an ancient swamp tree. Pelmen ducked back into his unorthodox position and struggled to regain the lost link. For some reason, Dorlyth now saw his friend's silly contortions as the most natural sight in the forest.

"There, it happened again!" Tohn broke in. "Didn't you feel it?"

"Feel what?" Flayh demanded.

"Yes, what?" Jagd echoed.

"Another—presence. Someone listening in on our conversation!"

"I have told you, Tohn, that is impossible!" said Flayh.

"Impossible? How could you know? How could you say what is possible or not possible with this magic device? I didn't make it, I don't know what its capabilities are. Can you really believe you do?" Tohn was less angry than he was frightened. He decided he didn't like the magical instrument. It seemed to invade his most private thoughts, and to broadcast his desires. It revealed more to these other men than he chose to reveal. He preferred the old methods, the messenger birds and the fire signals. They were more polite—and more dignified.

"I know what my trading captains have told me," Flayh was saying, "and not all are liars like my nephew. The man from whom they purchased these three objects swore to them that messages could not be intercepted. I question whether anyone is listening in, cousin Tohn. I fear you have simply developed what those hill people call a conscience. A worthless thing, Tohn, especially when you begin to listen to it. You've grown so isolated from the real world you've forgotten that conscience is a luxury we merchants cannot afford."

"I'm tired, Flayh, and I'm not well. I will break this link now—"

"No!"

"—and I will consider your suggestion."

"Don't break the link, Tohn," Flayh threatened.

"If I choose to attack Dorlyth's castle, I will notify you by blue flyer. Good day, gentlemen."

Tohn held his head in his hands a few moments after breaking the link, then jerked around, half expecting to see someone standing behind him. There was no one there, and he sighed, wondering if his imagination was running away from him. He stumbled out of the room and down the dark stairs, finally making his way out into the courtyard. "You," he said to one of the young boys he found wrestling in the dirt, "go fetch the captain of my guards. Do it!" he added when the boy hesitated.

"But—he won't listen to *me*, Uncle Tohn," began the boy, whose name Tohn couldn't remember. There were so many, how could he?

"Tell him I'm angry, lad," Tohn said. "He may not believe you, but he'll come just in case." The boy's chest swelled with pride at being the one selected, and he took off. "Lad!" Tohn stopped him. "Go to my falconer too, and tell him the same thing. Run now!" The boy shot away toward the main door of the inner keep, kicking dust up behind him with every barefoot stride. The other boys stood in a silent semicircle around Tohn, watching him, wondering what he would do or say next. Tohn noticed their dirty-faced stares, and stepped out of the way. "Excuse me. Sorry to break up the game." They continued to look at him, unsure of what he would have them do. Tohn thought for a minute, then grinned. "Anybody want to wrestle?" he asked.

When the captain of the guard arrived breathless in the courtyard, he found Tohn mod Neelis wrestling in the dust with the little boys.

Pelmen uncurled from his fetal position, and took a long, deep breath. Then he looked up at Dorlyth, and held out a hand to him, palm up. The hand glowed again briefly, and Dorlyth experienced another weird sensation—as if moss were falling from his body.

He blinked twice, sighed, and muttered, "My boots are soaked."

Pelmen ignored his scolding tone. "So are mine. Shall we go change them?" The two retraced their steps through the stream, then stepped out onto dry land, their boots squishing in unison.

"Would it be nosy for me to ask what you were doing back there with your tail in the air?" Dorlyth rumbled.

"I was listening," Pelmen replied.

"To the grass growing? To an army of ants?"

"To a powerful conversation between our enemies." Dorlyth frowned. "How did you manage that?"

"I had been told the merchants could communicate with one another without the aid of messenger birds. It's true. They can."

"The powers?"

"Yes, it is some magical device that traps and focuses the powers, though how it works I certainly don't know."

"Yet you managed to listen in?"

"I was only able to hear one side of the conversation. I couldn't tell if he spoke to only one man or two. Somehow he realized my presence and broke the contact."

"He, who?" Dorlyth asked, ducking under a branch.

"Tohn mod Neelis," said Pelmen, and Dorlyth nodded.

"And those he spoke to?"

"Only Flayh for sure. Who else, if anyone, I couldn't tell."

"Probably the elder of Ognadzu in Chaomonous."

"Possibly," Pelmen began, "and yet I doubt it. My guess is that Talith has arrested whoever holds that position now. I doubt he would carry a device this valuable into the dungeon with him."

"Then who?"

"I don't know," Pelmen said as they reached the edge of the small wood and stepped into the meadow west of Dorlyth's castle. He slowed, looking up at the battlements of the keep and the guards who stood there, more interested in their private conversations than in the business of watching the horizon. "But I do know this. You and your house are in grave danger."

Dorlyth wasn't the slightest bit surprised. "When you

show up, trouble can't be far behind. Did he say when he would march?"

"I don't believe Tohn has even made the decision to attack yet. Someone—Flayh, I'd wager—seemed to be pushing him to. Even so, I think it is time for me to take the girl and be gone."

"You just got here!" Dorlyth argued.

"Nevertheless, it's time to go on. If Tohn does choose to come, he will not find me here. You can let him inspect your dungeon and your keep and send him on his way. That should give us a two-day head start, enough to reach the forest."

"I take it you're going south?"

"And I hope Tohn thinks the same thing," Pelmen smiled. "We're riding north—to Lamath."

❧ Chapter Four ❧

"LAMATH!" Bronwynn exploded as they ate the evening meal. "What are we going to Lamath for? You plan to sell me to the King of Lamath yourself?" Her blue eyes snapped angrily. Rosha, seated across the table, found those eyes far more bewitching than his peas. She caught him watching her. "And what are *you* looking at?" she spat. His peas weren't so bad to look at after all, he decided, and focusing on his plate alone he began to shovel them in.

"We are going to Lamath because that's the safest place to go," Pelmen explained, his patience wearing thin.

"How can you say that? They're the ones who were trying to capture me!"

"Then they certainly won't be expecting you to come there, will they?" Dorlyth asked quietly, stuffing a chunk of meat into his mouth.

"But why can't I go back to my father?" she demanded of Pelmen.

"Because it was someone in your father's castle who made a captive of you in the first place."

"How do you know that? You can't prove it." She slammed her spoon down on the table and sat back in her chair, crossing her arms petulantly. She waited for Rosha to look up so she could say something nasty to him, but the young man had better sense than to do that. All she saw was the top of his head and the movement of his fork from plate to mouth and back again.

"I'm going to have to ask you to trust me in this," Pelmen said gravely, trying a new tactic with the girl. "I've not betrayed you yet, have I?"

Bronwynn wouldn't look at him. She took another bite of meat and chewed it without tasting. "All right," she grumbled, but her fury was still quite evident. She was tired. Tired of running away, tired of meeting new people, tired of trying to get Pelmen to notice her the way she wanted him to. She was also tired of this simple food. She liked variety in her diet, and was used to delicacies from the kitchens of a King. This all tasted bland. And she resented, too, the way the savage youth across from her was stuffing it in. She pushed the plate away, and folded her arms again.

"Better eat," Pelmen said in as kindly a way as possible.

"I'm tired of your telling me what to do! I am heir to the throne of Chaomonous and am fully capable of managing my own life!" She jumped up from her seat and stomped toward the door. There she hesitated and looked back. "If anyone wants me, I'll be with my falcon." Then she was gone.

Pelmen gazed angrily after her, missing the snicker Dorlyth and his son exchanged across the table.

"You're going to take her to Lamath, are you?" Dorlyth teased.

"I'm tempted to carry her to Tohn and beg him to take her off my hands."

"She's still a girl, my friend. Keep reminding yourself. Do you really expect anything different from Talith's daughter?" Pelmen said nothing, deciding he would enjoy his dinner regardless of the conversation. Dorlyth waited for a moment, then cleared his throat. "Rosha and I have talked this over, Pelmen, and we've agreed. You're going to need help handling this lady." Pelmen looked up at Dorlyth, suspicion written in his knitted eyebrows. "You said yourself the lad was ready. I'm sending Rosha with you."

Pelmen grimaced, then pleaded, "Already I'm burdened with a predatory Princess! Would you force a love-struck lad on me as well?"

"Love-struck he may be," Dorlyth said, watching Rosha's face flush once again, "but you've watched him practice. He's a formidable swordsman, as you've said yourself."

"But the two together—!"

"—may help keep one another in line. Pelmen, I'm sending the boy not for his own sake alone. I send him for you as well."

"You think I may need a swordsman."

"Yes. Oh, not in the Mar, certainly—a powershaper has no more need of a warrior than he does of a flint. But you are not always a powershaper, Pelmen, and you travel to Lamath."

"Where my actions are suspect?" Pelmen asked, smiling grimly.

"Where your actions are confusing, to say the least. You've said yourself you have no way of knowing who you might be there or what you might do! I send my son with you only because I can't go myself."

"You may find you need him here. Who can say what might happen next?"

"I've made my choices, old friend. I wish him to travel with you. Rosha!" Dorlyth said, turning to his son.

"Yes, F-father?"

"Go. Prepare yourself to ride with Pelmen."

"I'm al-r-ready r-ready," the boy grinned.

"Oh. Well then—go prepare some more."

"W-why don't you j-just tell me to leave?" Rosha chuckled.

"All right, I will. Leave!" The boy hauled himself

out of his chair, shook his head good-naturedly, and left
the room.

"On his way to the aviary I'll wager," Pelmen muttered.

"Pelmen," Dorlyth began with an intensity that demanded his friend's attention, "it's time for the boy.
Take him with you."

"But what if war should come to Dorlyth's castle——"

"Especially if war comes to this keep do I want him
with you!"

"Oh," Pelmen nodded.

"Teach him, Pelmen. I've taught him everything I
know—but that's not enough. He's more than I was.
He'll be worth something—if he lives."

"Dorlyth—I don't understand. I'm going to Lamath.
I don't know what I will become there—I can't be
trusted even with myself. And yet you want me to protect the boy?"

"No!" Dorlyth thundered, frowning. "I want you to
teach the boy. If I thought anyone could protect him,
I'd keep him here. No one can. But it is possible to
teach him. When he learns—I wager he'll protect not
only himself, but you and the girl as well."

"What is it you want me to teach——" Pelmen began,
but Dorlyth raised a hand to stop him.

"Let him travel with you, Pelmen. That's all the
teaching I ask you to give." Dorlyth jumped to his feet.
"If you're leaving early we'd best get to business. I believe you promised me a game before you left?"

Pelmen stood slowly and looked around the hall. It
was a relaxed group of guards and freemen who conversed in the warmth of their Lord's hospitality. He
longed for the freedom to linger. Well, he would enjoy
the evening, at least. "If you're so anxious to be beaten
again, let's get to it."

Once again the council chamber of the King of Chaomonous was filled with the coughing and shuffling of a
crowd of advisors. Few were ever asked for advice—
none dared to volunteer any. But the King was no less a
player than Pelmen, and he enjoyed his sizable captive
audience. It meant that Talith kept few secrets, but the

King seemed to accept that as a part of the natural order. Of course, others knew everything he said and did. He was the King; they were supposed to know. It rarely crossed his mind that this lack of secrecy could prove dangerous to him. Yet perhaps Talith was not as foolish as some believed him, for he realized his enemies would always be able to ferret out his secrets, whatever he did. Why shouldn't his loyal advisors know them as well?

Kherda, exchequer of the royal treasury, nervously watched as Talith paced the dais. Perhaps the King could afford to share his secrets, but Kherda could not. To be caught in conspiracy with the King's mistress would cost him his head. If the King should discover he had aided in the kidnap of Bronwynn—Kherda hated to imagine the torments Talith might invent for him. And Kherda genuinely expected to be discovered any day. He could not escape the conviction that Ligne was just using him, and that soon she would discard him as being of no further value to her. Yet each time he was with the woman he found himself agreeing to yet another ridiculously dangerous assignment, simply to win a smile from those lips. And if Kherda feared her turning on him, he feared more the result of failing her. At times like this Kherda wished he had just stayed in his vaults with the money.

He clenched his notes with both hands, trying to draw some security from them. They had been prepared long in advance—notes regarding the expenses involved in mobilizing a mighty nation for war. His figures told how many warriors could be drawn from each province within the nation, and how many could be impressed into service from the conquered lands to the south. They told what available ships of the merchant fleets could be quickly transformed into troop carriers. They listed foodstuffs available to feed an army, and the arms on hand to equip it for battle. Kherda had even taken the liberty of suggesting a possible strategy for invading Lamath, though he hadn't a hope that the King would really consider it. Kherda had taken great pains to plan an invasion that would insure the maximum loss of Chaon men and equipment.

For what was really of most importance to Kherda

was not this set of notes he clutched so tightly, but that other set of notes, hidden safely within the King's own treasure house, that plotted the overthrow of Talith's government. While the King fought a wasteful war with Lamath, a small army organized by Kherda under Ligne's prodding would march into Chaomonous and assume control. Ligne would open the palace to this conquering troop, and with little or no bloodshed at all Kherda would rule the mightiest nation in the world! Gradually then he would begin to shut off the supplies flowing north. By the time Talith realized the trick, his army would be so overextended and undersupplied he would never be able to recover. Kherda expected him to lay siege to the city, but by that time the capital would be so well stocked and so well defended Talith would never recapture it. Then, of course, there was Ligne's assassin. When the time came, Talith would be cut down.

Kherda didn't know himself who this assassin was— Ligne had chosen not to share that information with him. As a result, he feared everyone. Should Ligne choose to get rid of him, now that the plan was so neatly laid, the knife could come at him from any direction.

Kherda saw Joss watching him from across the room. Since the night of Bronwynn's kidnap the Chief of Security had been eyeing him that way. He struggled to wipe the anxious look from his face, and slowly placed his notes on the lectern in front of him. Did Joss read thoughts? He decided to clear his mind completely of plans for the coup. Perhaps he would survive all this.

"Then you've learned nothing!" the King was screaming. This was directed to his Lord of the Dungeon, a large, slow-moving fellow who hid a razor-keen mind under a façade of oafishness.

"No, Sire, not a thing. I'm sorry, Sire."

"Sorry!" the King exploded, and the heavy-built warden took a step back and held up his hands.

"They all claim they knew nothing of the kidnap until after it occurred. Said they'd been kept completely in the dark by other members of their family. Isn't that what they told you, Joss?" He turned his head toward the General, directing the King's eyes there as well. It pained Joss to see how successfully the warder had shifted the responsibility.

"Well, Joss?" the King snapped.

"That's what each has said. And I begin to believe them."

"What?"

"They all hold to their story with great integrity, even in the face of torture. I must believe they are telling the truth, for some would gladly have confessed, had they known anything to tell. None has revealed any knowledge whatsoever of the events surrounding the kidnap."

"It's that family pride, that clan unity!" the King raged, pacing the dais.

"Perhaps—but I doubt it," Joss said firmly. The King rewarded him with a scathing stare, but Joss went on. "They claim to have been betrayed by their elder in Lamath. It seems there is some factionalism even in the trading houses."

"If that were so, who took my daughter?" Before Joss could reply, the King answered himself with a flourish of his hand. "I know! I know what you'll say. That somewhere in this assembly of advisors there lurks a traitor." Joss sighed quietly as Talith gestured over the heads of the rows of counselors. The King pointed one out. "Does that look like the face of a turncoat?" The man who owned the face in question sought to look as decent and innocent as possible. "Does that?" Talith pointed to another. "Does this?" The King had gripped Kherda's chin and now squeezed his cheeks, and Kherda felt very faint. Joss half smiled at Kherda's discomfort, but remained attentive to the King. "These are my people, Joss," the King said grandly, loosing Kherda, who promptly melted over the lectern as Talith turned away. "I trust them. They are privy to every decision I make." Suddenly Talith's expression turned black. "So don't even imply conspiracy, unless you have specific accusations to make!"

Joss nodded curtly and replied, "I have none at this time, my Lord. I will continue to seek the information you desire."

"Do that. And increase your surveillance along our

borders with Lamath. I want to know their army better than their generals do!"

"You're planning war?" Kherda asked quietly.

"I'm always planning war, you stupid banker! I want to see Jagd!"

"He waits outside—" Kherda began.

"I know he waits outside," the King snapped. "I sent for him myself! Do you think I don't know what's going on in my own palace?" Kherda turned very pale. "Jagd!"

The doors flew open, and the guard began, "Jagd of Uda, to see—"

"I know all that! Let him in!" The guard's spear clattered to the floor, and he scrambled to pick it up while Jagd brushed past him. "There you are, my friend." The King smiled, and he seated himself on the throne that crowned the platform. "Sit here, and tell me the news."

Jagd sat in the chair to the King's right, and began to speak quietly to him. Kherda leaned forward to hear. "My Lord, the news is serious."

"Bronwynn?" the King yelped anxiously.

"No, my Lord," Jagd said quickly. "I know nothing at all of that situation. I have a caravan passing Dragonsgate tomorrow carrying messages of inquiry to my colleagues there. Of course we have exchanged messenger birds, but it is difficult to tie a large document to the leg of a little blue flyer. All I know is that Pezi's column arrived safely at Ognadzu holdings in Lamath, and that he immediately left for the capital. I assume the girl was with him." Jagd watched the King's face for Talith's reaction. It was slight, but significant. There was a clenching of the jaw, and Talith's right hand formed a fist. Jagd went on. "The troubling news is this. My fellows have observed great troop movements in Lamath. There are growing concentrations of warriors along Lamath's southern border."

Joss looked sharply at the wrinkled little merchant, while Talith looked just as sharply at Joss.

"Why haven't I been told of this?" the King roared.

"Because I knew nothing of it," Joss responded. "Nor am I sure I believe it!"

"Gentlemen," Jagd said quietly, "please let me explain. These are very late troop movements, and the news has only this afternoon come to me. As you know, we merchants are often able to see and hear things government agencies have no way of discovering."

Talith and Joss both resented this dig so characteristic of a merchant, but they knew, too, that it was true. Neither replied.

"It is to your advantage that I feel your cause so strongly," Jagd continued. "When you are backed by a merchant house, your intelligence problems are cared for. All that remains is the organization of fleets and battalions."

"I take it, then, that you counsel war," Talith said quietly.

"What other course is there?" Jagd asked. Kherda's heart leapt into his throat. This merchant was playing right into his hands. Unless of course Ligne had already—

"And my little girl? What of her?" Talith growled.

Jagd shrank down in his chair and shrugged helplessly. "I'll do all I can. But don't you see that Lamath is simply baiting you by stealing your daughter? They obviously feel themselves strong enough to conquer you, or they would not have troubled with so careful a plot."

"Lamath!" Talith shouted, and on his lips the word became a curse. He stood and paced a moment, then pointed at Jagd. "It's that Pelmen who has planned this! He's an agent of Lamath, I know he is!"

Jagd's eyes glowed. Obviously Talith hated the player. Perhaps Pelmen's interference could somehow be turned to an advantage. "I do know this," Jagd intoned quietly. "When Pezi reached his uncle's house in Lamath—Pelmen was no longer with him."

"That's it! He is masterminding this whole plot against me! Why, even now he is probably moving brigades into position for a mountain invasion! Kherda!"

"Yes, my Lord."

"I want a list of every available militia unit we can bring under arms! I want every merchant vessel outfitted with battle rams and grappling hooks, with crews of trained marines posted to each! I want supplies to feed, clothe, and arm the greatest fighting force to march since the days of the last great rebellion!"

The audience of counselors leaned forward in their seats to watch the climax of the King's speech, and Talith rewarded them with a worthy performance. Legs spread wide in a wrestler's stance, he raised a fist to the ceiling and followed it with his eyes. "I am a man of peace. But the throne of Chaomonous is a sacred trust, and an heir to that throne is the spirit of the golden land itself! Shall I stand idly by while the spirit of my nation is stolen away in the night? No! Let Lamath throw its best at me, I will have my Bronwynn back! To war! Any man who pleads for peace is no Chaon!"

The audience burst into wild applause, and the King nodded his head slightly to show his appreciation of their support.

Kherda gathered his papers together and spread them on the lectern for the sixth time. His relief knew no bounds.

Pelmen patted the powerful flanks of Minaliss and rubbed the animal's ears. "Seems rested enough," he said.

Dorlyth grunted. "Good horse. Merchants usually ride the best. You have provisions enough?"

Pelmen looked at the packhorse, heavy-laden with food and goods, and grinned. "No room to carry anything else."

Dorlyth waved his hand, dismissing this contribution. "Just want you to be prepared."

Pelmen reached out and put a hand on each of Dorlyth's shoulders. "You'll do as I've asked?"

"Let me see. I'm to go on about my business until Tohn arrives. When he comes I welcome him like an old friend and let him inspect the keep, the village, and the entire surrounding area. I delay him by making him stay for a feast and then I point him toward the south."

"What I'm asking is, will you do it?"

"Of course," Dorlyth said, smiling. "You don't think I want to get involved in this business, do you?"

"Just see that you don't."

"And as for my son—" Dorlyth hesitated.

"Yes?"

"Just teach him—anything. Tell him your funny tales about the foundation of the kingdoms."

"You always laugh when I speak of that," Pelmen smiled.

"So will he, if he has any sense. But tell him all the same."

"T-t-tell me what?" Rosha asked, coming up behind them.

Dorlyth turned around to get a good look at the boy. He was dressed warmly against the chill of the morning in a fur cap and warm bearskin coat. He carried the ever-present greatsword over his shoulder. Dorlyth clapped him on the arms, and forced a grin. "What's in here?" he asked, thumping his son's chest.

"The c-ch-chain mail vest, and it's h-h-hot!"

"You wear it to *bed*, boy!" Dorlyth ordered.

"You gave him your vest?" Pelmen asked.

"Why should I need it?" Dorlyth shrugged. "I'm to invite my enemies to a feast, remember? Ahhh!" he smiled, looking past the other two. "The lady."

"I don't look much like a lady," Bronwynn growled through teeth clenched against the cold. "And I don't feel much like a lady, either. It's still dark outside. Why are we leaving now?"

"For just that reason," Pelmen said. "Here, a gift from Dorlyth." Pelmen wrapped a furry cloak around the shivering girl's shoulders.

"Thank you, Lord Dorlyth," she said sweetly. "It's refreshing to find that someone in this land knows how to make a lady feel respected."

Dorlyth noted the sharp look she shot at Pelmen, and looked away, scratching his beard. "Yes, well, marriage does teach some things. Rosha."

"Y-y-yes, sir?"

"You ready, my boy?" Rosha nodded. Dorlyth felt his mouth suddenly go very dry, and under his beard his cheeks began to warm. "Good. Be off with you then." Rosha waited a moment, then turned to mount his horse. "I'll give you a hand, boy," Dorlyth said quietly, stooping to grab hold of the lad's boot, but he grabbed

Rosha instead, and hugged him hard. Though he fought to blank his mind, he could not help but remember sending Rosha's mother off so many years before. He jerked his son around to face him and stared into his eyes. "You survive, you hear me? What good is a dead hero, hmm?" Rosha stared at him, then the boy's lips turned up in a grin that Dorlyth's face answered with another. "Good riding, my boy. Come back." Dorlyth clapped Rosha on the shoulders again, and stepped out of the way. "Well, go on!" he grunted, and Rosha mounted his sleek black war-horse.

"What about my falcon?" Bronwynn asked Pelmen, and Dorlyth welcomed the chance to interrupt.

"It's on its way, my Lady. I already gave the order to bring it."

"Dorlyth, a falcon?" Pelmen complained. "This is no meadow outing!"

"This is no foolish bird, either! It's a hunting falcon, and you're going to take it," Dorlyth said, and Bronwynn smiled gleefully. Pelmen said nothing, but mounted Minaliss. The falconer finally arrived, out of breath, and handed the leather glove and the falconet to a delighted Bronwynn.

"Just remember, my Lady, we'll be riding very hard for the next two weeks," Pelmen said.

"I can ride with the best in Chaomonous," Bronwynn snapped back. "I can surely ride with you two." She mounted her brown pony and tossed her head proudly, then kissed the hooded bird. "I thought you were in a hurry?" she snapped tartly. Wheeling her mount, she made swiftly for the stable door. Pelmen jerked around to follow her.

"You see why I'm sending the boy?" Dorlyth called as Pelmen and Rosha thundered after her and out into the dark sky of the early morning. "She's too much for you, powershaper!"

Rosha smiled through the tears that had somehow crept onto his cheeks. He liked the feeling of his father's laugh following them into the night.

Dorlyth walked to the stable door and watched the little group disappear toward the south. Pelmen would continue southward to the nearest stream, then would

follow the path of the water to the west and turn north
once again. He would probably leave a number of con-
fusions to divert Tohn. It was a pity to waste all that
good magic. But it couldn't be helped. Tohn would
never have the chance to be fooled by those illusions, if
Dorlyth had his way.

"What of the fire summons?" he said quietly to the
falconer who flanked him.

"Issued it last night from the greater tower, while you
were at game."

Dorlyth winced. "It was a sacrifice, believe me."

"Did he beat you badly?" The bird handler chuckled.

"Have you ever known me to win? But it will be
worth it—if I can give them a good start. The warriors
should be assembling by noon. What of provisions?"

"We're not at siege standards by any means," the falconer answered grimly. "But we could handle a
hundred warriors for a week if the seneschal has figured
correctly."

"That should be enough." Dorlyth nodded. "And the
blue flyer to the High City?"

"I tossed the bird before lighting the signal fire. It
should arrive in the high palace of Ngandib in an hour,
depending on wind conditions."

"So if that sloth on the throne chooses to read his
mail today, he'll get my message."

"He should, my Lord."

Dorlyth sighed. "One can always hope." He patted
the falconer on the shoulder and turned to walk toward
the keep. "By the way," he said, hesitating, "would you
check around in the armory and find me an old leather
battle jacket? Just in case Tohn should get aggressive,
you understand."

"What of your famous mail shirt, my Lord?" the bird
handler asked in surprise.

Dorlyth scratched his neck. "I guess I just outgrew
it."

"Is that it? Or did someone else grow into it?"

Dorlyth smiled. "Are there no secrets in my keep?
Come, there's much to do, and too little time to do it."
The falconer closed the stable gate, and they planned
defenses all the way to the greater tower.

* * *

The dust hung motionless in the fetid depths of the cave. The dragon brooded in silence. The heads had never been able to agree on anything. Their bickering had finally worn them both out. Now the dragon fixed all eyes on the long road down into the southern valley, waiting for a caravan he knew was coming. He was hungry and hostile, and each head used the quiet to revile the other mentally.

An eternity passed in that murky den. The only noise was an occasional scrape of scales across stone as a head shifted position, or a low rumbling in the beast's giant belly, which impatiently awaited a meal. The entrance to the cavern was fifty feet up the sheer northern cliff face. By simply resting his heads on the rocky ledge that protruded porchlike from the opening, the dragon could see in any direction. He had spent many happy hours sunning his scaly skulls on this bone-littered shelf. That joy seemed dreamlike to the giant lizard now.

There. Movement far below him drew the attention of all eyes. Not a word was spoken between them, but the heads cooperated in squeezing the hulking body out of the mouth of the cave and lifting it gently into flight. The dragon settled to earth just as quietly. It took the better part of two hours for the caravan to reach him. Neither head spoke through the duration of its climb.

At the head of the caravan rode a young man clothed in the brilliant scarlet and dark purple of the world-famous house of Uda. He was an experienced trading captain, having passed Dragonsgate twenty times and more, but not since his first passage had Tahli-Damen approached the beast with such trepidation. Jagd had informed him of the possibility of his meeting a mentally unbalanced dragon this trip. Since the dragon had never exhibited a great deal of coherence by human standards, Tahli-Damen expected the worst. There was a blue flyer seated on his shoulder, bound to him by a leather thong he had tied securely around his wrist. From one of the bird's feet dangled a tiny parchment on a string. In addition to the reins of his horse, Tahli-Damen clutched a stylus, for he had instructions to scribble a message describing the dragon's behavior on the parchment and to release the bird as soon as he had completed his bargaining. It all seemed highly unusual, but he had been forced to admit that these were unusual times. He often despaired of ever attaining the high position he dreamed of. If only the world would stand still a day or two! All he wanted was his chance to make it!

His eyes were not good, so Tahli-Damen leaned forward, straining to see some expression on the dragon's faces. The beast seemed less playful than usual—more solemn. Vicia-Heinox appeared rooted in one spot, looking like one of the statues of himself that lined the boulevards of Lamath. As they climbed the last few hundred feet they were delayed by the normal number of fainting slaves. Since he was headed for Lamath, Tahli-Damen carried mostly Maris today. He preferred the runs to Ngandib-Mar. The country was nicer, and the Lamathian slaves carried on such trips were generally more relaxed at the sight of the beast and less resistant to being eaten. It had something to do with their religion. Some seemed even to appreciate Tahli-Damen's feeding them to the dragon—which did nothing to discourage the general opinion of all the merchant houses that Lamathians were a race of lunatics.

Now he heard a low growl emanating from the beast, and his heart fluttered uncharacteristically. Tahli-Damen had never heard Vicia-Heinox growl thus before. It was most unsettling. He suppressed his feelings, straightened himself in the saddle, and led his column to within twenty feet of those four gleaming eyes.

"Far enough," Vicia warned.

Tahli-Damen stopped his horse dead with a jerk on the reins. "Your Dragonship," he began, "I have brought you—"

"I can see," Heinox snarled, cutting him off. Vicia swiveled slowly to eye his twin, and Tahli-Damen wished he had been more attentive while learning the subtleties of dragon expressions. It seemed incredible, but was that a look of hatred the heads had just exchanged?

"I offer you the standard contract—" he began again.

Heinox interrupted. "No contract."

"Of course a contract!" Vicia snapped. "Am I trying to destroy *all* my relationships?"

"I am trying to establish new relationships—ones not subject to interference from any other head that might possibly occupy this body!" Heinox growled back.

"In other words, cutting the other head out?" roared Vicia.

"I'd prefer to cut the other head off!" screamed Heinox, and they were at it again.

Up and down the line, slaves were dropping like ripe apricots on a windy day. It wasn't from the heat, for there was a brisk spring breeze blowing up from the valley below them. It was the mere sight of those giant jaws snapping at one another above their heads, and those great, gleaming teeth—

The man of Uda jerked the parchment down onto the saddle and began to scribble. The messenger bird squawked and beat at him with its wings, making writing extremely difficult. The canyon pass was filled with noise, what with bellowing dragon heads, the screaming slaves, and a shrieking bird, but he did manage to write his reports. He broke the band that held the bird to his arm. It shot into the air in a streak of azure.

Vicia-Heinox paused in mid-argument to watch it hurtle past, bound for the blue sky beyond the cliff tops. The dragon hung there in the air for a moment, while Heinox slid down to ask, "What was that?"

"A—a messenger bird," Tahli-Damen replied.

The dragon thumped as he hit the ground with all four feet. "What for?" Vicia inquired.

The young rider cleared his throat. "There's been some talk that you have been acting—confused."

"Confused!" Vicia snorted.

"I, confused?" Heinox chortled, but he stopped when he saw Vicia's dirty look. "I am not confused. Merely—out of sorts with myself."

"Nevertheless," Tahli-Damen continued bravely, "the merchant families need some report on your condition, since it will certainly affect business. That bird bears my observations to the Council of Elders."

"What did you say about me?" Vicia asked eagerly.

"Yes, what?" asked Heinox.

"Why, I told them the truth."

"Which is?" Vicia asked again, edging down to look Tahli-Damen in the face.

"Yes, what is the truth?" Heinox put in.

"I've been having the most dreadful time deciding what the truth is, you see," Vicia went on pleasantly. "I haven't been able to put my talon on what it is, but I have the strong impression that things are just not the same anymore."

"Things haven't been the same since that Pelmen passed this way," Heinox growled, craning around to look west, as if he could see Pelmen somewhere out there among the mountains of Ngandib-Mar.

"Yes," Vicia hissed loudly, teeth snapping together so angrily that the clash touched off a whole new wave of fainting down the line of slaves. "Since that time I haven't been myself. Am I myself?" Vicia suddenly asked Tahli-Damen.

Before the man could reply Heinox interrupted. "Of course I'm myself! I cannot believe that I would sink to such a state that I would ask a merchant who I am!"

"I wish I could get it through my other head that I am *not* well! I need help!" Vicia yelled.

"Your Dragonship!" Tahli-Damen bellowed at the top of his lungs, hands cupped together before his mouth. It was a loud yell—loud enough to attract the attention of the arguing heads.

"Yes?" Heinox asked.

"What is it?" Vicia added, quite civilly.

"Perhaps I could offer you a bit of assistance in sorting this matter out." Tahli-Damen had visions of a promotion. To be the man who soothed the dragon and restored business as usual could open the door to the very Council of Elders itself.

"How?" Heinox sighed, his eyes lidding dangerously.

"It seems obvious," the man began, then paused to phrase it as delicately as he could, "that—ah—a rift has—ah—arisen in your relationship."

"My relationship to what?" Vicia asked.

"To—ah—to yourself."

"Myself? How could a crack appear in my relationship to myself? I'm me!"

"Yes but—there are—two heads . . ."

"Oh, I see. It's because—" Vicia stopped. "What did you say?" Vicia's eyes were flashing.

Heinox yawned, again dangerously. "He said there were two heads."

"I thought you were going to help me!" Vicia snarled. "Instead you insult my integrity!"

Tahli-Damen's eyes grew wide, and he cleared his throat and tried to explain. "No—oh no, your Dragonship! You don't understand! That's not an insult, it's just—"

"It is an insult! It has always been so, ever since that first smirking merchant called me a *two* before I was fully grown! I don't know what a *two* is, but I can tell from your face it is not complimentary!"

"But it is! I mean—it's not— Wait! Wait!" Tahli-Damen pleaded as he caught sight of Heinox, drooling hungrily. "It has to do with counting! Can't you count?"

"Shall I swallow him now?" Heinox asked calmly.

"In a moment," Vicia muttered. "You say this *two* means something in counting?"

Tahli-Damen was a brave man, but he felt himself weaving in the saddle. The blood had all drained from his face. His dream of a seat on the Council had been vaporized by Heinox' casual comment. It mattered little what he said now, and he replied almost absently. "Yes—counting. When I say two, I mean— It's as if you and—and you are each a different dragon."

"That's it!" Vicia trumpeted in sudden understanding, and he shot straight into the sky. It was fortunate for Tahli-Damen that he did, for Heinox was at that moment swooping down to chomp the rider off at the waist. Vicia's reaction jerked him up short. Razor teeth crashed together two feet above the man's head, and Tahli-Damen froze in the saddle.

"That's what?" screamed a frustrated Heinox, as he watched the ground recede below him.

"The answer to our problem!"

"*Our* problem?" Heinox puzzled, not at all happy at being dragged hither and yon by the excited swoops and dives and back flips of his Vicia-controlled body.

"Yes! Our problem!" Vicia sneered, then laughed. It was Vicia's first good laugh since the encounter with Pelmen, and he enjoyed it. Heinox seized the opportunity and took control of their wings, and the dragon settled back to the ground.

"Now," Heinox asked, a little dizzy, "what is this I'm blithering about?"

"I've no idea what *you* are blithering about," Vicia laughed wickedly, "but *I've* found the answer to the question that has been plaguing us!"

"Which is?" Heinox roared. He was in a terribly foul temper by this time. He hated to be made to feel foolish.

"That you, Heinox, are *you,* and that I, Vicia, am *I!*"

Heinox reeled back, then shot down to Tahli-Damen. "What is this? What's going on! Tell me or I'll swallow you!"

"No, you won't," Vicia snarled, wiggling between Heinox and the rider, "for *I* intend to protect him!"

Of course it didn't happen—it is questionable if such a thing was even possible—but Heinox screwed up those movable elements of his face and *appeared* to shed a tear or two. It was shocking enough to jolt Tahli-Damen out of his trance. "What's happening?" Heinox bellowed.

"Please excuse my partner's incredible dullness," Vicia cackled to Tahli-Damen, "but his skull is terribly thick, you know—"

"No! I will not be torn in half!" Heinox roared, and now *he* leapt into flight, and it was Vicia's turn to be dragged about. The dragon bounced from here to there off the canyon walls, very much like an inflated balloon when released. Heinox' control of the dragon's body was so chaotic that Vicia was only beginning to realize their awful predicament. No longer did their body respond only to coordinated commands from both heads. Suddenly it could be directed by either head alone—but only through overpowering the impulses of the other. It dawned on Vicia, as his rival's erratic flight pattern bounced him off a jagged cliff edge, that he now faced his most formidable adversary ever—himself.

Tahli-Damen watched in amazement. The noise passed as suddenly as it had begun—the dragon cleared the high cliffs, and was into the open sky beyond, no longer visible to the caravan. The merchant gradually became aware of the babbling voices behind him. At last one particular voice got through to him.

"Sir? Couldn't we—perhaps—move on? Maybe?" It was a slave who was speaking, one who obviously preferred the idea of bondage in Lamath to digestion in the dragon's belly.

Saying nothing, Tahli-Damen urged his mount forward. Within a few minutes they all reached the level plateau that was the center of Dragonsgate. Then they heard a subtle whir of wings, and once again Vicia-Heinox stood before them.

"Where do you think you are going?" Vicia scolded. Heinox said nothing, holding back and eyeing the rider angrily. Tahli-Damen hoped Vicia would not turn his back on Heinox—so to speak. It wouldn't take that other head more than a second or two to swallow the merchant.

"I—thought you—had—" he began lamely.

"We've settled our differences," Vicia announced.

"That fast?" the rider answered, neglecting to hide the disappointment in his voice. Heinox growled, and Tahli-Damen's horse backed up three paces, nearly treading on a bewildered slave's toe.

"Yes," Heinox snarled. "That fast. I have been forced to admit that an alien presence occupies my body, and that I and it are not the same."

"There will be trouble when the Lamathians hear this," Tahli-Damen muttered under his breath. "Very well," he spoke out, "what kind of deal do you wish to make?"

"We'll take all of these slaves—" Heinox began.

"All! But you never take all! How can I make a profit if you—"

"You forget," snorted Vicia. "Now we have two mouths to feed."

"But you only have *one* belly!" Tahli-Damen argued.

"It's the principle!" Heinox snarled. "We get equal

shares in everything—until I can figure out how to divest myself of *him*."

"It is I who shall get rid of you, Heinox," Vicia chuckled. "But it may take some time. Until then we share."

"But—" the merchant started to protest.

"As for *you*," said Vicia, "I wish to enlist the aid of your house in dealing with this menace I'm carrying around with me."

"No!" Heinox snorted, moving in so close behind Tahli-Damen's back that the merchant could feel the warm breath through his robes. "*I* must have the aid of Uda! It's a matter of life and death!"

"You aid *him* and I'll eat you," Vicia said flatly.

"You help *him* and *I'll* eat you!" Heinox retorted.

Tahli-Damen gulped. "And if I refuse to help either one of you—"

"We'll tear you in half." Heinox smiled.

Tahli-Damen gulped once more. "I hope it doesn't anger you for me to point this out, but—"

"But what?" Vicia demanded.

"But if you should manage to kill him, you'll die too." The merchant looked over his shoulder at Heinox and nodded. "Yes, it works the same the other way around."

Both heads jerked up and away, and they conversed together in low tones. The merchant looked around. The slaves seemed to have come to terms with their fears of being eaten. The biggest threat now was that the dragon would talk them to death.

"All right," Vicia said finally after both heads had returned to Tahli-Damen's side. "We've agreed we can't do anything to one another—yet."

"But it's going to be difficult for us—" Heinox interrupted.

"—since we will constantly—"

"—be fighting—"

"—for—"

"—control!" Heinox had gritted his teeth and forced the word in ahead of Vicia. They growled at one another.

"What about business?" the merchant pleaded.

"We have agreed on one thing," Vicia began.

"We hate Pelmen the Player!" Heinox snarled.

"Bring him to us!" Vicia roared.

"We want him soon!" Heinox screamed.

"He's the one who caused all this!" Vicia bellowed, then cleared his throat and dropped his voice. "Bring Pelmen to us, and we'll give your house a monopoly on all trade through Dragonsgate."

Tahli-Damen's eyes flew wide open. "I'll get on it immediately!" he blurted, and he turned his horse to ride back down to the south, to tell Jagd the news. Already he could see it: *Tahli-Damen, Elder of Uda*, engraved on a mother-of-pearl nameplate—

"Of course," Heinox whispered, coming alongside him again, "if you can think of a way to rid me of this aggravating growth on my shoulder—"

"I am not a growth!" Vicia shouted. "And you remember, merchant of Uda, it was I who kept you from a terminal case of being swallowed!"

Tahli-Damen could see another argument brewing, and he kicked his horse to urge it more quickly down the mountainside and out of the line of fire. Then it struck him. He was abandoning his caravan. He slowed his steed and twisted around to shout at the dragon heads above him. "But what about my slaves? My goods?"

"You just worry about Pelmen," Vicia said, smacking his jaws together hungrily.

"Yes, do," Heinox urged. "We can guarantee—these slaves will be well taken care of."

❧ Chapter Five ❧

THE DAY THAT BEGAN so cold warmed considerably as the sun climbed in the sky. Dorlyth's castle lay far to the north when Pelmen finally yielded to Bronwynn's plea for a rest. They stopped in a grove of trees, and the girl doffed the heavy coat she'd been wearing, carefully moving the falcon from one arm to the other and back again to avoid disturbing it.

"Why are we going south?" she asked.

"To fool Tohn mod Neelis," Pelmen answered firmly. He was in no mood for conversation. Surely the girl knew that; he had ignored her questions all the way from Dorlyth's castle. But she was Talith's daughter, to be sure. Stubbornness ran in her blood.

"Who's that, and how will it fool him?" she persisted.

"Tohn mod Neelis is the Elder of Ognadzu in Ngandib-Mar. We're trying to make him believe we are riding south, to take you back to your father."

"Why don't we just fool ourselves instead and go back to my father? If you think he'd imprison you again after rescuing me, then you don't know him. He'd welcome you as a son!"

Pelmen made a face, and Rosha chuckled. By the time Bronwynn twisted around to glower at the lad, he had taken a deep interest in something on his saddle horn; he wouldn't look at her.

"We're going to Lamath, my Lady, in spite of your persistence," Pelmen said. "It's the safest place for all of us, it appears."

"Then why are we wasting time going south? Shouldn't we be headed north as quickly as possible?"

Pelmen sighed, and peered out through the trees. He pointed at a small stream that divided a meadow that was yellow with buttercups. "I'll show you a little illusion when we cross the stream, the same illusion Tohn will see when he follows us here. Perhaps you'll understand then why Tohn may become a bit confused. Let's ride."

"Not again!" Bronwynn complained. "We just stopped!"

"Bronwynn," Pelmen began sharply, then stopped himself. Maybe Dorlyth was right. Maybe the girl was more than he could manage.

"Yes?" she asked innocently, eyes wide.

"Let's ride." He spoke softly to Minaliss, and the horse carried him out of the trees with a crash of breaking brush. There was nothing to do but follow him, so Bronwynn urged her horse into pursuit. She had stopped paying any attention to Rosha, since he seemed determined to ride behind her. They all crossed the meadow at a trot, stopping at the water's edge.

Pelmen turned to look at Rosha. "Ride through, lad."

Rosha was quick to obey. He urged his horse down into the stream, feeling a strange chill from the water, as if he crossed ice instead. Riding up the opposite bank, he turned to Pelmen to await further instructions, and gasped in surprise. His hand went to the pommel of his greatsword; it was out of its scabbard and into the air more quickly than a sneeze. Pelmen and Bronwynn were gone! He kicked his mount and was back into the water. As suddenly as they had disappeared, they were there again.

Pelmen was smiling, but Bronwynn's face wore an expression of shock Rosha knew mirrored his own.

"Where did he go?" the girl was shouting. Then she saw him reappear. "How did you do that?"

The powershaper grinned. "I told you, my Lady. The powers."

"But how—"

"It's a little trick done with light and wind." Pelmen shrugged. "A very useful illusion. Watch now." Both young people followed his pointing finger with their eyes; they sat in breathless amazement as four invisible sets of hooves tore the turf beyond the stream, making a trail that exactly matched the tracks the little troop had left behind them.

"But—" Bronwynn began again, in obvious dismay.

"Another trick." Pelmen chuckled.

Though there was no sound, the tracks appeared so regularly, receding from them across the clearing, that Bronwynn's imagination supplied the rhythmical hoof-beats. "Who's making them?" she pleaded, tugging at Pelmen's sleeve.

"I told you, my Lady. The wind. Tohn will surely follow us here and, crossing the stream, will follow those tracks yonder. A mile, maybe two, and those winds you see will spin away, once more their own masters. As for us—we will be gone, far to the northwest. Come now."

"But where did Rosha go? Where will we go, when we cross the stream?" Bronwynn begged, tugging so hard on her pony's reins that it began to back away.

Pelmen shrugged. "Across the stream," he said simply, and turned the head of his extraordinary horse to guide Minaliss into the water.

"P-p-pelmen?" Rosha cried. It was his first word since leaving the castle, and Pelmen looked up at him. "My m-m-mount seems un-sh-sure—" Indeed, Rosha's powerful black horse was almost skipping with anxiety, and the young man was having to fight to keep control of it.

Pelmen leaned across the horse's neck and spoke softly in its ear. That calmed the anxious animal immediately, and it raised its head to look at Pelmen. Was that a look of recognition? Bronwynn wondered.

"Now, together," Pelmen commanded firmly, and they all three splashed into the water, pulling the pack-horse behind them. Bronwynn had fixed her eyes on those phenomenal tracks before them; but as she experienced that same chill Rosha had felt, the tracks winked out like a snuffed flame. The earth was renewed—torn flowers blossomed again. Once more Bronwynn's pretty mouth fell open. Pelmen, watching her reaction, chuckled low in his throat. Though each act of shaping cost him dearly in energy and attention, there were times when it was all great fun.

"Look behind you," he said quietly, and the girl tore her gaze away from the reconstituted grass and looked back where they had come. The far side of the meadow now looked as virgin and untouched as did this side.

Bronwynn shook her head to clear it, and looked at him questioningly. "Where did they go? Where did they all go?"

Pelmen urged Minaliss into a trot along the stream toward the west. "Think of it this way, my Lady. Imagine that we arrived at the stream today—but are departing yesterday!"

Minaliss broke into a gallop, and Bronwynn had to kick her pony to catch up with him. She could hear Rosha's laughter behind her, and decided the sorcerer was teasing her. A black mood settled onto her again. Though it was a gorgeous spring morning in a breathtaking land, she longed for the hot, noisy avenues of Chaomonous. No one ever laughed at her *there*.

A few hundred yards from their point of crossing, the stream ran into an evergreen wood, a spur of the Great South Fir. They continued some three miles along the south bank, ducking pine needles and picking their way through stretches of rock. The two young people soon grew accustomed to the whirling wind that followed in their wake, erasing every trace of their passage. Neither spoke, leaving Pelmen free to concentrate on guiding that unruly power that trailed them. He chose finally to turn north, and they crossed the stream once more. He maintained the wind until midafternoon, when they were twenty miles farther north. Then it seemed that a burden lifted from his shoulders, and he settled back in his saddle and began to enjoy the day.

"I really don't know where the ability comes from," he was saying, "or how it settled on me. I only know that I am aware of forces—we call them the powers—and that if I can rightly focus my thoughts, these powers will do as I ask them."

"Bu-but how did you d-d-discover this ability?" Rosha asked. He was riding close beside Pelmen now, trailing the packhorse behind him. Farther back came Bronwynn, who was in deep conversation with her falcon about how mistreated she had been.

"It was just there, my friend. I tried to do something, and I did it. It was as much a surprise to me as to anyone."

"How did it happen? I mean, what f-feat did you p-perform?"

"It was in the Great North Fir, late one wintry night. The ground was covered with snow, and my fellows and I were freezing. We were all without flints for some reason, and were trying to summon a fire from the friction of sticks. But the wood was all so wet and our hands so numb we had no success at all. I was so angry I grabbed up a handful of fir needles I had dug from under the white blanket. As I held them up before my face, I screamed, 'Light!' They did. Burned my hand, they lit so quickly. I dropped the flaming needles into the fire pit we had wrested from the snow, and watched as the fire blossomed into a warming blaze. No one spoke of it then, but later each one asked me privately, 'Pelmen, how did you do that?' "

Rosha leaned closer to the powershaper to hear the tale's conclusion. "And what did you s-s-say?"

"I told them I'd frightened that fire into starting." Pelmen chuckled, then more reflectively added, "And that may well have been the truth. I really don't know myself. But it seems to me now so familiar, so easy to summon the powers, that I sometimes forget that others are unable to."

"Then why did you never reveal them in my father's court?" Bronwynn challenged from behind them.

Pelmen slowed Minaliss so that the girl could catch up to them. "You've finally decided to join the party?"

"Some party," Bronwynn snorted. "I asked a question."

"I never revealed the power there because I don't seem to have it there. Only while in the Mar am I able to shape the powers—and especially so the closer I come to the Great North Fir."

"Then your power is growing?" Bronwynn asked.

Pelmen wore a smile different from any smile she had seen. It was not the cynical smile so common to her father's court, or the joyful smile she had watched dance across Pelmen's face so frequently in his conver-

sations with Dorlyth. This smile spoke of a keen, proud
confidence. Pelmen's smile seemed the involuntary ov-
erflow of a power that energized him from within. Her
memory flashed back to crown performances in the court
of her father, when a thin, pasty-faced actor would strut
and posture and speak his lines before them. Could this
man who sat so confidently in the saddle beside her bear
any relation to that pale, skinny player?

"Growing is not the word. Waxing is better. As the
moon sometimes is full of light and other times is
empty, so my ability fills me, then passes from me. And
somehow it centers in the Great North Fir—somehow
. . . " Pelmen's voice trailed off, and his eyes narrowed
as if to pierce through the very mountains themselves to
see that fabled forest beyond them.

"D-d-do you think—I m-m-might—" Rosha began,
then grinned and shook his head.

"You might be a magician?" Bronwynn brayed, then
laughed derisively. "You could never pronounce the
spells!"

Rosha said nothing, but the look he fired across Pelmen at the girl spoke eloquently for him. Undaunted,
Bronwynn raised her head proudly and returned his
gaze, remembering how he had laughed at her. A wind
whirled suddenly around them and it was some moments before they realized that Pelmen had stopped and
they were riding on without him. When they broke their
staring match and looked back for him, his casual smile
was gone. He sat stock still astride a motionless Minaliss, his visage grim.

He waited for the two to ride back to him, then spoke
in tones quiet but full of authority. "Have you children
any notion—any notion at all—of the forces at work
when you bait one another in such a way? We ride to
the Great North Fir, children! Even the dullest of men
can sense the powers in that forest! In the Great North
Fir, Rosha, such looks can kill! You ask, will you have
power there? I say each man has power there! Whether
you'll shape the powers there depends on what you are.
But know this, you two, and know it well. Much of
shaping is in focusing power by will. If you should

argue there, and focus such ill will at one another, someone is liable to get hurt!"

Bronwynn blinked. "You mean, I could injure him with a look?"

"Don't take the possibility lightly, Bronwynn," Pelmen said. "And don't plan to test it either!" he continued, reading her mind.

"I won't!" she lied, and she shot a furtive sneer at Rosha.

She had planned to look away, but his fierce eyes caught hers and held them. She realized then how very much like her falcon Rosha looked. Then she jerked as, eyes gripping hers, he slammed his greatsword home into its scabbard.

The lightning seemed to open the sky ten feet above their heads—and that on a day so cloudless as to call the very existence of clouds into question. The noise was deafening; the impact knocked them from their horses. The source was Pelmen. Now as they gazed up at him, he looked like one of the mythological gods he played so frequently on the stages of Chaomonous. For the first time his youthful companions saw Pelmen as his enemies saw him. Here, truly, was a man to fear.

Bronwynn got to her knees and began to pet her bird, but it seemed unaffected by the shock. The horses, too, were calm, as if the thunderclap had been inaudible to them. Rosha and Bronwynn both looked away from the frowning sorcerer, who was silent for several minutes.

Then he spoke. "I'll warn you both once more. Someone could be injured—and I will not allow that. Is that understood?"

Both Rosha and Bronwynn nodded. Pelmen waited until they had mounted their horses again, then shook his head. "Rosha, you will never be a sorcerer. Your focus is in your hands and arms. Prick your spirit and that blade is in your hand—it is the only extension of your will you will ever rely on. I worry more about you, Bronwynn." Pelmen looked sharply at her. "You may discover you have the ability, only to find you've no worthwhile reason to use it."

He flicked his reins, and Minaliss sprang forward. They rode many miles in silence.

* * *

The southwesterly wind rippled both the tall grasses and the brightly colored pennants, as Tohn's small army mustered in the fields before his keep. "Boys," Tohn muttered to himself, "all boys." Yet they did indeed look grand, their helmets and bucklers flashing in the morning sun, their greatswords drawn in salute. Their uniforms were bright blue and lime, pleasing to the public eye but worrisome to an old, experienced warrior. There was no dirt on these uniforms, and no blood. The lads inside the finery had fought only one another. Were he riding into battle, he would trade them all for a small troop of veteran cutthroats. But Tohn did not expect a battle. Dorlyth mod Karis was among the finest warriors in the three kingdoms, and he had proved it repeatedly in one border skirmish after another. But he was certainly no fool.

If he could but surprise Dorlyth, Tohn thought to himself as he answered the salute with his own sword, perhaps he could put a swift end to all of this and get back to the business of living. It was a pitiful time for a skirmish anyway, what with fields to be plowed and seed to be sown. He'd feel far better to see these lads in work clothes, instead of prancing around in these fancy pants and tunics. Still, if he could strike now and have it done, it would be worth the delay in planting. If the problem was allowed to fester, there would be no harvest this year to need work.

If he could capture Pelmen! Now that would be a tribute to this fresh-faced troop. And it seemed feasible, provided the man was not preparing for his arrival. Tohn rehearsed the scenario of capture in a dozen different ways; but in each variation, success hinged on the element of surprise. And what if he had not been imagining the uninvited listener to his magic conversations? What if Pelmen himself had been listening in?

"I'm a crazy old man," he muttered angrily to himself.

His captain, not understanding him, barked out a crisp, "Yes, sir!"

Tohn looked at the fellow in surprise, then chuckled. The captain worried that he had missed something, but was somewhat reassured when the gray-haired merchant patted him on the shoulder and murmured, "That's right, son, keep reminding me." Tohn turned away and went to mount his horse. He heard the captain shouting orders behind him as he slipped his foot into the stirrup and swung himself up. When he turned to look at his battalion, they were mounting in spectacular precision.

"Beautiful sight," Tohn mumbled. "Not worth a snail, but a beautiful sight." He spurred his white mare, and she trotted down into a small gully and up onto a little rise. The wind blew his hair into his face and Tohn thought about donning his helmet; then he decided wild hair in the wind was preferable to a hot helmet and sweat, so he left it off.

What if Pelmen had heard him? There were others who could shape the powers besides Pelmen. The trouble was that Tohn knew none of them, and he basically mistrusted powershapers anyway. They had a callous disregard for a person's privacy, what with their mind reading and all. It didn't matter who may have been listening in—it couldn't be good.

Tohn sighed. Probably was just his imagination after all. Or what was that his cousin had said? A newly developed conscience? Little chance of that, Tohn thought. He summoned his squire to his side. "You have that bag I gave you?"

"This one, sir?" the boy asked, holding up a bag of blue velvet, knotted shut by a golden drawstring.

"That's it. You didn't look in it, did you?" the old man growled.

The boy shook his head vigorously. "I know it's something sharp though, sir," he volunteered.

"How do you know?"

"It poked me in the leg!"

"Here—you'd better give it to me then." It wouldn't do to have the lad concentrating on the mysterious object when Tohn's co-conspirators tried to contact him this afternoon. He took the bag, hung it by its string from his saddle horn, and smiled his dismissal at the squire. As the boy rode off, Tohn looked at the bag and told it, "You poke me in the leg and I'll toss you off the first bridge we cross."

The tiny army was riding past Tohn toward the west. The passing riders heard the old man talking to himself, but they paid no attention. All were used to his eccentricity.

"Six hundred men," he was saying. "Well, that'll be plenty—if it's a surprise."

A thousand feet above the snow-shrouded peaks of western Ngandib-Mar flew a bright blue messenger bird. A tiny sheepskin page, rolled into a tight cylinder, had been tied to the bird's leg by Dorlyth's falconer. This flyer was bound for the High City, and would not rest until she reached it. Throughout the night she had coasted along the air currents, finding the swiftest wind paths and spreading her wings to let them catch her and carry her onward. Dawn found her gliding along the treetops of a small forest, ignoring the calls of other birds as if they spoke a foreign tongue. She was not like other birds—she had a mission to perform. For she was a messenger bird, far removed from the life of the forest. She dwelt in the palaces of kings.

Blue flyers had been so long domesticated that few people now remembered their wild origins. Those whose business it was to know such things believed the species had been born in the Great North Fir, in the days before the coming of the dragon. But that was perhaps only speculation, formed on the basis of the flyer's peculiar power. It was indeed a magic bird, for it could take an impress from any human mind. If a man could form a visual image of a place and fix in his own mind the direction and distance to that destination, the bird by some marvelous ability could absorb that knowledge and fly there. How long it took depended to some degree on the bird's health and on the weather, but the primary factor in prompt communication was the clarity of the bird handler's mental directions. Once tossed into the air, a blue flyer would deliver its message or die in the attempt; many a bird had perished as a result of fuzzy directions.

Now this brightly feathered creature began to beat the air in strong, swift strokes, rising up the face of a sheer mountain cliff. A road crisscrossed that rock wall, carved of the stone itself. It was the major thoroughfare of the King of the High City, known to most as the Down Road. It was heavily trafficked this morning. Those passing downward looked in considerably better spirits than those who trudged up, for the road was certainly one of the steepest in the world.

But the blue flyer ignored the Down Road, shooting ever higher with each powerful stroke, until at last she topped the cliff. She flew above a broad plateau that stood some five thousand feet above the valley floor. Below was Ngandib, the High City, capital of the Maris. It was a beautiful sight, or would have been if the bird thought in such terms, for the city had that slightly wild flavor of the people of the highlands, and its architecture reflected a heritage rich in magic. Ngandib-Mar had been the dwelling place of shapers for as long as the city had stood on this spot. No one knew how long that had been, since the Maris had little use for history. Their only concern was for now.

Though the traffic on the Down Road was heavy, it appeared deserted in comparison with the bumping and pushing and selling and stealing going on in the marketplace. No one noticed the flyer as she passed over, her small black eyes seeking everywhere for the landmarks Dorlyth's falconer had impressed upon her mind. Her flight took her over most of the city, for the citadel of the King was in the center of the table land, while the main city rimmed its eastern edge. The palace stood on a mesa, carved from living rock by an extremely powerful magician in times long forgotten. Its parapets rose another six hundred feet above the plateau itself. It was inaccessible, except by a cavelike entrance cut into the rock at ground level. One had to enter the castle from inside, by climbing a closely guarded flight of stone steps.

Yet with a flick of its tail and flash of feathers, the blue flyer soared even above the pinnacle of the King's own tower, looking for a place to alight. This was her destination; having reached it, she felt at last the urgent need for rest. She finally spied the picture Dorlyth's falconer had planted in her mind—a window in the tower with a large blue circle painted around it.

She flew through that circled window, and joined a

line. For others had sent messengers to Pahd mod
Pahd-el, the High King of Ngandib. And since no one
in Pahd's court did anything very quickly, the messengers tended to stack up. All these flyers were tired and
hungry, and now they set up a chirping that must wake
every sleepy head in the tower. At last a barefoot servant came padding across the straw-covered stone floor,
his mouth wide in a yawn. He was not particularly gentle in his handling, but he did finally slip the cylinder of
parchment off the flyer's leg, and the bird followed the
others to a trough filled with seed. They belonged to no
one in particular, these birds. They simply were servants to men, flying wherever they were told to fly. Yet
it was a rare man who truly appreciated this wonder.

Dorlyth's message had been the last one to be removed, which was fortunate. It became the top missive
in the stack. The pile of letters changed hands several
times until it reached that golden tray for its final trip
into the King's chambers.

"Your messages, Sire," the serving lady said, curtsey-
ing before his Majesty, Pahd mod Pahd-el.

He was the fourteenth Pahd mod Pahd-el to rule
Ngandib, if anyone cared about such things. Pahd certainly didn't. Nor did he care about his mail. His answer
was a low snore, and a few grunts and groans as he
rolled over in bed, turning his back on both the lady
and her tray. The serving woman had expected this, and
she placed the tray on a small table and tiptoed out, just
as happy not to wake him. If he did wake, he would just
send her after something. This would give her another
hour to sleep.

"You mean you're not up yet!" screamed Pahd's
mother as she powered her way through the door. The
noise blew Pahd out of bed, just as it had done all his
life. Chogi lan Pahd-el was built like a bulldog. Her
bark was bad and her bite was much worse. Nothing
could make Pahd get out of bed except his mother, but
his mother always could.

"Of course he's not up yet, he's never up by noon."
This was the voice of Sarie lan Pahd, Pahd's own lan,
or wife. Between the two of them, these women made
Pahd's life miserable. At least, he thought he was miser-

able. He couldn't be sure. He was constantly asking them if he were.

"I have a headache—" Pahd began.

"Of course you do, dear," Sarie soothed. "You always have a headache in the morning."

"Shouldn't I go back to sleep? Maybe it will go away—"

"No, you're not going back to sleep!" Chogi belted out, grabbing the covers off the bed, wadding them into a large ball and tossing them into the corner.

"You want me to get up, Mother? Is that it?"

Chogi didn't answer him. Instead she sat on the bed, picked up the mail, and began to sort through it. Sarie pulled Pahd to his feet.

"It's a beautiful day," she was saying as she pushed him toward the window. "Isn't it?"

"Is it?" Pahd asked, looking out. He blinked at the harsh sunlight and stumbled quickly back into the room. "What do you think, Mother?" he asked.

"I think you need to have your head examined," she muttered without looking up.

"Didn't we already have my head examined?" Pahd asked his wife, and Sarie smiled sweetly.

"Yes, dear, we did."

"Ah, I remembered. And what did we decide?"

"We decided you need more exercise!" the young woman exclaimed brightly, raising Pahd's hands above his head.

"We did?" he murmured absently.

"We did! What would you think about taking a nice ride through the city?"

"We—we could," Pahd said, "but on the other hand, we would have to get dressed—and that would take the afternoon—and by the time we were ready to go it would be getting dark, and—"

"Then how about some practice in the armory? You need some, you know—"

"I—I could, but I'd have to get dressed, and get out the sword, and notify the swordmaster, and—"

"Give up on him, Sarie," Pahd's mother said. "He's not worth the effort. There's a message here from Dorlyth mod Karis."

"Dorlyth?" Sarie asked. "Isn't he the Lord who knows the sorcerer well?"

"Yes, he's Pelmen's friend," Chogi replied. "We sent that ugly slave master—who now?"

"Admon Faye, wasn't that it?" Sarie offered.

"That's the name. We sent Admon Faye to him to try to find Pelmen."

"Why are we trying to find Pelmen?" Pahd inquired with moderate curiosity. His mother moaned at his question and buried her face in her left hand.

Sarie smiled bravely, patiently, and put her hands on her husband's shoulders. "We decided you need a court magician, remember? We had a long conference with the advisors and the local Lords of the Confederacy and decided we would invite Pelmen to be your personal powershaper, remember?"

"We did?" Pahd asked.

"Yes, dear," Sarie answered, forcing herself to smile her brightest, cheeriest smile. "And we asked this Admon Faye to locate him, and sent him to Dorlyth, remember? And then he told us that he had heard Pelmen was in Chaomonous, having been sold into slavery by the King there."

"Really? Why would Pelmen let them do a thing like that, if he's a shaper?"

"Give up, Sarie," Chogi advised tonelessly, mulling Dorlyth's message over in her mind.

"We explained that, don't you remember? That Pelmen isn't a magician in Chaomonous."

"That's curious," Pahd observed, his eyes on the soft contours of his down-stuffed bed.

"Anyway, we sent this slave master to Chaomonous to buy the magician for us and bring him here," Sarie finished.

"Why?" Pahd asked simply.

"To try to bring you out of your stupor!" Chogi exploded. "To give you something to be interested in besides this bed!"

"Would he be able to do that?"

"We hope so." Sarie sighed. Then she winked at her husband. "Maybe this is good news Dorlyth sends us! Maybe Pelmen has been found."

"No," Chogi grunted, "it's not good. It's bad news. Listen: *Tohn mod Neelis, Lord of the west before Dragonsgate and an elder of Ognadzu, marches against me, breaking the confederacy. Your Majesty, may I count on your sword?* It's signed Dorlyth, and there's an added note: *Speed is essential—decide now.*"

"That's presumptuous!" Sarie exclaimed, rubbing her husband's neck. "To demand that Pahd decide today—"

"Presumptuous maybe, but it's certainly practical," said Chogi. She looked at her son, who was lost in thought. "Well?" she demanded.

"We do have an agreement, don't we?" he asked.

"The King of the Mar has agreed to defend his Lords against those who break the Confederacy, yes," Chogi replied.

"And he is sure Tohn rides against him?"

"Dorlyth wouldn't lie about such a thing."

"And he says he needs my sword, does he?"

"He does." Chogi shook her head in dismay at this son of hers. Such a splendid physical specimen, and such a sloth! The fact was that, once roused to war, there was no finer swordsman in all the Mar than Pahd mod Pahd-el, Lord of the High City—unless it might be this same Dorlyth. But what did it take to rouse him? She had to build a small fire under him just to move him from this room. Perhaps a sorcerer could aid him, create some interest in the outside world within him, tell him stories, show him tricks—something.

"But if I go," Pahd was saying, "I'll have to raise an army, and you know how much of a bother it is to raise an army—"

"You have a standing force housed in the caverns below this castle!" Chogi yelled. "All you need do is order them to war!"

"Yes—I could do that, but it would take most of the afternoon to get the order worded just right, and I haven't even eaten breakfast yet—"

"It's dinnertime, dear," Sarie whispered.

"Dinner then—maybe—"

"Yes?" Chogi lan Pahd-el sighed, knowing what was coming.

"Maybe if I started first thing in the morning—how

would that be?" He was ringing the bell to call for service, and the serving lady appeared, bleary-eyed, in the
doorway. "Do you think you could find me something
to eat? I'm not dressed to come to the table—" The
woman curtseyed and went out, and Pahd looked once
again at that bumpy, inviting mattress.

Chogi had gone back to the mail. She knew him well
enough to know his mind was made up on the question
of aid to Dorlyth. He would wait to decide later.

"This is bad news, too," she growled. "Production is
falling off in the diamond mines. Whatever you've got,
Pahd, it's catching."

"Oh really?" said Pahd. That was just before his
head settled back into his favorite pillow. Before the girl
returned with his tray, he was snoring again.

As Dorlyth had said, the assembly of warriors began
around noon. Throughout the morning men and women
had scurried about the keep, making preparation for
their arrival. Wood was gathered for a fire in the inner
court, and barrels of pitch, set aside long ago for just
such an eventuality, were rolled out of storage. The pul-
ley system was rehung on both the towers for fast transport of the heated pitch from courtyard to castle walls.
Sheaves of arrows were carried to the battlements and
placed loosely, tip down, in baskets spaced at ten-yard
intervals. Certain of the warriors coming to join Dorlyth
were powerful archers; in the initial battle shock, these
bowmen would take the highest toll on the enemy. Tohn
would not be expecting a siege situation, and a large
number of early casualties could dissuade him altogether from further aggression.

There was a small village to the southwest of Dorlyth's castle, where many of Dorlyth's freemen lived
with their wives and children. By ten in the morning,
the village was deserted; all of its inhabitants had
moved inside the keep. The children had arrived first,
driving sheep and goats before them. These were
housed in the stable. Older children and youths were
then sent to the fields and the woods to collect all the
fruits, nuts, and berries that could be found. There was
little that was ripe, for it was still early in the season,

but Dorlyth was less interested in providing food for the castle than he was in keeping it out of Tohn's hands. Thus the children, though they complained about the waste, obediently returned with half-filled buckets of unripe foods.

The women worked together to help one another transport what was left of their winter stores to the storage rooms of the keep. The dirt road from village to castle was thick with dust from the constant motion of ox carts traveling back and forth.

The men of the village helped to strengthen the fortifications, and then dug pits and set traps in the surrounding areas, more for nuisance value than anything else. All bushes and shrubs within fifty feet of the castle walls were cut down, to rob the enemy of any possible cover from watchful eyes above.

Dorlyth's greatest interest centered on filling the water cisterns, carved of the stone under the floor of the lesser tower. There was no well, and the precious liquid had to be piped from the stream to the base of the rock the castle stood on. There it flowed into a cavern below the lesser tower, and was hoisted up to floor level, bucket by bucket, by means of a water lift. Dorlyth feared that Tohn would cut his main pipe. Though buried for most of its length, it would still be quite evident to a careful observer on the river bank. Dorlyth cut down all the trees between the castle and the point where the pipe entered the water. His archers on the lesser tower would have their main responsibility in keeping the merchant's people away from that line of pipe. If they failed, the water in the cisterns would have to go a long way—and already the keep was getting crowded.

It grew more so through the afternoon, for warriors from the surrounding areas began to arrive at the gates in twos and threes, then in groups of ten and twelve. By dinnertime, a hundred and fifty experienced fighters crammed the banquet hall, laughing and joking and enjoying the reunion. All had fought beside each other under Dorlyth, but they rarely had the chance to gather together anymore. Only at the winter holiday did many of them see one another, and then only in small groups, for Dorlyth's castle was really too small to hold this many men in peacetime. But a new war had come; some soul as yet unknown to them was bringing them a battle; and so they jammed the tables of their friend and lord and ate happily what was placed before them. That wasn't much—Dorlyth's seneschal had not expected so many. Now he fluttered at the doorway into the kitchens, telling the servers who passed in and out to cut back on the portions.

"Feed them well!" Dorlyth thundered, overhearing his steward as he came into the dining hall.

"But Lord Dorlyth," the steward began anxiously.

His voice was drowned in the greetings and cheers. These warriors knew Dorlyth's gravelly bass voice, and they roared their approval of his appearance. The cheers and applause went on for several minutes, and Dorlyth beamed back at them, choking a bit, wishing only that Rosha could be here with him to hear this welcome. Then an expectant hush settled over the room, as they waited to hear from Dorlyth whom it was they were fighting, and why.

"I want you to eat well," Dorlyth began, and there was another round of cheers before he could go on. "This is the best we could put on the table—"

"And that's plenty good for me!" a warrior in back shouted, and there was noisy agreement from all parts of the room.

"But it may well be the last good meal some of you ever eat," Dorlyth finished. Some men nodded assent to this, but there were no more shouts. It was a sobering thought. "I wish I could offer you more. You are my friends, my fellows—in many ways my family. But we're facing a siege, and this castle is not well prepared for siege."

"Then why don't we just meet them and beat them out on the field?" someone asked from the back of the room.

"We may be forced to, depending on how long they decide to stay and on our water situation. But the real victory in this conflict rests in making it last a long time. I see some puzzled looks. I know you are fighters, not sitters. I'll explain. Tohn mod Neelis, whom some of you know personally and all of you know by reputation, is marching against Dorlyth castle."

"Why?" someone asked.

"He's the best warrior among the merchants, that's sure," someone in another corner of the room observed.

"He's breaking the Confederacy then?" an old warrior near the front asked. "Have you informed the sloth?"

"The King has been notified," Dorlyth answered. "I hope," he added under his breath. "You all are well aware of the King's problem so I won't bore you with it. If Pahd comes, he comes, but I don't expect him. What we do, we must do ourselves, and I've chosen to defend rather than attack—"

"But why—"

"I'm getting to that. Tohn mod Neelis has broken the Confederacy on the orders of the Council of Elders."

"I told you a merchant couldn't be trusted," one soldier growled to his neighbor, then cursed.

"He *is* a merchant, and it was well known to the Confederacy before he joined that his real loyalties were elsewhere. So be it. There's nothing we can do now except defend against his coming. He marches against me because he believes I am sheltering a fugitive the merchant families want badly."

"Are you?" someone shouted.

"If I were, I'd fight to protect him!" Dorlyth yelled back, and there was a roar of Mari approval. "The fact is, I no longer am. The party is in the process of escaping the area. I want to give them all the time I can."

"And that's why the siege strategy?" a young warrior asked.

"Look here," Dorlyth chuckled. "Even Venad mod Narkis is starting to think like a general!" Laughter greeted Dorlyth's comment, and the young man grinned good-naturedly. He was known for his skill with the bow, not for the quickness of his mind.

"Our problem is our water supply," Dorlyth continued. "If they cut that, we'll be forced to take to the field." There were some scattered cheers in reaction to that, too, but Dorlyth shook his head. "No, that's not what I want!" The room grew quiet. "My wish is to keep Tohn tied up for as long as possible without engaging him in battle. The longer we stay inside and the longer he waits, the more time our friends have to get away. And it is imperative that they escape, not only for their safety but for our security as freemen!"

All listened grimly to Dorlyth now as he paced behind the head table that lined the length of the platform. Many of these men had been slaves, whose freedom had been bought or won for them by Dorlyth. They knew little of the relation of other bondsmen of Ngandib-Mar to other lords, and cared less—but their bond to Dorlyth had been forged out of a struggle for personal freedom. They valued it—and listened closely:

"It is the purpose of the merchant houses to force total economic slavery on us by crushing our governments and replacing them with merchant kings. This attack is only the first flexing of merchant military muscle, and if we can weaken them now, I say we should do it." Dorlyth stopped pacing, and looked out at this gathering of dear friends. "But I won't risk your lives if I can avoid it. We'll hurt Tohn's army as much as is necessary to drive him home—and hope that he chooses to stay home next time. But I won't waste lives by going out to meet him in the field."

"Yet if the water—"

"We'll face that if and when we have to," Dorlyth said. Then he held up his hands to stop further comments. "That's enough for now—your dinner is getting cold and so is mine. Let's eat it."

Dorlyth sat and began to tear into a slab of beef. Soon the kitchen crew was back in business, and the seneschal had gone back to his worrying.

As Dorlyth finished, the bird handler stepped into the room and walked quietly to his side. The man bent and whispered in the swordsman's ear, and left again. It took a few minutes, but enough of the company had witnessed the exchange that soon the room grew quiet again. Dorlyth, forced to comment, stood once more.

"My falconer shared some news that you may be interested in. I sent a rider half a day's journey east with orders to watch and count. Tohn mod Neelis will arrive two hours before tomorrow's dawn." He waited for a

moment, but no one went back to eating. He smiled.
"You want the count. He brings a force of six hundred.
Against this crowd, I feel sorry for the man!" There
was laughter then, and Dorlyth sat down to sop his
plate. He felt a weariness in his bones, and he looked
forward to sleep. It had been a long day, and tomorrow
would be longer.

They rode from before dawn to well after midnight,
with precious few stops. What few moments of rest they
had taken were too short by half, in Bronwynn's estimation. All three riders were exhausted, and the last few
hours of the journey had been especially tense with the
passing of the light. The night was moonless; and
though the stars were brilliant, they did little to light the
way. Instead they dazzled the eyes, making the ground
and trees seem only more black and shapeless. Pelmen's
commands took on a sharp edge, for the rough terrain
seemed determined to part them from one another. He
spoke only when necessary, so deep was his concentration on holding them together. Rosha, of course, said
nothing. There were times when Bronwynn felt herself
all alone in the universe, and several times she said silly
things just for the sake of hearing a human voice tell
her to be quiet. She tried to content herself with the
muted shuffle of horses moving cautiously through
moist new grass and mud. She rubbed her cheek along
the feathers of the falconet that stolidly rode her shoulder, and passed the time by quietly voicing various
names for the bird. She settled finally on Sharki, though
she really didn't know why that appealed to her. It did
seem to her, though, that she had heard sailors tell her
father of a great sea creature by that name that was as
graceful and deadly in the water as her falcon was in
the air.

"Sharki I'll call you," she whispered to the bird.

"Quiet!" Pelmen scolded.

They rode on.

She sang songs in her head, counted hoofbeats, rehearsed a score of biting replies she would give the next
time Pelmen hushed her—and she sighed a great deal.
What about this Rosha, what does he think about? she

wondered. He was back behind her again. Pelmen had appointed him to keep her from getting lost—and she one of the best horsewomen in the whole Chaon court!

Just when Bronwynn was ready to scream in frustration, Pelmen decided to stop.

"Quietly now," he said, "I know you're both exhausted, but I need your help. We are at the edge of the Great North Fir. Dismount and come here beside me."

Bronwynn swung her right leg over her pony's rump, and was about to drop to the ground when she felt strong hands clasp her waist. Startled, she yelped.

"J-j-just me—" Rosha whispered quickly.

"Well, warn me next time," she snapped. The loudness of her voice surprised her.

Pelmen warned her again, "Quietly, Bronwynn!"

Unfortunately, she had so unnerved herself that she couldn't remember any snappy replies. Instead, she jerked free from Rosha and walked, hands outstretched before her, in the direction of the black shape she knew was Pelmen. Rosha followed closely behind her. As they neared the magician, each imagined the dark shape was moving his hands before him. Then they realized that he was indeed, and that an orange glow was forming two feet from his face, at eye level.

Soon it was a ball, and Pelmen caused it to rise above his head. "Look around. Gather all the firewood you can find and place it directly under this light—and please do it quickly!" The young people moved off to obey, Rosha vigorously, Bronwynn reluctantly. The powershaper knelt on the ground and closed his eyes. While sustaining the fireball in midair, he concentrated most of his power elsewhere. By the time he opened his eyes, the boy and girl had returned, and Rosha was building a cone of small logs below the fireball. The girl sat and watched him, her face drawn, her eyes heavy.

"Very good," Pelmen announced loudly, and both looked up at him, surprised. He had been kneeling for half an hour, and Bronwynn had assumed he was sleeping. "How about a little fire?" he murmured, waving his hand. They all watched as the fireball dropped onto the carefully stacked wood. It burst almost immediately into

a nice little blaze, and Pelmen smiled at Bronwynn.
"Now that was easy enough, wasn't it?"

"For you maybe." She shrugged. "You didn't have to
carry the wood." She wrapped her fur cloak around her,
and moved as close to the fire as she could stand. The
night had turned cold. Pelmen shook his head, and he
and Rosha moved swiftly to put up the tent. It was a
fine shelter, made of that costly fish-satin acquired with
such effort by divers in a land so far away no one included it when the world was discussed. Packets of food
were broken open and shared out. Bronwynn wolfed
hers down without a complaint about its quality.

Once warmed and fed, the little group felt their spirits improve considerably. Pelmen began to tell stories
that set Rosha to giggling, and Bronwynn relaxed and
dreamed of other places. After a time the conversation
between sorcerer and fledgling warrior took on a more
serious tone.

"I don't know what the relationship is," Pelmen said.
"I only know there are powers, and then there is the
Power. Powers one may shape, if one has the gift. But
the Power seems to work on men as a magician works
on the wind and fire."

"The P-p-p-power is greater than m-men, then,"
Rosha concluded, taking a bite of a crust of bread.

"Perhaps—if you say that which controls is more
powerful than the object it controls. But it isn't always
so, you know. I can shape the wind and yet it can still
blow out of my control and possibly harm me. I am not
greater than the wind—I don't compare myself with it.
Perhaps I shouldn't compare myself to the Power, either. I may sometime find ways of controlling even
that." Rosha raised an eyebrow in comment. "And yet,"
Pelmen continued, as the boy had expected he would,
"perhaps I tease myself when I say that. The wind may
blow me, but it has no soul. The Power—"

Rosha looked surprised. "The P-p-power has a s-s-
soul?"

Pelmen smiled. "A bad word, maybe. The Power has
conscious being, something the powers lack."

"B-but how did you f-f-find it?"

Pelmen chuckled. "I didn't. It found me."

"Where?"

"In this forest."

"B-b-but—didn't your ab-ability find you in this f-forest, too?"

"Yes, in a way. But my ability I wished for. I did not wish for the Power to control me."

"C-could it be that the P-p-power gave you the ability?"

"I suppose—"

"Or that you c-could ask the Power to c-control you, and that it would?"

"I don't know," Pelmen said, truly surprised at the depth of the young man's thinking. "I don't know if I could enter that state by trying—"

"Don't try!" Rosha said, pushing his jaws together fiercely to form the words. "If you are n-not in control, then we m-may fall into d-danger!"

"You're right, of course. I won't. But I need to warn you, Rosha. The deeper we travel into this great forest, the more chance that this Power will take me. It is a risk we run—"

Rosha snorted derisively.

"Why did you do that?"

Rosha struggled to answer. "M-my father said 'Let it b-be his risk, for he s-s-somehow is p-p-pulled to it. You ca-can't stop him, but d-do d-d-defend him.'" Rosha looked almost angry.

Pelmen reflected a moment. "Your father knows me well," he said finally. "Rosha, I do not know as yet what I shall become in Lamath. I found a book there, once. Your father will say it drove me slightly mad—or else he'll argue I'd grown overfond of magic and drove myself insane, and that the book became the fetish of my insanity. Tell me, truthfully. Did he tell you he thinks the powers have possessed me?"

Rosha nodded, then stammered forcefully, "What if this P-p-power that p-pulls you so is evil? What then?"

Pelmen was quiet for a moment. When he began again, his voice seemed to come from far away. "Some years ago, I was worn out by my powers. I used them so fiercely for so long in those wars of confederation you've heard so much about that I was exhausted. I came back to the North Fir—not to experiment with new forms of shaping, but just to be cradled in the birthplace of the old. I went deep, my friend, toward Lamath, and every step I took I became more convinced something there had summoned me. Somewhere between here and there it seized me, Rosha. A Power, but not one formed and sent after me by an enemy sorcerer. This was a Power drawn from earth and water, not from the fire and the wind. Fire and wind are fleeting, my friend. This Power rooted me to the ground I walked on. History, Rosha! It seized me and shook me with the nature of history, and left me dazed and dizzy—but with a new curiosity. Where did we come from, and when, and why, and what value is there in a day?"

Rosha stared across the campfire at the shaper, his eyes wide. He blinked, and would have answered, but Pelmen held up a hand, stopping him. "That was when I realized that this Power had being—why should history be important to a soulless force? You may listen to the wind—hear it? It rocks the trees gently or shakes them, according to its mood. The sound is so meaningless—it's empty. It passes and leaves nothing behind. Or the fire, crackling, throwing itself up into the air—" Rosha's eyes followed the sparks as they struggled upward, only to die away. "—and dying. Leaving nothing behind but ashes. But this, Rosha—" Pelmen now grabbed a handful of dirt. "This has history. As you do. You're not a wind any more than I am. You are Rosha, the treasure of Dorlyth, who was the treasure of his own father Karis."

"B-b-but what . . ." The boy let his words trail off. He didn't really know even the right questions to ask, so strange was all of this.

"I went to Lamath, Rosha. I became a monk of the Dragonfaith, a participant in the cult of the Dragon."

Rosha reeled back. "M-my father never—"

"Your father never knew. He thought I was wandering through the woods, feeding off nuts and berries. But I was searching for that history in the earth, scratching the soil with a rake day after day, just looking. And in the dead of night in a cavern beneath my monastery, I

found a book. The Power seized me again, then. Rosha,
I swear I didn't dream it! Through the weeks that followed I searched other books in the monastery library,
finding finally a grammar in characters resembling
those in the pages of my strange and attractive volume.
And I learned how to translate those runes."

"My father s-s-said you f-found it in the f-forest."

"So I told him."

"B-b-but why lie?"

"Why involve Dorlyth in a thing he needn't know?
Your father has carved his own history into the life of
Ngandib-Mar with the sharp edge of his greatsword. He
has carved his name in the lives of the people he has
loved there. He is content with the skill of swords and
the knowledge of powers. But you, my young friend—
you are not so fortunate. You travel with me toward
Lamath. For you it will be important."

"What d-d-does this b-book say?" Rosha asked, his
face wearing that intense expression he usually reserved
for his swordplay.

"Where's Bronwynn?" Pelmen asked suddenly. Both
men jumped up and searched around them. Rosha threw
open the flap of the tent and rushed inside. There was a
look of shock and vengeance on his face when he reap-
peared.

"She's gone!" Rosha cried.

Talk, talk, all they do is talk, Bronwynn thought to
herself as the two men philosophized. She was used to
that—being forgotten by men who adored her as they
wrapped themselves in meaningless phrases and called it
philosophy. Neither man saw her stand, and walk to her
horse. Neither saw her press a forked branch into the
damp earth and then place Sharki, hooded and already
sleeping, on one of the forks. Neither watched her tug
her coat around her shoulders and walk away from the
warmth of the fire toward the edge of its light. The stars
were different, she decided, when you could stand still
and stare up at them. She looked now for the striking
constellation known in Chaomonous as the Butterfly,
with its easily recognized body of three stars in a row.
Then she remembered—that was a winter constellation.

This was spring. She looked instead for the Diamond Cluster . . .

The light from the fire, scant as it was, caused her difficulty in seeing. She moved a few paces farther from it, and clutched her cloak more tightly as the cold seemed to deepen. No, she couldn't find the Diamond either. Pity about the Butterfly not being out. Those were the only two constellations that meant anything to her. The others she couldn't make any sense of. She turned to walk back to the campfire—and it was gone.

Panic seized her, at first. But Bronwynn was nothing if not quick. She gathered her coat around her and walked toward the dark center of the clearing, and burst through the wall of chill into the firelight.

"Bronwynn!" Pelmen yelled, and breathed a sigh of relief. Rosha's face lit up with joy. Bronwynn noticed, and decided she quite liked that.

"You've hidden us," she exclaimed to Pelmen as if nothing out of the ordinary had happened.

"Did you really think I was sleeping while you gathered firewood?" Pelmen asked sternly. "The next time you—" He stopped. Why did he feel such a compulsion to lecture the lady? He turned on his heel and walked into the tent.

For lack of anyone else to talk to, Bronwynn looked at Rosha. "It's just like the wall of cold at the stream this morning! No one can see us, or hear us!" Rosha smiled shyly, and looked away. "A little startling at first," she went on, "but I kept my head and just walked back through it."

Rosha looked back at the girl, and smiled again. "I am g-g-glad you ca-came back. I m-missed you." He turned away, looking for his blanket, and left Bronwynn standing there. She was cold, for the night was chill and the fire was dying. And yet she felt strangely warm.

❧ Chapter Six ❧

THE LONG HALLWAY that ran from Talith's tower to Ligne's apartments was glass-lined on both sides. This had certainly not been the King's idea, for everyone in the court could see him when he made that trip. It served Ligne's purposes, however, that the King be seen, and she had insisted on it. It was the only door into the rooms. Everyone knew there were other doors out, but only Ligne and a chosen few knew where they were located, and it was Ligne who controlled them. The King was not one of the chosen; but since he assumed he knew everything there was to know about Ligne already and had judged her to be loyal to him, he was totally unaware that a chosen faction even existed. He did wonder, however, when Ligne installed a hanging forest of sparkling cut crystal along most of the hallway's length. The strings of glass got in his way; as he knocked them brusquely aside when he walked to her room, they set up the most hideous tinkling. When he asked her their purpose, she just shrugged, and said, "I don't like surprises."

On the morning two days after his declaration of war, Talith stood in Ligne's bedroom tying a golden sash around his royal waist. "I don't see how they got her out," he was muttering to himself. "With all the guards at the doors, and that noise in the hall—it doesn't make sense!"

"Must that be the topic of every conversation?" Ligne snarled as she sat brushing her hair before one of the many mirrors in the room. "She was kidnapped by merchants, Talith. Obviously they bribed the guards, or distracted them somehow with some new bauble. You

122

have the guards in your dungeon. Why not ask them yourself?"

Talith glowered at the woman. "It seems strange to me that they would take her and leave you here!"

Ligne turned around to face him, red lips open in surprise; then she brightened and danced to her feet. She glided toward him and slipped her arms around his neck. She kissed him on the cheek. "Thank you! What a sweet thing to say!"

"What?"

"Oh, but I'm sure the Lamathians didn't realize your love for me is so great that you would go to war just to win me back."

"What are you talking about?"

"Otherwise I'm sure they would have kidnapped me instead of poor Bronwynn. You can be sure that if they had, I would have kicked and screamed all of the way. As it was, I got those two horrible bruises I showed you when they knocked me down." Ligne nibbled on the King's ear, and whispered, "You want to see them again?"

Talith cleared his throat. "Not right now. Affairs of state you know. A war to plan." He started for the door.

"Your crown's on the chair," she reminded him, and he turned back to grab it and jam it down over his forehead. Out the door he went, knocking the crystal hangings aside so that a delicate tinkling followed him all the way back to his tower. Ligne smiled to herself, stroking her hair absently as she waited for the noise to cease.

"He's gone," she said to one mirror after the hall was quiet again.

"It's hot in there," the man grumbled as he opened the mirror out into the room and stepped from a compartment concealed behind it. The woman winced in disgust at the sight of him, but managed to smile through her grimace. How could anyone be so ugly?

"You wear too many clothes, Admon Faye," she said. "Shed some of that finery and perhaps you would breathe more easily in these lowlands."

"My dress is fine for the climate of Chaomonous, my Lady. But only a flower could thrive in this greenhouse of yours." He gestured at the hanging plants that ringed the circular room, one for each of the tiny windows, set high in the wall for the sake of Ligne's privacy. "But of course," he continued, "clothing isn't essential to the function of this room, is it?"

"Sit down," she snapped, seating herself with a toss of her long green gown, "and we'll speak of things that are your business. My life is not."

The slave raider's face was so grotesque that even his smile chilled the heart. He sat on the edge of her bed and propped one boot upon it.

"I don't like mud on my bedspread," Ligne said as menacingly as she could manage. "Do you mind?"

"No, I don't mind mud at all, my Lady. I sleep in it every night. Now can we get on to our business?"

Ligne flared. "I hired you—"

"To be an assassin, not another of your human house-plants," he finished for her, his eyes boring into hers. "As long as that relationship is worthwhile to me, I will continue it. But I have been waiting long enough, and I have other matters to deal with this morning."

Ligne glared at him for a moment, then forced herself to laugh. "Admon Faye," she said, "you are a very powerful man."

"I'm also ugly and impatient!" he growled, starting to rise.

"I want you to kill someone," Ligne said quickly, and he settled back onto the bed, dropping his foot graciously to the floor.

"Who and where?" he demanded.

"I want you to murder the heir to the throne of Chaomonous," Ligne announced quietly. If she expected some reaction from him she was disappointed.

"Where?" he said again.

"Don't you hear any news? She has been kidnapped and taken to Lamath."

"I hear a lot of news, my Lady, much of it not true. I assume your sources are good?"

"The best," she said smugly.

"Dealing with the merchants then." He nodded to

himself, then went on. "And are you sure the lady arrived in Lamath?"

Ligne jerked. "Of course she did! Why would you ask that?"

"I said I hear a lot of things. I've heard some rumors that she never arrived. But you say the merchants told you she's there?" Ligne nodded uncertainly, hiding her shock and quickly stifling her fears. "They could be lying, of course. But I'll find her." He started toward a hidden door.

"I, too, hear rumors," Ligne said, stopping him. "It's rumored you are seeking Pelmen the player. He was sold into slavery and carried off to Lamath with the girl. Should you happen to see him, I will pay you extra to kill him as well. He's said some very unkind things about me in those plays of his."

"Yes, Pelmen always was an honest sort," Admon Faye sneered, and Ligne's temper flared again. "You want him dead and Pahd of Ngandib wants him alive. When I do find him, I'll sell him to the highest bidder. How's that?"

"Get out!"

Admon Faye chuckled, and crouched to duck through the low doorway concealed behind her marble washbasin. Then he stopped, and looked up at her. "Next time you want to see me, make it after the King's visit. I'm not going back in that closet." Then he was gone as silently as he had come, leaving Ligne to stew in silence.

Later that day the King's crystal-maker was ordered to replace some mirrors in Ligne's apartments. When the King threw things in anger, he tended to grab an unbreakable object. Ligne wouldn't throw anything unless there was some shattering of glass involved. If people couldn't see and hear your rage, what was the point of flying into one?

Tohn swore aloud, and swung himself up into the saddle. The sun had just come up, but it was already promising to be a hot day. Tohn cursed this changeable weather, cursed his horse who was inexplicably in the mood to prance this morning, but most of all he cursed whoever it was that had warned Dorlyth of his coming. Not only was the bearded swordsman not surprised, he was fully prepared for a siege! Every report Tohn received drove him deeper and deeper into depression. It had to be the magician's doing. Tohn stood in his stirrups to get a good view of the small keep, and dropped back into the saddle with a heavy thump that did nothing either for him or the horse. He jerked on the animal's reins and rode back to the brightly striped blue-and-lime tent that would serve as his command post. "Boy!" he bellowed, and his freckle-faced squire tumbled out of the tent, legs tangling in the unfamiliar flaps. "You bring me my helmet." The boy started inside. "And my sword," Tohn added.

"What, sir?" the lad asked, popping his head back out.

"Sword! You've heard of a sword, have you?"

"Yes, sir," the boy said, and he disappeared.

"And my standard, I'll need that, too," Tohn added.

The boy appeared at the door flap again. "What, sir?"

"My standard! How's Dorlyth mod Karis to recognize me without my standard!"

"I don't know, sir," the boy said, then hesitated at the door.

"What are you waiting for?" Tohn bellowed. Then he remembered something else. "And bring me that object in the blue bag . . ." He trailed off as the boy came out of the tent with helmet under one arm, sword and standard under the other, and the blue bag clutched in both hands. "How'd you know I wanted that before I called for it?" he roared.

"Simple, sir. It was the only thing left in the tent."

"Give me that," Tohn grumbled, grabbing the helmet the boy offered him. He looked at the sun climbing higher in the sky and muttered, "That magician's cursed me, I know he has."

"Remember, it'll be hot for the enemy too, sir," the lad offered with a smile.

Tohn looked at the boy. "Did I ask for encouragement? Did I?" he asked. The boy smiled at him, and Tohn finally chuckled and rubbed the youngster's head.

Then it was back to business. "Sword." The boy passed him his greatsword, and he unsheathed it in his left hand. It flashed brightly, and Tohn was pleased. He had drawn it for effect only. He wouldn't use it unless he absolutely had to. "Standard," he murmured, and the boy placed the butt of the stock in its holder on the saddle and pushed the pennant up for Tohn to grab it in his right hand.

"What about this?"

Tohn looked down and saw that the boy was holding the pyramid bag up to him.

"Can't you see I've got my hands full? Hang it around the saddle horn." The boy obeyed, and stepped back to look at his master, resplendent in blue-and-lime. "Look pretty good for an old fellow, hunh?" Tohn asked, and the boy grinned back. Tohn mod Neelis wheeled his horse, shouting, "Captains!" He rode toward the castle.

The word was passed quickly along the battlements. Tohn and three others rode close to parlay. Dorlyth donned his own helmet and walked out onto the arch surmounting the door to the keep. He waited until Tohn was twenty yards away, then shouted, "Enough." Tohn and his captains stopped their horses.

"I would welcome you to my property, Tohn mod Neelis," Dorlyth began, "but I see you have already made yourself at home." Dorlyth waved a hand at the semicircle of colored tents stretched across the eastern hill of Dorlyth Field. "I take it there's a reason for this display?"

"I seek only a man and a young lady," Tohn shouted back courteously. "They were guests of my house, but seem to have disappeared."

"If they chose to disappear, perhaps your house should improve its hospitality. That does not speak well of Ognadzu."

"Perhaps not," Tohn replied, "but that is hardly our concern here. I need this man and woman, and have come asking if you have some information concerning their whereabouts."

"You need six hundred men to ask a question, Tohn?"

"I felt there might be some need for wide consultation," Tohn replied.

"Then are your war councils growing as large as those storied councils of the golden south?"

"A lot of advice in a time of crisis can be most worthwhile, Dorlyth mod Karis."

"I quite agree. That's why I've invited these, my friends, to join me in my keep. To share advice."

"I trust they advise you to aid me in my quest for Pelmen the powershaper and a girl in his company named Bronwynn?"

"Actually they've been rather insistent on my not aiding you. As you say, good advice is most worthwhile."

"As long as it is good advice, Dorlyth." Tohn was threatening now. "If you choose not to aid me, my searching could prove costly to you. It would seem that with the relative size of the forces involved, the better part of wisdom would be for you to help me."

"Tohn, I give you freedom to search," Dorlyth called back.

Tohn brightened. "Is that an invitation to approach your gate?"

"It's an invitation to try to take it, if you choose." There was a murmur of agreement from the soldiers who lined the battlements.

Tohn's pony pranced while its rider decided to make a different appeal. "We are old men, Dorlyth," he began. "We have no business scrapping with one another as two boys would roll in the mud. Let us be reasonable."

"I'm listening," Dorlyth called back.

"Give me the man and the girl. It is simple enough a gesture, and think of the savings in life, in time, in crops. We're farmers, you and I, and neither of us has time for a siege."

"I quite agree that a siege would be foolishness," Dorlyth yelled back. "But I cannot choose for Pelmen and the Lady Bronwynn. If they chose the house of Dorlyth over the house of Ognadzu, who am I to send them packing?"

"Dorlyth—"

"You say we are old men, too old for fighting. I

agree there, too. The laws of the Confederation agree. I have no wish to fight you, and indeed I won't lay a hand to the sword. All I ask is that you pack your tents and return to the western lands before Dragonsgate."

"I will do that when I have Pelmen and the girl," Tohn yelled, calmly evaluating what force it would take to splinter the gate of the keep.

"They are free to go with you when they so choose," Dorlyth answered back, pointing down toward the gate with a hand hidden from Tohn behind the wall. Several warriors below him reinforced it still further, and a pair of thickly muscled local freemen carried a large vat of boiling pitch up a nearby stairway.

"Do you have any estimate as to when that might be?" Tohn smiled gravely.

"I am sure they will be ready to go with you in several years," Dorlyth smiled back.

Tohn chuckled. "As I said, I'm an old man. In several years I may be dead."

"Of course, there is that other possibility," Dorlyth called back, adrenaline rising through him and making him incautious.

"Which is?"

"That in several minutes you might be dead," Dorlyth called out brightly, and there was laughter all along the line of the wall.

"Or that you may!" Tohn called back, realizing that the battle was inevitable.

"Perhaps I will die today," Dorlyth replied loudly, "but I shall not raise my hand against you unless attacked."

"Well then," Tohn answered sadly, sheathing his greatsword, "I suppose I shall have to raise mine against you." He turned the head of his horse and made to ride away, then decided he wanted to add a word to the powerful warrior standing astride the gateway. "One thing, Dorlyth. This is not my idea."

"Mine, either," Dorlyth called back, and Tohn and his captains rode back to the striped tent on the hillside.

No assault came that day, but Dorlyth had really been expecting none. Tohn was no hot-headed youth, itching to prove his leadership by slaughtering his own men needlessly. No, the merchant was a tough old fighter of rich battle experience. Not only had he ridden with warriors of all the three lands, but some said he had battled with dragons. Dorlyth retired to his rooms to wait for the event he felt surely must come—Tohn's attack on his water line. The water lift in the lesser tower had been kept pumping since Pelmen's departure, but the cisterns were still far from full. When an old soldier knocked on his door and informed him that Tohn's warriors were in the forest behind the castle, Dorlyth recognized that the blow would come sooner than expected.

"Probably tomorrow," he whispered to himself. "Send Venad mod Narkis to the lesser tower now. We need his bow to defend our water."

"He's already there, Lord Dorlyth," the old man said softly, "and he's already claiming first blood."

Tohn and his captains were sitting solemnly in the command tent when the news arrived, followed quickly by the body. Tohn cradled the young man in his own arms and carried him to his own cot. "Get out!" he growled, and all others left the tent. "What am I going to tell your mother, lad?" the old fighter asked quietly, then he bowed his head across his young nephew's chest and wept.

The young man had been nineteen years old, one of the many Tohn had wrestled with and coached. He had been inspecting the stream on the far side of the castle, unwary, and had taken an arrow through the neck. In these few moments of quiet, Tohn did not blame the archer. He blamed himself for bringing such a youthful army so far for so little—and for deciding to remain and press the point.

"An old man should spend his days reflecting on life, my boy," Tohn said quietly, "watching the wheat grow. Not killing off his sister's babies."

And yet he realized he wouldn't give it up. Death or no death, Tohn had committed himself to this way of living, and he'd sat in too many tents with too many bodies of the first-slain to believe that this time he would yield to the temptation to pack up and go. He would be no hypocrite, and beat his breast and sob. Decisions made were decisions made. To second guess decisions constantly would only bring greater pain.

As he walked to the door of his tent and called for men to carry the body away, Tohn could not help but wonder if the continuation of the family business was really worth all the family blood. Once his captains rejoined him, he would need to thrust the question aside and get on to practical matters. But while he waited, shielding his eyes against the afternoon sun and examining once again the castle that was his target, he let his mind wander freely. Did the boy's personality ride now on the winds, a new power to be dealt with? Or was he just gone, a fleeting bright fire of a life, drowned by a bucket of his own shed blood?

"We raised no sword against them!" he heard one captain say angrily as they rounded the corner of the tent in a group. "And yet they ambush us from the battlements!" Tohn turned away and ducked back into the tent. The man continued his tirade as he followed the old merchant in. "What manner of man is this Dorlyth that he says one thing and does another! When we take this castle we should—"

"Quiet," Tohn said, and the man obeyed, a bit surprised. Tohn waited until they were all assembled, then addressed himself to the red-faced speaker. "You are saying he fights unfairly. So do you. So do I. Have some integrity as a soldier, son. He's done nothing you wouldn't do if you were outnumbered and your keep surrounded. Perhaps you must get steamed up about something before you can fight. Well, go ahead then. But don't let it color your respect for your enemy, or he'll kill you." Tohn turned to the others, and shrugged broadly. "We've lost a man. We'll lose others. At least the boy's death wasn't totally a waste. It provided us with some helpful information."

"What information?"

"Show me the spot where the young man died. I'll show you where we can cut off Dorlyth's water."

It rained during the night. When the sun rose the next day the colorful uniforms of Tohn's army were no

longer so bright and clean. The field between the tents
and the castle gate *was* bright, the bright green of new
grass; but though it looked as smooth as a hand-tied
carpet, Tohn knew it was full of treacherous potholes
and hidden puddles. He urged the long column of riders
to move closer, trying to minimize as much as possible
the distance of the charge while staying out of bowshot
range until all was ready. One unit of two hundred men
stood abreast of him on the eastern edge of Dorlyth's
field. Their mission was ostensibly a frontal assault on
the castle gate, but Tohn knew in advance they
wouldn't breach it. Not unless Dorlyth had built the
thing of green wood. The real purpose of this attack was
to draw defenders to this side of the castle. Tohn didn't
expect it would work, but he needed to try it in order to
achieve his main objective.

The second force was stretched along the bank of the
stream to the castle's north. This force of three hundred
warriors was armed for mêlée with axes and knives,
and each pair of riders carried a homemade ladder
slung between them. The wall was lower here than elsewhere, due to the slope of the knoll on which the keep
sat. If it were possible to scale Dorlyth's stone barrier at
all, this was the best chance, for the wall along this section rose no higher than twenty-five feet. Part of this
force would attack the lesser tower directly. Tohn worried about this strategy, realizing that it would be here
that he would suffer the bulk of his casualties. But it
was essential somehow to engage the defenders of that
smaller tower in the main battle, or the third arm of his
attack was doomed.

Tohn's third force hid in the forest to the west, armed
not with bows and swords but with good Lamathian
spades. Tohn had not come to war unprepared. While
he had hoped to avoid battle altogether, he had filled
several wagons with tools his experience told him might
prove useful. Tohn realized that soldiers did not end
sieges—engineers did.

Dorlyth stood on the lesser tower, watching the
woods for movement.

"There—" he pointed, but Venad mod Narkis shook his head. "You didn't see that?"

"No, my Lord Dorlyth. I saw nothing. Perhaps I discouraged them?"

"What, win a battle with one arrow? Wishful thinking, my friend."

"Maybe the merchant will surprise you and do something foolish." Venad smiled.

"No, they are there. I just can't see them yet."

"Nor can I, and my eye is as nearly perfect as that of a—"

"Yes, you've told me. There?" Dorlyth pointed again, but Venad only smiled at him and shook his head. There was some noise on the far side of the keep, and Dorlyth turned to look across the court at those who guarded the gate. Someone was shouting at him.

"Lord Dorlyth, Tohn mod Neelis calls to you!"

"What can he want?" Venad wondered.

"He wants to get my attention off the forest and on that side of the wall," Dorlyth grumbled. He gave one last sweep of his eyes to the forest, and jerked around to make his way down through the tower to the wall below them. "Keep pumping!" he called to the team of freemen who were driving the water lift with all the energy they could throw into it.

Venad mod Narkis watched as Dorlyth came out of the tower below him and onto the wall, then began to move along it toward the gate. He saw Dorlyth give a pat on the shoulder here, a word of encouragement there. Then Venad notched an arrow on his bowstring and turned to scan the forest again. He heard the two lords exchanging words far behind him, but he couldn't make out what was said. Suddenly he saw movement in the forest—and there they were. One hundred lime-and-blue warriors, half of them armed with shovels and the other half with bows and bucklers to protect the diggers. For the first time in a long while, Venad mod Narkis felt a chill scamper up his back.

Tohn shook his head at the needlessness of it all, then checked his lines of men. Signals traveled down the line and around to the other side of the castle, where his engineers waited. All was in readiness. Tohn gripped his sword with both hands, and slashed it over his head.

The scream rose first in the east and arced quickly around to the warriors gathered in the forest. As they broke from cover and splashed through the stream, Venad raised his bow. He picked his point carefully and loosed the arrow. The lead rider kicked his horse and the animal lunged forward—carrying its rider into the arrow's path, and death. Venad did not see him drop. He was already notching another shaft.

Tohn loved charges, but he quickly came to hate this one. Some riders went down under a hail of arrows from defenders above the gate. Others dropped when their horses tripped in the deceitful mud beneath the grass. He began to wonder if any of his warriors would ever reach the gate, much less breach it. Screams and shouts distracted him but he bent low in his saddle and merged himself with the rhythm of the pounding hooves. It seemed an age, that ride to the gate; but then he was there and off of his horse, shouting orders as he sought some cover under the lip of the gate itself. There he stopped, sheltered by the overhang of the battlement. Leaning against the heavy wood, he held a hand to his pounding heart. He was far too old for this, he thought. Far too old.

Dorlyth had no time to return to his position on the lesser tower. When the charge began, he grabbed up a bow and positioned himself astride a basket of arrows, pausing in his firing only to shout encouragement to those around him. He soon realized that it was here at the gate his aid was most needed, for the battle raged thickest along this short stretch of eastern wall.

The first battle of the siege of Dorlyth's castle lasted no longer than an hour. But neither commander had anticipated how costly the short conflict would turn out to be. Through the first half-hour Tohn despaired, watching helplessly as warrior after warrior was tossed from the wall or thicketed with arrows. His orderly commands turned first to anxious cries, then to hoarse screams as the rising level of noise took its toll on his voice. The battle was lightest at the lesser tower, for

Venad and his fellows concentrated their fire on the engineers across the field, while Tohn's soldiers discovered they had underestimated the height of the wall. The barrier proved too tall to be scaled, and those clustered at the foot of it soon shifted around the base of the keep to take the places of friends who had fallen before the gate. The pace of the battle there slowly wore away the strength of the castle's defenders. During the latter half of the hour Dorlyth too suffered, for he watched the fall of many loved and trusted friends and realized his responsibility in their deaths.

Time and again it seemed Ognadzu would scale the northeastern wall, for the blue-and-lime warriors had discovered that here their ladders could reach the lip of the battlement. But each time fresh reserves of pride and rage drove Dorlyth's defenders in to fill the gaps. The boiling pitch bubbled merrily in the courtyard, forgotten, for there was no time to raise it to the parapets. There was only time to thrust a sword, or fire another shaft. At the moment when Dorlyth acknowledged that they could stop the flood no longer, Tohn gave in. His blue-and-lime wave had been reduced to a trickle, and he croaked a retreat and ran for his own horse. A few of Dorlyth's battered companions managed a slight cheer at the sight of so many enemy backs, but most were able only to lean against the walls and gulp lungfuls of air in blessed relief. Ognadzu's retreat was far from orderly, but there were no fresh defenders to take advantage of the confusion of their flight. The battle—for the moment—was over. That was all that mattered.

Dorlyth leaned across the wall and gazed at the carnage below. How was it that he always remembered the glory and color of battle, but rarely recalled the horrible visions of those sacrificed to the powers of war? He gasped for breath, and put the sight and the thought behind him.

Now he ran along the wall, stopping to inquire about a slashed arm, wincing at the sight of a treasured comrade stretched lifeless on the stone slabs of the courtyard below. He put that behind him as well, and bolted into the lesser tower.

"Is it—" Dorlyth stopped. There was no sound of the

water lift being turned. Then he saw Venad slumped across the stairwell wall, gazing downward. The young archer turned to face his captain, wiping an embarrassing tear away in the same movement. Dorlyth put a hand on his shoulder.

"I failed you, my Lord," Venad mumbled. "The water flow has been stopped."

"What? Failed me, Venad?" Dorlyth said softly. "Never that, my friend. No, you think you've failed yourself—and only that because you expect far too much of Venad mod Narkis. It would have taken a miracle to keep them from destroying that water main, once they found it." Dorlyth sighed. Then he looked through a window that faced north. "And it's our miracle worker whose escape we fight to protect. Come."

With an arm around Venad's shoulder, Dorlyth led the exhausted warrior down the steps and out into the inner court of the keep. The siege had been launched. There was nothing left now but to lick the wounds, and wait.

Later that day Dorlyth sat alone in the greater tower. The curtain was open, and he gazed sadly out across his wheat field, sprinkled not with seed but with blue-and-lime tents. Was this a mistake, he wondered to himself? On the table before him lay a list his seneschal had prepared—a casualty list. Forty-three warriors were wounded, but that figure bothered him less than the other number scrawled on the sheet. Eighteen men were dead. Was it worth it? These eighteen lives for the sake of Pelmen's escape? So many decisions came back to haunt a man long after they had been made and left behind. Would this decision? Could he still end it all by simply announcing to Tohn mod Neelis that the party he sought had moved on? Tohn would want to inspect the castle, naturally. Perhaps that wouldn't be so bad.

No! Could he sit still while a supposed ally, a member of the Confederation of Mari Lords, ransacked his apartments and strolled through his keep like a conqueror? Tohn was no evil man, that Dorlyth knew well. But those who had ordered him to battle, those who controlled the Council of Elders—Dorlyth was convinced they were evil. He would not step aside and let

evil men roam the land he loved without calling them
into check.

Dorlyth's decision was made. He would not change
his mind now—that was not the Mari way. By the powers, the battle would come eventually, and he would
whittle away at the enemy now, while he and the Mar
still had the chance!

But—eighteen Mari dead. Dorlyth rose and walked
to the window. He had plenty of time to rehash the argument in the days that followed—and so he did. Over
and over again. Still, he stayed within Dorlyth's castle,
the gate tightly locked.

Flayh bustled down a long colonnaded walkway,
thrusting people out of his path. The slaves were used to
his foul moods, but no one could remember a series of
tantrums quite so severe as those of the last week. "Why
won't Tohn communicate?" he railed at the serving girl
who brought him his tea in the morning. "What is taking Pezi so long?" he shouted in the face of his barber,
giving the nervous little man fresh pains in his stomach.
"Nobody listens to me!" he screamed at the captain of
the guard, who sat up straight in his seat and endeavored to be as attentive as possible. Flayh was impossible to please.

He banged open a door at the base of his tallest spire
and turned to scowl at the slaves who had watched him
do it. They all went back to their chores—clipping the
roses, sweeping the walk, changing the torches—and
only looked again as he slammed the door shut behind
him.

Slumped in his darkened room, he stared at the blue
pyramid and thought angry thoughts at Tohn mod Neelis. The fool! The finest communications tool in all the
world and the old fool wouldn't use it! Wouldn't say
what he was doing, wouldn't tell where he was, no news
about the girl, no news about Pelmen, no news about
anything!

There was a chirp from the draped window. It drew
an immediate response from the little man, for he
bounced to his feet and jerked the black hangings aside.
A blue flyer sat on the window ledge, a parchment at its

leg flapping in the slight breeze. Flayh grabbed the note and read it quickly, oblivious to the fluttering flyer. In a very unsteady hand it read:

Dragon is unstable, advise extreme caution in all approaches to Dragonsgate.

It was unsigned, but obviously it came from the trading captain of Jagd's caravan. It was just enough news to be aggravating. How was the dragon unstable? What was the beast doing? And why hadn't he heard from the caravan leader himself? Surely he had arrived in Lamath by this time. Obviously the bird had been delayed by the captain's inability to give good guidance to Flayh's estate, but where was the man himself? Flayh wanted hard facts, not tantalizing tidbits! He paced his airy cell, pausing every other moment to gaze out the window, watching for some action on the road south to Dragonsgate, or the road to the southeast, where the Lamathian estates of Uda were clustered. Nothing.

There was another sudden flutter of wings, and Flayh cursed the stupid bird and reached out to grab the feathered creature. Then he realized there were now two blue flyers on his window ledge, and the latest arrival bore a message tied in the orthodox cylinder around its leg. Flayh tore the message off and shot a mental picture of his aviary at the two birds. They wasted no time leaving his company.

Flayh unrolled the message, and nodded. It was in the large scrawl of Tohn mod Neelis:

You will be pleased to note I have taken your advice. Have left this morning to visit Dorlyth mod Karis with an entourage of six hundred. Will keep you informed by carrier. —Tohn.

"By carrier!" Flayh exploded. Then he sat again before the blue crystal object on the table, and focused his malevolence into it. "Perhaps you won't talk to me, Tohn mod Neelis, but at least you will be aware that someone is talking to you—and that the words are getting nastier every day!"

As they rode deeper into the Great North Fir, Pelmen withdrew into himself a little more each day. It was barely noticeable at first, for the two young people were giving progressively more attention to one another. But it soon began to register with them that oftentimes now he would go for hours without speaking, and that he occasionally appeared to forget they were with him.

Other than the slight sense of insecurity this odd behavior birthed in them, the forest journey proved nothing short of idyllic for the boy and girl. At the southern edge of the great tangle of trees and shrubs, the powerful firs mixed with trees of other kinds. But the deeper they pushed, the more the evergreens took control, until at last they rode on a floor of needles alone, surrounded only by giant firs. Bronwynn had never seen trees so big, or forest glades so dark. They had spent the first day ducking low limbs and avoiding brambled bushes. Now they rode freely where they willed, for the nearest branches interlocked twenty feet above their heads. They spoke of the Fir as a vast green temple, with thousands of columns rising into an emerald ceiling, frescoed by light and shadow. They laughed at the antics of nervous squirrels, and compared their childhoods at length. Rosha taught Bronwynn what little he knew of falconry, and they freed Sharki to give him exercise as they rode. Swooping between the massive trunks, the bird looked less like a falcon than it did like a bat darting through subterranean caverns. The girl attempted to describe for Rosha the ocean and the beach, but succeeded only in making him angry.

"You t-t-tease me! There is n-n-not so much water in the w-world!"

"I'm speaking the truth! Just because you have never trav—"

"You think to m-m-make a f-fool of me!"

Bronwynn made a face at him. "No one needs to make a fool of you! You do it so well to yourself!"

Pelmen was riding some distance ahead of them. At this he turned Minaliss around and sat looking back at the young pair. His look wasn't scolding, just curious. He hadn't heard the argument, only the noise.

"Is there s-s-such a thing as a—a—an ocean?" Rosha demanded, frowning fiercely. Bronwynn said nothing. She knew she didn't need to.

"Of course. It bounds the eastern edge of the three lands."

"F-f-full of water?" Rosha protested. He didn't look at Bronwynn. He didn't care to view her smug smile.

"And fish, and shells, and salt. You mean Dorlyth never told you of the ocean?" Rosha shook his head angrily. "No—under the circumstances I suppose not. We didn't have joyful experiences there."

"What circumstances?" Bronwynn piped up. Pelmen's comment had been laden with meaning, and Bronwynn sensed a story hidden within it. Bronwynn loved stories.

"Well," Pelmen said after a moment, "Rosha's father told me to teach him. I suppose this is as good a time as any." The powershaper turned his horse back to the north, and his youthful companions reined in beside him. Through the rest of the afternoon he told them stories of adventure, stories of love, stories of failure that made the tales of victory seem more grand. He told them of the days he and Dorlyth had spent as slaves, and how they first encountered a man named Admon Faye.

"Ad-m-mon F-faye? He's the one who c-c-came to see m-my father."

Pelmen looked sharply at Rosha, surprised by this— then recalled Dorlyth's cryptic statement about being in touch with the man. "Yes, Dorlyth did get on better with him than I did."

"Was he captain of the slave raiders that captured you?" Bronwynn asked.

"Oh no, he was just a slave himself then, a helper to the land pirate who stole our freedom from us. Tried to befriend us, even as he helped put the shackles to our wrists."

"That ugly thing?" Bronwynn protested.

"He wasn't ugly then. Evil comes to carve a man, Bronwynn. The ugly face he wears today was not inflicted on him. Somewhere along the way, Admon Faye chose evil—and in that choosing, chose the ugly face as well."

The conversation wound through different subjects much as they wound their way through the massive trunks. Rosha listened earnestly, his mind a-jumble with facts and concepts that vaulted beyond his poor imagination. As dusk came, they found that the forest had thinned around them, and realized they had been climbing for some time. A break in the branches revealed the peak of a breathtaking mountain towering above them, and Pelmen slowed his horse to gaze upward, transfixed by the vision.

"We'll stop here," he muttered. Without a further word, he dismounted and walked to the center of the clearing, eyes still fixed on that crown of snow turned pink by the setting sun. Bronwynn looked at Rosha and shrugged, then hopped off her horse and stretched. She was becoming used to these rugged days of riding, and was proud of herself for it. She began to pick up what wood was lying around, and called to Rosha to do the same.

But Rosha remained seated on his horse. The day's conversation had benumbed his mind, but that was not his concern now. He worried about Pelmen.

The powershaper was changing. Dorlyth had warned him it could come, Pelmen had warned him it would come; but even so, the young man could not escape the uneasiness this change produced in his heart. He dropped from his horse, drew his greatsword, and vowed that this night he would not sleep.

Bronwynn was puzzled. She dropped the wood in the middle of the clearing and put her hands on her hips. "You would think someone else might help!" she complained, looking back and forth between the two men. Suddenly Pelmen began to walk, climbing up the slope and entering the trees.

"P-pelmen!" Rosha called, wanting to run after him but hesitant to do so.

"Where's he going?" Bronwynn cried, aware now that something was happening she didn't understand. Rosha ran to her instead, and put a protective arm around her shoulder.

"I d-don't know that. But I do know he's not p-p-protecting us tonight."

"I'm cold," she said quietly, and Rosha felt a shudder scramble through his body. He raced to the packhorse

and fetched her coat, then ran back to wrap her in it.
He set up the tent while there was still some light, and
he bundled Bronwynn in piles of wraps and put her inside it. "No fire?" she asked.

"N-none tonight," Rosha growled. A picture burned
in his mind, a picture of his father and Pelmen, trussed
like bagged bucks and tied across the saddles of slave
raiders. It was all the warmth he needed to keep his
eyes wide open and his hands clenched on the pommel
of his sword.

Pelmen spent the night on the mountain.

"Onions!" Pezi exclaimed, and took a long, deep
sniff. His companions, other merchants of Ognadzu,
looked at one another and snickered. "Well, can't you
smell them?" he asked. "Someone has an onion patch
along here, and I intend to find it."

"Pezi, you are beginning to smell like a vegetable
vendor," one mocked him. "You've bought out every
garden we've passed since we left the desert!"

"Don't remind me of the desert! I don't ever want to
hear about that desert again!" The Telera Desert
stretched across much of the southeastern section of Lamath. One had to cross it to get to the more populated
areas in the northern river valleys. The five merchants
had been three long days crossing it.

"Come now, cousin, it was good for you," another
merchant joked. "I'll wager you dropped forty pounds
back there in the form of sweat!"

"But he'll replace it with forty pounds of potatoes as
soon as we get to Lamath," another man cackled.

"And why shouldn't I?" Pezi blustered. "You have
your vices, your recreation. Why shouldn't I have
mine?"

"It's a pity the games don't include a meat-to-mouth
competition. Ognadzu would be assured of at least one
first prize every year!"

"I warn you, cousin, I'm not to be trifled with!" Pezi
threatened the last speaker.

"Yes, be careful, Malchar. Woe betide if Pezi should
decide to sit on you!" More laughter greeted this, but it
was cut short by the ring of steel scraping steel. The

merchant named Faliar, a barely bearded youth who was Pezi's second cousin, sighted down a sword blade that hovered at his nose.

"And should I decide to sit on *you*, Faliar—woe betide?" Pezi said quietly. A cruel grin spread across his broad face as he watched Faliar ransack his vocabulary for a reply that would get him out of trouble with the least amount of embarrassment. Pezi dropped the tip of his sword and lightly tapped Faliar's chin with it. "These new whiskers. They perhaps make you think yourself a man now, who can scoff at others without threat of injury? Perhaps I should shave them for you?" Faliar gulped involuntarily, and pulled tightly on the reins of his horse. If the beast should become frisky and jerk forward . . .

"My apologies, Pezi," he blurted, choking on the cockiness he was forced to swallow.

Pezi said nothing, but sneered meaningfully. He sheathed his sword. "Now to the onions," he muttered, standing in the stirrups to peer down the rows of crops that lined each side of the King's Road.

"Your uncle may not be pleased with you dallying over foodstuffs while he waits for news," Malchar said coldly.

"And who would be so foolish as to tell my uncle such a thing, Malchar?" Pezi inquired.

"You mustn't think, because my young brother backed away from your drawn sword, that I will, cousin," Malchar said, his hand on the handle of his own blade. Pezi met his gaze.

"Threaten me again sometime when I'm not hot and hungry," Pezi said at length. "We'll see who backs away then." He looked at the others. "Come on, we ride to Lamath."

"You've decided your visit with the King is top priority?" Malchar said snidely.

"That is my mission, cousin," Pezi replied with insulting politeness. "But first priority is a saddle-maker I know."

"A saddle-maker?" Someone asked.

"Since that thief stole my horse, I've had to use one of your skinny little saddles that doesn't amount to anything. It's like riding on a rail, I tell you! It's about to cut me in half." Someone giggled. "What are you laughing at?"

"The dragon has one body with two heads. Can't you picture Pezi with one head and two bodies?"

"There's certainly enough of him for two!" someone whooped, and they were all cackling again.

Why fight it? Pezi thought. His sword remained in his scabbard, and he sighed for the passed-up onions.

Pelmen came back to camp before the sun rose, and was there when Bronwynn awoke. A fire was made, and breakfast cooked and eaten, without a word passing among the three of them.

They bypassed the mountain, skirting its base to the east and then back around to the north. Even after they were well past it, Pelmen kept craning his neck to look back at its towering summit.

It was during that afternoon that the dread fell on Bronwynn. She began to believe that things were watching her. The forest had opened up again, and they rode once more in the realm of the big trees. Bronwynn could see long distances in all directions, yet she still felt uncommonly tense. She convinced herself that there were watchers behind every trunk—invisible watchers, who kept hiding behind the trees. She pulled Sharki down off her shoulder and began stroking his feathers. If it annoyed him, the bird didn't show it. She searched the limbs above for squirrels, but saw none. Except for the three of them, the forest was abandoned. We are riding through the land of the dead, she thought, and a tremor swept through her. She swiveled in her saddle, seeking reassurance from the powershaper who rode behind her, but found no help there. She saw that Pelmen was turned away too—back to the mountain. What fascinated him so about that pile of rock? Then she saw his face as he turned around again, and her heart quailed. His forehead was furrowed with lines of uncertainty, and his normally vibrant eyes looked lifeless and lost. His lips moved. He's talking to himself, she thought. The powershaper is unsure of his power. She turned to look at Rosha and edged her horse closer to his. The young warrior was fighting to stay awake. The day passed in deathly silence.

And yet when they stopped to make camp that night, Pelmen seemed his old self. He called fire out of the air and made it dance to amuse Bronwynn. He slapped Rosha on the shoulder and taunted him for being a sleepy head.

"You are Rosha Pahd-el, that's who you are," Pelmen teased. "You've caught the King's disease." Rosha grinned wryly, but said nothing of the cause of his exhaustion. He was profoundly grateful finally to see Pelmen kneel in the ritual that would draw a wall of invisibility around them. But his thanksgiving gave way to anxiety again when, more than an hour later, Pelmen hadn't budged from that position. Rosha sat by the fire and watched his father's friend, feeling some responsibility to protect the man—and realizing how unequal he was to the task.

"I'll bet you're hungry, aren't you?" Bronwynn asked. Rosha began to reply that indeed he was, but stopped when he saw she wasn't talking to him but to her bird! "Go on, Sharki. Take off!" She tossed the bird up into the air, even as Rosha was crying out.

"Wait!" The cry echoed away.

Rosha stood slowly, shock and disappointment etched on his face. Bronwynn looked at him curiously. "What's wrong with you?"

"P-p-pelmen has p-put up the cloak of p-protection! How will Sharki find us in the d-dark?"

Now grief tore through Bronwynn, and she cried, "My falcon! I've lost my falcon!" She darted for the edge of the tiny clearing, but Rosha leapt out and caught her by the wrist. "He won't know where to find me! He'll be lost!" she said, tears spilling onto her cheeks as she struggled to get away.

Rosha clung to her, whispering to calm her. "We'll f-f-find him. We'll step outside the c-c-cloak and wait for him to return!" Then he slipped his arm around her shoulders. Glancing back once more at the kneeling figure of Pelmen, he guided her through that magic wall of chill they had come to take for granted. The fire winked out behind them, and they sat on a fallen log and looked back at the now darkened meadow. There were no stars tonight, nor did the glow of a moon pierce the heavy cloud cover overhead. Rosha drew his greatsword and propped it on the log beside him.

"We'll be able to see him here?" the girl asked anxiously.

"I g-guess so. I'm no p-p-powershaper, I d-don't know."

"I wonder if Pelmen is, anymore," Bronwynn said, her eyes searching the sky. "Has he talked to you about last night?"

Rosha shook his head. "I m-meant to sp-speak to you about that—"

"Slow down," she murmured, laying a hand on his arm. "You get nervous and then you talk fast, and your stutter gets worse."

Rosha looked at her, a new appreciation of her dawning in him, then nodded and continued, more slowly now. "I—have—been—watching—him—all day. He is—changing."

"Into what?"

"Into—whatever—he is—in Lamath."

"That makes no sense. He's himself, isn't he?"

"Yes. But—my—father—says—his—self—is different there. He d-doesn't—he—doesn't—shape—p-powers in Chaomonous, d-does he?"

"Slowly! No. But there aren't any powers in Chaomonous."

"No—powers?"

"I've never seen any. But, of course, there are things like lightning and wind. Our learned men don't call them powers, though, and they don't try to shape them by magic."

"Then—how?"

"By—understanding them. Experimenting with them. Mixing things together. You understand, don't you?"

Rosha shook his head. "Sounds like m-magic to me."

"But Pelmen doesn't do that there. Or he didn't, when I knew him."

"What—did—he—"

"He was a player." Rosha cocked his head in puzzlement. "He put on plays for all the people to come watch. He wrote some himself, I think. They were funny plays, until he began to make fun of my father. That's what caused my father to enslave him." Bronwynn thought for a moment, then said, "Oh no, he's not going to turn into a stupid actor again when we get to Lamath, is he?"

Rosha shook his head, and partially smiled. "He's— not what you—think he is."

"By that you mean—?"

"He's m-more." Now it was Bronwynn's turn to be puzzled, and she waited for Rosha to elaborate. "M-my father—told me, but I d-didn't—believe him. Last n-night—I—left—you—for—a little while. I followed him. He was—kneeling—like he is n-now. Only he was—talking to someone."

"Who? Who was there?" Bronwynn asked anxiously, the dread springing again to her mind.

"That's—j-just it. There was n-no one there!"

"But there's someone here, laddie-buck!" a voice said behind them, and suddenly Rosha and Bronwynn knew what fishnets looked like to a fish.

The men were experts at this quiet capture, and struggle was futile. Rosha still gave it a try, fighting to get his hands past the rope that bound them within the net and onto the handle of his greatsword. A foul-smelling man kicked the sword and sent it flying well beyond Rosha's reach.

"Fetch it, laddie-buck," he laughed, but his laughter froze in his throat. He had kicked the sword into the meadow. Before it hit the ground, it disappeared. "This meadow is witched!" he whispered urgently. "Let's take our treasure and begone!"

Bronwynn screamed and Rosha fought, but the net was too strong and the hands that held them too experienced. Soon they were both bound hand and foot, and were each carried away by a pair of slaves, their bottoms dragging in the fir needles.

Pelmen woke from his reverie when the sword came spinning into the clearing and landed with a clatter. "Rosha?" he called. "Bronwynn?" There was no answer, and a memory flashed through his mind—

remembrance of the night he and Dorlyth had been ambushed in a forest, and their lives irrevocably altered by bondage. "Rosha!" he called, running for the spot where the sword had appeared. He crashed through the wall of cold into darkness.

The wall had effectively silenced his voice. The slavers hadn't heard him, and they continued to whisper among themselves as they wrestled their catch across the forest floor to the spot where their horses waited. Pelmen could hear Bronwynn screaming for him, and he pulled himself to his full height, flung his cloak around his shoulders, and began to chant.

Then he stopped, his body shaking. "No!" he groaned violently. "No, please! Not now—" His face twisted into a grimace as he pleaded, but the one whom he entreated wouldn't listen. The Power had possessed him. Pelmen the Prophet sprawled trancelike beside the log.

❧ Chapter Seven ❧

By MORNING, Bronwynn had given up hope that Pelmen would rescue them. While they remained in the forest she clung tenaciously to the knowledge that it was here that Pelmen had gained his ability, and that surely he knew this forest as well as anyone alive. But she soon realized that the slaver, dull-witted as he seemed at first to be, was no fool. They came upon a low outcropping of rocks just as dawn began to turn the treetops from black to green. Tied as she was, belly down across a saddle, Bronwynn could see little, but she did catch a glimpse of an opening at the base of the pile of rocks. When she was finally untied and allowed to stand, wobbly-legged, beside her horse, she understood with dismay that it was the mouth of a cavern. Without a word, a slaver grabbed her and thrust her toward the cave. When she would have turned to run he whacked her across the shoulders with a staff. She stumbled and fell into the dirt, but the man just dragged her up again and booted her forward, saying, "Get in there, lad, or your back'll make unpleasant acquaintance with my stick."

As feeling came slowly back into legs that had been fully numb for hours, Bronwynn waddled forward, thanking Pelmen for having had the foresight to clothe her as a boy. As long as the slavers didn't know the truth, she would try to keep that knowledge hidden from them. Her shoulder began to ache where the slaver had clouted her, but she bit her lip and put on a brave face as she ducked to enter the cavern.

Rosha was already inside. At the sight of him Bronwynn forgot her own troubles. He was being pushed along in front of her, his hands tied behind him. His head sagged to his chest, so dejected was he, and Bronwynn could see from the shape of his bare back that he had felt that stick already—and much more severely than she. His bare back! They had taken his father's precious mail shirt from him!

The narrow cave opened out into a wide cavern, where torches along the wall guttered for lack of oxygen, and breathing became a chore. The floor was littered with fir neddles and people. A couple of harsh shoves, and Rosha and Bronwynn had joined them. None of the other captives met their eyes, and Bronwynn was sure one man, at least, was dead.

"Now, lads," the man with the stick began, "two rules to know, that's all. No talking. No getting up." He glanced meaningfully down at his club. "Or I'll whack you again." Then he ducked back outside, and Bronwynn could hear him talking with the other ruffians. There was a sound of farewells being offered, and the stirring of horses.

"I'm beginning to get tired of being kidnapped," she whispered to Rosha, trying to make her tone joking. It didn't really come out that way, and he said nothing. He didn't even look at her. "You could at least grunt so I know you're alive," she whispered again, but again there was no response. She realized then that he wouldn't look at her because he couldn't look at her—that the weight of his shame burdened him as nothing had ever done before. "It wasn't your fault—"

"Ho there, someone breaking a rule already?" the man growled as he ducked back into the cavern. "Which one of you, hunh? Hunh?"

"I s-s-spoke!" Rosha snarled, jerking his head up to look at the slaver, who brought his staff crashing down across Rosha's shins. Bronwynn yelped at the impact, but the young man's only reaction was a narrowing of the eyes. The slaver stepped back and looked at him, then shook his head.

"You're going to give me trouble all the way to Lamath," he said. "I can tell already." The man ambled over to a bag he had tossed onto the cave floor and opened it up. Then he sat, his back against the rock wall nearest the exit, and pulled out a garment that glistened in the torchlight—Dorlyth's mail shirt. Bronwynn glanced back at Rosha, but he'd dropped his eyes again and gazed listlessly at the dried-up needles. "Nice piece, this," the slaver muttered as he fingered the finely wrought links. "Must come from Chaomonous. I've never seen such fine work in Lamath." He tossed it in the air and caught it. "Light, too. Must have been expensive, hunh, lad? Only a hero would wear a mail shirt this fine." He looked up at Rosha and sneered. "So what hero did you murder to get it?"

Bronwynn snorted angrily, and looked at Rosha. The boy was gazing at the man again, but saying nothing. If there was rage behind his quiet look, Bronwynn couldn't detect it. He just lay calmly in the prickly needles, and looked up at the slaver.

"Because you're no hero," the man scoffed, holding the mail shirt up to his chest to see if it would fit him. "No hero would sit in the middle of the Great North Fir after dark and talk like he sat in a castle. Come on, tell me, boy. You stab him in his sleep? Poison him?"

Rosha continued to stare at the raider, and it seemed to Bronwynn that he almost smiled. She decided he had more sense than she had given him credit for. At least he knew enough not to get his legs beaten bloody. The man gave up trying to bait him into talking again and settled down against the wall to wait. He pulled a knife from his belt and a chunk of cheese from his bag. He didn't offer to share.

How do we get away? Bronwynn wondered to herself. But no ideas came. Then she recalled Pelmen's words of the nature of the Great North Fir. He had said she might have the ability, and he was a powershaper—sometimes. She lay back on the floor of the cave, thankful that her own hands were tied in front of her rather than behind, and began to focus her attention on summoning some aid through the use of the powers.

She strained the muscles of her body, pushing her head out above her as if that were the key to making things happen. She succeeded only in making herself very dizzy, and had to quit. She sighed, and gave in to the feeling of despair and hopelessness that had nagged at her throughout the night. Then she thought of Sharki, and that depressed her even more.

As if cued by her thought, there was a powerful beating of wings; suddenly the cavern seemed filled with the presence of a flying creature. Bats? Bronwynn wondered. A small dragon?

"Sharki!" she cried, and tears of joy exploded onto her cheeks. The slaver leapt to his feet, swinging his staff to try to knock the bird from the air, but he was no match for the aroused falcon.

"Ow!" he yelped as the bird darted between his hands and pecked at an eye. The man stumbled backward, and the falcon came at him again. He squealed in pain and clapped his hands over his head. His stick clattered to the ground. Rosha finally got Bronwynn's attention.

"The knife," he said quietly, as the bird continued to swoop around the small cavern, dropping to peck the man again at every pass. Bronwynn saw now that the slaver had dropped his knife in the confusion and she lunged across the room to scoop it up in her bound hands. She was back cutting through Rosha's ropes before the slaver even realized she had it.

"No!" he yelled, batting the falcon away and diving for the knife himself. But Rosha's hands were already free, and the raider's face met the lad's balled-up fist in midair. He dropped to the floor, dazed, as Rosha leapt to his feet, his hands closing tightly around the end of the man's staff. The slaver stood, but only for a moment. Using it as he would a greatsword, Rosha thrust the end of the staff into the man's belly, driving him up against the cave wall and doubling him over. With three quick cracks of the wood on the man's head and shoulders, Rosha reduced him to an unconscious, bleeding pile on the needles and the dust. The other slaves, Bronwynn discovered, were not dead, for they yelled their encouragement and danced in a frenzy of excitement along the opposite wall. Rosha wore that same calm gaze in his eyes—he expressed his rage and vengeance with his arms, not his face. Stroke after stroke rose and fell, and he would have killed the man had not a strange thing taken place. The falcon flew up into his face; using its wings alone, it beat Rosha away from the man. Suddenly the bird dropped to the floor and walked away, and Bronwynn saw that Rosha's face was changed. He gazed about in shock mixed with triumph, and he looked no more at the unconscious slaver, but rather at the ragged band of slaves clustered at the far end of the cavern. He dropped the staff and picked up the knife, then motioned them by him, cutting the bonds of each as he passed. They ducked on out of the cave as soon as they were free, and Bronwynn could hear their whoops of joy coming from outside. Rosha retrieved his mail shirt and started to put the knife in his belt.

"Aren't you forgetting someone?" Bronwynn asked. He turned and looked at her, blushing, and immediately cut her bonds. Then he took some scraps of the rope and went to truss the unconscious slaver. Bronwynn reached for the falcon, but it walked away from her. "I knew I could do it, Sharki," she said as she followed the bird and tried again to pick it up. Once more it walked out of reach. "What's wrong with you? Come here." But the bird was walking out of the cave, and she had to duck to follow him out. "I knew I had the ability, I just didn't know how to focus it," she said, shuffling down the rock corridor. Then she chuckled. "I'm so glad I brought you along! And after Pelmen said . . ."

"I said what?" asked the magician, who was suddenly standing before her. She was so surprised that she bumped her head on the opening of the cave. Rosha cackled behind her and reached out to rub her head. She blocked the sun out of her eyes and looked around for her falcon. "Where's Sharki?" she asked.

A grin danced across Pelmen's face and then was gone. "I sent him home," he said seriously. "He'll be happiest back there with Dorlyth."

"No, I want him here!" she cried, shielding her eyes and searching the sky for some sight of beating wings. How had he flown away so fast? It wasn't until she caught the look Pelmen and Rosha exchanged behind her back that she realized. The falcon in the cave hadn't been Sharki. It hadn't been a falcon at all.

There was a mammoth stretch of flatland north of Chaomonous. In years long past it had been a parade ground for mighty armies, a staging area for great invasions to the north and south and west. In the time since it had been divided and subdivided, and parcels had been owned by many different landlords. But the ground had proved singularly infertile, and squatters had finally taken it over, erecting squalid little hovels within easy walking distance of the grand avenues of Chaomonous. But now, suddenly, the hovels were gone. The great field had been swept clean of its ramshackle huts, and hordes of displaced refugees now watched in dismay as their homeplace was renewed again to its glorious position as the mustering field of the Golden Kingdom. In place of the crooked rows of narrow streets, there now stood straight lines of stiff new tents. Powerful men rehearsed the arts of war where gangs of happy children had run and played only days before. One thing remained the same. The dust still hung in a thick cloud over the plain, choking everyone who breathed it.

Kherda was proud of his accomplishment, and felt justified in his pride. As a squatter township, the field had been an eyesore. As a parade ground, it was soul-stirring. But for the dust, of course. Everywhere he looked, golden pennants fluttered on the small breeze.

The sight filled him with patriotic fervor. He had to remind himself that he was plotting the destruction of this very army. Guilt was his frequent companion these days, and it rejoined him now for another round. "But I'm doing it for Chaomonous," he lied to himself, and his guilt left him again. Kherda was becoming a splendid liar.

"What a sight! What a magnificent sight!" the King gloated from behind him, and Kherda very nearly jumped the railing. It would have been his death if he had, for they stood on the highest level of a reviewing stand, two hundred feet above the ground.

"My Lord, I wasn't expecting you so soon! The platform isn't even completed yet, and the ceremony doesn't begin until noon!"

"I couldn't wait," Talith chuckled, striding to the railing to look down. The scaffolding was built like a staircase. The lowest levels extended well out into the field. "Those below us will be able to see me?"

"Certainly, my Lord. Please, step away from the edge. It may not be secure yet!"

Talith turned to Kherda and grinned widely. "You, Kherda. You are too loyal to be suspect."

"Suspect, my Lord?" Kherda gasped.

"Yes, yes, Joss has me believing all manner of strange things. He wants me to think that everyone is out to overthrow me and take my crown. He even suspects you."

"Me, my Lord?" Kherda stammered. He managed a weak smile.

"Yes! But if you were out to murder me, what better way than by pushing me off of a faulty scaffold?"

Was the King teasing him? Had Talith uncovered the plot? "I . . . I don't know, my Lord—"

"Of course you don't, Kherda. You don't think in those terms. Joss does—but of course that's why I need him. I cannot be too careful these days. After all, someone did steal my daughter."

"Yes, my Lord . . ."

"That's why I'm not going to lead the army myself."

"You're not going to—" Kherda stammered.

"No, Joss says it would be too dangerous. So when is

this platform to be finished, hunh? The parade is in less than an hour!"

"Yes, my Lord, I have all the workmen I could gather busy—"

"Very good, I don't need the details. But they will be able to see me, won't they? My people?"

"Everyone, my Lord," Kherda said absently, hiding his panic. The King was not going to lead the army! The plan was in shambles!

"How do I get down off of this thing?" the King was muttering, and Kherda led him toward the steps. As he escorted his monarch down the bare wooden staircase, he was wondering how to get loose from Talith—he had to get to Ligne with this news. But the King was not about to let him go. "How many warriors have we assembled?"

"Ah, thirty-seven thousands, my Lord, with more arriving every hour and many thousands still days away—"

"And by the end of the week?"

"I expect, ah, seventy-five thousands, my Lord—"

"Wonderful! And ships, how many ships?"

"Ah, I believe my Lord will remember I said some fifty-two ships will be sailing under the golden flag of—"

"Will that be enough?"

"If you mean to carry the entire army, no, my—"

"I mean to defeat the Lamathian fleet!" Talith yelled.

"Why, yes, my Lord, I believe it should be—"

"Good. Now where's that wife of mine?" Talith was craning his head in all directions, seeking Latithia in the midst of the already gathering crowd below.

"Your wife, my Lord?" Kherda asked, trembling within. These sudden changes!

"Protocol, Joss says. He checked the records. It seems that it must always be the official Queen who names the King's commander."

"I thought that protocol was my domain," Kherda said stiffly. Joss had certainly been busy. Something had to be done about that man!

"You've had a lot on your mind, my friend. I don't expect you to remember everything. There, is that her?"

It was indeed Latithia who made her way through the

crowd. She was given a wide berth by the milling populace, for she was escorted by a troop of the King's
guard, and they were notoriously ungentle when moving
people aside. The King eyed her progress distastefully.
She was certainly beautiful enough, with that blondish
hair and proud patrician's chin. But she caused so much
trouble! Why did she have to argue with everything he
said?

"Is this grandstand ready yet?" the King snapped at
Kherda, who sighed in reply.

"It appears it must be, my Lord, since the court
seems already to be assembling on it." The exchequer
gazed around him. Workmen scrambled up and down
the bare beams like monkeys, unwinding golden bunting
behind them as they climbed. The nobles of Chaomonous, along with their families, were already badgering
those in charge of seating arrangements. It seemed no
one had been placed quite as close to the King as he
thought he ought to be. Soon several families took it
into their own hands simply to move themselves higher
in the grandstand. The arguments grew heated, and new
arguments began as more highly ranked families found
their seats occupied. Kherda saw the coming chaos and
knew that soon he would be called on to begin arbitration. If he were to get away for a private conference
with Ligne before the parade, he would need to go now.
Ligne had to know of these changes!

The King exchanged icy pleasantries with his wife at
the foot of the stairs, but the racket soon grew so loud
he couldn't hear himself. He glanced up angrily to see
what was causing such confusion. "What's happening?"
he snarled at Kherda.

"People aren't satisfied with the seating arrangements, my—"

"Then satisfy them!"

"But, my Lord, you agreed to the arrangement as I—"

"Then tell them to get to their proper places! Look
at those crowds above us! Don't you realize what could
happen if too many people get onto the upper levels of
this platform?"

"Yes, my Lord, it could fall. That is why—"

"Are you trying to kill me by letting half my kingdom fall on top of me?"

"No, my Lord—"

"Then straighten out the problem!" Talith thundered. Kherda bowed slightly, then hustled up the stairway, clutching his robe to his waist to keep from tripping over it. "Now where were we?" Talith said pleasantly to his wife as he took her by the arm and led her up the stairway at a more dignified pace.

"You were telling me whom I was to name as your champion," Latithia answered quietly.

"Ah yes. Rolan-Keshi is my choice. Young man. Untested. But I feel he will be able to handle the task. You know the man?"

"By name only. I rarely get out anymore." Her voice was like acid, so bitter was she. It was Talith who had confined her within the palace.

"Yes—well, he's a very fine general—"

"I thought you were leading your army of deliverance."

"I was, but Joss talked me out of it."

"He did, did he? And how did he convince the enraged father to yield command of the largest rescue force in all of history to a pup?" She mocked him. Not light, friendly mocking. Latithia wanted to wound Talith if she could.

"He's heard some rumors that certain men of my court are plotting against me. He says it wouldn't be wise for me to leave the capital."

"You're sure it was *men* that Joss said were plotting against you?" she asked snidely.

"There it is again, your jealously—"

"My jealously!" she snapped. "Rather your blindness!"

"If you please!" he fumed. Then he added more quietly, "We are in public."

She sealed her lips in a tight, humorless smile and smiled and nodded at subjects all the way to the uppermost platform. There Kherda awaited them, sweat dripping off his nose, the result of his hurried ascent.

"All is now in order, my Lord," he panted. Talith

said nothing, taking his seat on a portable throne placed at the very peak of the parade stand. He looked around below him, then clutched the arms of the chair tightly and swallowed. "A man could get dizzy at this height," he observed.

"But certainly not a King," his wife snipped as she took her seat beside him. They were flanked by liveried trumpeters; beyond the trumpeters on either end of this highest level, giant golden flags flapped noisily in the wind. The dust was boiling up thicker than ever now, as the lines of warriors began to form far below them. The crowd noise was growing more intense.

Kherda massaged aching temples and wished the day's events were already over. He leaned over the rail and happened to see Ligne in the level below. She stared up at him with that cold, angry gaze that so terribly frightened him. Did she think it was his fault she was there and Latithia here, rather than the other way around as he had planned it? He tried to mouth an explanation to her, but she couldn't read his lips. He could read hers, however, and he reeled away from the rail, shocked that a lady would even know such words. He looked up to see that Joss had joined them on the uppermost level and was again watching him. Kherda straightened his shoulders, fixed an official smile on his face, and walked stiffly to his appointed seat.

"When is it going to start?" Talith was shouting at him, but as Kherda opened his mouth to reply Joss interrupted him.

"While we wait, perhaps the King would like to hear some important news from the merchant of Uda. Jagd has some information that may have a great bearing on the course of the war."

"Bring him to me," the King growled, annoyed by the interruption but realizing the necessity of granting Jagd an audience. Joss waved his arm, and Jagd and a young man climbed to the high platform. Both men wore ceremonial gowns of the purple and red of Uda.

"My greetings, your Majesty." Jagd bowed, then he indicated the young man with him. "This is Tahli-Damen, my Lord Talith, a merchant of my house who is showing great promise. He is the only survivor of the last caravan I sent through Dragonsgate." Tahli-Damen smiled at the King, pride swelling through him.

"He lost an entire caravan?" Talith snorted. "Doesn't sound very promising to me."

Tahli-Damen's smile died, and he turned a little red. Jagd put a hand on his shoulder and said, "Nevertheless, my Lord, he is a valuable servant, to me and I think to you. He is the last man to speak with the dragon. Tell the King what you told me." Jagd stepped away and nodded Tahli-Damen forward.

The young merchant felt light-headed. Perhaps the climb contributed, and the seeming instability of this platform, but Tahli-Damen would have attributed it to the awesome company in which he found himself. Here was Talith, believed by many to be the most powerful regent in the world! Next to him stood Queen Latithia, legendary for her beauty and her sharp tongue! And there was Kherda, and behind him Joss. On this platform stood the mightiest of Chaomonous—and he stood among them.

"Come, come, lad, I have a parade to review!" Talith snapped, and Tahli-Damen plunged into his story.

"The dragon is divided."

"He's what?" the King shouted, and the others on the platform responded with equal shock.

"He is divided, my Lord. The heads are at enmity with one another."

"That's impossible!"

"And so I believed, my Lord, until I saw and heard. The two heads compete with one another for control of the beast's body. They fight with one another as if they are two beings, rather than one! There is only one thing they can agree on."

"Which is?" the King asked, leaning forward to hear every word of this shocking announcement.

"That Pelmen the player must be found and brought to him. —Ah, them."

"Pelmen!" the King exploded, and he jumped up from his throne to stride across the dais to the railing. The parade stand faced north, and the King now gazed beyond the swirling dust to the northwest and Dragonsgate. Of course he could see nothing but the vast north-

ern plain of the Golden Kingdom, but it was a dramatic
posture, and it put him very much into the public's
view. The great crowd below him began to cheer at the
sight of their leader, resplendent in sparkling gold vestments. The King raised his fist high above his head and
brought it down onto the railing with a crash. "Pelmen!" he bellowed again, and the crowd below him
cheered more loudly still.

"I wish you wouldn't pound the rail like that, my
Lord—" Kherda began fearfully, but Talith ignored
him, turning to look at Tahli-Damen, who was watching
him, mouth agape. The young merchant had not expected such a violent reaction.

"Then I and the dragon agree!" the King shouted,
his eyes narrowing menacingly. "I want the player myself!"

"The—the dragon said he would grant a total trading
monopoly to the house who brings Pelmen to him,"
Tahli-Damen explained, and immediately Jagd thrust
him aside and took over the discussion.

"Don't you see what this means, my Lord?" Jagd
asked quietly but urgently. "If we can persuade the
dragon that our army is marching to Lamath in pursuit
of Pelmen, the beast may allow us free passage through
Dragonsgate!"

Talith was excited, but cautious. "*Our* army, is it?
This is my army, I believe."

"Yet we are allies, my Lord." Jagd smiled slyly.

"For as long as you choose to be," Talith observed,
and Joss nodded grimly. The King was beginning to understand, Joss thought to himself.

"You wrong me, my Lord," Jagd protested, feigning
hurt. Then he smiled again and moved closer to Talith.
"But if you truly suspect my sincerity, let me help to
clarify the situation in your mind. A trading monopoly
for the house that brings Pelmen to the dragon! My
Lord, you can be assured of my loyalty on this account
alone! I have not the wherewithal to capture Pelmen
myself. I must depend on you. Together we will capture
the player and reclaim your daughter, and put an end to
the house of Ognadzu. You come away with the prize
you seek, in addition to the conquest of the Kingdom of

Lamath. I come away with my prize—a monopoly on trade! We both have so much to gain!"

Talith thought for a minute and looked meaningfully at Joss, then shrugged. "It sounds so easy."

"And it shall be easy. Instead of a wasteful campaign in the mountain wilderness of the Spinal Range, the golden army can simply march through Dragonsgate and descend on Lamath en masse. The fleet conquers the coast of Lamath, and their army is trapped and crushed between the main army and the troops from the coast! Instead of lasting years, the war could be ended in a matter of weeks."

"And I would be the King of the entire coast," Talith murmured, his eyes glazing over with greed.

"I had heard that the purpose of this war was to regain our kidnapped daughter!" Latithia suddenly interjected, dragging Talith out of his pleasant fantasy.

"And so it is!" he growled at her. Then he smiled a conspiratorial smile at the wrinkled merchant of Uda, and added, "But since they began this war and not I, haven't I every right to take back what is mine—with interest?"

"With the combined strengths of Chaomonous and Lamath at your disposal, the eventual fall of Ngandib-Mar would be assured. Then you would be—"

"King of the World!" Talith cried, his eyes flashing. "My father was never *that*!" He turned to Jagd and clapped him soundly on the back. "Then it is agreed. My ships will sail with the next good tide, and within the month my army marches to Dragonsgate. Let the parade begin!" The King pointed at the trumpeters, who suddenly came to life. Latithia clenched her jaws and covered her ears, but still the noise was deafening. Though there were many parts of official life she had missed during her period of disgrace, this was not one of them. How could anyone enjoy such terrible noise?

Talith stood at the railing, his arms stretched wide as if to embrace all of his army and all of the throngs of people who watched below. The trumpet call was picked up by trumpeters on every level of the grandstand, who relayed it to the massed bands on the field. The crowd roared its approval of the Golden King, and he beamed back at them, waving his arms and laughing. Never had Talith been so excited. Never had he felt so powerful.

Jagd pulled his young employee to the stairway and motioned him down. Tahli-Damen attempted to ask a question, but the roar of the crowd was too loud. It wasn't until they reached the base of the scaffolding that he was able to ask, "I thought you told me Pelmen was in the west rather than in Lamath—"

Jagd spun on his heel and cut him off. "Silence!" The young merchant quickly shut his mouth. Jagd looked around. The crowd was far too interested in the display on the field to pay any attention to them. He leaned over and whispered in the younger man's ear. "You show promise, Tahli-Damen, but you are not an Elder yet. You will understand these things when I'm ready for you to. Until then, you will keep your questions and observations to yourself!"

They moved swiftly through the crowd to their carriage and were away. Jagd wished to be in his offices by sundown, in the hope that Tohn mod Neelis would yield and make use of the pyramid tonight. What stubborn men these merchants of Ognadzu were proving to be! What a lack of simple business sense! When the opportunity arose, Jagd would use their stubbornness against them. Until that time, they were more useful as allies than as enemies.

The King tired at last of waving his arms to the throng, and he came to take his throne once more. He was chuckling as he leaned over to speak in Latithia's ear. "I've decided to send the contents of my dungeon with the army. A kind of peace offering for the dragon."

"You seem to be taking all of this rather lightly," Latithia said tonelessly.

Talith sat back in his chair and gestured at the field below. "Look there! My father never formed an army this large, nor my grandfather either! Isn't that cause enough for my mood of celebration? Why can't you let yourself enjoy it along with me?"

"All I can think about is that someone has my Bronwynn in chains! I keep imagining her, languishing in a dungeon somewhere—or worse!"

"As do I! Why do you think I've formed this invasion force?"

"To become King of the world!" she spat out bitterly. "What do you know of dungeons? Nothing, save that you intend to feed the unfortunates in yours to the two-headed beast! Well, while you've been posturing and proclaiming yourself something special, I've been sitting in my locked apartments, a captive in my own palace. I know what my child is experiencing, and it causes me to weep myself to sleep each night!"

"Woman, I have told you I intend to rescue her!"

"Ha!" she snorted. "Rolan-Keshi will rescue her . . . perhaps—if he can spare the time from conquering the world for you! You haven't even arrested those who kidnapped her!"

"I assure you, Latithia, that when Pelmen is apprehended he will be thoroughly punished . . ."

"Pelmen! Pelmen was in your dungeon the night she was stolen, or have you forgotten that too in your blindness?"

"What blindness?" Talith snarled coldly.

"The blindness that takes you daily to the bed of the one who spirited my daughter away!"

Talith laughed harshly and sneered at her. "There it is, that jealousy again. I knew when Joss told me you had to be seated with me that it would come to this." The King slouched on his throne, fingering his wispy beard angrily.

Latithia's pale complexion was suffused with a crimson glow. Her proud, handsome jaw was clenched tightly, and her eyes were wide open with rage. Yet when she opened her mouth to speak, her tone was relaxed, almost lighthearted. "Perhaps you aren't blind at all. Maybe it is I who have been blind. Blaming Bronwynn's kidnapping on poor Ligne, when actually you had her abducted to give you an excuse to conquer the world!"

"Guards!" Talith screamed, leaping to his feet. Instantly there was a swarm of warriors standing on the uppermost platform. The King was livid. "Escort the Lady Latithia to her chambers, immediately!"

"My Lord . . ." Joss began.

"She is not to leave them, nor is she to see anyone save myself! Move!"

With a guard on either side of her, the Queen turned her chin up and walked gracefully to the stairway. A hush was settling over the crowd as row after row turned from the parade to watch the drama unfolding on the high platform.

"My Lord," Joss said urgently, "it is traditional that the King's Lady announce the choice of the King's champion—" Joss realized too late his unfortunate choice of words. The King turned to him with a look of mocking triumph.

"And so she shall!" Talith gloated, and he walked to the railing and leaned over it. "Ligne!" he called. The woman had not taken her eyes off the King since the beginning of the day's events. Now she responded to the awaited cue. In moments she was standing by his side, throwing kisses to the roaring multitude. "You are to nominate Rolan-Keshi as my champion," Talith whispered to her as they both smiled and waved.

"I will not," she whispered back, and Talith jerked around to stare at her.

"Listen, woman, I have already had one argument on this platform today—"

"I wouldn't nominate anyone save you, my love," she smiled at him, laying a hand on his shoulder. "Rolan-Keshi indeed! You would allow that ridiculous farm lad to rob you of the glory intended solely for you? You must be the conquering hero of the Lamathian war! You are the King!"

"But—"

Ligne stopped him with a hand on his mouth and whispered, "Make a hero of Rolan-Keshi and you make of him a rival. Conquer Lamath yourself—and no man on earth will be able to stand next to you!" Ligne pointed to the trumpeters, and they sounded the horns immediately, without questioning her authority. The King was lost once more in his dreams of glory, and his pride conquered his judgment. As Ligne announced that the King would lead his own army of deliverance, the marching warriors joined their cheers to those of the crowd.

Kherda cheered as loudly as a twelve-year-old caught up in the highest frenzy of hero worship. But his accolades were not for the King. Rather, he cheered the slim brunette who stood at the monarch's side. Once again, Ligne had turned disaster into victory with a whisper and a quiet touch.

With the pandemonium at the parade grounds, few people noticed the small chartered boat slipping out of the port and turning downriver to the sea. On the deck a large man stood leaning on the mainmast. Admon Faye was bound for Lamath.

The Lamathian farmer wiped his forehead and replaced his hat without breaking stride. Once he got this old ox started plowing he didn't like to stop it unless it was absolutely necessary. As he followed the plow he sighted on an oak on the far side of his property, doing his best to cut a furrow that would be straight. But his mind wasn't really on his plowing. It had to be done, if he were to make his living, but that didn't mean he had to think about it. He thought instead of the queer new religious ideas he'd been hearing bandied about in the village, and wondered where people got the time to cook up such weird notions.

A shadow flicked across him as something passed between him and the sun, and he casually glanced up to see what it was. Then he shook his head to clear it, his forehead creased with concern. He needed to get out of the sun. What would the other men say if he told them he'd actually seen the dragon fly overhead? Such visions were for priests and for giddy young wives. He decided he should concentrate harder on his plowing. Of course, he would keep his mouth shut about this apparition. He had his reputation to protect.

"There was another one," Vicia said sourly, longing to wrest control away from his heedless twin.

"Too scrawny," Heinox said, dismissing him. "Couldn't make a light snack off that, much less a decent meal."

"You could have had the cow!" Vicia complained. "I would have settled for the farmer."

Heinox snorted, "You know I don't like beef."

"Then I'll eat the cow. I'm hungry!"

"We'll find something soon. Keep watching." Heinox altered the dragon's course slightly with a lazy flip of its left wing, and Vicia settled back into foul-tempered impotence. He hated being dragged about like this.

"Now I know what a tail feels like," the surly dragon head commented.

"You said it, not I," Heinox told him rudely, carefully studying the valley floor. It was crisscrossed with the etchings of thousands of tiny plows, but nowhere did he see any concentration of humans worthy of his interest. There were hundreds of villages scattered across the northern river valleys of Lamath, but most were small, and all seemed to be hidden in the trees. Those villages he had spotted seemed deserted. "These Lamathians are being most uncooperative," he said at length.

"I told you we should have gone south. The villages are bigger, and the people have a tangy flavor!"

"I don't like all that spice in my belly."

"It happens to be my belly too, and I like the flavor of Chaons!" yelled Vicia.

"Then fly there—if you're able," Heinox baited him spitefully.

Vicia gnashed his teeth and lidded his giant eyes, and dipped into his imagination, seeking a new trick to regain control. This had been the continuing pattern of the last few days. Vicia would find some means of throwing Heinox off balance and would seize command, and would hold it until Heinox thought of a way to distract Vicia. The game was growing more intense with each exchange; once a trick was used, both heads took pains to guard against that particular tactic in the future. The moments of critical importance were those immediately preceding sleep and immediately after waking, for while one head did not sleep unless the other slept as well, each head harbored its own thoughts and responded differently to the sleep experience. This morning, for example, Heinox had awakened with a start, refreshed and rested and ready to go, while Vicia, exhausted from a long day of struggling to maintain control, had difficulty leaving behind his pleasant dreams of less complicated times. Now he suffered for it, and strained to come up with a new ploy. His eyes popped open. He had it.

"Give up?" Heinox sneered.

"I'm too hungry to fight with you, you irresponsible, unreasonable lizard!"

Heinox did not reply. He was enjoying himself enormously.

"Drop down a bit, I think I see our dinner," Vicia lied, and Heinox coasted down off of the current he had been riding and hit a pocket of air. Normally air pockets caused the dragon no problem, but this was not a normal time. Vicia still had complete control of his own neck and head, and now he shot himself up at a right angle to the rest of the dragon body and opened his mouth wide. The sudden shift in wind resistance threw Heinox off course, and Vicia shifted back downward, struggling to clutch dominion once again. But Heinox wouldn't yield, and for several seconds the giant body plunged forward and down without effective guidance.

"You're causing us to . . ."

Several peasants in a hamlet three-quarters of a mile away were exchanging pleasantries when they heard a loud fluttering, a sound like canvas being torn by the wind, and felt a slight concussion as something big made a heavy impact on the earth. All shielded their eyes against the sun and looked toward the southwest. It seemed a cloud of dust was rising from that quarter.

"Came from over by the monastery," one peasant observed.

"Lot of strange goings-on at that monastery this year," another drawled. Though all were curious, no one said anything more about it. It wasn't smart to get too involved in this religion business. Especially not lately.

". . . crash!" Heinox finally finished his sentence with a growl, tasting the dust caked around his teeth. Vicia reeled a bit, but he had not taken the blow as hard as his companion. While Heinox had warned, Vi-

cia had positioned himself to absorb the shock. Heinox'
forehead had made a most convenient cushion. Vicia
chuckled as Heinox wobbled up out of the dirt.

"It's fortunate we landed in a plowed field," Vicia
said. "If we'd hit a patch of rocks we could have been
skinned up rather badly." He was in complete authority
over the workings of their body, and felt quite proud of
himself. Heinox was understandably cross.

"What's this?" Heinox snarled.

Across the furrowed field came a line of figures, all
wrapped in robes of sapphire blue. They came slowly,
stepping from one crumbling ridge to the next. Vicia-
Heinox was rather pleased, at first. The dragon was un-
accustomed to this kind of reception from humans when
he went foraging abroad for food. But as the group
picked its way closer, Heinox grew anxious.

"What are they doing?" he said. "Can't they see I'm
a dragon?" Vicia did not reply. It was indeed puzzling.

The column of blue-clad men and women formed a
semicircle before the dragon, and the leader, who appeared to be either a very young man or else a woman,
stepped forward to speak.

"We offer ourselves to you, Lord, and count it an
honor that you would choose us!" The voice quavered,
but the words flowed smoothly. Had the dragon been
more acquainted with such things, he would have realized the speech was rehearsed. The robes hid all but the
faces of the small group, and these were all chalky
white. Fear Vicia-Heinox could understand. It was
these words that didn't make sense.

"What are you offering yourselves for?" Vicia asked
curiously.

"He speaks," several cultists murmured in awe, and
the leader turned to hush them.

"Please excuse the disbelief of my brothers and sis-
ters," said the speaker. It was now clear that she was a
woman. Her voice trembled as she bravely answered the
dragon's question. "We offer ourselves for any purpose
the Lord commands."

"What lord?" Heinox asked, rising up and over the
gathered group and swiveling around to look at these
strange people from behind.

"Why does the Lord ask who he is—" a young man whispered, but the leader quickly cut him off, her impatience heightened by her own terror.

"He's testing us, don't you see? The heart of the creed, together now, recite!" The entire group fell to its knees in unison, and all struck the same pose. Both hands were formed into the shape of the letter *C*, as a child would when making shadow animals in the candlelight. Both arms were raised above the head and then crossed, hands opening outward. Heinox looked at Vicia inquiringly.

"What are they doing?"

With a hint of a dragon smile, Vicia replied quietly, "I think they are doing an imitation of us!"

"I believe in the Dragon," they all began together. "May he preserve us. May he hold the stars and earth together in tension. May he hold good and evil together in tension. May he hold my interests and his interests together in tension, until such a time as I shall pass over or be chosen. May the Dragon live forever. So be it." The rhythm was unnatural. The words had been repeated so many times throughout the centuries that they had really lost their meaning.

Heinox snorted, and a number of the quaking monastics twisted around to squint up at him. Never in any imaginative vision of their god had they pictured just how large and pointed his teeth really were. Though the dragon's size had been greatly exaggerated down through the ages, the paintings and statues of him never captured this feeling of threatening immediacy. This was no terra-cotta figure, this was a real live dragon! Not only did his teeth glisten and his eyes flash, but he had remarkably bad breath. Could anyone blame the two cultists who fainted into the furrow? "You believe in the dragon, do you?" Heinox snarled. His jaw was aching where he had slammed into the dirt, and he seized this opportunity to ventilate his frustration.

"Oh, yes, yes, we do!" a dozen devotees cried out as they turned, still on their knees, to face him.

"I say, that's rather rude, to turn your backs on your own god," Vicia said huffily, and now the entire group swiveled back around to face him, still kneeling.

"One moment, please!" said Heinox. "I also happen to be a part of this dragon, and I deserve an equal share of the attention!" The cultists were in a quandary. They huddled together for a moment, and the leader turned to address the dragon once again, doing her best to make eye contact with both heads at once.

"Lord, do you think it might be possible for both of your heads to stay on one side? I mean, it is very difficult for us and we're getting our robes all dirty—"

"What sort of priestess are you, anyway?" Heinox teased, angling down into the girl's face. "First you say you offer yourself to me, then you try to tell me what to do!"

The girl was petrified. She stared for a moment into those great, faceted eyes, and gave the only response she knew to give.

"I believe in the Dragon, may he preserve us, may he hold—" She was back in the crossed-arm posture, eyes shut, quoting the remembered scripture as loudly and earnestly as she could. The others quickly joined her.

Heinox pulled away, and glided back across the heads of the feverishly muttering monastics to counsel together with Vicia. "My jaw hurts."

"Mine does, too," Vicia replied.

"How could it, you didn't hit yours!" Heinox groused.

"No, but you were clumsy enough to hit yours, and your jaw is my jaw too, remember?"

"But it doesn't hurt you as much as it hurts me!"

"Would you stop worrying about our jaw? I'm trying to listen."

"Listen to what?"

"To what my worshippers are saying about me."

Heinox stared hard at Vicia, then snorted. "I knew it."

"Knew what?"

"I knew as soon as these curious humans started calling us a god that it would go straight to your head."

"Why not be a god?" Vicia asked, preening their shared body proudly. "Who else in the world would qualify?"

"Oh no," Heinox groaned, and he laid himself backward into the dirt. "Not this. Anything but this."

"Tell me," Vicia began loudly, and the chattering was silenced. All eyes were fixed on him. Vicia arched his neck vainly and asked, "How long have you been worshipping me?"

The question seemed simple enough to Vicia, but the monastics appeared thunderstruck, and there were several minutes of serious theological debate before an acceptable answer was formulated.

"We have been faithful before you!" the leader replied piously.

"That hardly answers my question," Vicia sniffed, touching off another debate that went on even longer than the first.

The community historian won this one, and now he spoke up, his voice cracking nervously. "We have been faithful to the true belief for over three hundred years, Lord! This order has stood firm on the issue of your coherence, and has staunchly denied any Divisionist heresies!" The little speaker scrambled backward after his speech, hiding himself in the group.

Vicia was perplexed. Heinox cackled, rolling himself in the brown earth, gently massaging his jaw into the soil.

"Three hundred years!" Vicia marveled. Then he slipped over to Heinox and asked, "How much is three hundred years?"

"You know I can't count."

"We're going to have to learn how to do that. It seems to be very important."

"I thought you were hungry."

"I am!"

"Then let's cut out this nonsense and eat these people!"

"Would you please have a little patience? I've never been a god before."

"You aren't one now."

"How do you know?"

"We are a dragon, Vicia. Dragons are not gods."

"Am I a god?" Vicia asked the crowd.

"I believe in the Dragon, may he preserve us, may he hold—" they all began in unison, and Vicia looked smugly at his twin as the litany was repeated.

"They are people! Are you going to believe their word over that of your very own other head?" Heinox asked.

"My very own other head has been nothing but a nuisance lately!" Vicia snarled back.

"Very well then, be a god," Heinox snorted, "but I intend to remain as fully dragon as it is possible for me to be—under the circumstances. Would you be quiet!" he roared at the droning devotees, and they stopped their recitation and looked up at him. "If you must do that, do it to yourselves. It's getting on my nerves!"

"The—the creed displeases our Lord Vicia-Heinox—?"

"I am not your Lord, nor anyone's Lord. I am not a god in any form, though I seem to be having difficulty convincing the other half of me of that."

The assembled monastics reeled in disbelief. One finally managed to stammer, "Then—the Divisionists are right?"

This unleashed a flurry of loud discussion. "Heresy! Heresy!" the historian shouted. "You blaspheme the Dragon!"

"But he said himself—"

"The Dragon is testing us," the leader cried, her own voice tinged with uncertainty.

"We must not let the Divisionists know he's said this!" another shouted. "You know what kind of interpretation they would put on it!"

"I shouldn't think the Divisionists will hear any of this conversation," Heinox began, "whatever Divisionists are—" The dragon was interrupted by a chorus of amens and sighs of relief, but managed finally to finish, "—for I intend to eat you all."

A sudden hush fell on the cultists.

"Come now, is it fair to devour *all* of them?" Vicia asked his bodymate. "They have been most entertaining."

"But I am most hungry," Heinox replied.

Vicia dropped down to eye level with the leader,

whose face was once again very pale. "Just between us
. . . are there many who worship me in Lamath?"

She curtseyed slightly and murmured, "The Lord
Dragon knows that all of Lamath worships him." Her
eyes were glazed, an expression of mixed fear and ec-
stasy playing across her features as she anticipated the
joy of total union with her god.

Vicia rose high into the air and turned to Heinox. "It
seems," he said, "that if all of Lamath worships me—
these few surely won't be missed."

"Is he sick?" Bronwynn whispered to Rosha, watching Pelmen sway to and fro in the saddle some twenty
feet beyond them. Rosha shook his head and smiled to
reassure the girl, but in fact his fears had all returned.
The brief, glorious explosion of action experienced in
the cave had given way once more to the hushed, cautious plodding of horses through yellowing mulch, and
the sparkling-eyed sorcerer appeared again to be a broken, tired fugitive. His mind seemed ever to be elsewhere, and Rosha bit his tongue to keep from crying
out in protest. Why? Why did they continue to journey
into Lamath, if this was to be the outcome? Was this
what Lamath did to a man?

Bronwynn felt much the same. An hour after their
rescue, the excitement began fading; three hours later it
was all but forgotten. They retraced their steps until
back on the right path, but she really didn't notice. The
thick trunks and the branches above had grown so mo-
notonously common that she told Rosha she hoped
never to see another tree as long as she lived. Depression settled on the band, enveloping even the horses.
They no longer reacted to one another or to their riders,
choosing to plod wearily forward as if shielded by blind-
ers from the sight of anything save the dry ground
ahead.

"Some magic forest!" Bronwynn spat, and Rosha
grinned wryly.

"N-n-not happy, m-my Lady?"

"I'm not happy and I'm not your lady." Bronwynn
snarled, and he drew back, his face hardening, his soft
expression of boyish curiosity giving way before her

bitter mood. She kicked her pony savagely, impatient with its sluggish response. Quite suddenly Minaliss wheeled before them, and Pelmen, sitting straight in his saddle, stared at the two of them. Their horses slowed to a distinterested stop, unaware of their riders' shock.

Bronwynn felt as if she really saw Pelmen now for the first time. As they watched, the transformation that had been taking place so gradually over the past few days raced to completion. They were eyewitnesses to the change.

What color had he been wearing? Bronwynn struggled to remember, but the memory got lost in the gentle drapes of a fish-satin robe of sky blue. It was the color of the cloudless horizon at noon on a hot summer's day—it was dazzlingly blue. His face was gaunt. Had she never noticed that graying at his temples? The thick brownish hair that fell in waves to his neck? Had she never before noticed eyes so blue they cut? His cheekbones were so high and hollow as to suggest twin cliffs, from which those blue beacons beamed out a message to all that saw them. And that strangely compelling message in his eyes seemed to say, "Trust me, for I know." And Bronwynn trusted.

No longer the laughing magician—still less the mocking performer—Pelmen the Prophet regarded these two bickering children quietly. He said nothing for a long time. Then he smiled gravely.

"It *is* a magic forest, Bronwynn. But magic is not always pleasurable. It can wrap you in dark folds of gloom as easily as in colored light. It will steal from you as much as it gives, my Lady. The powers always balance." He looked away, gazing toward the north and frowning slightly.

Bronwynn and Rosha glanced at one another, and she at last gave breath to the question they both were asking. "What—has happened?"

Pelmen looked back at her, his gaze steady and clear. For days his eyes had flicked from one point to another, settling on nothing, always in flight. Now he was at rest—and Bronwynn drew on that reservoir of calm, dispelling doubts and fears she didn't realize until that moment she had harbored. He smiled again. "The Power has come," he said.

"It has—taken you?"

"It has been given."

"Do you—control it?" she asked fearfully. He was too different, this new Pelmen. She found herself trembling. She had been rescued from the dragon by this man . . . been tumbled from her horse by a thunderclap he had summoned . . . had chased him around a cave believing him to be her pet bird . . . and all that was manageable, somehow, for she had sensed in every instance that Pelmen was in control. Now she wondered.

"You have spent too much of your life close to political power, my Lady. You think too highly of control."

"Then you don't control it," she said firmly, not questioning but demanding. He gazed at her in mute reply, and the hush between them was broken only by a telltale stirring in the trees above. "Then you are a slave to it," she finally said tonelessly, feeling the dread like a cloak draping itself around her shoulders once again.

Pelmen glanced up at the wind in the trees, then back to the girl. "There are many kinds of slavery, my Lady. In most cases, one is free to choose what he will be in bondage to. A storm is coming from the north, and we must be in our tent before it strikes us." He looked at Rosha. "Here we will camp."

"B-b-but—the horses. They n-need water, and there is no stream—"

Pelmen did not look away from the boy, but held his right hand out to his side, palm down. A shifting wind touched the mass of pine needles below it. Strangely, the wind scooped some aside, and beneath the organic cover a bald patch of stone appeared. A wet stain began spreading across the slab of rock, and then—a trickle. Pelmen's eyes had not left the face of his youthful companion.

"You do control it!" Bronwynn cried out with glee. "You are still the same Pelmen!"

His eyes flicked back to her, and her excitement subsided into an awkward silence. "I do not control it, my

Lady. I mediate it. And as to my being Pelmen—was that ever in doubt?"

A smile twitched on her lips, and she shrugged childishly, robbed of any reply. But as he swung himself to the ground, blue folds whispering, and as the horses bent to lick the growing stream of water that now nibbled at the dry mulch, she reflected on his question. And yes, she had to answer, there had been doubt in her mind. What's more, that doubt remained, for this was another, different Pelmen, the third she had met. How could she ever come to know a man who constantly shifted character? Of one fact she was sure, however. She knew she would follow him.

❧ Chapter Eight ❧

IT WAS a horrible storm. Through the skin of the tent they would see nothing but black, then at once the white light would flicker beyond its walls, and they would see clearly the outline of their shelter's bright stripes. Then would come the crashing crescendo of noise, booming through the giant trunks as if wishing to rip them from their age-old stands by force of sound alone. With each sense-shattering blast Bronwynn would gasp or moan, and clutch Rosha more tightly. As each wave of thunder reverberated past them, she appeared surprised that she still had not been swallowed up and carried away. Rosha, too, recoiled at each blast, but in between shocks he was having a wonderful time hugging Bronwynn to him and teasing her.

"You s-say it is not the p-powers trading insults, so why sh-should you be afraid?"

"Because it's frightening!" she snapped angrily, but she made no move to leave his embrace. Another flash—another crash—she shuddered again.

"But your scientists have told you it is n-nothing but force j-jumping from cloud to cloud. If there's nothing malevolent to it, why s-shake so?"

"Just because I can explain something doesn't mean I can laugh at it!" She screamed at him, fingernails digging into his hands. "It could still kill us!"

"But it won't," he whispered softly, and she followed his eyes to Pelmen, who sat entranced on the far side of the tent. Rosha spoke the words so comfortingly and so sincerely that she almost relaxed—until another blow from the angry skies struck the muddy earth. Giant raindrops came fiercely, then subsided, then came again, beating so mercilessly on the fish-satin that it seemed certain to Bronwynn it would tear.

She glanced again at the kneeling Pelmen and muttered, "How can he sleep through this?" Then she yelped, as another stroke of the hammer of god echoed through the forest.

But Pelmen wasn't sleeping. He listened to a conversation carried on the airwaves of the spirit, a conversation between three who willed to rule the world. Tohn mod Neelis had finally given in. He spoke to his co-conspirators through the pyramid.

But there was a difference now in Pelmen's reception of the conversation. Perhaps because of the storm—perhaps because of the intensity of the discussion—perhaps because of the Power that was upon him—for some reason, Pelmen now heard and saw all three.

"It's easy for you to give suggestions, my scrawny cousin, seated in your spire in the safety of Lamath!" Tohn was shouting. "You've not been sitting in a sweltering tent day after day, watching as the dandelions carpet the battlefield with yellow, and still watching when they turn white and blow away!"

"If you spent less time watching dandelions and more time watching Dorlyth's movements, you could crack this tiny acorn of a castle and give us what we want!" Flayh replied, smiling viciously.

Jagd groaned, his chin resting in his hands, his elbows propped on his own triangular table. "My forehead is splitting. Can we please get on with the work and hold the bickering until after the business is settled?" The other two saw the wisdom in Jagd's plea and each man held his tongue. In order to keep the pretense of working in partnership, they would have to hold their bile inside.

"Dorlyth is out of water," Tohn grunted matter-of-factly. "Any day now he'll be forced to take the field, and sheer numbers insure our victory."

Many miles to the north in a dripping forest, Pelmen winced at the news. Surrounded by a torrent of water, he felt his own throat constricted by his brother's thirst. Dorlyth had broken his promise!

"Be cautious, you old fool," Flayh snarled. "Remember, he has a magician in there with him."

Jagd was surprised. Tohn did not bristle, but replied, "I don't think so."

"What?" Jagd asked.

"I don't believe Pelmen is here."

"What do you know?" Flayh screamed. "Where could he have gone?"

"It's a big world," Tohn muttered.

"You lie!" Flayh exploded. "He's slipped through your fingers, and you lie to cover your failure!"

"He didn't slip through my fingers. He wasn't there to begin with!"

"He wasn't—"

"I can't *feel* him!" Tohn bellowed. "I've fought in this country all my life! I've battled witches and sorcerers, the whole lot, and I can tell when someone is shaping the powers against me. I can sense it." Tohn paused. "Pelmen isn't here."

"Where is he, then?" Flayh demanded.

"He could be in Lamath for all I know!" Tohn roared back. Flayh hurled a stream of curses across the dark void at his cousin, and Pelmen opened his eyes a moment to clear his mind. The young couple still whispered and clung to one another for support. When he dipped back into the conversation, Jagd was speaking.

"We have an opportunity here we cannot pass by. With the dragon confused and angry, we have a passport through his passageway. Our armies will say they march in search of Pelmen. Talith prepares to march from the golden city and I assume the plans are in motion to bring the dragonhordes of Lamath to Dragons-gate as well?"

"They'll be there," Flayh snorted, hoping this time Pezi would not fail. If he did, Flayh would drop him down a deep shaft and let him starve to death. Of course, that would take longer than usual—Pezi had so much to go on.

"We can manipulate the two-headed beast to allow both armies passage to Ngandib-Mar. Once they come into contact with one another, battle is a certainty. We'll let Lamath and Chaomonous whittle one another down on the eastern plains of the Mari highlands, while their governments fall to carefully planned coups at home."

Tohn bit his tongue. He thought of the fields around his castle. His green lands to become the battlefield for a wrestling of giants! At least now there would be no damage to the harvest. How could there be? There had been no planting.

"It is certain the lazy man of High City will make no move," Flayh chuckled. "My informants tell me he spends his days folding artificial birds of parchment sheets and launching them from his castle casements."

"No, there's nothing to fear from Pahd mod Pahd-el," Jagd agreed, "and that is to our advantage. Once we control both Lamath and Chaomonous, Ngandib-Mar will tumble to us like a squatter's shack in the whirlwind."

Tohn winced at that, but said nothing. He was thinking of his fields.

"From his vantage point within his castle, Tohn will be able to witness the entire conflict." Jagd smiled, and then chuckled low in his throat. "When it is clear which force has won the day, Tohn can attack the victor."

"If he's returned in time," Flayh goaded.

Tohn had been lost in thought. Now he looked back into the blue object he balanced on his palm and answered quietly. "I can leave today. I assure you I'll not miss this place."

"And break the siege?" Jagd asked, startled.

"What purpose is there in continuing if Pelmen isn't here?" Tohn argued.

"If he isn't there, why does Dorlyth resist you so strongly?" Jagd argued back anxiously.

"I don't know. Pride, I suppose. After all, he is a Mari."

"Yes, and Maris are a pigheaded race," Flayh injected.

"I would not expect you to understand pride, Flayh," Tohn shot back. "You have, after all, so little to be proud of."

"I insist you continue the siege," Jagd urged, attempting to get everything said before the mounting animosity broke the link again. "Perhaps Pelmen is not there. But maybe he is, and wishes you to think him gone. He may be witching you yet. Remember he's a powershaper! Then, too, even if Pelmen has fled, the girl may still be in the castle. That Princess has been our primary pawn in this entire enterprise. Her recapture would be of great value still! I implore you, Tohn. Don't break the siege!"

"Very well." Tohn sighed. "We'll stay. But it cannot last much longer. I know Dorlyth's water is gone. He will have to yield soon, or else take the field against me."

"Which leads me to my last point," Jagd rushed on. "After which you two may insult one another until you both have your fill of bile. If we can force this war into Ngandib-Mar, we have nothing to fear from Pahd. Our only danger lies with that one you have bottled up in his castle."

"Danger from Dorlyth?" Tohn mumbled.

"He is the only Mari outside of Pahd who could unite those clans against us. Pahd won't. Dorlyth, given the chance, will."

"And so?"

"When the opportunity arises, Tohn—kill him."

There was a long pause, then Tohn answered quietly, "I'll do what I must." The old warrior tossed the crystal object across the tent and buried his face in the hand that had held it. The link was broken again.

Pelmen opened his eyes. The interior of the tent, devoid of light, nevertheless glowed with an eerie blueness. He realized at last that it emanated from himself. His two companions still held one another tightly, even in their sleep, though the storm had evidently passed. Pelmen stood slowly, quietly, and tossed a wet tent flap aside to step out into the moist night air.

Water ran along the ground and dripped from every branch. It filled the trench they had carved around their shelter, and—yes, it still dribbled from the rock in a steady stream that had not existed yesterday.

Water, thought Pelmen. While Dorlyth went thirsty.

By his own manipulation of the powers he could shape himself into the swiftest of birds, and be in Dorlyth's keep by noon. By the Power, he mediated, he could call forth a stream from the bare rock beneath Dorlyth's castle.

"Would that I could do both, at once," he murmured, as the water-laden branches of the giant pines showered him. But he could not. "Why must I always be forced to choose?" he groaned quietly.

"Dorlyth," he said, thinking of the lad wrapped in blankets in the tent yonder. "I must save Dorlyth." Impulsively he raised his hand above his head in the classic stance of the magus—a pose not taught him by book or man but by his own intuition and his years of practice. But as he would have focused his will—as he would have mumbled the words and shaped himself into an eagle—he hesitated.

He had not been made to stop. It was not that he couldn't. It was rather that—though torn by love for his friend and brother and for the son that lay in the tent—he wouldn't.

Instead he lifted his other arm as well, and opening both hands in supplication he implored of the Power beyond the dark silhouette of the trees. "All right! If I cannot, then you do something!"

There was silence in the clearing, but for the steady rhythm of moving water. Then, as if in answer, there was a soft roll of thunder from far away in Lamath. Water dripping from the brilliant blue cassock, head drooping on his chest, Pelmen the Prophet made his way back to the dark shape of the tent, and sleep.

Many miles to the south and west, the same storm that poured torrents on the Great North Fir shed a fine mist across the high plateau of Ngandib. The cobble-stones and courtyards were slippery with the wet, and the moist gloom muffled the usual noises of castle life. It was a good day to stay in bed—and, of course, many of the servants of Pahd mod Pahd-el did just that.

But not Pahd. "Not today!" Chogi lan Pahd-el ex-ulted, and she dragged the King's young wife out into the damp courtyard to listen to the sweet sounds coming from the armory. "You hear, Sarie? Hear that?" Pahd's mother barked happily to her daughter-in-law, and Sarie replied with a surprised yawn. Though muffled by the cloak of dampness, there was still the unmistakable noise of sword clanging on sword.

Sarie wrapped her robe tightly about her and asked uncertainly, "You're sure that's him?"

"Of course that's him. I know my own son, don't I? Dragged him out of bed at daybreak!"

"Daybreak? How could you tell?" Sarie wondered, eyeing the dark sky and yawning.

"Had seventeen opponents lined up for him to face. Took me the better part of last night to blackmail them all into appearing, but they showed. Made him promise he'd practice with each swordsman before he quit."

"Seventeen!"

"Not to worry. He'll work through them by noon; they're none of them very good. But at least he's getting some exercise!" Chogi grinned her elation, her hands propped on her wide hips as she enjoyed the music of the rhythmic clanking. Sarie cocked her head, also lis-tening. Soon she began to frown uncertainly.

"He's very—regular in his exchanges, isn't he?" she asked.

"Regular?"

"Of course, I know very little about swordplay, but it seems there would be a bit more action. This constant 'clank, clank, clank.' Somewhat boring, don't you think?"

"Greatswords, dearie, remember," Chogi growled. "Takes a lot of effort to swing one. Come on, we'll watch. Perhaps when you see the flash of the blades, and the careful body work, it won't seem so boring to you." They walked across the cobblestones to a stairway leading down to the armory. The nearer they came the louder was the clashing of swords. But Chogi, too, now noticed that the strokes fell with a rather numbing uniformity. "He must be tiring," she muttered as she opened the armory door.

In fact, Pahd mod Pahd-el wasn't tiring at all. There was little chance of that, stretched as he was across a wrestling rug piled in the corner of the stone-walled room. His seneschal, though, was ready to fall over. The poor fellow feared his arms would soon fall off, for he had been standing next to the window beating swords together for a full half-hour, and the King would not let him stop.

"What is the meaning of this?" Chogi bellowed, and Pahd raised his head off the mat to look up at her.

"Oh, hello, Mother. You can stop now, Plari."

"Thank the powers!" the seneschal moaned, and two swords clattered to the floor.

"You promised to duel seventeen opponents! On your word as a King!" Chogi yelled.

"Tell her, Plari," Pahd sighed, laying his head back. The seneschal advanced to the Queen Mother, swinging his arms to loosen cramping muscles.

"You mustn't scold him, my Lady," he puffed, "for I can attest that he kept his promise to the letter." Plari stopped to gasp for a breath.

"Seventeen opponents?"

"They weren't any good, Mother. If you're going to make me practice, would you at least find me some decent competition?"

"Such as?" his mother challenged.

"I don't know. Muldi mod Sag, of the northwest . . ."

"Killed by a cavern bear," Plari put in. "Up in the mines."

"What was he doing there?" Pahd asked.

"You sent him," the seneschal replied simply.

"Oh yes, now I remember," Pahd said uncertainly, trying to remember. "But isn't Muldi a bear's-bane?"

"He *was*." Plari shrugged. "Apparently, bears don't put as much stock in such titles as we men do."

"Go on," Chogi urged, tapping her foot impatiently. "Name me another."

"Ah, Dorlyth mod Karis, or—"

"Ah-hah!" Chogi gloated, and Pahd looked at her, puzzled. "Dorlyth mod Karis is locked in siege with Tohn mod Neelis, or have you forgotten?"

"Of course I haven't forgotten," Pahd protested, having forgotten. "Why did he lay siege to Tohn mod Neelis?"

"He didn't! Tohn attacked him! He sent you word almost two weeks ago. Don't you remember anything?"

"I remember how to sword-fight," Pahd sniffed, offended. "Tell her, Plari."

"Oh yes, my Lady, he certainly does. It took him not more than four strokes for any man. One to engage, one to disarm, one to feign the death stroke, and a whack across the backside for each with the broad edge of his blade! It was a splendid exercise, with—"

"Spare me, Plari!" Chogi begged. It was a request, but the threat in her voice told Plari he had no alternative but silence. He smiled at Chogi, and closed his mouth. "Nevertheless," Chogi began, turning to her son, "that wonderful ability of yours is of little value here. I wager Dorlyth mod Karis could use your blade this minute—if he hasn't already fallen. I did tell you that he notified us of his lack of water. I know I did."

"You did?"

"She did," Sarie agreed.

"Oh, hello, dear." Pahd smiled lazily. "What are you doing up?"

"The question is, are you going to lie there and just let one of your vassals, whom you've sworn to protect, be overrun by the armies of this renegade merchant? Are you?" Chogi demanded loudly, her face turning orange-red.

"Of course not." Pahd shrugged.

"Then what are you going to do about it?" Chogi shouted.

"I'll—rescue him, naturally," Pahd replied.

"When?"

"Well, we could go today—" Pahd began.

"Wonderful!" Chogi sighed and turned to stalk triumphantly from the room.

"—on the other hand, it's raining today. By the time we got a nice-sized army gathered from the city, it would be late afternoon, and it isn't good to leave for war in the late afternoon, so probably it would make better sense to wait until tomorrow morning, when it may not be raining and more people would be willing to volunteer."

"Are you finished?" Chogi snorted. She leaned in the doorway, waiting for him to make up his mind.

"Why do you always ask me that, Mother? Why can't you just let me take my time?"

"The army!" she demanded. "Shall Plari give the order to muster the army or not?"

"Always rushing me!"

"Take your time, darling," Sarie soothed, kneeling behind him on the rug to massage his neck.

"I think I will," Pahd said defiantly, leaning back into her fingers and closing his eyes. They popped open again to look at Chogi. "Don't worry, Mother, I'll get to it." Then he lay back into Sarie's lap.

"If there's anything left to get to," Chogi muttered sourly, and she left the armory. As if that weren't aggravation enough, she slipped climbing the steps back up to the tower.

But there was no rain on Dorlyth's castle. Though Dorlyth pleaded with the powers to send moisture his way, none fell. He stood on the battlements, gazing north at a large black cloud, feeling the promise of rain in the sticky way his robes clung to his body. But the cloud passed him by. And the blue-and-lime tents stayed on the hillside beyond his unplowed fields, awaiting his decision. To fight? Surrender? Where was Pelmen by now? Where was Rosha? Vainly Dorlyth watched the storm bypass the boundaries of his lands. His mind was made up. He skipped down a stairway to the stables and found his captain-at-arms.

"It's time to move," he murmured quietly, and the captain managed a grin between parched lips.

"I'd drink to that—if there was anything to drink."

Dorlyth nodded. "A general summons, then. We'll make our plans together."

Across fields now a foot and a half deep in grass, Tohn sat waiting for some sign. Finally his patience was rewarded. "Action on the battlements," a soldier informed him through the walls of his tent, and he stepped out into the muggy day to see for himself. There was the crisp, clear note of a horn being blown within the walls of his target, and his wrinkled face cracked open into a smile.

"Blow our own horns, lad," he ordered his squire, and the boy rushed off to deliver the old merchant's instructions. "Now what, Dorlyth?" he said softly, unconsciously fingering the edge of the knife he had been sharpening. He glanced down at the knife; realizing its import, he felt a heaviness come over him. He hid the knife within the folds of his tunic, where it would be easy to reach, and ducked back into the tent to prepare for battle. "Funny," he continued, speaking only to himself, "I used to feel elation when I finally broke a siege. Why is it now I only feel old?" Trumpets began to sound on all sides of him, and he lost himself in the noise and the detail of making ready for battle.

"I wish to see the King," Pezi announced, bowing stiffly. It was not a deep bow. Pezi hated deep bows, for he was afraid someday he would bow so deeply he couldn't straighten back up again. He looked neither to right nor left, his face frozen into an official-looking frown. There were certain rules of behavior in the Lamathian court, and Pezi had studied them all in preparation for becoming a merchant. He concentrated on remembering all of them now. He realized his career depended on how effectively he carried out Flayh's orders, and that meant he needed to be well received here. But it was difficult for him to keep a confident manner in the rarefied atmosphere of the court of Lamath. It was, of course, no more magnificent than that of Chaomonous—less so—but it was new to Pezi, and quite forbidding. The walls were of white marble streaked with veins of blue and coal-black, and they glistened in the light of lamps that burned the purest of olive oil for fuel. Most impressive were the forty-foot dragon statues that guarded every corner and every door. Pezi's last meeting with Vicia-Heinox had left unhealed wounds on his psyche. He didn't enjoy being reminded of the monster's existence every forty feet!

"You . . . want to see . . . the King," the reply came at length from the vizier of Lamath. When the man said no more, Pezi felt a need to fill the silence.

"Yes, I wish to see the King." There was more silence, and the vizier sneered politely. It was permissible to express any emotion in the Lamathian court, as long as it was done politely.

"You!" More silence. This time when Pezi opened his mouth the vizier quickly cut him off. "What possible business would you have that would interest the ruler of the entire world?"

It was Pezi's turn to sneer, but he hadn't mastered politeness. "You might tell the ruler of the world that the King of Chaomonous is preparing to bury him!"

The vizier raised an eyebrow, not at the news but at Pezi's breach of etiquette. "What a quaint turn of phrase." The vizier smiled. "I am sure you probably believe it to be a true statement, but—"

"It *is* true. At least fifty thousand Chaons, and they're probably marching across your borders already!"

"It is not considered proper to raise one's voice to an official of the Lamathian court." The vizier frowned, both eyebrows raised. It was quite a noticeable gesture, for the vizier was totally bald, and his bushy eyebrows, bright red in color, were the most prominent feature of his otherwise uninteresting face.

Pezi throttled his temper, realizing that his voice had echoed loudly among the pillars and the dragons, and replied more softly, "Pardon my impatience, I just think the King should be informed that his land is under attack."

"I'll add that to my list," said the vizier, showing Pezi his bald head as he made some illegible scratches on a parchment before him.

"Your list?" Pezi asked.

The vizier's head rolled back up slowly, the tiny eyes

locking on Pezi's. "Yes, my list," he sneered. Then he produced something from within his vestments. Pezi saw it was an instrument of some sort that hung around the vizier's neck on a silver chain. The bald official brought it to his lips and blew two notes, one a shrill high whistle, the other thin but sweet. There were at least a dozen doors opening onto this circular room. The one far to Pezi's left now slammed open and a guard in the livery of Lamath marched across the floor to the vizier's side. "You will go with this man," the vizier said to Pezi, reading another parchment as he spoke.

"To see the King?" Pezi asked brightly.

The vizier's eyes shot back up to glare at the fat merchant—but politely, very politely. "Of course not. To see the Chieftain of Defense and Expansion."

The vizier turned back to the page he'd been reading, but Pezi risked one last comment. "Will you tell the King he's at war?"

The vizier dropped the parchment in polite exasperation; as it fluttered out into the room, he scowled. "I *said*," he murmured quietly, "it is on my *list*." At this he turned his back on Pezi and motioned the uniformed guard to take the merchant out. Pezi felt an insistent hand clinch onto his upper arm, and he went along with no further comment.

The guard led him through a maze of halls and doorways; in a matter of minutes he was hopelessly lost. His opinion of the might of Lamath grew at every turn, for nowhere had he ever seen such a wealth of polished marble or more artistically wrought statuary. He was passed from one guard to another, and felt he had walked two miles by the time the last guide in the series turned to motion him into a small, high-ceilinged office. There were two windows, but they were no more than three-inch slits cut through the wall, running from floor to ceiling. Beside them stood baskets of blue-feathered arrows, and bows hung from pegs in the marble walls. Pezi realized this room fronted on the outer walls of the Lamathian palace, and that from this vantage point two good archers could very effectively defend the palace gates below. The Lamathian King at least had the sense to place his best soldier's office where it would be of some practical value.

There was no one in the room, so Pezi seated himself next to a cool wall and waited. He loosened his lime-colored belt, and struggled to get comfortable. It was a humid day in Lamath.

Suddenly a man burst through the doorway, tossed a sheaf of bound parchment onto an already messy desk, and turned to look at Pezi.

"War then," he said. "Where? How many?"

"Ah, approximately, ah, fifty thousand—"

"Who?"

"Ah, ah, Talith of Chaomonous—"

"Why?"

"Ah, because he thinks you've stolen his daughter—"

"Ridiculous. Why would I want to steal his daughter."

"Ah, he doesn't think you've stolen his daughter, he—"

"Then who?"

"Ah, the King of Lamath—"

"More ridiculous. Who really took her?"

"Ah, ah, how should I know who—"

"You're a merchant, merchants know everything. Who took her?"

"Ah, I don't think—"

"Can't tell me. Very well, where will the attack come?"

"I, ah, I really don't know—"

"I believe that. Any flotilla involved?"

"I—I'm sure there will be some—"

"Estimate how many ships."

"I couldn't really say—"

"Don't know much for a merchant. Fifty thousand Chaons, possible flotilla, trumped-up accusation which points to imperialistic expansion as the prime motive. That's it?" This was the first ordinary question the man had asked him. The others had been demands. Pezi took a deep breath and started to reply.

The warrior interrupted him. "Captain!" he shouted, and another warrior in a blue tunic was immediately at his side. "General alarm, immediate status, arrest any merchants lately from the south, including this one, for interrogation—house arrest after you're convinced they are not actively involved. Send the standing Third Column south to secure the King's Road, then cordon off Dragonsgate and stop all caravan traffic, in or out. Notify all watches along the Spinal Range to relay any unusual troop movement directly to this office by blue flyer. Alert all naval vessels under Lamathian colors that they must be battle-ready within three days, and contact the naval commander and have him see me regarding forcible impression of all available merchant vessels into service to our King."

"Yes, sir," the captain snapped, and he turned to hurry out.

The Chieftain of Defense stopped him short. "And, Captain."

"Yes, sir?" the man replied, turning in the doorway to face his superior.

"It's happened," the Chieftain said quietly, and for the first time his expression changed. "It's finally happened! We're going south!" By the time he had finished his sentence both the Chieftain and his assistant were giggling like two excited schoolboys, slapping one another on the back and cackling with elation. Pezi stared, openmouthed.

"That is all," the Chieftain said, and all was business-like again. They snapped salutes at one another and the captain departed quickly.

Pezi thought the salutes rather weird, but said nothing. He didn't realize it, of course, but it was the same gesture of respect Vicia-Heinox had thought so curious when his worshippers did him homage: both arms raised above the head, then crossed, fingers curved into little dragon's mouths. Must be difficult to salute with a sword in your hand, Pezi thought, but said nothing.

The Chieftain of Defense and Expansion now turned back to Pezi, seating himself behind his cluttered desk. "I'm sure you feel a little nonplussed at the speed of that operation, but wars don't wait on anyone, and we try not to fall behind in our preparation. I'm Asher, General of the Army and Chieftain of Defense and Expansion."

"Ah, Pezi's my name, Pezi of Ognadzu."

"Evident by your colors."

"Ah, yes, so it is. I must say, I'm impressed with your organization. I, ah, I had some fears for your entire culture when I was told the King wouldn't see me——"

"The King sees no one. I've never seen him."

"Never?"

"Only spoken to him through a fabric partition."

"Quite a contrast with the fellow from the south," Pezi grunted, recalling the vanity of Talith. "Will he be told that he's—ah—at war?"

"If he chooses to hear the vizier today, yes. He is a very secretive ruler, Pezi, and quite a worried man."

"Worried? What about, if not about war?" Pezi asked, pleased that Asher had remembered his name.

"About death, and about the destiny of his soul."

"What?" Pezi chuckled. "Worried about religious things? Why?" Pezi's hearty laughter faded quickly when he saw Asher was not laughing with him.

"Why not?" Asher asked frankly, eyes fixed on Pezi's.

"I—well, of course he would be. Wouldn't he?" Pezi smiled questioningly.

"There's a great deal of religious unrest in the land. A priestess from the northern regions has set the Lamathian Dragonfaith astir with her preaching of renewed devotion. Great hosts of people follow her wherever she goes, and always her teaching is the same. Ultimate devotion demands ultimate personal sacrifice."

"Sacrifice?"

"Yes. She prepares her followers for consumption."

"She gets people ready to be eaten by the dragon?"

"Of course!" Asher snapped. His handsome young face was hard now, his jaw set, his mind far away to the north with Serphimera, the Priestess of the dragon.

Suddenly he turned on Pezi, and spat out, "*You*, you merchant! You seller of slaves! Surely you've fed a few bodies to the dragon yourself, have you not? Lamathian bodies?" Pezi said nothing, for he suddenly found it difficult to swallow. "You don't think your Chaon soldiers are capable of truly capturing so many, do you?"

Still Pezi kept silence, but he remembered now many

discussions in various merchant kitchens around the world, concerning the willingness of Lamathian slaves to serve as dragon fodder. The thought sent shivers down his spine. "They *want* to be eaten?"

"Yes!" Asher thundered, then he looked away, peering through one of the window slits at the street below and the capital city of Lamath beyond. "And now the King wonders and worries about where the ultimate reunion with the dragon is to be, if not in the twi-beast's belly?"

"And—what about you?" Pezi asked cautiously.

Asher's voice softened. "I've seen her. Serphimera. Weaves a spell around a crowd like a Mari witch over a brewing potion. Touches . . . smiles . . . frowns . . . and they all belong to her. To her and to the dragon."

Pezi thought of the horrible stink of Vicia-Heinox's combined breath, and wondered aloud, "Has she ever talked with the dragon?"

"She lives still, doesn't she?" Asher snapped, and Pezi shrugged helplessly. "The day she meets him, she will be inside him. But her people won't let her go, you see, fearing that if they lose her they will lose his palpable presence with them. So she stays behind and sends others in droves to your Chaon soldiers—and the dragon." Asher took a bow off the wall and tested the tension of its string absently. "And me? Ah, yes. I wonder too. I've watched her move, Pezi. She walks with the liquid motion of a woman who is sure of her lover." Asher sighed. "But her lover is the dragon, and no man. And me? I'm the one who must stop her."

Asher looked at Pezi. "You shouldn't think this war with Chaomonous is a fearful thing to me. No, no. It is a relief! At last I can lead my warriors against the true enemy and spatter Chaon blood on the granite barrier between us!"

Pezi gagged a bit at the force of the image, but said nothing. He was imagining how his uncle would manipulate all this information to the profit of Ognadzu, and pleased that he would have so much to share with the cruel old buzzard.

"So tell me, Pezi," Asher demanded, planting himself

astride Pezi's outstretched legs, "Where can I expect
their attack?"

"I, ah, can't say—"

"Can't? Or won't? Well, perhaps a stay in our guest
room will help you to recall some more helpful information. Guard!"

"Thank you, General Asher, but I've rented some
rooms in town and—"

A guard appeared at the door, and Asher thundered,
"Conduct this merchant to his quarters!"

"Come on, then," the guard said to Pezi as he swag-
gered into the office. "It's a long walk to the dungeon."

Dungeon! Who'd said anything about a dungeon?
Asher had said the guest rooms, not— Pezi was jerked
from his seat and dragged out the door, where the first
guard was joined by two others. Soon they were in the
lower levels of the palace, and Pezi noticed that down
here the walls weren't marble, but were carved out of
the rock. As they slammed a heavy door behind him,
one could hear Pezi's plaintive call echoing down the
hallway: "But he said I could stay in the guest room . . ."

They poured down out of the foothills of the Spinal
Range, and walked for days just to glimpse her. Wherever she passed, villages went empty, cattle went hungry, plows gathered the dust of spring. Across wide
fields, painted yellow-green by the glowing sun, she led
her following—and every night beside giant bonfires
she lectured on ultimate devotion. Each night the group
was watched by Asher's soldiers. Yet every evening two
or three pilgrims managed to slip past the watch, unnoticed, and started the long trek to the south and slavery—hoping. Her pattern took her from one monastery
to the next. She slept always in the chapel, before the
dragon statue that was an obligatory part of every chapel's decorations. It mattered little what stream of Dragonfaith the monastery espoused. She visited all in
turn—Divisionists and Dichotomists as well as the more
orthodox Coalescence mainstream. And there were cas-
socks of every shade of blue among her following. No
segment of the Dragonfaith went untouched by her
teaching.

She was always smiling, her long dark hair gleaming in the sunlight. Her own robe was the blue of the midnight sky when it encircles a full moon. Around her neck she wore the white vee, and it draped across her breasts as a symbol to all that, doctrinally, she stood with the Coalescence party. But her mind was never on doctrine, only on the dragon. Whenever a cloud obscured the sun, throwing its shadow across her, she would toss her hands up to shade her eyes and search the sky for some sign of the flying twi-beast.

Understandably, she and her whole following surged forward with excitement at the news received from a small village in the heart of the Lamathian mainland. The population of an entire monastery had disappeared one day, and a local farmer swore that on that same day he had seen the dragon himself flying over his fields. Then there was the great dent in the earth only a few hundred yards from the monastery's gates. A number of peasants reported they had heard a loud blast coming from that direction, but laughed at the idea that it had been the sound of the dragon crashing. In fact there was much discussion over whether the notion of the dragon crashing out of control was blasphemous or not.

Serphimera did not participate in the discussion. She sniffed the air at the site of the crater, then went down into it to feel along its banks. She slept that night before the statue in the monastery. When she emerged the next morning her statement was unqualified, uttered with unshakable confidence. "The Dragon was here. Those of this monastery were the first to be found faithful."

Overnight, the empty monastery filled with newly sworn initiates. In the absence of an abbess, Serphimera lingered. Within a week, she decided that here she would make her abode. The name of the little village nearby had never been firmly fixed. Now it took on a new name, one that was whispered throughout the length of rural Lamath. Serphila, it came to be called, home of the Priestess Serphimera. It quickly swelled in size. Perhaps the local farmers were not totally believing—but all found new occupations serving those who came to Serphila to await the return of Vicia-Heinox.

* * *

"Amazing," Bronwynn murmured wearily. "Bushes and shrubs do still exist." They rode down out of the forest in a line, Pelmen leading the way. Their two-week journey through the Great North Fir was ending. "Seems like it's been six months," she grumbled.

"W-where are we g-g-going?" Rosha asked.

"And what are we going to do when we get there?" Bronwynn added. It was not the first time they had asked Pelmen this question, but there was always hope he would finally condescend to answer.

And answer he did. "You'll see it in a moment."

"Really?" The girl grew excited for the first time in days. "Can we see it from here?" She stood in her stirrups, trying to peer past Pelmen's head.

"W-what *are* we g-g-going to do?" Rosha asked from behind. Bronwynn had noticed a strange tension between the two men, but nothing had been explained to her. In fact, it seemed from her conversations with Rosha that he himself didn't really understand why it existed. It was just something that had seemed to grow between them since the storm a few nights before. Rosha dismissed it as more of Pelmen's strangeness, but Bronwynn wondered if there weren't more to it than that. It seemed to her that Pelmen was hiding something.

They rode down into a small forest bowl, fighting through a tangle of roots and brush, then up the other side. Here, abruptly, the trees stopped, though there were stumps and small bushes in abundance. In a moment they stood atop the last hill, looking down on the giant central river valley of Lamath.

"It's like home!" Bronwynn exclaimed, her eyes misting over unexpectedly. "But not," she added.

"Much greener than Chaomonous at this time of the year," Pelmen said quietly. "Then again, maybe there are parts of Chaomonous that are greener. I haven't seen all of your land."

"That's it . . . it's so *green*!" the girl gushed.

"And s-s-so flat," Rosha snorted. The lad turned his mount to look back at the forest longingly, already missing its cool covering.

Pelmen knew what the lad was thinking. Rosha scorned Lamath because he feared Lamath. "Too big a land to be someone in, Rosha?" he asked.

Rosha wheeled his horse back to face him. "Too b-big? I n-never said that."

"Good." Pelmen smiled. "Because it's not too big for you." There was a minute or two of silence on the hill, as the two men regarded one another. Bronwynn quickly grew impatient, and her pony seemed to sense her urgency, for it began dancing around. Finally she interrupted.

"You said we would see where we are going?"

Pelmen glanced at her, then pointed out across the countryside to the northeast. The recent rain had settled the dust and washed the horizon blue. Four or five villages with their own local fields were easily visible from this height, as was a broad blue strip of river that curved through the countryside on its way to the east and the sea. "The village there . . . in the bend of the Mashab River."

"That little place?"

"No. Look out from it—north. You see a low white wall?"

Bronwynn shaded her eyes and squinted. "No," she said frankly.

"I s-s-see it," Rosha murmured.

"Of course you see it," Bronwynn said. "Anyone could see from the shape of your nose that your grandmother was an eagle." Rosha chuckled, and Bronwynn was pleased with herself for easing the tension. "What is it?"

"It's a monastery of the Divisionist faith."

"That tells me a lot!"

"You'll have plenty of time to learn more." Pelmen spoke a word to Minaliss and was off again.

"You are always welcome here, my brother." The old holy man smiled toothlessly. "And these with you as well. Though I must confess I am a little startled at your sudden reappearance after such an extended absence." The Elder of the monastery sat on a three-legged stool in the center of the library, sipping a hot bowl of thin soup between sentences. Pelmen also sat on a stool, but the brethren had provided soft, pillowy stuffed chairs for Rosha and Bronwynn. This luxury, together with the warm, protective atmosphere of the cloister and the soft drone of the conversation, rapidly put them to sleep.

"It was time," Pelmen said simply, "though I cannot tell you how I knew."

"Indeed, it is time, my brother." The old man's eyes narrowed and he leaned forward to stare at Pelmen. "If you've come to do the thing at last."

Pelmen did not look away, but he had to fight to keep his eyes from filling with tears. "I have, my brother," he answered, "yet I wonder still why it must be me?"

The Elder chuckled, a melodious laugh that seemed incongruous emanating from that toothless mouth. "Who else then, Pelmen? Who found the book and deciphered it? Who but you could do the task, and tell the tale?"

"I never asked the Power for this—"

"Do you think I asked for this?" the old man asked, gesturing at the bare room and slopping his soup in the process. "Oh my," he muttered, setting the bowl on the floor and sopping up the spillage with the hem of his grimy blue robe. "But this is what came," he continued, not looking up, "an old man and a group of men to guide spiritually." He glanced up at Pelmen. "More or less." He grinned. "Nor do I complain anymore. Why should I?" He gestured again at the books. "Look at the wealth I possess . . . and the friends!" He stood and made his way to the door to open it. He whispered something to a brother outside and soon in came a group of men to bundle the boy and girl up in robes and carry them off to their rooms. "Exhausted, they were," he muttered to Pelmen, scolding him. "You brought them too far too fast."

"No choice in that, Elder. They both must grow well beyond their days in a hurry if they are to match the burdens being thrust on them."

"Yes." The old man sighed. "Yes. The changes do come, don't they?" He seated himself on his stool, lowering himself in sections to avoid complaints from aged joints. "Well then. What will you do about the woman?"

"What woman?" Pelmen asked, puzzled.

"You don't know of the Priestess from the north? Where have you been, boy?"

"I've not been in Lamath, if that's what you mean— my father." Pelmen grinned as he added this last. It had been a long time since his teacher called him boy.

"Playing magician again, I suppose." The Elder sighed. "And I thought it was her appearance that had brought you back. I underestimate you again!" the little man called out loudly, and Pelmen realized his teacher spoke not to him, but to the Power.

"Perhaps I should know of the woman?"

The Elder quickly sketched the details of Serphimera's appearance and the sudden explosion of her popularity. The news troubled him, but what concerned him more were the stories of what happened in the wake of her visitations to monasteries.

"Burned parchments. Burned codices. Burned libraries, all over Lamath. And naturally the most virulent reprisals against Divisionists. She is, after all, orthodox." The little man chuckled, but there was no joy in his laughter.

"Has she been here?" Pelmen asked urgently.

"Look around, boy." The Elder smiled, gesturing again at the rolls and books. "Use your head a little. No, your precious codex has not been destroyed . . ." The old man's voice softened. "Though Power knows I've wanted to do it myself, knowing the grief it's caused you."

"No!"

"I haven't," the Elder soothed.

"Where is it?" Pelmen asked eagerly. The Elder rose slowly from his stool and moved his bowl to one side; then he moved his stool and bent to lift the edge of a woolen rug, to flop it out of the way. The process took a full two minutes, and Pelmen fought impatience.

"It's in the cavern, then?"

The Elder sighed. "Well, of course, it is. Go ahead." He waved Pelmen to a stone slab in the floor. "You know I can't lift it." Pelmen quickly grabbed the inset handle and lifted the slab out of the floor. A cold gust of wind blew up into the room, and the Elder stepped away from the edge of the black hold. "It's where you found it," he muttered, and Pelmen nodded and reached for a lamp. "Watch out for bears, and don't stay all night, you need your sleep, too!"

"Yes, my father," Pelmen replied absently, stepping onto the top rung of the ladder.

"Before you go—"

"Yes?" Pelmen replied, stopping with his head at floor level.

"What about the boy and girl? Who are they? What am I to do with them?"

"The girl is the heir to the throne of Chaomonous. Clothe her in blue and hide her at all costs. The boy—his father asked me to teach him all I know. I've done better. I've brought him to my own teacher."

"Pelmen, I—I am old. If it is your responsibility to teach him—can I bear that?"

"There is the matter of time, my father," Pelmen replied, laying a hand on the old man's sandaled foot and looking up into his eyes. "There are priorities."

"Yes. Well, for now then. But protecting the girl—Pelmen, this Priestess could come any day now . . ."

"Let me deal with the Priestess," Pelmen said quietly. "Just clothe Bronwynn in the blue of an initiate and keep her hidden for a time. As for truly protecting her, your mind can rest at ease. Protecting Bronwynn is something the boy won't have to be taught. Good night." Pelmen descended into the cavern below the cloister, and the old man watched him down.

"Good night," the Elder said at length, and then he added, "my brother."

Tohn mod Neelis stood at the head of his mounted army and waited for Dorlyth to venture out. Three columns of riders waited behind him, responding to the order for absolute silence by carrying on their inevitable prebattle conversations in whispers. Tohn's archers lined the northern edge of the field, their flank shielded from arrows by wooden barriers constructed in the long days of the siege. His best cavalry unit waited on the southern tip of the hillock Tohn had camped on. He would not bring them in until after the general mêlée began. It was his plan to drive Dorlyth south with a volley of arrow fire and squeeze him then between the main force and this reserve cavalry. It was a fair plan, Tohn decided. Nothing fancy. What really mattered was how his soldiers responded to this, their second battle. He hoped some at least had learned something from the first.

"Boy, I want you to stay well back from the action," Tohn growled at his towheaded young squire.

"Yes, sir," the lad replied, but he never looked up at his master. The gate was all he was concerned with, the gate of Dorlyth's castle. There was a breathlessness in the boy that told Tohn he would not stay back—no, could not stay back.

"You do as I say, lad!" Tohn said sharply, and the boy looked up at him in surprise.

"I said I would," he protested.

"It isn't what you think it is, lad. This grunting and sweating and hacking at one another won't make you the man you're in such a hurry to be."

"Did I say I was in a hurry, sir?"

"Every boy is in a hurry, lad. Then he's an old man, wanting to stop hurrying but not knowing how."

"Sir?"

"Just stay put when we charge!"

"Yes, sir."

There was a cry of "Gate's opening!" down the line, and Tohn looked again at the castle.

"By the powers, it is. Very well, lad. Pass my lance up."

Similar orders were mumbled up and down the line, until the rows of mounted soldiers resembled a living picket fence. The whispering stopped. There was much nervous coughing. Tohn's own blood was pulsing rapidly though his aged veins, but he set his jaw and thought calming thoughts.

The gates were fully open now, and a line of riding warriors came slowly out and down the earthen ramp to the level of the field. One could say it was a ragtag army, and scorn its lack of discipline. On the other hand, one could view it as a collection of heroes, individualists who chose to dress and act as they liked, but who had chosen in this case to fight side by side. The second view, Tohn feared, was nearer the truth, and he felt his lips go suddenly very dry. The warriors flowed forth from the mouth of the castle in two rows, one turning south and one north, and all rode with the deliberate pace of men in control of themselves and their animals. Psychologically speaking, it was a most effective ruse, Tohn thought. Sweat trickled down his ribs inside the oven of his mail shirt. He fought his impatience.

The lines were fully extended now, and Tohn watched the fellow he had come to know as Dorlyth ride from the gate. With that mass of curling hair framing his face, he looked like a bear. The old merchant wondered briefly if the man's nature was as violent as one of those denizens of the underground. Then Tohn lurched forward in his saddle, dumfounded. Dorlyth mod Karis was unarmed . . . and he rode past his line of soldiers toward the middle of the field. There the man stopped and dismounted. In a gesture that amazed all of the gathered host of Ognadzu, he slapped his horse on the rump and sent it riderless back to its stable. He then knelt on the grass and tugged a weed from the ground; inserting it between his lips casually, he began to chew it. It was obvious he was waiting for Tohn to meet him.

That sharpened knife was still tucked away inside Tohn's battle shirt, within easy reach. "When you get the chance, kill him," Jagd had suggested, and Tohn intended to do so. Tohn measured the distance, and calculated that he could easily strike the man down and return to his line before Dorlyth's warriors could react. A bow-shot could fell him, perhaps—but it would demand a brilliant bowman and a lucky shot. The deed needed to be done. There would be no better time.

"Here, lad," he muttered, passing his spear back to the boy. "And here." He handed the squire his greatsword, and took the reins to ride toward Dorlyth.

"You did it, my Lord!" The boy beamed up at him, eyes full of the purest respect and admiration.

Tohn stared at him, shocked at this intrusion of virtue into his dark scheming. He felt himself grin foolishly, and in disbelief heard himself say, "Leading is easy, lad. You just have to believe in yourself."

Then he had kicked his horse and was riding forward, his attention fixed not on the crucial confrontation with Dorlyth, but strangely on the self he had seen reflected in his squire's adoring eyes.

As his horse cantered toward Dorlyth, Tohn mod Neelis wrestled with a dilemma. Who was he, really? In his earlier days he had been trained to ignore the ethical dimensions of any question that involved the family. What was good for Ognadzu was good for Tohn mod Neelis. But now, as he felt his squire's admiring gaze on his back, the greater glory of Ognadzu was the last thing on his mind. He was within speaking distance of Dorlyth now—if he were to strike the man down, now was the time—

Tohn reined in his horse, and got off.

Dorlyth eyed the older man intently as Tohn walked stiffly up to face him and knelt across from him in the grass. Dorlyth spoke quietly. "I hoped you would come."

"Yes, well . . . What is it you want?"

"That's what I was going to ask you."

"You know what I want," Tohn said gruffly. "Pelmen and the girl. Give them to me and my troops and I will leave you in peace."

A glimmer of a smile flashed behind the veil of Dorlyth's beard. "I think we both know better than that, don't we?"

Tohn raised an eyebrow. "Know what?"

Dorlyth sighed. "Pelmen isn't here. Neither is the girl. You must know that by this time, Tohn. If I had a powershaper within my walls, why would I need to be here, talking with you?"

Tohn shifted his eyes toward the long line of his blue soldiers, and shook his head. "You have me there."

Suddenly Dorlyth was speaking with a hushed intensity that drew Tohn's eyes back to his face. "I know why you're here, Tohn. I know who sent you. What I don't understand is why you, a Lord of the Mar, would allow

yourself to be manipulated by flatlanders! Tohn—"
Here Dorlyth broke off, sighing, then continued more
quietly. "What do *you* want? Really?"

The old warrior again turned his gaze away, staring
at his nephews and cousins in uniform. "Me? I want to
go home and plant my crop." There was a long silence
between them.

"Why don't you?"

Tohn shook his head. "Isn't that easy. I'm a merchant, Dorlyth, and the Council of Elders—"

"Tohn, you're a Mari! Mari to the heart! I can't believe you mean to threaten that—"

"I'm both, Dorlyth!" Tohn exploded, then calmed
himself a bit and went on, "I'm either both, or neither."
But even as he said this, Tohn realized it really wasn't
true. He thought for a long time then, reflecting on
what he should tell Dorlyth and what he should with-
hold.

In the end he told him all. Thinking of the towheaded
boy in the ranks behind him, he shared with Dorlyth
every detail of the plot, and finished with this: "I just
want to be left out of it, Dorlyth. I'll neither fight with
you nor against you. If my fields and harvest must be
sacrificed as a plain of battle, let it be so. But I want my
children to live—and I want them to live as I have, as
Maris."

Dorlyth nodded, and smiled a friendly smile. "Tohn
mod Neelis," he said, "you're the first merchant I ever
met who had a conscience."

As they grasped hands to seal the peace, Pahd mod
Pahd-el arrived on the field of battle, at the head of his
palace guard. He would have arrived sooner, of course,
but . . . he'd overslept.

❦ Chapter Nine ❦

THE CAVERN was so familiar Pelmen could have found his way in the dark, but he appreciated the illumination of the lamp. So intent was he on rediscovering his prize that the thought of creating a ball of flame to light his way never entered his mind. He was no longer a power-shaper—not here. He was back in the caverns of La-math, back in the Dragonfaith blue, and it was as if the intervening years of his travels were but dreams without meaning. The cavern looked as old as it had always looked, and the bear stench was as strong and unpleasant as ever. Truly, it could have been yesterday that he last closed the book and wound his way out of the sub-terranean maze to dinner.

He slipped quietly around a corner and went down to his knees to enter a narrow tunnel, pushing the light before him as he wiggled through on his belly. Then he stood, holding the lamp above him to survey the room that had been his study for so long, so many years ago.

A natural shelf of rock had served as his desk, a small stool as his seat. He tested his weight on the stool carefully and found it sturdy still, then reached into a crevice on the wall and withdrew a case of beaten metal. There was no lock on the box. He flipped it open quickly and pulled from it the leather-bound volume that had been uppermost in his mind since the moment he had again laid eyes on the monastery. He placed it on the shelf and hung the lamp on a peg. Then he opened the book and began to read, translating the strange characters into thoughts.

Glorious things. A world of strange names, but easily recognizable events. People who so far preceded him in linear time as to have no connection to the reality of the present—but who nevertheless were people, just as he, whose lives had intersected with one another and with catastrophe. People who had experienced life, and struggled to prolong it.

He skimmed through material already read and pondered, renewing his memory of the whole by dipping more deeply into selected sections. He came at last to the place where he had left off reading, to ideas and symbols that had so threatened him that he had fled the monastery and Lamath. Tears sprang to his eyes as of old, tears of frustration and despair. For each passage read only deepened his conviction that the words spoke of him. How could it be, he asked himself—and Pelmen realized anew the presence of the Power in his tiny cell, answering simply, "It is."

"Then why do I constantly talk of choice?" Pelmen asked glumly of the wall, and he was startled by the way his words echoed out into the passageway behind him. He suddenly felt very tired. Unhooking the lantern from the wall, he walked to the narrow entrance. Before he stooped, he turned and spoke again, spoke aloud, spoke to the book that still lay open on the rock. "I already said that I would!" Just that. Then he knelt once more, and was crawling out of the passageway.

"Where is she? She was told to be here at midday!" The speaker was a young man of twenty-five, very intense of face and bearing. His garment was so rich with costly jewels one could say it was encrusted with them. It was a very heavy robe, and noisy when he paced like this. It was far too long for him, and the hem dragged the floor. Emeralds clacked along the mosaic tile with every step he took. It had been thrust upon him, along with the sapphire hood of office and the keys of dominion, with the untimely passing of his father less than a month before. He was Naquin, High Priest of the Unified Dragonfaith—and he was scared senseless by the suddenness of his rise to power. One day he had been a slightly tipsy poet. The next he was spiritual father to a nation. "She calls herself Priestess! Who made her Priestess?"

"She says she was made so by the Lord Dragon himself . . ." answered a voice from a row of attendant advisors. There were nine of these, all shrouded in shades of blue. Naquin could see none of their faces. They were his anonymous advisors, chosen from obscurity by each separate branch of the Dragonfaith. It was the tradition that they remain forever unknown to the High Priest they advised, so that none would be favored over the others and so that the Priest would feel no political compulsion to listen to any one. He, of course, could do as he chose in any case, whether it suited his advisors or not. The advisors followed Naquin throughout the day, commenting as a chorus on his every action, offering advice freely, whether asked for it or not. Naquin was sure they were plotting to drive him crazy.

"That's absurd!" Naquin shouted. "The dragon cares nothing for priests or priestesses, he cares nothing about our faith!" There was a chorus of tongue clicks and murmurs of "shame," but no truly violent verbal reaction. Nothing like the response Naquin got when he called Vicia-Heinox an overgrown gecko.

"Whatever your evaluation of the woman's authority, you must confess that her influence with the people warrants her claim to being Priestess."

"I don't have to confess anything to you parasites, I wish you would get that through your heads. Assuming you have heads under those veils. I honestly don't see how you get around. Don't you trip over things in the dark?"

"No," the answer came back from several directions, but the idea was already planted in Naquin's mind. He would have rocks cemented into the floor throughout the temple, rocks that would rise two or three inches above the level of the tile. It would do him good to watch one or two advisors go down in a whirl of vestments as they scurried to keep up with him.

"She is come," someone said, and Naquin glanced up to see the woman gliding toward him. Her robe skimmed the floor before her, giving the illusion that she floated rather than walked.

"More blue," Naquin sighed. "Doesn't anyone here ever wear anything but blue?"

" 'It is the color of the water—' "

" 'The color of the sky—' " began the chorus, quoting the ancient lines regarding the sacred color.

"All right, enough!" Naquin snorted, stamping his foot. "Leave us!" he commanded imperiously, and his nine naggers obediently left the room. Naquin surveyed Serphimera with a pained expression, and said, "I suppose if this movement of yours gets any larger, you'll be wanting to make it ten?"

"Ten what?"

"Ten advisors, of course. Every other movement is represented, why not the 'ultimate devotion' party?"

Naquin's sarcasm was not lost on the Priestess, but she disregarded it. He was, after all, still a boy. "I had no wish to start a new movement, only to restore the old to its original passion."

"No doubt, no doubt. So did all the other movements when they started." Naquin was not pious by any means, but he did know his history.

"But this won't be another movement." Serphimera smiled knowingly. "The true end of ultimate devotion has nothing to do with religious practice. The true end is to be swallowed by the Lord Dragon."

"And that's what confuses me in all this," Naquin replied. "When the aim is to be consumed by the dragon, and when so many adherents are flocking to captivity in the south in order to accomplish that dubious purpose, how is it that your following continues to grow?" Naquin smiled sarcastically. "Could it be that a lot of them preach what they fear too much to practice? I notice their leader is still undigested . . ."

"It has been given to me to prepare the faithful," Serphimera replied patiently, condescending to his skepticism. "When the proper time comes I hope to make my own pilgrimage. Like you, I hope that time is soon."

"Like me?"

Serphimera laughed brightly and tossed her dark mane over her shoulders. "I quite understand that my disappearance would be cause for great rejoicing within this temple—and within a host of monasteries still untouched by my devotionalists."

"I would never think such a thing!" Naquin lied. "My only concern is that you've gotten the King into a lather over this, and for the welfare of the country I wish you would make some proclamation or something that would set the old fellow's heart at ease."

Serphimera's eyes flashed with excitement as she smiled triumphantly. "But you see, my concern is not with the welfare of the state. I'm far more concerned with the welfare of the Lord Dragon!"

Naquin smiled back, a thin smile, then weakly called out, "Advisors?" Within moments his nine blue shadows trooped back into the room. "Would you please discuss this situation with the lady? I've remembered an important task of office I must attend to." He turned on his heel then and walked out of the temple, his robe clacking all the way. He really had nothing else to do, of course—what could be more important than the welfare of the King? But it was just too much for him today. Too much. He needed to get out of this jeweled lizard skin and be himself for a while.

The Elder climbed cautiously down the ladder into the cavern, sniffing for bear at every step. He realized it made little difference if he did smell one, for the beast would get him before he could get back up the ladder. Still, he felt it might be worthwhile at least to know what was getting him before it did so. He thanked the Power that bears never came up into the open.

He walked quietly, holding the lantern above his head and trying to remember the way. At last he found the entrance hole, and saw a light glowing from within. "My brother?"

"Yes, my father?" Pelmen replied from within. The closeness of the place made his voice sound distant.

"I hate to disturb your study, but there is another one waiting in the anteroom." There was a short silence, then the old holy man heard Pelmen sliding through the passageway.

"You didn't disturb me," Pelmen answered gravely, shaking dust from his clothes.

"That's a lie, of course," the Elder said, "but a gracious one. You seem to be bearing up well under the burden." They shuffled back toward the ladder. "I wish one could say the same for your young friends." Pelmen stopped walking and looked at his old teacher.

"What can I do? What other choice is there?"

"Oh, I didn't say you had a choice. I do think that perhaps you could help their adjustment somewhat if you would spend a little time with them. You seem to have it for everyone else . . ."

"Yes. You're right, as always."

"Do you think we could walk along as we talk?" the old man asked. "After all, we could visit in the library all night and never even smell a bear . . ."

Pelmen chuckled, and they moved on. "I'll speak with the two of them as soon as I deal with this new seeker who has come."

"Oh, no need to wait."

"But—"

"You see, I lie rather graciously myself." The old man put his hand on the ladder and passed the lamp to Pelmen. "You take this prophecy business so seriously. What other lever do I have to get you to fulfill your responsibilities?" The Elder was old, but he wasn't dead. This close to the library and safety, he wasn't about to give any passing bear a chance to render him so. Pelmen was amazed at how swiftly the little man scrambled up the ladder and out.

"We just don't understand," Bronwynn said when the three of them were together. "We've been a part of everything you've done up until now, why can't we be a part of this?"

"But you are a part of this. Look at your robes, look—"

"What difference does it make what color robes we wear?" Bronwynn protested. "All right, so the good brothers have told us the significance of the sacred blue. But Pelmen, we have no interest in this religion business, we want to be a part of what you're doing!"

"Rosha? You're saying nothing?"

"I speak for both of us," Bronwynn said, and Rosha nodded to indicate this was true.

Pelmen sighed. "If you're not interested in all of this, what makes you think you would be any more interested in what I'm doing?"

"You." It was Rosha who said it, and even he seemed surprised that he'd spoken.

"Me?"

"It doesn't matter what it is," Bronwynn said, her tone pleading as she sought to make him understand. "If it is this important to you, it is important to us as well."

Pelmen gazed first at one young face and then the other, then stood to stroll around the room. "Very well," he said finally. "I will make you my first initiates." It was such a serious pronouncement that Pelmen expected more reaction from the young couple than he received. They simply nodded. "If there's nothing else then—"

"One more thing," Bronwynn said.

"Yes?"

"Rosha wants to know if you have any news about his father."

Pelmen's grim expression grew more so. "Why do you ask this, Rosha?"

The young man cleared his throat. "I had a—dream. The n-night of the s-s-storm. I dreamed that you—heard a c-conversation about m-my father. D-did you?"

Pelmen stared at the lad. "Yes."

"Why d-did you hide it from m-me?"

"Your father did not do as I asked. He has been under siege by Tohn mod Neelis—probably since the day we left."

"D-don't you think I kn-know that?" Rosha stammered, his eyes angry. "I kn-knew that before you d-did! My father t-told me his plans! M-m-my father t-t-t-*trusts* me!" Rosha glared at Pelmen, and the Prophet felt his stomach knot up. He had underestimated the son of his finest friend, he now realized, and it grieved him.

"I'm sorry, Rosha. I was trying to protect you."

"I c-can protect m-myself!"

"I realize that. Better now than before, my friend."

"Then t-tell m-me what you have heard!"

"The three men who plotted Bronwynn's kidnap have also plotted Dorlyth's death."

"D-d-did they succeed?" Rosha asked, stony-faced.

Pelmen shrugged helplessly. "All I heard was the plot."

"Then they d-d-didn't," Rosha barked fiercely, "for I know my father, and he has b-b-better sense than to g-get himself killed."

In spite of the weightiness of the conversation, Pelmen was forced to smile at that. "I see the son trusts the father as well."

"Why didn't you go and help him?" Bronwynn asked softly. Her face expressed faint distaste—the sad smile of one betrayed. "You could have . . . couldn't you?"

"I could have," Pelmen admitted.

Bronwynn waited for him to explain further, but he said no more. "I don't understand," she said finally, shaking her head and turning away, no longer able to meet his eyes.

"If you are to be my initiates, you will soon."

Bronwynn said nothing, nor did she turn back to him. She did nod slightly, as if to say, "We'll see." For the moment it was the best she could give.

Pelmen looked at Rosha. "I should have known better than to try to hide anything in the Great North Fir." With that, Pelmen started for the door.

"P-p-pelmen—" The Prophet stopped and looked back at the powerfully built young man. "When d-d-do we start?"

Pelmen grinned slightly and motioned toward the door. "Now, if you wish."

Rosha hopped from his cot and grabbed Bronwynn's hand. "We're r-ready," he grunted.

Bronwynn glanced up at him in surprise. "I thought we agreed I would speak for us!"

"Then t-t-tell him we're ready s-s-s-so we can g-get on with it!"

Bronwynn looked at Pelmen and shrugged—then out she went through the door.

As they trooped into the library and down through the floor, they passed the Elder, who appeared to be lost in the reading of a sizable volume. Rosha entered the pit first, then Bronwynn.

As Pelmen put his foot on the top rung of the ladder and started down after them, the little holy man spoke, his eyes never leaving the pages of his book: "I don't know why you ever thought you could do it alone in the first place."

Vicia-Heinox groaned and rolled once more onto his back. He thrashed his tail from side to side, sweeping swirls of dust high into the air. As it settled onto the expanse of the dragon's distended belly, Heinox snarled an accusation he had been repeating all morning long. "It's your fault!"

"It isn't my fault, it's your fault!" Vicia snarled back. "You ate all those diseased ones!"

"They weren't diseased, they were just underfed!"

Vicia moaned again, and whimpered, "I wish I was underfed—"

"Well, if you hadn't insisted on eating all of those fat young fools we wouldn't be in this condition!"

"But they were so tasty—"

"So you kept gulping them down. I told you then you were eating too fast!"

"You didn't help any by swallowing all the scrawny ones! Especially when there were so many volunteers."

"There you go, trying to rob me of one of the few pleasures left me—savoring the taste of a helpless, shivering human!"

The dragon rolled over onto its stomach and flapped his wings feebly. Rather, Heinox flapped the wings.

Vicia just groaned. "That's not going to help either."

"What is?" Heinox demanded.

"How should I know? We've never had a stomach-ache before!"

"We shouldn't be having this one. But you insisted—"

"They were begging me to swallow them, Heinox!" Vicia relished the memory for a moment, then added grandly, "How could I refuse them their wish?"

"Don't get started on that god business again," Heinox growled. "If I hear one more word about that I will go mad."

"You simply lack the capacity to understand spiritual things, Heinox," Vicia goaded. "I think it's because our soul resides in me."

"What soul?" Heinox spat out.

"You see? You just aren't capable of comprehending."

"I'm going to get you, Vicia," Heinox threatened. His belly burned so fiercely he could not put much inflection into his threat, but he meant it from the bottom of their shared heart.

Vicia chuckled derisively. "And how will you manage that, since it is so evident from the condition of our stomach that whatever affects me affects you as well?"

Heinox rose slowly into the air to gaze menacingly down on his counterpart. "I'm going to destroy Lamath, and all your worshippers with it. Then we'll see how much like a god you feel!"

Now Vicia rose up to face him. "Without me you aren't capable of destroying a hamlet, let alone a splendid and cultured civilization." Vicia felt any nation that had the good sense to worship him was obviously splendid and cultured.

"Perhaps not," Heinox replied, with the dragon's equivalent of a smile. "But the nation I favor is capable."

"What nation?" Vicia snapped. Heinox raised his head as high into the air as his neck would allow, and turned to gaze arrogantly to the south. Vicia understood, and snorted his reply. "Chaomonous? You would pit those feebleminded fumblers in the gold helmets against the faithful of Lamath?" Vicia cackled. "Why, less than a month ago I burned out an entire column of your little golden heroes!"

"Keep in mind, Vicia, that it works both ways," Heinox answered smugly. "You can't do a thing to Chaomonous without my help."

Vicia pondered that. "Are you suggesting that we encourage these nations to battle one another? As our champions, perhaps?"

"Why does it take you so long to catch on?" Heinox mocked. "I think it's because the brains reside in me!"

Vicia growled softly but chose to ignore the taunt. "We would encourage this war, but not participate in it?"

"I intend to participate in any way I can," Heinox snarled. "Whatever I can do to aid Chaomonous, I will do. But since I assume you'll do the same for Lamath, I rather think our efforts will cancel one another out, don't you? Or is that too big a thought for your tiny mind to swallow?"

"Would you please not mention swallowing?" Vicia groaned.

"The question is, how to get Chaomonous to attack Lamath," Heinox said to himself.

"Obviously I don't have that problem. All I need say is, 'Attack!' and my faithful will leap to obey me!"

"You don't know they'll leap to obey you. All you know is that they'll leap down your throat. Doesn't sound like a very stable sort of warrior to me."

"You just want humans to quake and tremble before you eat them."

"They taste better that way!" Heinox argued back. The dragon's attention shifted once more to his stomach, and the beast rolled around in silent misery for several minutes before Vicia spoke again.

"It occurs to me that we should learn to cooperate a little before it's too late."

"Why should I cooperate with you?" Heinox grumbled, though his stomach insisted painfully that there was at least one reason.

"What hurts me hurts you—and without my help you can't protect yourself. What happens if one of these armies should decide to attack us instead of each other?"

It didn't take long for Heinox to get the point. In spite of their aching stomach, the two heads spent the rest of the morning relearning how to focus heat—in self-defense. By the time he finished venting his hostilities on the landscape, Vicia-Heinox felt remarkably better.

Pezi sat in the straw in a corner of the dungeon, trying not to pay attention to the insults being hurled at him from down the hall. Fortunately his cousins had been imprisoned in another cell. They all blamed their predicament on him, and now they competed with one another to see who could call him the vilest name. Far and away, the victor in this contest was Faliar, the young cousin Pezi had threatened on the road a few

days before. Safely protected by two locked doors and
walls of stone, Faliar's acid tongue was free to wag its
worst.

But there were some advantages, Pezi reminded himself. At least he didn't have to suffer Faliar up close.
Besides, his other cousins were angry enough to do him
real harm; had they been imprisoned in this cell with
him, he would scarcely avoid a beating, or worse. The
dungeon of the crown of Lamath was a great improve-
ment over Flayh's. Though Pezi certainly wasn't feast-
ing, he wasn't starving either. In fact, were there a little
more food and a little less noise, Pezi thought he could
come to like the place, damp and dank though it was.

He heard footsteps in the tunnel, but he stayed in his
place on the straw. He had run to the door for nothing
too many times to believe these steps heralded his release. But he wasted no time getting to his feet when he
heard a key scraping in its lock.

Pezi gasped when he saw the contingent that had
come to remove him. These were not soldiers; they were
spectres, wraiths, beings without faces! Four figures
clad from top to bottom in blue robes stood waiting for
him, their faces hidden by veils of blue gauze.

"Come with us," said one in a funereal tone, and Pezi
gulped and backed away.

"Are you the—the executioners?" he managed to
stammer, and was surprised to hear muffled laughter
from beneath those solemn cloaks.

"No, my son. We are advisors to the High Priest of
Lamath. Our master would have words with you."

The High Priest! Flayh had instructed him to make
contact with the High Priest, but Pezi's imprisonment
had made that impossible. Now the High Priest had sent
his ghouls after Pezi! The fat merchant began to quiver
inside, wondering what this Priest would be like, and
what weird twist this adventure would take next. Pezi
decided right then that he hadn't the stomach for diplo-
macy.

"The master is waiting," another voice said ominously, and Pezi steeled himself and walked forward
into the hallway.

Pezi had been expecting the High Priest to look like

his advisors—only more so. He was hardly prepared for the youthful countenance that squinted out at him from under an ill-fitting, blue-jeweled hood. It appeared, in fact, that Naquin was as afraid of Pezi as Pezi was of Naquin.

"Welcome, Pezi!" The High Priest smiled warmly, and he motioned the chubby merchant to a chair. As Pezi sat, the four beings who had summoned him gathered in a semicircle behind him. This made the fat little man most uncomfortable, and the feeling wasn't helped any when these four were joined by five others. They seemed to be inspecting him. Pezi wanted to return their stares, but instead he smiled weakly at Naquin.

The High Priest noticed his discomfort, and a frown creased his forehead. "Shoo! Shoo away there!" Naquin said angrily, flicking his hand at his dark advisors as if they were flies on the pudding. All stepped back obediently, but Pezi remained very aware of their presence. "Just imagine they're not there," Naquin advised. "It's the only thing that helps. Now, where were we?"

Pezi cleared his throat and said, "Well, I was in the dungeon—"

"Oh, I don't mean that. I'm Naquin, High Priest of the Unified Dragonfaith. And you're Pezi, a merchant of Ognadzu."

Pezi nodded in agreement. The High Priest had everything right so far.

"And you've reported to my Lord the King that Chaomonous is mobilizing for war." Once again Pezi nodded. Naquin chuckled, pleased with himself. "You see, I know a great deal about what goes on in the palace." Naquin leaned forward and winked. "I have my advisors, you see. I realize they're strange, but they do get the job done. Besides, they're loyal to the Hood. That's, ah, this blue thing I have on my head," Naquin explained, tapping the sapphire-studded headpiece and then readjusting it self-consciously. "Hasn't been sized yet." He chuckled nervously, then sat back in his opulently stuffed chair and endeavored to relax himself. "My father died recently. I've only lately come under the Hood. Naturally, that has left me with a lot to learn.

My advisors have informed me that my father was great friends with your uncle Flayh."

"Friends?" Pezi blurted out in surprise. "With Flayh?"

"Ah, perhaps allies would be a better word. My father was a very difficult man to get along with. I never managed to."

"I never get along with Flayh either," Pezi confessed quietly, then looked over his shoulder again to see if anyone were taking notes.

"Don't worry," Naquin smiled, and he tapped his headpiece again. Pezi settled cautiously back into his seat. "We should be great friends then, shouldn't we, Pezi?"

Pezi smiled slowly, with extreme anxiety. He feared this young ruler was about to make a fool of him, but he couldn't help himself. Pezi liked to be liked.

In fact, Naquin was making a strong bid for real friendship. He was so isolated in this giant holy place, so cut off from the outside by the constant attendance of his nine wardens, that any glimpse of the world beyond the walls came like a shaft of light through the stained glass. Now he leaned forward earnestly and laid his hand on Pezi's knee. "Tell me then, friend Pezi. How is it with your uncle—and what news do you bring me?"

Pezi shifted uncomfortably, then leaned forward to meet him. "Do they have to stand there? Can't they stand across the room or something?"

"Over there!" Naquin commanded imperiously, and the nine blue-cowled figures shuffled to the wall and formed a line against it. "Now."

Pezi sought to remember what Flayh had ordered him to say. Haltingly he began, "The—ah—the King of Lamath has—ah—he's blasphemed the dragon. And—ah—he's sending his army to attack the beast. Ah—if you don't move now, to—ah—weaken the morale of the army, you'll lose your—ah—Hood." Pezi glanced nervously around at the advisors, who were whispering among themselves. That made him feel more insecure than ever, and he looked back at Naquin for some indication of the High Priest's response.

Naquin stared at him for a moment, blank-faced, then shook his head and murmured, "There was more nonsense in that one statement than I've heard from all my advisors combined since my father died—and that's a whole lot of nonsense!"

Pezi choked, but said nothing. Already he was speculating on the nature of Naquin's dungeon. Doubtless he would be spending some time there.

Naquin gazed down at the hem of his robe where it bunched heavily around his ornate sandals. "It sounds as if Flayh is at least as big a liar as my father was," he murmured, then added, "Maybe bigger." The High Priest glanced up at Pezi's white face and smiled warmly. "But apparently, Pezi, you are a terrible liar! You ought at least to be a trifle creative with the general outline your uncle gives you, or you could get into a lot of trouble. You see, the King is anything but a dragon blasphemer. In fact, the old man's gone so holy on us he's wishing he could get himself eaten by the beast!"

"Oh, I knew that," Pezi blurted out. He really knew of nothing better to say.

Naquin examined him curiously. "Then why all this other foolishness?"

Pezi shrugged sheepishly. "That's—ah—just what my uncle told me to say."

Naquin was amazed. Far from being annoyed with Pezi, he felt positively pleased. Here was living proof that he was not the only incompetent in a position of responsibility. What he needed to learn, Naquin decided, was how to gather the Pezis of the world around him and manipulate them to insure his continued position. Perhaps he could keep this Hood yet.

"Thank you, Pezi, for your honesty. I appreciate that in a man. I'm going to need your help in enacting a plan I think will benefit both your house and myself." Naquin leaned forward and spoke so softly that only Pezi could hear. "The King wishes to be consumed by the dragon in an act of ultimate devotion. How could the High Priest be any more loyal than to help the King get his wish?" Naquin's smile curled into a sneer, and Pezi's face now twisted to mirror Naquin's expression back at him.

"Yes—how could he be more loyal?" Pezi agreed.

Naquin sat back on his throne and folded his hands on his lap. "Yes, Pezi," he affirmed, "you and I are going to be great friends."

Bronwynn pored earnestly over the characters in the flickering firelight. So hard did she squint, so deep were the furrows of concentration plowed into her forehead, that her delicate eyebrows nearly touched over the bridge of her nose. She read out loud, her voice now halting as she unraveled skeins of words woven into complicated passages, then skipping as she raced through fragments easily understood. Pelmen nodded frequently, mouthing the words along with her and helping her when she stumbled. Rosha sat against the wall, his arms locked around the one knee he had drawn to his chin, and leaned his head against the stone. It was hard to tell whether he was visualizing the passages as Bronwynn read them, or daydreaming.

"It's easy, Rosha," Bronwynn exclaimed. "It's in our tongue, only the runes are different." Rosha grunted to prove he was awake, and the girl raced on, excited. "Perhaps it is a bit difficult at first—the characters are so oddly shaped—but it doesn't take long to learn. Why don't you try it?"

Rosha opened one eyelid and looked at her, then shook his head and leaned against the wall once more.

"When he chooses to learn there will be time," Pelmen told her. Then he pointed to the place where he wanted her to begin again.

"But why is it in our speech?" Bronwynn asked.

"Why w-w-wouldn't it b-be?" Rosha challenged her.

"There are other lands, Rosha, and many use tongues other than ours—" The girl turned again to Pelmen. "But I don't understand why, if these people used our speech, they made use of these strangely shaped runes."

"I think the fathers of all our lands used these same characters in the time long past. I think they chose deliberately to change them, when the one land was divided into three."

Rosha sat up at that. Bronwynn looked puzzled. Both waited for Pelmen to explain.

"Have you never thought it strange," he began, "that though the three lands hold one another in ridicule, still the speech is the same wherever in the three lands you may travel?"

"The s-s-speech is not the s-same," Rosha muttered. "I can barely under-s-stand the b-b-brothers."

"Yes, the dialects differ," Pelmen agreed, "but you *can* understand. Certain words may sound strange on the lips of the brothers, but their meanings stay the same, whether here or on the streets of the High City, or on the plains of southern Chaomonous."

"Aren't the merchants responsible for that?" Bronwynn asked thoughtfully.

"Responsible for preserving the common speech, yes—very possibly responsible for our present alphabet as well, after these runes disappeared. But could merchant houses influence any of our lands to adopt this tongue on the basis of trade alone?"

"But if the three lands were once united, why would they choose to divide?" Bronwynn wondered.

"P-p-perhaps they d-didn't choose," Rosha muttered. "P-perhaps it was chosen for them."

"It was both chosen for them and they chose, Rosha. Few changes that great occur from a single cause. Many factors worked on our fathers of old to destroy the one land. All are described in that book Bronwynn holds."

"Please, Pelmen, tell us! It's so much easier to hear you explain it than to try to read it all."

Pelmen nodded, then reached out to take the book from her and seated himself on the stone shelf. Bronwynn scooted the stool away to give him room. Then she leaned against the wall beside Rosha. The small cell seemed more so with all three of them crammed inside, but to Pelmen it seemed the safest place to pursue their study.

He placed the lamp to one side, closed his eyes, and began. "It's hard to condense factors without making generalizations, but the breaking of the one land resulted from our fathers' inability to integrate all they discovered in the one land's last age. There were so many people then—many more than live today—and so much happened so fast. Various groups of men began to cluster around ideas they held in common. There were those who saw the powers of the air as inanimate forces that could be controlled by physical means. They built devices to harness the powers and hold them in tension. Others viewed these powers as spirits of the wind and fire, that could only be controlled by magic. These were the ancient powershapers, who scoffed at using tools to bend the powers. Still others clustered around various leaders, men who taught that the powers aided only those who worshipped them. None of these groups could live with the others.

"Too much took place to sketch here—that's why I want you to read the book, my Lady—but it seems that man is foolish enough to believe that if he can hurt another man sufficiently, that other man will come to agree with him."

"There was war?" Bronwynn asked.

"Many wars, Bronwynn. Certain men of great authority devised a plan that would separate these warring factions from one another, hoping that with separation would come peace. It was never their intention that this be permanent—they only wished to keep men away from one another's throats until the race learned to integrate all these parts of its personality. Their plan succeeded beyond their expectations—and well beyond their wishes as well. The capital city of the one land disappeared."

"Where was it?" Bronwynn asked excitedly.

"N-ngandib-Mar? On the high p-plateau?" Rosha suggested.

"I bet it was somewhere in Chaomonous," said the girl.

"I've never found it," Pelmen replied quietly. "It disappeared, along with its history, its art—and its writing. Except for the book," he added, patting the volume absently.

"What was their plan? Does it say?"

Pelmen opened the heavy codex, flipped through it until he found the page he wanted, and passed it back to the girl. "Read there."

Once again Bronwynn knitted her brows together and read: *"We have succeeded in crafting the beast through our unified efforts. The power of the subject can only be guessed, but it seems clear from our experiments that it will be fully capable of dominating man's history for at least a short period—long enough, perhaps, for our race to come of age."* Bronwynn glanced up at Pelmen, wide-eyed. "What beast?" she asked. He motioned to the page, and she read: *"We have taught him the rudiments of common speech, and given him a name. From this point forward we will attempt to increase the natural hostility of the beast with calculated cruelty. When we at last unleash Vicia-Heinox on the world, we trust he will be enough of a challenge to mankind's existence that dealing with him will demand the best energies of all cooperating factions."* Bronwynn stopped incredulously. "They *made* the dragon?"

"And the dragon unmade them." Pelmen stood, his head bumping the low ceiling, and stretched his arms before him. "How long it's been since those words were written, I've no idea. This, though, is the section of most concern to me." Pelmen leaned over and flipped through the pages once again. He read upside down, for the book lay in Bronwynn's lap, but at last he found his place, and pointed.

The young lady cleared her throat and read: *"The thing is done. It cannot be undone now. But one will come, the Power assures us, who will set things right again. You will know that one has come when the dragon is divided."* Bronwynn bit her lip thoughtfully, then looked up at Pelmen. "The dragon is divided now." Pelmen nodded. "Then is this speaking of you?"

Pelmen sighed. "It appears so."

Every day, two or three seekers would come to the monastery to inquire if there was a new prophet in the land. Pelmen met with each one, but volunteered nothing more than he was asked. If one had an illness that needed curing he cured it. If there was some quarrel that needed arbitration, he judged it. He did not explain where his power originated, nor did anyone need to ask. The prophetic tradition in Lamath was a long one.

When there was a prophet available to give counsel or aid, the people of the land sought him out. Pelmen asked only one thing of these whose lives he touched— that they not take it upon themselves to proclaim his presence publicly. When the time was right, he assured them, he would do it himself. Most seekers willingly abided by this condition, for until he became known, a prophet was a local preserve, a natural resource which need not be shared. But there were a few who could not contain their wonder. A new prophet had come, and they were witnesses to it! So the news continued to spread, and each day seekers arrived from farther away.

Occasionally he was asked to travel. Wherever he went he was always accompanied by an oddly matched pair of initiates. One was fair and slight and seemed so delicate in his movements the seekers deemed him effeminate. The other hid broad shoulders under the folds of his robe, and more. A telltale billowing of his gown at the hip suggested that beneath it he wore a sword. This was so contrary to the calling of an initiate that many who saw that sword-shaped bulge denied to themselves they had seen it. But it was noised around that while the Prophet himself seemed holy enough, the two with him were somewhat unusual.

The three rode one afternoon to the home of a local aristocrat, ostensibly for the purpose of blessing his crops. The wealthy farmer's true motive was to get a look at this miracle worker who had so unexpectedly appeared in his own back yard. He was leery of the presence of a prophet in his neighborhood, for Lamathian prophets had always been notorious for favoring the poor over the rich. But as a local leader he had a responsibility at least to meet the man. Perhaps the fellow could be of some practical financial value.

The hot, muggy weather had held Lamath in its grip for days, but this looked like the day it might change. Clouds had moved into the region the night before, and now they piled one atop the other into charcoal-colored towers that threatened a violent storm. Rosha's eyes were on these storm clouds as the farmer led them across his acreage, and he turned to mutter his suspicions to Bronwynn.

"If there was any danger, Pelmen would surely warn us," she whispered back.

"S-such c-c-confidence may p-prove excessive," Rosha warned her, but she was no longer listening. Even when the wind picked up to the point that it was wrapping their robes tightly around their legs, and Rosha had to turn his back on the others to keep his greatsword from showing up in bold relief, Bronwynn still would not speak with him about it.

They had completed the tour and turned to ride back to the landowner's modest palace when a shout went up from among the entourage. Panicked riders spurred their horses around those who led the group, and raced one another to the main gate. Pelmen turned in his saddle to look backward.

Rosha saw the blood drain from the Prophet's face, and watched as he dug his heel into the flank of Minaliss and jerked forward. There was no mistaking the fear in Pelmen's eyes. Rosha shouted to Bronwynn to ride as he whipped his own mount into action, then he too swiveled his head to peer up into the black sky behind him.

A dark, living presence as tall as the heavens stalked the earth behind them. It was as if the giant clouds, black with rage, had chosen to chase them down, and now leapt from point to point along the ground on a single colossal whirling leg. Each place that funnel-shaped foot touched down, trees and fences were torn asunder. Yet the presence within the wind took no interest in these inanimate playthings, tracking instead the tiny creations that fled its charge on horseback. Rosha whipped his horse again, his blood pounding as he urged his mount to an ever faster pace. When he glanced back again the tornado had hopped a mile to the south, leaving a once proud silo littered along the ground behind. Then it was again pursuing them, and Rosha saw clearly that he would never outrun it. Yet he raced onward past Pelmen, who sat astride a strangely calm Minaliss, facing into the oncoming cloud.

"You'll be killed!" Rosha screamed, the thought so clear and the need so immediate his lips would permit no stutter. Then he was past, his horse flying forward so quickly that he feared to try to stop it. Instead he dropped down to cling to the horse's neck, and clinched the beast's flanks between his knees with all the strength left to him in the wake of his fear. The wind roared in his ears, and he realized his scream could not have been heard. He'd seen enough in that brief glimpse to know that Pelmen's face was still as white as ground flour— the fear still clutched him. Why, then, did he stand his ground?

Bronwynn loomed up before Rosha, and he saw she too had turned her horse back toward the wind. As he passed her, Rosha leaned out to reach for her reins to turn her, but his reach fell short and he was forced at last to tighten up on his own steed to try to turn her slowly. Over the roar, he heard Bronwynn shouting at him.

"Look, Rosha! Look!" But Rosha could not look until he had controlled his mount and turned her around. Still trembling, he cast a quick glance up at the black funnel, then sat up straight to search the horizon for it. He didn't see it. The whirling wind was gone.

Reality returned slowly. The world gradually came back into focus. Rosha shook his head to clear it, and realized that speech was audible once more. Bronwynn was shouting in his ear.

"Did you see him? Did you see? He stood his ground in the face of the storm and the winds divided around him! Rosha, Pelmen destroyed the storm!" As she shouted she rode toward that figure on horseback who still stood quietly in the roadway. Rosha patted his horse, and thanked her quietly as he had seen Pelmen do, and urged her back toward the mounted Prophet.

"You've done it, Pelmen!" Bronwynn shouted as she reached him. "You've controlled the storm."

Rosha reined his horse in to face the Prophet, and murmured, "Are y-y-you all right?"

Pelmen looked up, his face still ashen. "Yes."

"You've controlled the whirlwind!" Bronwynn repeated loudly. Rosha noticed Pelmen was shaking.

"No . . . not I," the Prophet said. His voice was somewhere between his lungs and his throat. "The Power . . ." He struggled to get it out.

"Yes, but you mediated the Power," Bronwynn began.

Abruptly the Prophet's voice returned, and he cut her off. "No!" Pelmen's eyes were sharp again, Rosha noted with relief, and the Prophet's attention came again into the present. "I did not mediate it," Pelmen explained. "I stood in the wind's pathway expecting to lose myself inside it. I raised no hand against it. The Power destroyed the wind, Bronwynn. For its own reasons the Power has preserved me."

Bronwynn stared at him in awe. The religious sense within her, stifled in her childhood, experienced a renascence of life. Bronwynn was becoming a believer.

Rosha sat idly in his saddle, waiting for some indication of what to do next. His father's best friend—and his own teacher—had just survived certain death in the face of cyclone winds. He felt no sense of awe. He only felt an urgency to move on to the safety of the manor. This storm had passed them by. There was no certainty the next would.

❧ Chapter Ten ❧

ADMON FAYE was not so foolish as to ride his chartered craft all the way into the harbor of Lamath. The river between the capital and the sea was lined with little fishing villages, and each village had its own businesses that catered to the needs of the sailor. Some miles east of the city Admon Faye paid the pilot the last of his fare, and asked to be put ashore. He made his way into one of these establishments, a dark little beer hall filled with the smells of brew and spices. His eyes adjusted quickly to the dim interior—indeed, he preferred the darkness to the day—and he quickly found an empty booth to occupy. His face discouraged any who might offer to keep him company. He sipped his brew in silence—and listened. After a time he had a fair idea of where the information he needed could be purchased, and he joined himself to a pair of drunken sailors.

They were rowdy men, that was clear to all. But they were daylight dwellers, and they lacked guile. After their initial shock at the incongruous smile on this stranger's hideous face, they shared with him all he needed to know—and more.

"Any unusual doings?" he asked, his voice taking on that peculiar edge common to Lamath, and especially to Lamathian sailors.

"They're all unusual in these times," the blond sailor grunted, gazing stupidly into his beer. "No peace for a sailing man. They all want to make you navy."

"Navy, yes," the other man agreed, drunkenly stabbing a finger into the air for emphasis. "This war, it is. Always the wars. Do I look like a fighter?" he asked, grabbing his tunic and looking imploringly at the ugly stranger. The blond found something hilarious in this, and convulsed onto the bar top in a spasm of giggling.

"I mean the supernatural." Admon Faye went on grinding his teeth behind his phony smile.

"You mean religion?"

"That, or magic."

"Quit there!" the dark-haired sailor yelled at his drunken friend, and he shoved him off the bar and onto the floor. "What was that? Magic?"

"Magic," Admon Faye repeated, his cold eyes meeting the sailor's firmly.

"Where you from?" the sailor muttered.

"Does it matter?" Admon Faye asked quietly, shoving several pieces of gold into the sailor's hand without any audible clink. The seaman's grip tightened around the coins, and he shook his head slowly from side to side.

"Any magic then, my friend?" the slave trader asked, eyebrows raised inquiringly.

"No magic in Lamath," the sailor whispered. "You show by that you don't belong, despite your accent. But there is religion, now, and plenty of it, and wonders worked regular these days."

"Where?"

"Seventy miles east of the capital, about. Ask after the Priestess, they'll all know where. Though why you should want to go . . ." He didn't finish his sentence, for there was no one to finish it to. In three long strides Admon Faye was out the door and gone.

He searched throughout the village for a horse, but found none available. He walked the two miles to the next village only to find the same result.

"All the horses are gone for the army," one man told him. "If you want one, you'll have to join the army, too."

The slaver scoffed at that, and walked another three miles toward the capital. When he discovered the man had spoken the truth, he didn't hesitate. Late that afternoon, Admon Faye, resplendent in newly woven Lamathian blue, sat astride a pretty white pony that had been issued to him by the Department of Defense and Expansion. Still later, the new uniform was stuffed into his handbag, and pony and rider rode swiftly through the night. For the first time in many days, Admon Faye felt at home.

From the walls of Chaomonous, the column looked like a golden snake that slithered ever northward to Lamath and to war. It was not as large as Talith had hoped, but forty-seven thousand was still a mighty fighting force, and the King would not allow this small disappointment to rob him of his sense of achievement. He rode now at the head of the column, but he frequently checked behind to see that his litter was keeping up. He wasn't about to let this conquering-hero business deprive him of the simple human comforts.

With him rode Generals Joss and Rolan-Keshi, the latter still chafing at being robbed of the command, the former wishing he had a late report on events inside the palace. Also traveling with them was young Tahli-Damen, dressed in his usual purple and red—he was the only man in the column not clothed in the colors of the King. He felt very out of place in this company.

Jagd had carefully outlined for Tahli-Damen the plan laid for Talith's betrayal, and had assured him that success in this enterprise would thrust Tahli-Damen into the highest echelon of merchant leadership. There was only one problem to all this, Tahli-Damen reflected. He would feel very fortunate if he survived.

On the walls of the Crown Palace of Chaomonous, other orders were being issued—orders every bit as treacherous as those Tahli-Damen labored to hide. Kherda clung to a stone abutment and watched in amazement as the column wound farther and farther north, passing around a stand of mountains and out of sight. He was trembling again, but no longer from fear. Now he shook with excitement. The day had come! He had succeeded in dispatching Talith to war without his plot being uncovered. He heard Ligne clicking off orders behind him, but he paid no attention. His job was done. Now he could rest.

He felt no elation as he heard the clatter of metal-shod feet on the cobblestones below him and in the hallways within. He felt no remorse as he heard shouts of alarm and cries of distress and pain. He had orchestrated this takeover of Talith's palace—now he listened as someone else conducted it, knowing in advance when new sounds would be added, listening for and hearing new clashes begin on cue. He clung to the cool stone, leaning his cheek against it and waiting for word that the coup had been successful, and that Ligne was in control of the palace.

Ligne stalked through the halls, her eyes flashing a warning to anyone who might accost her. For months she had been the Queen in effect—now she was the Queen in fact, and well known to each of the combatants who struggled in the corridor. No one bothered her as she pushed with purposeful stride past friend and foe alike. Bodies fell to her right and left, and there were cries of disbelief and screams of horror on every side, but she paid them no mind as she glided, pantherlike, to the door of her rival's apartment, and slammed it open.

"Welcome, Ligne dear. I was expecting you." Latithia's tone was light and trivial, as if the noise of the battle beyond the wall had nothing to do with her. Ligne glanced around at the carnage to assure herself that her forces were firmly in charge, then stepped into the room and closed the door behind her.

"You were expecting me? Really?" She smiled sweetly, taking her cue from Latithia.

"Of course I was." Latithia smiled back. "Won't you have some tea?" The deposed Queen poured Ligne a cup of the steaming liquid, and set it on the table. Ligne slipped into the offered chair, and fingered the rim of the cup.

"You surprise me, Latithia. I had expected tears, or pleas—you seem determined to take the fun out of this for me."

"I'm so pleased to have disappointed you," Latithia replied brightly. "I have always felt it becomes a lady of position to be able to cope with the inevitable."

"And my victory was inevitable," Ligne gloated.

"No. My husband's defeat was." Latithia rose gracefully, carrying her teacup in both hands. "Anyone could have overthrown him. He was a rotting apple, ripe for the plucking."

"You speak of him in the past tense, dear. Have you already consigned him to the grave?"

"Hmm?" Latithia asked, sipping her tea. "Oh no. Not him. Myself."

"You wrong me," Ligne protested unconvincingly. "I have no interest in taking your life."

"Yet." Latithia smiled. "That would be a bit much right now, wouldn't it? After all, you'll need to convince the peasants that your cause is just, and that your rule will be fair. Once your reign is secure, there will be plenty of time to behead the old Queen—" Latithia stopped, and pointed to Ligne's cup. "You haven't touched your tea."

"I don't intend to," Ligne snorted.

Latithia paused for a moment. She seemed to be listening at last to the clash of arms in the hallway. The noise was receding, as Ligne's trained insurgents swept away the last resistance of Talith's paltry guard. Just that morning, the King had reversed Joss' order to station more men in the palace. With difficulty, Latithia refocused her eyes on Ligne, and murmured, "Pity—I had hoped to take you with me." Then she clutched her stomach, squinting at the sudden pain, and toppled to the parquet floor.

Poison. Ligne pushed her own cup away with one finger, and softly chided, "I wish you hadn't done that. I was going to have such fun with you." Then she left the room as swiftly as she had come, ignoring the dying woman's groans.

She climbed to the battlements where Kherda waited, and announced, "It's done." Kherda turned to look at her. The woman's face was flushed, as if she'd come fresh from the bed of her lover.

Kherda nodded. He felt no different, now that the thing was done. The sky had not fallen. The ground had not opened up to swallow him. He had betrayed and overthrown his own King—yet he survived. He made his way to the reassuring confines of his familiar apartments. As the golden city fell, the man who had planned its conquest enjoyed the soundest sleep he had known in months.

Pelmen had planned to make a public announcement of his prophethood. That was the common practice, and he felt this continuity with Lamathian tradition might help to soften the blow of his unorthodox teachings. The experience of the whirlwind, however, made any public announcement unnecessary. Those who had witnessed it from the manor departed in every direction the moment the storm abated, and there was only one subject on their lips. A new Prophet had come to Lamath.

Everywhere the announcement was made it met the same response: "What will the Priestess say to this?" Within days, the news had made its way to Serphila, searching out new ears the way tree roots search for water—in order to continue to live. By the time the tale was told in the village, the story had grown like spring grass after the rain.

"A Prophet has come to Lamath! He wears no symbol, and they say he is a Divisionist, but he has power over nature and can bend the world to his will. He cut a tornado in half with a snap of his fingers! He laughed and stars fell from the sky. He cannot pass a burial place without bodies rising to follow him! No, I'm not

lying! It means that the Lord Dragon knows Chaomonous threatens us, and has sent us a Prophet as a sign!"

Those closest to Serphimera could scarcely contain
themselves when they heard the news. It was not that
they believed it. Instinctively they feared it. But the
Priestess certainly needed to hear. They raced one another to tell her, and found her tending the garden that
had sprouted in the field surrounding the crater made
by the dragon.

"Stay off the peas," she shouted to them as they
picked their way toward her.

"A Prophet has come to Lamath!" one shouted and
the others chimed in with their echoes. Serphimera ab-
sorbed the news with little more reaction than a blink of
the eyes, and held up her hands for silence.

"The Lord Dragon's garden is not the place for such
a tale. Let's make our way to the chapel."

There was much excitement and noise in the chapel
that afternoon. The Priestess had a vision of a Prophet
in blue being torn in two by the dragon. They were
powerful things, Serphimera's visions. Usually they
came true.

Pelmen was speaking quietly to Bronwynn and
Rosha, explaining a passage of extreme complexity,
when someone cleared his throat beyond the entry hole.

"Yes, my father?" Pelmen called through the wall.
He had heard that sound many times before, usually
when his teacher had wished to call him back from
vague speculations to the realities of the lesson at hand.

This summons proved to have some of that same
quality, as Pelmen discovered after he made the transit
on his stomach and stood beside the toothless little man.
"I hate to disturb your study again," the Elder began,
but his sardonic smile belied his words. "However,
there is a matter I felt you needed to be aware of. Your
fame has reached the ears of the Priestess of the dragon.
The lady is on the way here, it appears, and I was wondering. Do you think you could meet her somewhere
along the way? It would do none of us any good if she
were to discover exactly where you stay."

The old man loved Pelmen and he supported the new

Prophet's mission with the utmost enthusiasm. But he also loved the other brothers. Was it fair, he wondered, to penalize them and stifle their spiritual progress for this one, when there was no need even to involve them?

Pelmen nodded curtly. While it was too late to keep this place hidden, he too saw wisdom in disassociating himself from the monastery. "Rosha! Bronwynn! Come quickly." As the two young people slid noisily out of the chamber, Pelmen turned to the Elder and put his hands on the man's shoulders. "You know that you may store your library here if you wish . . ."

"What?" the little man said, his head jerking. "Why should the bears want to read my books? I certainly wouldn't be reading them down here!" Then the bald-headed scholar joined himself to Rosha as they all walked back to the ladder. The lad was the only one who had the good sense to carry a sword into this cavern.

Central Lamath was dotted with small farming communities, where life was slow and travel infrequent. How then did news travel so quickly? Without aid of crier or public proclamation, everyone seemed to know everything that was going on anywhere locally. Before Pelmen knew, before Serphimera knew, the locals had calculated exactly where their meeting would take place, and began to gather there to wait for the event.

"Give them plenty of room," a self-appointed crowd manager was yelling as he pushed groups of seated peasants into an ever-widening circle. "There'll be wonders and signs aplenty when these two meet, and we'll all want to be able to see."

Grudgingly people responded, outwardly complaining but inwardly glad that someone had assumed the responsibility. Behind the crowds petty merchants had set up tables, and now displayed their wares. Everywhere there were groups of young boys, and so quickly did these gangs run from one place to the other that there seemed to be twice as many groups as there actually were. In the absence of professional jugglers and acrobats, amateurs entertained the crowds. This was a spontaneous carnival, all realized, and since such events were rare, everyone made the most of the occasion.

"What is g-g-going on?" Rosha asked as they rode within sight of the growing throng.

"Looks like a fair," Bronwynn said matter-of-factly. "Can we ride around it?"

Pelmen felt an irresponsible quickening in his pulse rate, and fought to calm it. He was, after all, a player—or had been—and the excitement and noise of the crowd reawoke strange impulses within him. "We would disappoint them greatly, Bronwynn. From the looks on these faces, I believe we are the main act—or half of it." He referred to a group of boys who hid in the bushes beside the road. As the three riders passed, they would bolt from their cover and sprint ahead to hide in still more bushes farther along the way. Finally one ran all the way to the crowd, and from the sudden roar of approval Pelmen knew his arrival had been announced. "Shall we wait until the Priestess arrives before we enter the arena?" he asked mockingly. Bronwynn gave him a puzzled look, and they rode on.

A chill shook Pelmen a few moments later, when there was another great shout from the crowd and he realized that it was not for him but for Serphimera. His stomach began to knot up with tension. Try as he might, he could not stifle the self-doubt that sprang unbidden to his mind. He glanced over at Bronwynn and drew some reassurance from the expression on her face. She did not question that she rode beside the Prophet foretold in the days of the breaking of the one land. Bronwynn had no doubts at all.

But surely even she was affected by the sight of that surging flood of blue-gowned humanity that quickly filled up the hard-won space in the center of the giant circle. This army of believers had accompanied their Priestess, and they proudly took their places in front of the local peasants. As Pelmen dismounted from his horse and walked across the opening toward the lady, the air was filled with complaints and curses and the sounds of petty scuffles. There was such confusion that most of the assembled crowd missed the first few ex-

changes between the Prophet who had split the wind,
and the Priestess who had captivated even the King.

Bronwynn and Rosha flanked Pelmen as he walked
forward, Rosha watching the crowd of blue-robed figures menacingly, Bronwynn focusing intently on Serphimera and mentally listing all the flaws she could find in
the woman's storied beauty. There were not many. This
fact made Bronwynn frown.

Serphimera waited demurely for Pelmen to reach her,
then her lips parted in a coy smile. "I have heard much
of you, Prophet."

"And I of you, my Lady," Pelmen replied quietly.

"I am the Priestess Serphimera," she announced, her
voice loud enough to signal that she wanted silence
from the crowd. The people settled down to listen.

"So I have been told," Pelmen said, again quietly.
His voice had long been trained to project to all parts of
a vast theater. But he didn't use that booming voice
now, for he had chosen not to play to the crowd. This
lady he faced attracted him, and he sought behind her
sparkling eyes for the woman at the heart of the Priestess. Perhaps she had come to speak to the crowds. Pelmen was determined to speak with her alone.

"They tell me you do mighty wonders." She smiled,
arching an eyebrow in inquiry. "Is that true?"

"The Power works," Pelmen muttered. "Not I."

"I do no such signs," she proclaimed, walking away
from him and then turning back to look. She had widened the space between them to force him to raise his
voice. "However, I am frequently credited with mira-
cles. It seems the Lord Dragon has richly blessed Lamath in these days." She gazed at him, hungry to hear
his reaction.

Pelmen closed the gap between them again, a move
she had not expected. "It is not the doings of the
dragon, my Lady," he murmured. "It is the blessing of
the Power."

Serphimera laughed nervously, sharply, and stepped
away again. "What power do you speak of? There is no
power save that which issues from the Lord Dragon!"

"It is the Power that empowers me, my lady," Pelmen responded, again closing the space between them.

Then he whispered with intensity, "There is nothing to this worship of the dragon. You need to understand that."

Serphimera's mouth fell open in shock; then she screamed in her loudest voice, "I have a word on you! The Lord Dragon has told me you are against him! I hear now from you that it is true!" The crowd responded with gasps of surprise, and Pelmen was forced finally to play to them.

"When have you spoken with the dragon?" he demanded loudly.

"I have never spoken with the Lord Dragon. It is always he who speaks through me!"

"I have spoken with the dragon, face to face!" Pelmen added another "to face" in his mind, remembering that strange conversation as he gave the crowd time to react. "And I have news that all Lamath needs to hear." The crowd responded with silence. Pelmen took a deep breath. "The dragon is divided!"

Scarcely could a more inflammatory phrase be uttered in Lamath. The crowd was of mixed conviction; sprinkled through it was a liberal quantity of Divisionists. These now leapt to their feet crying, "Yes!" Pelmen's sentence was a watchword of their faith. Divisionists believed that while it was obvious that the Lord Dragon was only one, he needed to be viewed as being of a double personality, one good and one bad. This explained the presence of evil in the world without slipping into heresies of dualism.

"No!" cried out the orthodox Coalescents in the assembly, who believed the dragon could not be viewed as either one or two but had to be viewed as a coalescence of both one *and* two. Thus the universe was held in tension. These were far in the majority, and the meeting would swiftly have resulted in a hundred different fistfights had not Pelmen summoned all the reserves in that powerfully trained voice and bellowed, "Sit down!"

The words came like a thunderclap—so loud in fact that Pelmen was even a bit surprised himself. He glanced over at Serphimera. The woman's face was purple with rage. She was speechless at this heresy.

There was no turning back now, Pelmen reasoned.

He would add to his heresy a heavy helping of blasphemy. "When I say the dragon is divided I say not that the Lord is in two parts. I say that the *dragon* is in two parts, and that he battles with himself! And I say that the dragon is not the Lord!"

He had violated the basic tenet of the Dragonfaith. Theologically, Pelmen had cut his own throat. The cries and curses and shouts that greeted his declaration gave warning that there were many in the crowd who would be pleased to slit his windpipe physically, as well.

"Let me save the Lord this trouble!" one burly, blue-robed figure shouted as he leapt forward, arms outstretched to grab Pelmen by the throat and throttle him where he stood. But the cultist was met in midair by Rosha. As the man hit the ground, Rosha was jerking up his own blue gown and pulling out his blade.

"Hold!" he shouted, sword ready to thrust toward any quarter. Would-be attackers jumped back, and Rosha pointed the tip at the burly man's face and stammered, "P-p-perhaps you had b-best g-get back." The man looked up into the young man's face, confused and emboldened by the stutter. But there was no mistaking the intent of the youth's eyes. The fellow scooped his robes up around his knees and slipped back into the crowd.

"Yes, hold!" Serphimera cried, sweeping one arm dramatically over her head and drawing all eyes again to her. "For I have had a vision of this Prophet. I know his end!"

The crowd gave a great roar of approval, and then settled back to listen to the Priestess pronounce doom upon this charlatan. Pelmen turned to gaze at the woman, whose eyes now were as hard as emerald gemstones and just as shockingly green.

"I have seen you, Prophet!" she cried. "And I know your death! In a vision, in a dream, the Lord Dragon revealed to me the act to seal your life. You will battle him, and you will fail, and you who scorn the Lord and profane that robe you wear, you he will tear in twain!"

Pelmen felt dazed. The roaring of the crowd around him, so common and so manageable when he was but a player, now robbed him of his senses and very nearly drowned him. He could see all about him the snarling faces of the faithful, and beyond them the laughing features of those peasants who had cheered him. But he saw behind the sneers and laughter to a people without hope—people who sensed the earth was changing but could not comprehend it—people who needed something to believe in so much that they believed in death. And he saw that indeed the dragon did hold them, that it was no psychological phenomenon without basis in fact. The existence of the beast had mesmerized them; his double visage had stared at them from too many street corners and chapel alcoves for them to disregard him. The bond could not be broken from this side, for the dragon was more powerful than he. The bondage could only be broken at its source—in the act of the dragon's death. Perhaps Serphimera was still speaking to him—perhaps she was not, was waiting, rather, for his reply. Whatever the case, he spoke, not to the crowd, too tradition-bound to hear, but to Serphimera, who spoke with spirits.

"Why, my Lady, why?" he said, moving toward her with upraised palms. A troop of loyal believers closed the gap around her, to keep her safe from harm.

"I do not doubt that you must encourage your initiates to bear arms!" she shouted. "Clearly, you are beyond the care and protection of the Lord Dragon!"

Still he walked toward her, surprising those who cordoned her off from him, reaching over their heads to try to touch her, to make her see. "Serphimera," he whispered to her alone, "why believe only in yourself? What right do you have to share visions, visions of others' ends? I have a book, my Lady, in ancient script, that tells me what I know. *That* I can believe. My Lady, can't you understand? What use are visions without the knowledge? What use the heart without the head?"

She backed away from him, her eyes wide, stepping on the feet and hems of those who endeavored to protect her. They moved along with her as one tripping, stumbling body, too crammed together to move as individuals, treading on one another's toes. Abruptly she turned her back on him, and raised her arm high above her head. No longer looking, no longer caring, she pronounced that this new Prophet was dead. Then she pushed her way forward and out onto the road, her midnight-blue gown billowing behind her as she lengthened her stride and began walking east.

The meeting was at an end. Many ran beside the blue tide that surged onto the road behind Serphimera, while others pointed at Pelmen and his friends and laughed or sneered or cursed him. Rosha still held his sword unsheathed, one arm wrapped tightly around Bronwynn. Pelmen stood watching a long, long time, then dropped his head on his chest and sighed. When he looked back at his two young followers, they could see his eyes were moist and red.

"Let's go, then," he said. Without another word the three returned to their horses.

The dragon did nothing as the golden column climbed up the steep and rocky road from the south. Some may have taken that as an encouraging sign, but not Tahli-Damen. He had never known the dragon to sit so quietly. He wished to himself he were still a lowly courier in Jagd's castle.

As the head of the column moved within speaking distance, Joss issued the order to stop. It was quickly obeyed by the soldiers in the forefront. As far as they were concerned, it had come none too soon. They had been shortening their strides at every step for the last half-hour.

Still the dragon did nothing. Its only movement was the casual flicking of its monstrous, reptilian tail.

Talith sat in his litter, a quarter of a mile down the hill from the front of the column. Tahli-Damen waited for him to conclude his conversation with Rolan-Keshi.

"Then where would our ships be right now?" he was asking.

"Assuming the weather is good, they should be passing the Border Straits today, but—"

"What do you mean, if the weather's good? There isn't a cloud in the sky!"

"Not here, my Lord." Rolan-Keshi sighed. "But there could be grievous storms at sea—"

"I am not going to listen to such negative thinking

from one of my chief generals!" Talith snapped. "Get to the front and send Joss back to me." Rolan-Keshi jabbed his heels angrily into his horse's flanks, and started up the hill. Talith turned to Tahli-Damen. "And what do you want, merchant?"

"My Lord, the dragon will not wait all day—"

"Why won't he? He has waited thus far."

"Yes, he has, my Lord, but—"

"I am the King, Tahli-Damen. Kings do not cater to the time schedules of anyone save themselves."

"But, my Lord—"

"I have tolerated your unsought advice ever since we left the palace, merchant, but I have grown tired of your insistence that you are the only one who knows how to deal with this dragon. Now, I will treat with Vicia-Heinox—through you, of course—whenever I deem it—" Talith's eyes caught sight of something beyond Tahli-Damen's shoulders, and his words froze on his lips. The young merchant understood immediately, even before he heard the leathery flapping above him. Instinctively he ducked, and fell off his horse in the process.

King Talith was greeted by the sight of one dragon head staring in at him from the left-hand side of the litter, and another peering at him from the right. He finally found his voice. "Tahli-Damen?" he asked quietly. "Tahli-Damen, would you please come talk to this dragon?" The two heads moved in for a closer look, and Talith scooted down, attempting to hide under the cushions. "Tahli-Damen? Are you down there?" he called, peeking over the edge of the litter.

"So this is the mighty King of Chaomonous," Vicia snorted.

"I believe so," Heinox replied uncertainly. Then addressing Talith, he asked, "You are the King, aren't you?"

Talith gulped. "Yes," he squeaked.

"Yes, he is," Heinox told Vicia.

Vicia moved in even closer, and murmured, "Well, you may tell your precious King that if he marches one step closer to Lamath, I will swallow him alive!"

Talith suddenly had a very existential appreciation

for all of those tales of terror related to him by men who had spoken with the dragon. He trembled.

"You mustn't believe him," Heinox said matter-of-factly.

"I—you—I—ah—I mustn't?" Talith stammered.

"You mustn't," Heinox replied patiently. In all his dealings with human Kings the dragon had never been too impressed. Heinox had not been expecting much from this King, and Talith certainly didn't disappoint him. "You see," Heinox continued pleasantly, "he may threaten a great deal, but he can't really do anything to you unless I let him."

"Really?" Talith said eagerly. He was still nervous, of course, but this was encouraging news.

"Not exactly so," Vicia corrected. "It's true that I can't do anything to your army unless my other head participates. But I could very easily swallow you, before he could stop me."

Talith gazed up at the giant head in horror.

"Yes, that's true," Heinox admitted. "But he won't. He knows that then I would do something to his King."

"You surely wouldn't eat him, would you, Heinox?" Vicia mocked. "After all, he wouldn't be shaking and trembling before you."

"All Kings shake and tremble before me!" Heinox roared back. Then he swiveled to explain to Talith, who was shaking and trembling. "He seems to think his King would be more courageous than you."

"His King?" Talith murmured in confusion.

"For some reason he favors the King of Lamath," Heinox explained.

"The King of Lamath worships me," Vicia growled. "All of Lamath worships me. Does Chaomonous do as much?" Vicia almost came inside the litter, and Talith scooted as far from him as he could without falling off the edge.

"I could . . . make a decree . . ." Talith began.

"Do that, and *I'll* eat you," Heinox snorted, and Talith scooted back to the middle of the carriage.

"What are you doing here?" Vicia snarled. "I have never allowed armies to pass this way!"

"But I thought . . ." Talith began.

"He's going to attack Lamath, can't you see that?" Heinox growled at Vicia.

"How did you know—?" the King started to ask.

"Did you somehow send word to this sniveling human that you would try to sneak his army by me?" Vicia demanded.

Heinox snorted. "Of course not. Think I could sneak an army of this size through Dragonsgate? You certainly have a vivid imagination."

"Then what is he doing here?" Vicia demanded.

"How should I know?" said Heinox. "I know no more about this than you do. But I can tell you this, I shall make every effort to speed his army on its way!"

"You will?" Talith said in pleased surprise.

"Of course. The sooner you conquer his Lamathian army the sooner he's put in his place."

"Then my army may advance?" Talith asked hopefully.

"Certainly," Vicia snarled, "and I shall swallow you the moment you give the order."

Talith gazed up into those giant lizard eyes. "Oh," he said simply. Then he had an idea. Gesturing toward Heinox, Talith asked Vicia, "Do you think we could talk privately for a moment?"

Vicia's answer was a full-throated dragon roar that filled the canyon and echoed down into the valley. It was all the various commanders could do to keep the golden army from bolting home to Chaomonous.

"I see," Talith nodded, voice quavering. "Well then," he asked Heinox, "are there any other possibilities?"

"I would think it a fair trade, myself," Heinox offered. "Your life and the lives of a few of your supporters in exchange for the conquest of my enemies."

Talith laughed nervously, then choked his laughter down to keep from offending this monster. "Perhaps to you it would seem so, but my life is very important to me."

"More important than the conquest of my enemies?" Heinox asked, his head looming large in Talith's limited field of vision. Vicia-Heinox's two heads were so close by now that Talith could actually see nothing but dragon.

"Tahli-Damen, are you anywhere close by?" the King whispered, smiling nervously at those many teeth.

"Under the litter, my Lord," the young merchant replied honestly.

"What are you doing under there?" Talith asked angrily, the smile remaining fixed in place.

"Hiding," came the truthful reply.

"Do you have any suggestions as to how I can get out of this situation, merchant?" the King ground out between his clenched teeth. "A way," he added, "that doesn't involve my being eaten?"

"You might request a little time to think the idea over," the merchant suggested.

"Perhaps you two heads would be kind enough to give me the opportunity to think all this over?"

"Certainly," Heinox replied. "You have no objections, do you, Vicia?"

"No objections," Vicia replied. "One condition."

The King cleared his throat. "And what is that?"

"I'm hungry," the dragon replied, and the King nodded. He had expected that.

They haggled for another half-hour, then one squad toward the rear of the long golden column received word they were needed at the front. The King thanked each man personally, and promised each that his widow would receive a posthumous decoration.

By nightfall, the army of Chaomonous was encamped at the southern mouth of Dragonsgate. Talith threw many goblets and chairs in frustration that night, but those who knew him best considered him to be in quite good spirits. He had, at least, survived.

Few words passed between them as they rode to the monastery. Rosha battled to contain his frustration. Why did Pelmen not use his powers to prove to that dark-haired witch lady that he spoke the truth? Pelmen had gained nothing in the exchange. Rosha knew little of Lamathian religious politics, but that much seemed clear even to a novice. He said nothing. He was the initiate, not the teacher. But he vowed to stay constantly at Pelmen's side. There would be fewer seekers now, but Rosha wagered there would be many more assassins.

In the silent riding, Bronwynn thought of a hundred things she might have said to that raven-tressed phony who called herself Priestess. Some Priestess! The young Princess fantasized about creeping into this Serphimera's dwelling and stealing away her identity. Now if Bronwynn were the Priestess, this dragon cult would make some changes. How could they worship anything so ridiculous as the dragon, anyhow? She felt no awe of Vicia-Heinox. The giant monster was so foolish she almost felt sorry for him.

Pelmen gazed straight ahead, but he was very aware of the thoughts and feelings of these two who rode behind him. They were so young, so in need of a worthy teacher. And Pelmen felt so inadequate to the task. He had crammed everything he could into their all-too-short lesson periods. Bronwynn was already reading more swiftly than he could himself, and Rosha had taken to reading as well, once Pelmen discovered that it was fear of reading out loud that made the lad balk. That much he had accomplished.

But the changes were taking place too quickly. Open warfare between merchants and landowners in the Mar. Religious revival in Lamath that rivaled any such period in the Dragonfaith's history. Mobilization for war in all the lands, a war planned and pushed by avaricious merchants who wished to rule the world. And a dragon gone crazy. Tired as they all were, Pelmen resolved to take his two charges below the library tonight and continue with the lessons. The leisurely ride through the Great North Fir seemed dreamlike to him now as he considered the hard realities of his task here in Lamath. There was no more time for leisure. Only time for work.

The road they followed was really no more than a wide path, one of many that linked small villages together. The broadroads would be unsafe for them today, Pelmen had advised, for the majority of the surrounding villages supported Serphimera wholeheartedly, and news of her pronouncement of doom would fly most swiftly along the major highways. At times they seemed to ride through a leafy tunnel, for the grass grew thick to either side and the branches of the trees often intertwined above them. There was little noise— chirping birds, an occasional cricket, the soft plodding of their horses—nothing to disturb them as each rider remained wrapped in thought.

But it could not continue so. They had to cross the Mashab River to get home, and there were few bridges. They rejoined the main highway just a few hundred yards from the bridge they had crossed that morning. Pelmen jerked suddenly on Minaliss' reins, and the horse stopped immediately. There were soldiers on the bridge. "This looks unhealthy," Pelmen grunted quietly.

"That spiteful—" Bronwynn began. "You mean she's turned the army against us?"

"I believe the lady capable of that, yes," Pelmen answered. "Rosha, leave your sword where it is."

The young man had stealthily drawn the hem of his robe aside, preparing to pull his blade. He dropped the robe back down his leg, wondering how Pelmen had known, since he was directly behind the Prophet.

Now Pelmen turned in his saddle and looked him squarely in the face. "Never pull your sword against a troop of Lamathian soldiers. It's true they use stubby little knives compared to that greatsword you carry, but I assure you they are quite skillful with those little instruments. Two or three you could handle. A dozen? Best to remain a pious initiate."

"They're riding t-t-toward us," Rosha informed Pelmen quietly.

The Prophet turned around to face the oncoming riders, muttering, "I was afraid they would. How did she get to them so fast?"

The leader of the troop quickly answered Pelmen's question. She hadn't. "Greetings, Prophet. We've been waiting here all day for your return. How went your meeting with the Priestess?"

"She appears . . . quite powerful—" Pelmen began cautiously, and the soldier quickly cut him off.

"I am sure she would say the same of you. The Chieftain of Defense and Expansion has heard with joy the news of a new Prophet in Lamath, and has sent me to inform you that the King and the Dragonfaith are in

need of your services. A vessel waits below the bridge
and I am to set you aboard it."

The man spoke so swiftly there was no chance for
Pelmen to interrupt. Now he blurted, "But why?"

The soldier looked at him sharply, curiously. "There
is war in Lamath, have you not heard? And a prophet
in wartime sails with the fleet. Come, we've no time to
waste. The Chaon fleet has safely passed the Border
Straits and already harasses the southern coastline. You
must sail now, or our fleet risks being bottled in the
river." The leader made to grab Pelmen's reins, but
Minaliss wheeled swiftly out of his reach, unwilling to
let any man save Pelmen lead him.

The Prophet calmed the animal and nodded curtly.
"I will come. But may I speak a word to my initiates?"

"A swift word." The captain nodded; then he led his
group of riders a decent distance away to give the
Prophet a moment of privacy.

Rosha's look of horror was mirrored in Bronwynn's
pretty features. Both were dazed by this sudden shift of
circumstance. Pelmen spoke rapidly, reaching out to
grip Rosha's right hand and Bronwynn's left and
squeezing both to punctuate his commands.

"Ride to the monastery. Study the book! Don't leave
there, and don't let that book be injured. If Serphimera
should show herself, and I expect she will, hide in the
cavern. Do *not* confront her! Rosha, keep your sword
in its scabbard, and Bronwynn, keep your tongue in
your mouth! I'll come as quickly as I can." He gave
each hand a parting squeeze, then let them go.

"I'm going with you," Bronwynn said, and Rosha
echoed, "And I!"

Pelmen looked at them both, and thought about it.
"Impossible. Soldiers wouldn't allow it," he said, shaking his head. "Prophets are considered good luck in
wartime. Initiates are always a jinx. Besides, who would
protect the book?" He gave them no time to argue, but
bade them a quick good-bye and rode toward the soldiers. He turned to look back over his shoulder. "Take
Minaliss on with you! I'll have need of him later."

Then he gifted the stunned young couple with a smile
that hearkened back to friendlier days on the battle-

ments of Dorlyth's castle. Upset though they were, his smile was contagious. Bronwynn giggled, and Rosha's face cracked into a grin. Pelmen was off with the group of riders, and they watched him dismount and walk down the river bank and out of view. Their smiles died, and they just sat there for a moment, absorbing this surprise.

"At least he gave us an explanation this time," Bronwynn murmured. Then she looked at Rosha. "He didn't just tell us to go home."

"He m-might as well have," Rosha snorted, and he urged his horse into a trot and rode onto the bridge. Already the boat was slipping away to the southeast. Rosha followed it until it turned with the twisting Mashab and moved out of sight. On the deck a small figure clothed in brilliant blue lifted an arm to wave, then was gone. Rosha looked at Bronwynn, who had ridden up to join him. "We had b-best g-g-go on."

Minaliss stood in the middle of the bridge, looking puzzled. Bronwynn reached out to pat his nose, and he remembered her . . . a brown-haired slip of a girl he had carried a long, long way. He nuzzled up against her leg, and she patted his flank.

"Confused, aren't you?" Bronwynn murmured to the powerful beast; then she gazed downriver where the boat had disappeared. "So are we, old friend. So are we."

❧ Chapter Eleven ❧

SERPHIMERA did not stop walking when she arrived at Serphila. She passed through the growing township without a word of greeting to any of the hundreds who massed there to welcome her. Instead she made straight for her chapel and locked its doors behind her. Those

who had traveled with her explained her behavior to the
people who had waited behind. "The Prophet is a blasphemer!"

Never had Serphimera's followers seen her so anxious or so angry. The next morning she made an im-
promptu sermon to what villagers were awake that
early, then started east for the capital. She had concluded that this Prophet needed to be stopped.

As she hiked out of the city, word spread rapidly.
"The smile of the Priestess is gone. The false Prophet
has stolen it."

A large band swarmed after her as she walked pur-
posefully down the broad highway to Lamath. But an
even larger group surged out of town in the other direction, toward the dwelling of the false Prophet. The Divisionist monastery he occupied was obviously a hotbed
of heresy. It needed to be cleansed. Along with these
angry, threatening marchers traveled one who had only
arrived in Serphila the previous day. No one really
knew his name. All the way up and down the line he
was referred to only as the ugly man on the white horse.
It was chilling to look the fellow in the face, but one
thing was generally agreed upon throughout the line of
march. When they got to where they were going, he was
the one who would know exactly what to do.

General Asher was aware of Serphimera's approach
long before she arrived. The spy network he had constructed through the central plains of Lamath was un-
equaled, even among the merchant houses. He had recognized the rural penchant for gossip and simply harnessed it. He considered the result one of his foremost
achievements in office. But strangely, though he knew all
about the confrontation between Pelmen and the Priestess the day it occurred, he did not know the results of
that meeting until he heard it from Serphimera's own lips.

"The man is a heretic and a blasphemer."

Asher chuckled quietly and settled back into his canvas field chair. "I take it you two disagreed. There
couldn't be some, let's say, professional jealousy in your
evaluation of him?"

The Priestess did not blink. She transfixed the General with those forest-green eyes. "No. He is what I say."

Her gaze made Asher uncomfortable, and he pushed himself out of his seat and walked to the tent flaps. The camp spread for miles in every direction. Since his command post stood on the only hill in the area, he could see much of the camp's activity from his door. Everywhere there was bustling confusion, the delightful disorder of the preparation for war.

"He isn't sending Lamathian citizens away to be eaten, is he?" Asher asked, his back still turned to her.

"General Asher," Serphimera began, and a chill chattered through him. Her voice had taken on that seductive quality that had so mesmerized him in the past. "I know you are a believer. I can see it in your life, hear it in the way you issue orders. The dragon will reward you for that." He did not turn to look at her, so she came to stand directly behind him and continued to soothe in subtle tones as she worked to make her point. "You have expanded the realm of Lamath farther north than any war chieftain before you—surely you don't imagine you did that on your own? I know you don't. And I know, too, that were you to hear this counterfeit Prophet, you would be as anxious as I to remove him from Lamathian life." She placed her hands on his shoulders, an electric touch that made his back tingle. "General Asher, he has no tradition. He does not abide by the old understanding, but brings a new belief. And—he says the dragon is divided."

"What does he say?" The General turned to face her, and was nearly overpowered by her warmth and closeness.

"That the dragon is at war with himself!"

General Asher scowled. "At war with himself?"

Serphimera danced lightly away, her point made. "Simple heresy," she added, but she needn't have. The angry red glow in the General's cheeks gave evidence that he was already convinced. "He needs to be captured," Serphimera advised, "and locked away, so that he can do no more harm to others. Or to himself," she added quietly. "I know where you may find him—"

"Oh, I know where he is," Asher growled, cursing his own impulsiveness. "He travels with our own navy!"

"What for?" Serphimera demanded.

"It is the tradition that a Prophet in Lamath at wartime rides with the ships to battle."

"You could not have waited until after I met him?" she snarled bitterly.

"No. Time was too critical. I needed to rush our navy onto the sea before the Chaon fleet reached the delta and bottled us in the river."

"Can he be stopped?"

"Not now. Your meeting took place two days ago?"

"I came as swiftly as I could—"

"You are too late. His boat passed by here yesterday, and the fleet left the harbor of Lamath this morning. By this time it should be moving into the ocean—if not already engaged in battle." Serphimera clenched her jaws in frustration. Asher patted her on the shoulder, then immediately withdrew his hand, surprised at his own familiarity with this, the greatest Priestess of the land. "Calm yourself. If the Chaons sink his vessel, we need concern ourselves with him no longer. If he does return, I myself will meet him at the dock, and carry him from the victory celebration to the dungeon."

"Never had much dealings with prophets, myself," the wiry sailor remarked. "Always got a queer feeling when I passed one of them dragon statues."

"Does the same thing to me," Pelmen said merrily, and he drew a deep draught of salty air into his lungs. It had been some time since he last saw the ocean, and even longer since he had traveled on it. He noticed the sailor was eyeing him with curiosity, and smiled. The wind and the salt had somehow renewed his spirits.

"I take that as strange, I do," Erri the sailor observed. "Seems like a prophet fellow would get a real thrill out of one of them monsters."

"Not this Prophet."

Erri scratched his beard. "You seem a strange Prophet, at that."

"Oh, I hope so." Pelmen grinned.

"Aren't you afraid the Lord Dragon'll be displeased?"

"The dragon isn't the Lord."

Erri jumped as if he'd stepped barefoot onto a jellyfish, and looked around for a place to hide. "Listen, Prophet, a ship is no place to play blasphemy! Suppose the Lord Dragon decides to burn you with a little flick of lightning! What's to prevent me from being charred along with you?"

"Relax, Erri. I know that dragon, and he can't hear me. We're turning into the wind again," Pelmen added, and Erri jumped up to help trim the yards as the oars along either side of the vessel slipped out in unison and began thrashing the water like so many centipede legs. The sounds of a beating drum and groaning men rose through the boards of the deck, dampening Pelmen's cheerful mood. There had been a time when he, too, had worked an oar in the bowels of a battleship. He preferred to forget the experience.

Those who rowed below were mostly Chaon slaves. Ironic, Pelmen thought, that the Chaon fleet would be powered primarily by Lamathian muscle. He doubted there were many Maris below deck. Maris made poor oarsmen. They were too small, usually, to pull much weight, and they spent too much time being seasick. Setting a Mari to an oar was like trying to hitch a mountain goat to a plow. When sea traders went shopping for oarsmen, they usually chose slaves from the other seafaring nation. Of this Pelmen was sure, however: when the fleets closed for battle, Lamathian slaves would be cheering their Chaon masters, while Chaon slaves would show new loyalty for Lamath. Nationality had little meaning in the stinking hold of a battleship. What mattered there was survival.

Erri returned, swinging himself down to sit on a pile of rope. "So tell me, then," he continued, picking up the conversation as if he'd never left, "why are you a Prophet of the Dragon if you have such a low opinion of the beast himself?"

"I'm not a Prophet of the dragon," Pelmen replied evenly. Erri stared, his eyes and mouth very wide. Then he glanced up at the sky, fully expecting a cloud to appear suddenly in the clear blue and aim a fire bolt directly at them. Nothing happened, and he looked back at Pelmen.

"Nothing happened," he observed needlessly.

"Of course not."

"I don't understand. If you're not a Prophet, why pretend to be a Prophet?"

"I didn't say I wasn't a Prophet. I just said I wasn't a Prophet of the dragon."

Erri nodded, but his expression said he was puzzled. "I didn't know there was any other kind."

"Didn't it ever seem strange to you, all this noise and excitement about a dragon?"

Erri shrugged. "Not really. Religion is always strange. It doesn't have to make sense."

"It does to me," Pelmen murmured quietly.

"Yeah, but you're a Prophet, see. Religion is supposed to make sense to a Prophet." Pelmen didn't say anything. "Isn't it?"

"Has nothing to do with religion, Erri. Has nothing to do with the dragon, either. What's important is the Power, Erri, not the Dragonfaith. All the rest is just wrapping."

Erri chuckled. "See, you are a Prophet after all. I can't understand anything you say."

"Is that because you're afraid you shouldn't? Or because you do understand, and are afraid of what it might mean?" Pelmen's eyes had been scanning the southern horizon as they spoke, and now he saw golden triangles, far away—the sails of the Chaon fleet. "Better warn the Seachief, Erri. We're about to meet our brothers from the south."

At that moment bells began ringing on all the ships, and the salty air was filled with shouted orders. Erri scampered off to his station, but a thought sprang into his mind and he swiftly climbed back to ask Pelmen, "Just one thing. If you don't believe in the Dragon, how you going to help us in this battle?"

"The Power will have to show you that, my friend. At this point I really have no idea."

The oars pulsed more quickly, in rhythm with the increasing pace of the oarsmaster's gavel. It was good the oarsmen could not see what they were rowing into. The sea warriors who stood in the prow of the battleship watched with dismay as more and more golden sails appeared on the horizon.

Pelmen estimated that they were now fifty miles southeast of Lamath. Then he recognized a small harbor to starboard, and knew exactly where they were. It was a shallow little bay that he recalled from his travels along the coast—so full of treacherous shoals no Lamathian vessel ventured near it. He glanced to the east and the open sea and either saw or imagined a small cloud on that distant horizon. Suddenly an idea came, and he climbed a series of narrow steps to join the Seachief at the helm.

The commander of the fleet was a capable leader, but even he was distressed at the sight of that glistening armada. He smiled thinly at Pelmen, and muttered, "Any ideas, Prophet?"

"One small one. Veer toward the bay."

The Seachief started, then chuckled. "Let the sailors do the sailing, Prophet. You concentrate on getting some wind behind us! They have the advantage of a southwester behind them."

"I'll do my best—but you would do well to follow my suggestion."

"That shallow little bay would sink my fleet!"

"I didn't say move into the bay. I suggested only that you veer toward it."

The Seachief looked Pelmen over suspiciously, then gave a slight nod to the helmsman, and went to inform his signaler.

The Admiral of Chaomonous watched with interest as the smaller Lamathian fleet turned to make for a sheltered bay.

"Is that an inlet? Are they running? What?" He shouted at the captain who stood beside him, a merchant seaman who had been pressed into service by Talith, and liked it not a bit.

"I have no idea, my Lord," he grumbled. "It appears their commander wants to run his whole navy onto the rocks."

"Ridiculous! He just doesn't want to engage me in

the open sea. He wants to shelter in that little harbor and take us a few at a time."

"My Lord Admiral, that's a shallows you see, not a—"

"Wouldn't the Lamathian commander know his own coastline?" the Admiral bellowed. He disliked this merchant. The fellow always found some reason why the Admiral's orders were foolhardy. He would not allow this merchant's overcautious nature to rob him of a total victory. "Helmsman, to port and make for that harbor. With the wind behind us, we'll beat him there."

The eastern cloud grew larger, and Pelmen concentrated his attention on it. There was no sensation of making it grow, no feeling of shaping the powers of nature as he had in the past. It was only that he wished so for it to come . . . and it was coming.

"The Chaon fleet moves west to meet us!" cried a watchman hanging in the rigging.

The Seachief looked at Pelmen and asked, "Was that your aim?" The Prophet nodded, and the Chieftain rushed on, "Then can we change this course and make for safety?" He sounded annoyed. The man chafed at being directed by a Prophet.

"We're not in danger yet, are we? Why not ship your oars and just wait until he beats you to the bay?"

The Seachief considered that, then nodded, and gave the order to ship oars. The vessel coasted through the water, slowing steadily, even as the golden fleet made more swiftly for the shallows. Pelmen turned back to look east.

"Now," he said at length. "Turn hard to port . . . and row for that storm."

So intent had he been on the course of the enemy flagship, the Seachief had not noticed until that moment the sudden eastern squall. The southwester was dying away. Abruptly he realized what Pelmen had planned, and shouted with joy.

"You've done it! A Prophet in wartime *does* belong on the sea! Helmsmen, hard to port! Oarmaster?"

"Here, sir!" came the cry from below.

"Hard to port and full speed, *now!*"

The ship shuddered and creaked, then began pulling

slowly around to the east. Signals flashed from ship to ship throughout the Lamathian fleet, and all made the same slow turn. Some distance away, the Chaon war boats struggled to respond to this new movement of the enemy, but their wind was gone and already the innermost battleships were floundering in the shoals. The squall hit the golden fleet broadside, driving ship after ship into the rocks.

The Lamathians fought hard against the wind, oars working madly to meet its force. Sea warriors went below to spell tired slaves at the benches, and to keep from being blown into the swirling sea. The waves grew, and at times the ship seemed to run across a washboard, not an ocean. But the storm was brief. It passed swiftly over them and into the Lamathian coastal plains, where it dumped much-needed rain on some very thirsty crops. The Lamathian fleet rejoiced.

But the men of Chaomonous found nothing to cheer. Broken vessels littered the beach alongside the bodies of drowned sailors and slaves. How fitting it would have been had the Admiral's body been among them, but his ship had weathered the storm, and now led the flight for home.

Pelmen stood on the deck, leaning against the mizzenmast. Something dropped onto the boards beside him, making him jump. It was Erri.

"What is it you think I'm afraid of?" Erri demanded, and it took Pelmen a moment to realize that, once again, the sailor had resumed their conversation without thought to the interruption.

"Not of storms, evidently."

"Storms are part of life. This religion business, though. That's something else."

"Yes," Pelmen agreed with a smile. "Most of the time, I'm afraid it is!"

Bronwynn and Rosha didn't speak as they walked back through the cavern to the ladder. They had haggled incessantly since Pelmen had left them, and had just left a terrible argument behind them in the alcove. Rosha stamped along pouting, so angry with Bronwynn that he had forgotten to pull his sword from his scabbard. But as they neared the ladder, he slowed. Something seemed very wrong. He reached out to grab Bronwynn by the arm to stop her.

"Let go, you stubborn buffalo!" she managed to snap before he clapped a hand over her mouth.

"Look," he whispered, after she realized he wasn't trying to tease her into forgiving him. She turned her eyes upward where he pointed and drew a surprised gasp. The hole through the floor was closed. The stone slab that concealed this underground cavern had been put in place for some reason. Rosha drew his sword quietly and mounted the ladder. Bronwynn mouthed *Careful* to him, and he nodded. He climbed to the slab and tilted his head to listen, ear pressed to its underside. He looked down at Bronwynn and saw her mouth *Anything?* He nodded, and she covered her mouth with both hands. He heard voices above. Then there was a scuffle, and his eyes jerked wide open. He would have thrown all his weight against the stone and pushed his way up into the library, but Bronwynn caught his eye. Her face was fierce, and she shook her head violently from side to side. He nodded, and she panted for breath, her tension heightened by her inability to give expression to it. Rosha's muscles ached for action as well, due to his cramped position on the ladder. Suddenly something fell onto the slab, nearly knocking the ladder loose from its tenuous perch against the lip of the hole. Then there was silence.

Rosha waited a long time, it seemed; then he nodded and sheathed his sword. He thrust both palms upward against the heavy slab, grunting as he struggled to push it up. At last it began to budge, then abruptly felt much lighter as something heavy rolled off of it.

Rosha peeked cautiously into the library and saw nothing. He pushed all the way through and started to shove the slab backward when he saw a hand dangle over the edge of the stone, and he started with horror. He recognized that hand.

He was out of the hole in a minute and had lifted the form of the Elder from the floor, then scampered back down the ladder and stretched the little man's body on the cavern floor. Bronwynn gasped in hurt surprise and bent to examine him as Rosha rushed back up the ladder to reseat the concealing slab. He had not been in the library more than a minute, but that was long enough to see what had taken place. Serphimera's army had come—and from the sounds that came through the library windows, they were still at work.

The Elder's head lay in Bronwynn's lap, and she stroked his bald pate in shock. He smiled at that, but it was a pained smile. He was bleeding freely from a wound in his chest. The girl was sobbing.

"It wasn't Serphimera's people, really," the little man murmured rapidly. "It was an ugly fellow out of your master's past." He was almost babbling, smiling a strange, excited smile as he struggled to impart this last bit of information and advice. "You need to go. The fellow—someone called him Admon something—is hunting you too, little lady. And though I wouldn't tell him of the caverns, some of the other brothers may not be so bullheaded as I. Please," he asked, shuddering with pain. "Go now, quickly."

"Admon . . ." Bronwynn murmured, dazedly. Then the name sprang up at her and gripped her attention. "Admon Faye! Admon Faye!" she yelped, and Rosha realized she was edging toward hysteria. He grabbed her chin tightly and turned her face to look him in the eyes. Quickly, she regained control of herself. "Admon Faye has killed the Elder!" she cried, her heart breaking at the thought.

"He's n-not d-dead!" Rosha snarled, but the little man between them chuckled, and interrupted them.

"Oh, but I am, lad," he mumbled. "I am. But don't look so horrified. I think I might like it." Tears filled his eyes, and he continued, "They've taken all my books . . . they're going to scatter my brothers." He muttered again, through the tears. "What business do I have staying in this life?" He would have wept then, as the senseless tragedy of it closed around him, but he would not let himself. His instincts as a teacher went too deep. As he looked up into the crying face of this proud young lady, and watched her curly-haired warrior fight to control his own feelings, he could not resist the opportunity for a lesson that might truly stick. "Why weep then, my children? You've read the Prophet's book. You know there's a Power, you've watched it work! Now . . . I'll get a chance to know that Power."

The old man's eyes seemed to lose contact with this world and gazed elsewhere. Rosha thought he had passed from them. He lifted the body from the floor of the cave, and began to mount the ladder again.

The aged eyes focused again. "No, no, leave me here. You run . . . run . . ."

Rosha looked down at those lined cheeks, and wracked his mind for something Pelmen would say. Then it came to him, and he forced a smile onto his severe young face. "What? And leave you to the b-b-bears?" The old man smiled thinly in appreciation . . . then the life was gone. Rosha carried him into the library with great tenderness, and stretched his body along one of those shelves that had held his treasured books. Then he glanced around, as if to be sure no one was watching—though he knew no one would be—and kissed the old man on the cheek, as he remembered his mother kissing him, long ago.

Bronwynn waited for him at the foot of the ladder, her eyes red and swollen but her tears now dried. That was good, Rosha thought to himself. They would both need to be fully alert now. They would be traveling in a region that belonged to the cavern bears. Better that, he reasoned, than to meet with Admon Faye. For the first time in his life, Rosha knew what his father meant by fear.

General Asher stood on the King's Dock. It was named so because it was where the King of Lamath embarked when he traveled anywhere along the Lamathian waterways. It was an ornately decorated mooring, with reviewing stands and thick carpets standing under a vast canvas canopy. Usually the stands were empty and the canopy frame bare, but today the place was alive with color, and the victory celebration had drawn a large crowd.

The Seachief stepped first from the boat, and was greeted by thunderous applause. He was being touted as the newest in a long line of naval geniuses, and Asher greeted him with the dragon salute and an affectionate, if awkward, embrace.

"Well done, my friend," he murmured in the Seachief's ear. He was startled by the Seachief's uncharacteristically modest reply.

"Thank you, General Asher," the Seachief whispered back, "but I really cannot claim the credit. You were right about the Prophet. It was he who set up the victory!"

"You are very modest, Seachieftain," Asher said as he stepped back. "I'm certain that your contribution was far greater than you insist."

"Well . . . I *did* follow the man's suggestions." The Seachief smiled, his vanity getting the better of him. He certainly didn't refuse it when Asher hung a diamond-studded pendant around his neck and proclaimed him the Dragon's Friend. It was the highest honor any commander in Lamath could hope to attain, save of course the title of Chieftain of Defense and Expansion. But Asher had a stranglehold on that position, and the General was a relatively young man. If the Seachief chose to bask in the crowd's adulation for a time, it was because he realized how fleeting that love could be.

The crowd reacted differently, however, when Pelmen appeared. There were those who cheered, of course, for the story of his advice and the wind he had summoned had been shared a hundred times by sailors calling to friends on the shore. But most muttered curses and raised their crossed arms in an angry gesture usually considered obscene by Lamathian society. In different corners of the assembled crowd chants arose, one group shouting, "Proph-et, Proph-et!" while another group answered, "Doom, doom, doom!" The noise grew so loud that few people witnessed the exchange that now took place, or marked how unusual was Asher's greeting of the Prophet. Soon the lesser leaders of the victorious navy stepped off the boat to receive their own accolades, and the Prophet was forgotten.

A carriage was ready to carry Pelmen directly to the palace of the King. He was thrust in, to sit between two stony-faced guards who spoke neither to him nor to each other. Only one person in the great crowd seemed really to grasp what was taking place, and he ran alongside the carriage for several yards, trying to understand.

"Prophet, ho, Prophet! Where are they taking you?" Erri the sailor stopped and listened, but if Pelmen answered him he didn't hear it. All he heard was the clatter of hooves on the cobblestones and the bouncing of the carriage springs. Then Pelmen was gone.

Talith was talking and eating at the same time. This was not unusual for the King, and General Joss had trained himself to understand the garbled words regardless of what chewed foods they had been forced to struggle past on the way out of Talith's mouth.

"Do yoummsupposemmwemwon?"

"I don't know what the naval situation is, my Lord. As I said, I've not had any decent intelligence since we left the golden city."

"I got a letter today," the King observed, none too precisely. What he had received was a tiny blue-flyer scroll that simply reassured him of Ligne's continued love and support.

"From your mistress, of course."

"Of course! You don't think my wife would write me, do you?"

"She would not be capable, my Lord, locked as she is in her apartments."

"Her own fault," the King muttered, chomping into a chicken leg. "Why haven't you heard anything from the navy?"

Joss interpreted the question from among the grunts and smacks of the King at table. "I am concerned, my Lord. I fear some change has taken place in the palace that has altered the national political situation. I fear . . ." Here Joss paused for emphasis. ". . . that you have been overthrown."

Talith stopped chewing and stared. Then he closed his mouth and chomped angrily. He took a long draught of wine to wash it all down, his menacing eye never leaving those of his Chief of Security. Then he stood, and leaned across the table. "I said I received a letter from Ligne this morning!"

"Yes, my Lord."

Talith paced around the table. "You never have trusted Ligne, have you?"

Joss thought a moment, not about his reply, for he knew exactly what he thought of Ligne. Rather, about its consequences. "No, my Lord," he answered.

"You thought it was she who kidnapped Bronwynn, and now you think she is plotting my overthrow, don't you?"

"I don't think she's plotting it any longer, my Lord," Joss answered matter-of-factly. "I think she has accomplished it."

Talith smiled cruelly. "Then you shall ride back to Chaomonous tonight and see if your suspicions are correct. You certainly won't be missed, since we're doing nothing but sitting here."

"If that is my Lord's will, certainly I will obey it," Joss replied.

"It is, General Joss. And my instructions to the troop that travels with you will be to conduct you to the dungeon once they are sure that all is well in the palace. How does that strike you?"

"As my Lord chooses . . ." Joss began.

"So I choose! Go pick your troop and get out of my camp." Joss turned smartly and started out. "Joss," the King called after him, "I'll visit you in the dungeon when I arrive home."

The former Chief of Security turned at the door and bowed slightly to his King. "I will certainly be there, my Lord. Should you arrive home."

"Get out!"

Joss obeyed. He bumped into Tahli-Damen as he emerged into the moonlight, and the young merchant begged to be pardoned.

"Do you think he would see me?" the merchant went on.

"I'm certain he would." Joss snorted. "Just leave your self-regard at the door as you enter," the General muttered as he moved off into the night. Tahli-Damen thought about that, but it made no sense. He made his way through a series of veils and entered Talith's presence.

"What do you want, merchant?" the King demanded.

"I came to make a suggestion . . ."

"Then make it. There's still plenty of room in my dungeon." Tahli-Damen hesitated. "Well go on, boy," the King bellowed. "Say it or get out!"

"I suggest you approach the dragon again . . ."

"And get swallowed, I suppose. Guard!"

"No, sir, please listen!" Tahli-Damen dropped instinctively to his knees as two guards fought their way through the veils to enter the tent.

"Get out," the King muttered, and the guards fought their way back outside again. "Go on."

"I suggest you ask the dragon to let you pass, not to Lamath, but to Ngandib-Mar!"

"Why should I want to go there?" Talith mumbled, examining the wine that remained in his cup.

"The dragon would permit you to go there, for one thing. It is to Ngandib-Mar that the man Pelmen escaped, the day Pezi the merchant attempted to carry your daughter to Lamath."

Talith turned purple. Then he exploded. "Ngandib-Mar!" He seized Tahli-Damen by the throat, and once again the merchant found himself crawling most humbly on his knees. "You told me Pelmen was in Lamath!"

"No, my Lord, please!" Tahli-Damen implored. "We did not know! We have only lately discovered this from other merchants!"

"How have you discovered it?" Talith demanded. "I have had you watched, merchant, ever since we left Chaomonous. You've received no messages that I do not know about!"

"My Lord," Tahli-Damen pleaded, "I assure you we have ways of contact that no one knows . . . I just heard this from Jagd in the capital!"

"Jagd, hmm? And how go things in the capital, hmm? Answer, merchant!"

"All is well, my Lord!" Tahli-Damen yelped. "The country awaits news of your victory!"

"As I thought!" Talith growled, throwing the merchant from him and striding back to the table. Tahli-

Damen lay on the canvas floor of the tent, watching the King's face. "Joss *was* lying."

"Joss, my Lord?"

"Get up, merchant, and tell me what you've learned about Pelmen and my daughter. Then I want to know everything Jagd's told you since we left the palace."

Tahli-Damen lied that night as he had never lied before, and when he finally made his way back to his tent he collapsed in exhaustion across his cot. Before he slipped into deep sleep, he thought he heard Jagd complimenting him. "Well done, my boy," the dream Jagd told him. "You'll make a merchant yet."

Rosha held the lamp in one hand and his sword in the other, while Bronwynn kept close behind him as they shuffled through the silent hallways of stone. She gripped the book in both hands and argued with herself about bears. At last she decided to bring Rosha into the conversation.

"What do cavern bears eat?" she whispered.

"P-people," the young warrior answered frankly.

"Where do they find enough people to eat?"

"In Ngandib-Mar they d-dwell mostly in the c-c-caves near the mines. There they feed off of the m-miners."

"But there are no mines here. Why would bears want to live in this region?"

"How d-do you know there are n-no mines here?"

"I've never heard of any," she answered.

"I n-never heard of the ocean either." They turned a blind corner very cautiously, then continued.

"*Are* there mines here?" she asked, her voice hushed to dampen the dreadful echo.

"I've n-never heard of any." He shrugged, peering into the darkness ahead of him. Bronwynn frowned at his back.

"Then how do you know there are bears here?" she asked.

"The s-smell."

"I don't smell anything."

"That's because you've b-been smelling bears too long."

"Just because—"

A sudden snarl came from the nightmare black. Then what seemed to be two eyes with teeth leapt at their throats. The only thing that saved either of them was the fact that Rosha dropped the lamp as the explosion of his fright blew him backward. The oil spilled across the stone and flared, and the beast stopped on the other side of it. The spreading oil burned out quickly, but by then Rosha was back on his feet, greatsword clasped in both hands and pointed at the memory of those burning eyes. Nothing happened for a moment, as the three of them stood silently in the darkness.

"Bronwynn—"

"Behind you."

"Quiet—"

"I'm here . . ." Her voice quavered slightly, but she was getting good at controlling it, even when suffocating in horror. The beast made no sound. Rosha listened.

"Back up—" he whispered. "Slowly . . ." He listened some more. Sandals scraped sand on the stone floor behind him. He took a step back himself. Somewhere in front of him the beast growled low in its throat, and Rosha froze.

"Still backing?" he asked, his voice cracking as he choked the words out.

"Still backing," she whispered, and he could tell she was twenty feet behind him now. He waited, stiff and ready, but the beast still did not charge. Rosha had only glimpsed the bear briefly in the lamp's dying flare-up. It was surprisingly small. Rosha concentrated on how small the bear really was, for the darkness insisted that the animal was larger.

"Have you reached that last corner?" he asked, wondering if a loud noise could frighten the bear away. At least the tension seemed to have stopped his stammering for the moment.

"Not yet . . . not yet . . . not . . . yet," Bronwynn chanted as she backed into the blackness with her hands held behind her, fearing that another set of teeth might chomp down on them any minute.

"Quiet!" he ordered, and she stopped her chant in time to hear the cavern bear snort. "Just tell me when you get there." Rosha began to feel dizzy, standing motionless in the pitch black. His fear was changing to anger, anger at Pelmen for leaving them, anger at the bear for blocking their escape, and anger at Bronwynn for no reason at all. He entertained thoughts of springing savagely at the bear, hacking at it, biting if need be, crushing it in his grip. But he held onto his senses, and gripped his sword.

At last Bronwynn called softly, "I'm here."

"Good." His mind raced.

"What are you going to do?" Her voice sounded so far away! Could it be that far back to that last turn?

"I'm thinking." He took a cautious step back. No response from the bear. Another step, and an answering growl. "Bronwynn," he called anxiously.

"I'm here . . ." Her voice was calming. She had labored to make it sound so.

"Are there . . . depressions, holes in that wall behind you?"

"Yes," she murmured back after a moment. She sounded dreamy, almost drunk.

"Good. Step back to the left . . ."

"But . . ."

"Turn the corner, Bronwynn!"

"And leave you . . ."

"Now!" Suddenly he was running toward her, and she leapt out of the way. The bear was after him with a gut-shaking roar, and Rosha bolted ahead more quickly. He was panting loudly, then beginning to moan faintly as he ran blindly on, sure he would misjudge the corner and yet sure he knew just where to turn. Bronwynn marked the corner for him precisely when she screamed.

"Rosha!" Her voice told him where to turn, and Rosha danced lightly around the bend of the tunnel. As he spun, he whipped his greatsword up over his head and jammed its pommel into the far wall. It caught in one of those depressions, and momentum drove it in solidly, to hang with its point facing out. That same momentum bounced Rosha off a wall, and he sprawled beside Bronwynn, who crouched there. The rock had torn his shoulder open, but he felt nothing as he listened be-

yond the reverberations of Bronwynn's scream for a
sound that arrived right on schedule. The ruse worked.
The bear nearly spitted himself on the blade as he went
crashing heavily into the wall.

Rosha scrambled backward, pushing Bronwynn behind him, then hushed her to listen as the unseen beast
snarled in pain. He could hear the scratch of claws on
stone as the cavern bear struggled to right itself. He
could also hear a scraping noise that thrilled him—his
sword had lodged in the bear, and now the angry animal dragged it with him. Rosha waited, crouching on
his hands and knees, as the bear turned the corner and
began to push its way toward him, marking each step
with a scrape and a growl. Bronwynn clasped her hands
first over her mouth, to keep from screaming, then over
her ears to shut out the awful evidence of the bear's
approach. But Rosha waited eagerly. The bear was
wounded. There was a chance.

But not without his greatsword. Though it was valuable as an indicator of the bear's whereabouts, he
couldn't kill the beast without it. His only chance was to
leap toward the sound of it, pull it free, and plunge it
home again before being ripped apart. It wasn't a good
chance, but he had no alternative.

"Rosha, do some—"

"Shh!" he hissed, then tensed his body to spring,
fearing a charge. It didn't come. Only the continued
scrape-scrape-scrape of a wounded bear moving closer.
Rosha's muscles were knotting under the tension, but he
didn't notice. He waited . . . waited . . . jumped.

Boy and bear crashed heads before Rosha's fingers
closed on the hilt, and the blow threw Rosha to one
side. The bear roared and leapt forward, but Rosha
clung to the handle of the sword, causing the animal to
flip over the end of it. The blade came free, and Rosha
shouted in dismay. The beast was now between him and
Bronwynn!

"Run!" he screamed. Then he rammed the sword
forward into the darkness. It struck flesh, and at that
same moment he heard small feet scuttling away down
the corridor. His spirits soared. He hadn't hit Bronwynn, so he must have hit the bear. He jerked his

weapon free, slashed out again, and grinned at the answering yelp of pain. He stabbed again, twice more, then listened. The beast was silent, and the floor was slick beneath his feet. He took a running step in a direction he hoped was toward Bronwynn, and skidded down in the puddle of blood, landing on the bear's hairy back. He jerked away in revulsion, then reached out to touch the sticky, matted fur, and to listen for a sign of life. There was none. He had done it! He was a bear's-bane!

Bronwynn called out of the darkness. "Rosha! Rosha, are you all right?" In the black she misjudged the distance and she, too, stumbled over the bear. Rosha caught her in his arms, and hugged her, hard. He took a deep breath.

"I th-think we have safely established that there *are* b-b-bears in this cavern." Bronwynn convulsed into a fit of the giggles, and Rosha joined her in the aftermath of tension. They stroked one another as they giggled some more. At last they snickered into silence.

"What are we going to do now?" Bronwynn asked soberly.

"It m-makes no sense to g-go on," he said finally. "We've lost our light. We have n-no assurance that we c-can find a way out. We know there are b-b-bears ahead of us."

"But Admon Faye is behind us!" Bronwynn moaned.

"Then let him c-c-come!" Rosha fiercely challenged the dark. His fingers found the pommel of his blade. The grip was slippery so he dropped to one knee and wiped it clean on the long hem of his initiate's gown. Then he stood proudly, and announced, "I'm p-p-prepared."

"Prepared for what?" Bronwynn's tone was bitter. The gravity of their predicament had stolen her hope.

"P-prepared to face Admon Faye!" he shouted in the direction of her face. "I am the treasure of Dorlyth mod Karis! I will not die in a gopher hole!" He started down the passage, but she resisted, pulling down on his arm.

"Wait! Which way are we going!"

"We're going b-b-back, my Lady! B-back to where we came. I know n-now, we never should have run!" They started off together, he clutching his sword and she clutching her book, and each gripping the other by the hand. As they walked, Rosha reflected on what he had just said, and realized it wasn't quite true. He had fled into this cavern a frightened fugitive. He was walking out a bona fide bear's-bane. And with a witness!

"Congratulations on your victory, Prophet." Asher smiled sardonically. "I am sorry our discussion at the wharf was so rushed, but perhaps you noticed the crowd was of a divided opinion on you."

"I did notice," Pelmen acknowledged. He stood before Asher in the general's office, flanked by the same pair of burly guards who had escorted him from the King's Dock. His wrists were manacled together—hardly the reception one would expect for a victorious Lamathian Prophet. But Pelmen was not surprised. His only concern was for the safety of Rosha and Bronwynn. He reminded himself that they needed to learn life sometime. He had dismissed all regard for his own safety the day Serphimera pronounced her doom upon him. Deceived though she was about the dragon, and blind to the real nature of the Power, Pelmen still was experienced enough in the things of magic to know her visions could well come true. If she were convinced it was really his death she saw . . . who could alter visions?

"My Seachief modestly gave all credit for the victory to you, Prophet."

"The credit belongs to the Power."

"What Power?" Asher said sharply. "You talk like a magician! If you mean the Lord Dragon, then say so!"

"I don't mean the Lord Dragon."

"Then you are a magician?" Asher's eyes sparkled with excitement. If this Prophet confessed to sorcery he could be dealt with quickly, for the law stated clearly the penalty for such heresy. The drawing blocks in the heart of the city had not been used in generations. But unless the termites had chewed out their insides, they would certainly still perform their function.

"It isn't sorcery I speak of, General. But neither is it the dragon. The dragon was made and will pass. The Power has been and will be."

Asher studied this false Prophet a moment. Then, in a burst of temper that surprised even himself, he spat into Pelmen's face. "Maximum cage. *Now!*"

The two guards lifted Pelmen from the ground by his armpits and carried him from the room. As the tail of the flopping blue robe disappeared into the hallway, Asher fought the nausea that rose in his throat. Such national decay. And so quickly, too. Through the folds of his tunic, he fingered the carved Dragon talisman that had long hung around his neck and thought of Serphimera. Then he stripped himself of his ceremonial clothing and donned his battle gear. He gave his office a last glance before he closed the heavy door. There was nothing on his desk that needed attention—nothing that couldn't wait until after the war.

By late afternoon the army of Lamath filled the King's Road like a mighty, south-flowing river. Northbound traffic simply had to clear off and wait until it passed. The Chaon column had been sighted attempting to pass Dragonsgate. General Asher hoped to arrive in time to help the Lord Dragon demolish the infidels.

❧ Chapter Twelve ❧

ADMON FAYE sat quietly in the former library, watching the square-cut slab that hid the cavern below. His drawn sword lay across his lap, and his hands played absently with a wickedly curved dagger. Two or three brothers had died before he received the information he needed, but others had proved more cooperative. It was a pity the dead had been so stubborn. The slaver had had no quarrel with them. He would seize the lad and the girl eventually, anyway. Why should these monks waste their lives attempting to prevent the inevitable?

He had accepted, finally, that Pelmen had escaped him. But he felt sure that he knew who the girl was, and she would be worth plenty, either to her father or to Ligne. If he could, he would capture the boy as well, and use him somehow to entrap Pelmen. But if the lad resisted, the slaver resolved to kill him. One live prisoner would be difficult enough to smuggle out of this foreign place. Two could prove more than just a nuisance.

They had to come up sometime, he told himself. Surely they weren't stupid enough to lose themselves down there. Suddenly there was a faint scrape, and Admon Faye gripped his weapons tightly and moved around to crouch behind the stone.

The slab lifted out of place very slowly, but Admon Faye was patient. He hid himself behind the edge that acted as a hinge for the rest of the slab. There were muffled grunts and gasps, then he saw a hand with thin, tapered fingers—a woman.

Bronwynn heaved the stone up, and it flipped onto its face as Admon Faye skipped out of its way. The girl's back was to him, and she didn't see him until he had grabbed her. His knife hand slipped nooselike around her neck as his sword arm thrust under her left arm and around to grip her waist. She screamed as he lifted her off the top rung of the ladder and spun her in the air. He whispered menacingly, "Where's the boy?"

Bronwynn didn't answer. Her chest began to heave, and she whimpered instead. He crushed her against him harshly and demanded again, "Where's the boy?"

"He's dead!" Bronwynn yelled back, and tears washed out onto her cheeks.

"I don't believe you," the ugly murderer snarled into her ear. Then he craned his head around and bit her, hard, on the cheek.

"It's true!" Bronwynn screamed, and she kicked back at his shins with all the energy remaining to her. She missed. He swung her through the air and tossed her sprawling against the empty book racks. Then he dropped to his knees and peered into the hole. There was no light at all, but he thrust his head inside and strained to hear the sounds of breathing. He couldn't. Not with the girl's loud sobs.

He pointed his dagger at her and commanded, "You close your mouth!"

"How can I?" she screamed back at him. "He's dead! He's dead!"

"How is he dead?" the slaver demanded, vaulting the hole and thrusting his sword tip into her face.

"A bear!" Bronwynn wailed. "Don't you see the blood?" She raised the hem of her robe for his inspection. It was wringing wet with red-black blood, and for two seconds Admon Faye believed her.

That was time enough. The slaver heard rather than felt the blade-stroke that split the flesh of his back open. Fine hearing and trained reflexes kept it from being fatal, but Rosha had caught enough of the man to make the slaver drop his dagger. Bronwynn grabbed it and scrambled away on her hands and knees. Rosha leapt around between her and the killer, and deflected the wounded man's thrust easily. He didn't pause, but cut immediately under the slaver's blade and jabbed for the heart.

Admon Faye wasn't that hurt. His sword was shorter than Rosha's, a Chaon sword, and he was quick and cagey. He slammed his blade down fast, knocking Rosha's point toward the floor, and the young warrior had to dance sideways, briefly turning his back on the slaver, to avoid a slice that surely would have gutted him.

The elements of surprise and reflex response now exhausted, the swordsmen backed off and regarded one another. Admon Faye tried to force Rosha to circle far enough so that he could grab Bronwynn again, but the boy caught on, and indicated his refusal with two quick, capable slashes that drove Admon Faye back a step. Then the slaver recognized Rosha.

"Rosha mod Dorlyth, is it?" he muttered coldly. "You're a boy. I have no quarrel with you."

"B-but I have with you!" Rosha snapped back proudly.

The slaver's repulsive face broke into a crooked grin. "What's wrong, lad? Fear chewing you?"

"I am n-n-not afraid of you, Ad-m-mon Faye!"

"Rosha, don't talk!" Bronwynn warned from behind him.

"Don't talk? He *can't* talk!" Admon Faye chuckled. It was an attempt to draw Rosha into an exchange, true, but the slaver had not counted on the ferocity of the boy's response. With a flurry of strokes that came unbelievably fast, Rosha chased Admon Faye around the room, and Bronwynn was hard pressed to keep herself behind him. Admon Faye struggled to defend himself. When the boy finally slacked off, the slaver put an extra step between them. He resolved to say nothing more about the lad's stumbling tongue. He tried a different tack. "Give me the girl, swordsman, or I'll chase you into your tomb! I have no quarrel with you! Leave off, and I will make none!"

"The d-door!" Rosha cried, and he jumped forward again, fighting with a skill unrealized because it had been untested. He fought not with his arms and legs and back alone, but with his eyes, with his ears, with his mind. He beat Admon Faye back to the far side of the room, freeing the doorway, and Bronwynn bolted outside.

Admon Faye now felt the effects of that first deep cut. His back burned, and his strength was diminishing steadily. If he were to kill this boy, it would have to be by craft. And he would need to move soon or the girl would be away. He parried, then skillfully turned the boy's attack, driving Rosha back toward the open hole in the floor, herding him along with a fancy mixture of strokes. But as Rosha reached the edge of the pit he leapt nimbly backward, clearing it easily while his eyes never left the slaver's. Now Admon Faye jerked to one side and swooped his sword tip through the legs of the old Elder's stool. In the same motion he flipped it spinning straight for Rosha's face, and jumped across the yawning pit himself.

Rosha never hesitated. He thrust his blade forward to impale the stool, then brought it crashing down into Admon Faye's chest. He caught the man in the midst of his jump, and the slaver's feet came out from under him. Then he dropped, bouncing off one edge of the pit and jackknifing as he plummeted through it into the black of the cavern. Rosha tossed sword and stool aside, and stooped to grab the ladder, jerking it swiftly up into the room. As he gripped the haft of his sword and jerked it free from the stool, he heard Admon Faye groan.

That was unfortunate, Rosha thought to himself. Evidently the slaver had survived the fall. But Bronwynn was outside yelling for him to come, and he couldn't stay. He dashed from the building and jumped into the saddle of the white pony Admon Faye had stolen from the army. Bronwynn was mounted on Minaliss, and the powerful horse snorted with excitement as they turned and rode swiftly in the direction of Lamath. He seemed to know he was going for his master.

The cell Pelmen occupied was nothing more than a cage. It was a cubicle five feet square with one open side. This was closed off by a grill of riveted iron strips. A man could sit or kneel or curl himself on the floor, but he could not stand up or stretch out. Pelmen crouched in a corner, dozing. The guard assigned to watch him sat, pasty-faced with fear, on a stool facing the cage. He didn't like this at all. Imprisoning a prophet was never done in Lamath, even if he were of the Divisionist order. What with the army marching off to war and all, was this really a good time to aggravate the Lord Dragon?

"We will see your prisoner," someone said. When the guard recognized the speaker his ashen face turned whiter. Standing behind him was the entire council of advisors, along with the High Priest of the Dragonfaith himself!

"It's all right," Naquin told the guard, but the fellow wouldn't be comforted. "Go—eat something," Naquin ordered, and the guard scurried off to obey him. The High Priest turned to examine the man who squatted in the cage, whose eyes by now were wide and watchful. "Now, Prophet—for so they tell me you claim to be— help me to understand all this."

"I am addressing the High Priest of the Dragon-faith?" Pelmen asked, without changing position.

"You are."

"You really want to understand this?"

Naquin thought for a moment. "No," he answered honestly, "for I'm afraid you'll want to bore me with a lot of religious rubbish. Actually, I just came to see you for myself."

Pelmen smiled slowly. "Here I am."

Naquin raised his eyebrows, but did not comment. "It may be of interest to you that I am concerned about your welfare. It seems Serphimera finds your Prophet-hood most distressing. Why is that?"

"She worships the dragon. I don't." The gathered advisors muttered and whispered at that, but Naquin smiled.

"How interesting! I don't either. Perhaps we can be of some real use to each other, after all. I consider the Priestess to be a gigantic nuisance, and I appreciate any annoyance you may have caused her. Now, General Asher has decided that you are to be publicly drawn as an example to other false prophets, and he has sent that request to the King. He'll sign it, of course. The King loves Serphimera. Which leaves you in a rather nasty situation, doesn't it?"

"Does it?" Pelmen asked quietly.

"I think so, yes. You do know the function of the drawing blocks?"

"I do."

"You understand, then. Now, my feeling is this. Asher is gone to war and the King is hidden, dragon knows where. That leaves me as the most powerful man in the capital. If you'll agree to aid me in a little scheme my allies and I have worked up, I'll declare you an officially recognized Prophet of Lamath. Coming from under the Hood that should carry some weight . . . this hood is certainly heavy enough!" Naquin chuckled at his own joke, and Pelmen managed a smile. "What about it?"

Pelmen sighed, and looked around him at his situation. Then he tilted his eyes upward. "Whatever," he said. He was speaking to the Power.

"Very good," Naquin replied, interpreting that as consent. "My associate will explain the plan. Pezi? Come down here."

Pelmen sat up at this, looking beyond the hooded figures to see if this was the Pezi he knew. The first part of the rotund little man to come in sight was his belly. Yes, thought Pelmen. It was Pezi.

"He has agreed," Naquin muttered. "Explain the schemes."

"Now, Prophet," Pezi began. "First we—" Pezi stopped, his jaw agape.

"Hello, Pezi."

"Pelmen the player!" Pezi burst out.

"What are you saying?" Naquin asked him.

"This is no prophet! He is Pelmen the player! He's a crazy actor from Chaomonous!"

"A what?"

"An actor! He puts on plays!"

"What's a play?" Naquin asked his advisors, but none of them knew.

"This is a very dangerous man!" Pezi exclaimed. "In fact, he may well be responsible for bringing destruction on all the world!"

"Oh really?" Naquin said, amused. "This fellow in the cage?" The High Priest chuckled.

"It was he who confused the dragon!"

"He did?" Naquin looked in at Pelmen. "I'm coming to like you more and more!"

"My Lord, he is dangerous!" Pezi cried.

"Not to me, friend Pezi. To me he is a new prophet who may prove a very valuable resource."

"He is also known to be a sorcerer!" Pezi whispered anxiously in the High Priest's ear. Naquin stopped laughing, and looked at Pelmen with a new seriousness.

"Are you a sorcerer?" he asked. Pelmen shrugged. Pezi pressed his point home. "Didn't you wonder when they told you he controlled the winds?"

"Yes," Naquin agreed, watching Pelmen's face.

"And when the Seachief said it was this man alone who sank the Chaon fleet?"

"Yes." Naquin stiffened. "What do you want with Lamath, sorcerer?" he asked sharply. He suddenly felt very uncomfortable. The very mention of magic frightened him.

"I want only to see it free of this bondage you call the Dragonfaith."

"I see." Naquin turned to look at Pezi. "So. We let the order stand as it is, then?" Pezi nodded vigorously. The High Priest retreated hastily to the shelter of his giant temple, trailed by nine lanky spectres and one bouncing butterball.

Rosha and Bronwynn rode all that night and the next day. They stopped only for quick naps that were far too short to refresh them, and to beg chunks of bread in the villages they passed through. Though many villagers heaped abuse upon them for being so obviously initiates of the Divisionist sect, all provided some bit of food for the journey. It was the custom in Lamath to give initiates what they begged for and to speed them on their way. So Rosha and Bronwynn were well fed, but were left alone, and they rode unhindered to the capital city.

In the few weeks they had lived in this land, they had not traveled anywhere without seeing soldiers. Now the roads were empty, and by this they knew that the armies all had marched, and the battle at last was joined.

"Is he with them?" Bronwynn wondered aloud. Rosha wouldn't answer. But Bronwynn was lonely and needed to talk. "It is incredible to imagine that all this started when Ligne and Kherda had me kidnapped. Think of it—a war being fought over me!"

"Lamath," Rosha interrupted. "S-see the smoke?"

They rode harder then, and by sundown they reached the outskirts of the sprawling city. Bronwynn realized then why Rosha had been so silent. He was frightened.

They begged their dinner and found a deserted alleyway to gobble it down. "Where do we start looking?" Bronwynn asked, and Rosha shrugged.

He was oppressed by the buildings. Not by their height, nor by the skill of their construction, for in truth they were nothing but the hovels of rural squatters on the edge of the capital. What oppressed him was the sheer number of structures. They had ridden past row after row of shacks, yet seemed no closer to the distant palaces than when they had first entered the burgeoning township. There was a noise to his left, and Rosha's sword leapt into his hand as he spun around to face the danger. Bronwynn couldn't help but laugh.

"Wh-what is it!" he demanded.

"It's just a cat. Haven't you ever seen a cat before?"

"There are h-h-hordes of these cats!" Rosha yelled, and now Bronwynn saw them too—scores of cats, all of different colors, who ran along the piles of debris that filled the alley, who jumped from one squat roof to another, who slipped liquidly into hiding at the sound of Rosha's shout. "We must leave this p-place!"

"But cats aren't dangerous—"

Rosha sheathed his sword and stalked swiftly out of the alley. His companion ran to catch up with him, and soon they were mounted and again on their way.

"I d-don't like this city," Rosha snorted. Bronwynn was quick to agree, city dweller though she was. Never had she seen so many cats or so much garbage, and she began to long for the marble columns of Chaomonous.

They rode aimlessly through the maze of streets, becoming steadily more confused and frustrated. Vainly, they sought a main thoroughfare that would lead them to the heart of Lamath. The few people they met on the streets stared at them. Not only were they initiates, a rare sight in the city, but they were mounted. The two riders felt extremely out of place.

"Where are we going?" Bronwynn growled at last.

"D-do I look like I kn-know?" Rosha snapped back; but as she started to tell him that he certainly didn't, an idea came to him. "The river! P-perhaps some man who works with b-boats could tell us where P-p-pelmen has gone."

"We haven't been able to find a main street," Bronwynn complained. "How are we going to find the river?" But she had to admit that it was a better idea than any she had suggested.

They had made so many wrong turns, it was time for their luck to change. Rosha chose a direction and led them straight to the river. He tried not to gloat, but Bronwynn couldn't miss the intent of his pleased little grin. There, however, bad fortune caught up with them again; no one on the docks would admit to knowing anything about the Prophet.

"I know nothing," one tough old seaman growled, his religious sensitivities offended by the color of their gowns. "The only fool who bought the Prophet's line is that saltbrain, Erri. He swallowed the hook and the float as well!"

"This—Erri. He's—a sailor?" Bronwynn asked earnestly.

"Calls himself one," the seaman groused.

"Wh-where can we f-f-find him?" Rosha asked, and the old sailor glared at him silently in response.

"Please, sir," Bronwynn implored, "tell us where to find this man! It's very important!"

The seaman grimaced in disgust, then waved his arm toward a mooring some distance downriver. "The King's Dock, if you're a-mind. But you're fools." Then he disappeared up the rigging of his boat. A few minutes later, Rosha and Bronwynn stood face to face ith Erri the sailor.

"The Prophet? Of course I know the Prophet. I sailed with him, didn't I?" Erri looked suspiciously at these two blue-robed figures. "Might you be spies, come to entrap me somehow for my friendship with that man?"

"Not spies, not at all!" Bronwynn cried brightly. "We are his friends, his initiates! We've come from the country to find him!"

"You won't find him here," Erri grunted, and he started to climb back aboard his ship.

"Then tell us where we can find him," Bronwynn pleaded.

"You really don't know?" Erri asked. Then he grunted again. "Well, even if you were spies, I'd be giving nothing away. I'll tell you the truth. I really don't know myself. But if you truly seek him, you might check around the King's own dungeon. I've heard nothing of him these three days, and I'll wager that's where they hold him."

Bronwynn's face had paled. "Why?" she asked.

"Because he won a victory for us," Erri snorted. Then he cursed. "I don't pretend to understand it."

"C-can you d-direct us to this dungeon?" Rosha asked, and Erri studied the young man's face for signs of duplicity.

"You don't know that either?"

"We're from the country," Bronwynn explained, "we know nothing of this place!"

"Lucky, then," Erri commented, and he looked around him. The sun was setting. There was nothing to do aboard ship. Nothing in the bars but a brew and a brawl. And he had liked Pelmen. "I'll take you." He hopped up onto the deck of his vessel and disappeared below; but soon his head popped back out of the hatch and he jumped down to join them on the wharf. "Best not to ride these animals to the palace. The army will surely relieve you of them. I know a man who keeps horses—he has a few honest days each week. Perhaps tonight will be one of them."

The two travelers followed his advice and stabled the horses, promising the innkeeper a worthy reward when they returned. Then they were off on foot to the palace of the King. They drew fewer stares now, but they still made an unusual picture—two initiates in torn and grimy sacred blue, with a foul-mouthed sailor between them.

At first Erri refused to speak with the warder, and he tried his best to keep the young couple from approaching the man. "It's too dangerous! Better to wait at the dungeon gate and talk with the guards as they leave!"

But the young pair had ridden too far and been without rest too long to have the patience that plan required. They were going to speak to the warder whether Erri came or not. Erri wouldn't allow them to go in without him, so all three walked up to the gate.

The warder of the dungeon was no fool. He had heard the story of the Prophet's confrontation with the Priestess, and knew there had been two initiates. These two wore the same colors that Pelmen did. The warder arrested them without another thought. "And since we have plenty of room below—" he began, but Erri didn't let him finish. He shot out the door of the warder's office, running as fast as his short little legs would carry him. He knew he could never outrun his pursuers, but he surely could outclimb them. Alas, there were no handholds on the apartment houses that lined the street, and no ropes hanging from the lamp posts. A few minutes later he was sharing a cell with Rosha and Bronwynn, just a few paces away from the cage that held Pelmen.

"I knew I should never have agreed to aid you!" Erri screamed. "I knew it!"

"Erri, is that you?" Pelmen called from down the corridor.

"Pelmen!" yelped Bronwynn, and she dashed back and forth through their cell, looking for some crack or window through which she could see him. She found none.

"Is Rosha with you?"

"He's here."

"Why didn't you stay at the monastery?" Pelmen wanted to know.

Bronwynn related to him all that had happened since their parting, how Admon Faye had killed the Elder, and how Rosha had killed Admon Faye.

"He isn't d-dead," Rosha reminded her, wishing mightily that the girl's words were true.

"What about the book?" Pelmen called doubtfully.

The book! Bronwynn had left it in the bag on Minaliss' saddle! "I—I hope your innkeeper friend is as honest as you say," she said to Erri, who was sitting angrily in a corner of the cell, "because one of those horses carries a book that cannot be replaced."

"What? This old thing?" Erri pulled the book from where he'd stuffed it in the waistband of his pants, and Bronwynn danced joyfully across the straw of the dungeon floor to whisk it out of his hands. "I borrowed it," Erri explained defensively. "I like to read sometimes when my mates are off drinking. I was going to return it anyway, because it's no good. It doesn't have proper writing!"

"Pelmen, it's here!" Bronwynn yelled through the door, and Pelmen relaxed his grip on the bars of his cage and settled back onto the floor.

"Good," he called. "Then we have something to do

while we wait to—then we have something to do. We can read the book."

"Well, read it to yourselves!" an angry voice called from another cell. "We're trying to get some sleep here!" It was one of Pezi's cousins. Though Pezi had come to a position of influence with the High Priest, he had refused to argue for the release of his family members. One could hardly blame this cousin for his sour disposition.

Bronwynn and Rosha were too tired to read, anyway. They slept in the straw while Erri and Pelmen shared a quiet conversation about the nature of the Power.

"What good is this Power," Erri whispered down the corridor, "if it can't keep you out of prison?"

"Sometimes I wonder that myself," Pelmen replied. He shifted, seeking a comfortable position for sleep. But there would be no sleep tonight. Only memories of an old friend, lost to the dagger of Admon Faye.

While most of Lamath slept, its army continued to march. By morning, General Asher and his troops stood at the northern mouth of Dragonsgate.

Sometime in the night a small contingent of guards came marching down the corridor and unlocked Pelmen's cage. He was still half asleep as they dragged him from the tiny cell and carried him farther down the hallway.

Erri was awake when the key turned in the lock. He jumped up and scrambled to the door, and so was right in Pelmen's path as they tossed the Prophet into the room and slammed the door behind him. The two fell in a heap on the floor, and Pelmen immediately rolled off.

"Are you all right?" he asked.

"Fair enough," Erri answered, struggling to his feet. "I hope I made your landing a bit less painful. Why did they move you down here? And at this hour?"

"I've no idea—"

"Someone to see the Prophet," came a call from the corridor, and once again the door opened and someone stepped inside. There was no light in the dungeon, so

Pelmen didn't recognize her until a guard followed her in with a lighted torch. It was Serphimera.

"What's going on?" Bronwynn called sleepily from the corner.

"Someone to see the Prophet," Erri hushed her. "Go on back to sleep."

"The Prophet is here?" Bronwynn exclaimed, and she jumped from her pile of straw and ran to Pelmen. She hugged his neck, crying words of greeting, and he responded by wrapping her in his arms.

"Excuse us, my Lady," Pelmen smiled at Serphimera over Bronwynn's shoulder. "We've been separated for several days."

"So I understood from the warder." Perhaps it was the acoustics of the cell, but Serphimera's voice seemed tinged with jealousy. Pelmen gently pulled Bronwynn's arms from around his neck, and grinned at her.

"Where's Rosha?" he whispered.

"You know Rosha. He could sleep through an earthquake."

"I'm here," Rosha murmured from the corner. "Since I d-don't expect to be g-going anywhere, I'll let you greet your g-guest."

Bronwynn looked around at Serphimera and frowned.

"What's she doing here?" she asked.

"We're about to find out," Pelmen said quietly.

Serphimera cocked an eyebrow and surveyed Bronwynn's ragged, bloodstained garment. "Since when have the Divisionist brothers been accepting female initiates?"

"I asked that they conceal the girl among themselves, and they complied."

"Do you find that heretical, too, Priestess?" Bronwynn sneered.

"My mission here has nothing to do with you, my child," Serphimera said. "Would you excuse us, please?"

"I am not your child—"

"Bronwynn," Pelmen murmured, and the girl turned to look up at him. "Let me speak with her."

"Here, girl, I've made you a new pile of straw," Erri

called from a dark corner of the cell, and Bronwynn laughed derisively.

"I'm the child, being sent to bed, then?" she snarled. "Very well, my master! Perhaps in the morning you'll relate to us what the lady had to say?" No one missed the bitterness in her voice.

"Bronwynn, let them b-be!" Rosha called, and the sulking girl finally went to sit beside him. She whispered heatedly in his ear as Pelmen looked at the Priestess.

"Why *did* you come here, my Lady?" he asked.

"When I heard Asher had put you in that cage, I had to come," Serphimera answered quietly.

"Oh? I understood from the General that it was you who asked that I be imprisoned."

"Imprisoned yes, but not caged! It is for your own good," she continued defensively, "and for the good of the people of Lamath. You cannot be allowed to roam the land, attracting weak believers to your heresies."

"Yet you roam the land, my Lady."

"I share the truth of Lord Dragon! Yours is a message of lies!"

"So you have said. Did you come to this dungeon to argue with me, my Lady?"

Serphimera turned her back on him and walked toward the door. She did not wish these others to hear their conversation. When she spoke again, it was almost in a whisper. "I have come to offer you freedom."

"What kind of freedom?"

"Freedom from this place, of course . . . and freedom from death."

"On the condition that I follow you?"

Serphimera looked back at him. "I know well enough you could not follow me now. In these short weeks you have built your own following, and many remain stubbornly loyal to you in the face of all reason. No, I don't ask you to follow me. I only ask you to leave off your Divisionist heresies and serve the Dragon."

"Your devotion is impressive, Serphimera. But I have met your dragon, and he is no god. Please don't cover your ears!" He pulled her hands from her head to hold them in his own, and stooped down to gaze into her face. "Look at me, Serphimera—please." She had clenched her eyelids tightly against his words. Now they flickered open, and he saw great sadness in her eyes.

"Asher gave the order to the keeper of the tugoliths four days ago," she whispered. "The beasts are already prepared to draw you."

"I understand that."

"If you are a Prophet, you know the traditions. Five days from the giving of the order, the tugoliths draw. You will be between them tomorrow, unless you recant."

Pelmen thought a moment. "But Serphimera, what of your vision?" The Priestess dropped her eyes and tried to pull away, but he held her. "Did you not see me torn between the mouths of the dragon?"

"It was a dark vision . . ." she murmured, struggling weakly.

"Yet you said it was I! You spoke so certainly of my doom!"

"The man in my dream wore a robe of sky blue— Divisionist blue, like this robe you wear!"

Pelmen released her. "Few Divisionist monasteries still exist, so effective has been your teaching." He shook his head and paced away from her. "Most monks are midnight-clad, as you are. If the man in your vision was noon-clad, I've no doubt you dreamed of me."

"Draw no comfort from my vision, false one," Serphimera said. "It will not save you between the blocks!"

"Who can alter visions, Serphimera? Am I to believe that you are able?"

"It was a dark vision, I told you!"

"Who else but I would be clothed so?"

"Your initiates are two!" Serphimera snapped, and she gestured to the young couple lying in the straw.

"Rosha, Bronwynn—when I gave you those robes I told you the time would come soon to lay them aside. It has come."

"G-good," Rosha announced, and he jumped up from the floor and began stripping the garment over his head. Bronwynn now saw by torchlight that he had been clothed in tunic and mail shirt all along.

"No wonder you've been complaining about being hot!" she said.

"C-could n-never tell when t-t-trouble might come."

"That's all very well for him," Bronwynn told Pelmen, "but I don't have anything on under this!"

Pelmen smiled. "I imagine you are safe enough here, Bronwynn. But we've been discovered now. There's no longer any sense in hiding your womanhood."

"You seek to force the vision to apply only to yourself and thus insure your safety between the blocks," Serphimera spat out. "But if you were a true Prophet you would know that every vision is open to many interpretations. There are those who say the tugoliths are related to the dragon. Could they not fulfill the prophecy in drawing you?"

Pelmen gave Serphimera a slight grin. "Tugoliths related to Lord Dragon? Now that sounds like heresy to me!"

"Oh, stop this!" the Priestess shouted, and Pelmen's smile departed. "Will you waste your last few hours of life in sophistry?"

"My Lady," Pelmen replied softly, "it isn't sophistry. A Priestess of the dragon has pronounced my doom upon me. How can I but watch the horizon of the future for its coming?"

Serphimera sighed. "Then you will not recant?"

"I *cannot*, my Lady. If I have seen the truth, can I deny it? When you have seen a vision, can you call it a lie?"

Serphimera looked at the guard, and inclined her head to the door. He held it open for her, and she stooped to go out. There she stopped and looked back in at Pelmen. "You are a fool, Prophet." Then the door slammed shut, and they were in darkness once more.

Erri kept his mouth closed as long as he could, but finally could hold his tongue no longer. "You kick away a chance to be free just because you and the lady don't see things alike. Is that entirely necessary?"

"How should I know what's necessary?" Pelmen growled back, and the others heard him drop heavily onto a pile of straw beside the door. He would speak no more until dawn.

While conquering the northern lands centuries before, the armies of Lamath had discovered the great beast of burden they came to call the tugolith. It was a monstrous animal standing about fifteen feet to the shoulder, with an enormous horn protruding from the middle of its forehead and a hide as thick as dragon scales. Its skin and its size led those early Lamathians to assume the tugolith was a distant relative of the dragon. There was even a rumor that certain of the soldiers who discovered the creature attempted to worship it, but the army and the Dragonfaith kept that very quiet, for it was quickly seen that the tugolith was not terribly bright. Even the smartest of the beasts never accumulated a vocabulary much beyond that of a four-year-old. Certainly an animal so dull could not be related to the Lord Dragon!

Lamath needed a wall in the far north to hold off the attacks of barbarians, and soon the army put these beasts to work hauling the stoneworks into place. They proved so capable that a large herd of tugoliths was driven south to help in the building of the capital. There the concept of drawing was hit upon quite by accident, when an unfortunate handler gave an imprecise command and his two animals pulled apart rather than pulling together. Before many years passed, drawing by a pair of tugoliths became the chief form of capital punishment. It was considered especially appropriate for heresy.

But that had been long ago. The sects of the Dragonfaith had grown so numerous and so varied that heresy was impossible to define. Then, too, quicker and less expensive forms of execution had gained in popularity. Few people expected ever to see a heretic drawn, though there were many who argued about the necessity of keeping the drawing blocks. The announcement of the drawing of the false Prophet came as a shock to the entire nation, and a large number of rural peasants brought their children to Lamath to witness this rare event. The dungeon's occupants began hearing the crowd at daybreak, and the noise level gradually swelled through the morning.

Erri sat glumly in one corner, facing the wall. Rosha, too, kept to himself. He had never laid much stock in any visions of any kind, but he did know something of the laws of nature. If two monstrous animals were to pull Pelmen apart, the Prophet would be killed. That much was evident. What was not so obvious was what one could say to a man condemned to such a death. Instead of talking, Rosha played with handfuls of straw, and daydreamed of the snow caps on the mountains of Ngandib-Mar.

But Bronwynn was a believer. If Pelmen did not think he would die between the blocks, she didn't think so either. Something did concern her, however. She scooted over next to Pelmen. "What do you think of the Priestess? You've never really told us."

"Why do you ask me that?"

"I just want to know what you think. I would like very much to hate her—but I get the feeling you don't."

"No, I don't hate Serphimera."

"I don't see why not!" Bronwynn snapped. "She's trying to kill you!"

"No, she tried to save me. Remember? Serphimera is a very beautiful woman who thinks she knows something—but really doesn't."

"Then what do you think of her?" Bronwynn persisted.

Pelmen smiled. "Isn't that enough?"

The girl studied his face. "I don't think so," she said seriously. "Things passed between you two last night that had nothing to do with words."

"Who gave you permission to listen?"

"And I want to know this: do you love her?"

Pelmen cackled. "What a thing to ask a condemned man!"

"Well, do you?"

Pelmen took Bronwynn's hand and rubbed it affectionately. "You've been too long in your father's court, Lady Bronwynn. Like him, you mistake attraction for love."

"Isn't that what it is?"

"No. Love is much more than that. I'm a little surprised that you haven't discovered that already."

"But you do feel that for her?"

"Feel what?"

"Attraction."

Pelmen grinned. "Yes. What difference does it make?"

Bronwynn blinked a couple of times, and shrugged her shoulders. "Some," she said. "It matters some." Then she stood up, and drifted away.

Soon after, they all heard the tramping of guards in the hallway. Then the door flew open, and the warder and his personal staff filled the cell. "On your feet, Prophet. It's time to go."

Pelmen stood slowly, then looked around at his three friends. Rosha glided to his feet and came toward him. The Prophet noticed the lad had donned his robe again to protect the mail shirt from theft by the guards. Rosha hugged him forcefully, then stepped back to look Pelmen in the face. "D-do you want us to d-do anything?"

"You still have the book?" Pelmen asked. Rosha nodded. "Then keep reading it. Keep telling these people the truth."

"Come on, the tugoliths are driving their master mad! We don't have all day."

"Very well. Erri?" The little sailor hopped to his feet and took the hand Pelmen offered.

"Oh, yes," said the warder, looking at Erri. "You're to go with us too. The Seachief has cleared you of all complicity with the heretics, and you're free to go."

Erri raised his eyebrows, but said nothing. He muttered a quick good-bye to the two young people, then climbed out of the cell into the hall.

"Bronwynn?" Pelmen asked, opening his arms to the girl, but she wouldn't come. She stood on the far side of the cell and gave him an awkward wave.

"See you," she murmured softly.

He waved back. Then he, too, climbed into the passageway. The warder followed him out, and the door clanged shut again. Once more, the young couple was alone.

"Was that any way t-to say g-good-bye?" Rosha growled.

"I wasn't saying good-bye," Bronwynn snapped back. Then she turned away from him. "Besides," she said. "He's in love with Serphimera."

❧ Chapter Thirteen ❧

THUGANLITHA AND CHIMOLITHA were the two tugoliths who had been chosen to draw the false Prophet. Just now they were aggravating their handler to the limit of his patience. The creatures possessed only a four-year-old intelligence, it was true, but they had all the curiosity of a four-year-old as well. They were also very forgetful, and tended to ask the same question over and over again.

"Why am I here, Dolna?" Thuganlitha asked his keeper for the thirtieth time that morning.

Dolna screamed back his answer. "Because I brought you here!"

"Why?"

"So you can draw this Prophet, whoever he is!"

"Who is he?" Chimolitha butted in.

"What's a Prophet?" Thuganlitha asked.

"Please," begged Dolna, "one question at a time?"

"Me first!"

"No, me!"

"I'll horn you!"

"I'll horn you first!"

"Quiet!" Dolna shouted, and the two monstrous beasts obeyed. So did a large portion of the crowd closest to the platform, and they craned their necks to see who had yelled, and if the program were beginning. They saw no change in the personnel on the dais, so each returned to his own private conversation. Dolna sighed, and leaned against one of the blocks.

"I wouldn't have them myself," said the King's headsman, who also stood on the platform.

"Oh, they're not so bad," Dolna explained through a drawn smile. "When they're working, they say very little. It's this waiting around that makes them nervous."

"Dolna, this waiting around makes me nervous!" Thuganlitha said, and Dolna ran around to yell in the beast's face.

"I've told you before not to copy what I say! Now be quiet!"

"Dolna, why am I here?" Chimolitha called, and Dolna tilted his head back and pinched the bridge of his nose between his thumb and forefinger.

"Yes, Chimolitha. I know you need attention too. Just be quiet and I'll come around there to you." Now Dolna looked back up into Thuganlitha's gigantic face and threatened, "If you don't keep quiet, I'm going to do something very terrible to you when we get back to the pens!"

"What?" the tugolith demanded petulantly.

"Use your imagination!" Dolna replied fiercely. Then he stalked around the blocks to pat Chimolitha on the beast's giant chest. "Please be quiet, won't you?" The animal regarded him balefully, then nodded. Dolna staggered back to his place beside the headsman, and slumped down to sit on the edge of the old stone platform.

"Never have any trouble with my blades," the headsman murmured. Dolna made a face, but took pains that the larger man did not see it. "Have to sharpen them is all," the headsman continued. "No, my problem is with reprieves."

"Reprieves?"

"That's what I said. Terrible problem for a headsman. These government officials, they never can make up their minds. First they want to kill a lad, then they don't, then they do, then they don't again. I'd say three quarters of my trips to the block I never get a chance to swing my blade."

"What's a blade?" Thuganlitha asked.

"Are you using your imagination?" Dolna yelled back. There was silence from the giant animal, and Dolna smiled. "Go on," he nodded to the headsman.

"Gives me a queer feeling, talking to a monster," observed the headsman, and Dolna sprang to his feet trying to hush him.

"Don't say that!" he whispered. "These animals are very sensitive!" He straightened up and listened a moment, then nodded in relief as he called out, "Still using your imagination?"

"Yes," Thuganlitha said. His tone was surly. "Dolna, I don't like that man."

Dolna's relieved smile faded, and he rushed around to whisper in the animal's ear. The startled headsman used the time to plot his quickest route of escape from the platform. Soon Dolna appeared beside him again.

"It's all right," the handler said, patting the headsman's shoulder. "He promised he wouldn't horn you unless you called him a monster again. Thuganlitha is very sensitive to such remarks." Dolna dropped his voice to a whisper. "And his hearing is excellent." The headsman nodded, and tugged his hood down nervously. "You were speaking of reprieves?"

The headsman cleared his throat. "Ah, yes," he said, feeling he had just been reprieved himself. "These chieftains and priests—they can never make up their minds. They've no respect for my trade. They use me, you see, to bend men to their wishes. Never give a thought to my sense of fulfillment as a person! I can never be sure when I sharpen my blades if I'll get the chance to swing them or not. What kind of life is that, now? They pay me to look ferocious in my mask, you might say. But a headsman can't get no fulfillment out of posturing, can he?"

Dolna smiled politely. "I suppose not."

"But they don't care," the headsman snorted. "If my covered head and eye slits can scare a man into serving them, they let him off!"

"There's little chance of that today," Dolna said, watching the crowd. It continued to swell. The city square was filled with people jammed tightly together, and every apartment house or small mansion that fronted onto the square had its windows full of spectators.

"No, not today," the headsman grunted. "The order was given by the Chieftain of Defense, and how can he reprieve the lad when he's off for the wars?" The headsman's grin was clearly visible below the nether edge of his dark hood. "Pity, though, that I didn't get the job. I could do it clean, and never involve you and your beasties here. Ah, they don't mind being called beasties, do they?"

"They've never said," Dolna shrugged.

"Dolna, I don't like that man," Thuganlitha rumbled, and the headsman hopped to his feet.

"I meant nothing unkind, nothing unkind—"

"Dolna, may I horn him?"

"No, Thuganlitha, you may not! I have you harnessed where you are for a specific purpose and I don't want you ruining all my work just to horn someone!"

"How can I keep from offending these animals?" the headsman pleaded, and Dolna smiled.

"Try not saying anything." The headsman nodded, and closed his mouth.

"Why am I here, Dolna?"

"We're waiting for the High Priest, Thuganlitha. Just be patient."

"Dolna?"

"Yes, Chimolitha." He sighed. "What is it?"

"What's be patient?"

"I don't want to go out there!"

"But, my Lord, you must!" said an advisor.

"It is the tradition," said another.

"I don't care!" Naquin protested. "That man is a sorcerer! I may be—struck with lightning!"

"There's not a storm in sight, my—"

"—swallowed by an earthquake!"

"I assure you, my Lord, you are perfectly safe—"

"I'll wager that's just what the Chaons thought before this magician sank their fleet!"

"My Lord, please stand still—"

Naquin paced throughout the temple, his hands clasped behind him. His advisors chased him between the mighty pillars, attempting to surround him or to block his path, but he had been eluding many of these same advisors since he was but six years old. He had been raised inside this edifice. There was no corner of its vast acreage that was unknown to him. Still his advisors scurried after him, attempting to place the Hood of Office on his head, as if to do so would render him immobile.

"Take that thing away! I said I'm not going out there!"

"But the High Priest must show himself, or the execution won't be carried out!" The advisor was exasperated with this young man. Had his father been this much trouble to his advisors when he was newly come under the Hood?

"The High Priest must show himself?" Naquin asked.

"So I've been saying all morning long," sighed the advisor.

"Very well then, the High Priest *shall* be seen. Pezi! Pezi! Where is he?"

"Have you tried the kitchen, my Lord?"

"Good thought." Naquin darted to the kitchen door and slung it open. "Pezi? Pezi, I need you!"

Soon the merchant stood beside him. "Will this take very long? I left a plate of ribs—"

"Are you ready to watch this Pelmen be drawn?"

"Certainly, my Lord, just as soon as I finish my—"

"Put the hood on him," Naquin ordered.

"My Lord!" the advisors chorused in shock. "You cannot do this thing!"

"Put the hood on his head and help me out of this robe!" the High Priest commanded. The advisors complied, but they voiced grave doubts throughout the operation.

"Now then!" Naquin smiled. The High Priest drew a circle in the air with his finger, and Pezi turned around twice to model his new vestments. "How does he look?"

One advisor said, "Obese." Another used the term, "Fat." The other comments were similar.

"Nevertheless, the people need to see their High Priest, and so they shall."

"But what do I say!" Pezi protested.

"How should I know? Make something up. That's what I would do." There was a pounding at the door, and Naquin motioned them all out. "Time to go. Have a nice time. Be sure to remember everything that happens, so you can tell me all about it. Good-bye!" He pushed them all out the door, and slammed it on all their protests. Then he looked at himself, and giggled.

He wore Pezi's clothes. Rather, the voluminous garments swallowed him up. He turned across the mosaic floor, the robes billowing around him, and thought what it must be like to be Pezi.

"The ribs," he said, "I mustn't neglect those ribs." With that he was off for the kitchen. He could not remember the last time he had enjoyed himself so much.

Rosha pounded his fist on the walls in utter frustration. Bronwynn just watched. "I don't know why you're so worried," she said. "He told us he would be back."

The young warrior looked over at her with a pained expression. "How c-can you be so b-believing? What do you b-base such confidence on? On that b-book?"

Bronwynn had been hugging the book to her. Now she looked down at it. "This? Partly, I suppose. Though not really. My confidence is more in those who made the book than in the book itself. No, better still, I believe in the one who taught me to read it."

"You trust in P-Pelmen, then?"

"I trust in Pelmen," she affirmed quietly.

"D-do you . . . t-trust m-me?"

Bronwynn looked up at Rosha now, wondering at the unusual tone in his voice. "Of course I trust you. What do you mean?"

"You t-trust me to . . . t-to fight bears, or evil m-men. B-but do you t-trust me . . . c-could you t-trust me, like you t-trust P-Pelmen?"

Bronwynn laid the book aside and got to her feet. "Why are you having such difficulty saying this, Rosha?"

"You d-don't make it easy, m-my Lady . . ." He blushed and looked away from her. She put her hands on his shoulders and began to massage his rock-hard neck.

"I can't read your mind, you know," Bronwynn said, and he sighed heavily and walked away from her hands. "Are you still angry that I didn't embrace Pelmen when they took him?" Rosha shook his head, and sprawled on the straw in the darkest corner of the cell. "Then what?" She came and crouched beside him, and ran a hand through his hair.

Rosha didn't look at her. He laced his fingers behind his head and gazed intently at the ceiling. After a moment he began, "I . . . have so mu—so much I n-need to tell you. B-but it gets all c-closed up in-s-side me, and I c-can't speak well . . ."

"Take your time," she soothed, and she stroked his head again. That helped him to look at her.

"I remember m-my m-mother, some. And I—I remember that my father loved her, m-*much*. I m-may know n-nothing of love, but if I d-do, then I think that . . . I love . . . you, B-B-Bronwynn." His eyes flicked away from hers then, swiftly, and he looked for some crack or chisel mark in the cold ceiling to focus on.

"Rosha, I—"

"I kn-know you are a P-Princess, b-but I n-needed to say this. N-now it's said. So."

"Rosha?"

He dared to look into her eyes again. Imagine his shock when he saw tears on her cheeks. "Why . . . why do you cry?"

Bronwynn smiled, then half chuckled. "All my life, I've wanted someone to say that to me. And you just did." Rosha nodded. Her face crinkled into a smile again, and she leaned over and kissed him on the cheek.

"My Lady," he muttered, "you are a P-Princess—"

"No, Rosha." She hopped to her feet and spun around. "I am an initiate in the Divisionist order of the Dragonfaith—can't you tell by my robe?" She dropped to her knees and took the cloth of his garment in her hands. "I see you are too. Don't the brothers say we must love each other?" She smiled impishly at him, and he returned her smile with wonder. Then her expression changed. She showed him the girl she hid inside, and her eyes asked him how he could love one such as she. Rosha's arms slipped around her slim waist in silent reply, and he pulled her to him. They lay in one another's embrace then, as they had so many times before. But their embrace was different, this day, for both knew what it signified—and they rejoiced together in the gloom of the dungeon.

Waves of cheers broke on the platform, and Pezi could not hear himself think. He pulled the jeweled hood as low onto his face as he could, and hunched his shoulders, hiding behind the rich brocade of the High Priest's vestments. His eyes shifted from side to side, searching nervously for one who might shout out his name and expose him as a fraud to this throng. But those who watched him seemed content that he was truly their spiritual leader. They looked not at him, really, but at the robes and the hood of office. The High Priest rarely appeared in public.

The tugoliths danced impatiently in their harnesses, and demanded of Dolna that he release them and let them horn various members of the audience. The headsman stood at the top of the stairway, eyes following the progress of a small clump of uniformed men as they made their way from the dungeon gate to the platform. They surrounded a man in a bright blue robe, obviously the principal figure in this execution. The crowd swayed from side to side, carrying the soldiers back and forth, but on they came, plowing a way with shoves and curses and the occasional prick of a pike.

At last they gained the stairway, and the warder preceded Pelmen up the ramp. "I have brought your prisoner," he announced to the headsman in the traditional formal language.

"What?"

"I said I brought your prisoner!"

"Oh! Good. I'll get the keeper of the tugoliths."

"What?"

"I said I would get the keeper of the tugoliths!"

"Oh!" The warder plugged up his ears against the noise as the headsman went off to fetch Dolna.

"I am required to read the charges before you execute the man!" the warder yelled when Dolna stood before him, and the tugolith handler nodded. The warder pulled a scroll from inside his tunic and began to read. *"Inasmuch as the King has found this man . . ."*

"What?" the headsman called.

"I'm trying to read the charges!" the warder yelled back.

"Oh! Just read them to yourself, we all know why the King is killing him."

"What?" the warder yelled back.

The headsman waved his hand in disgust. He reached beyond the warder, pulled Pelmen around to the blocks, and cupped his hand around Dolna's ear. "You can go ahead now!"

Dolna nodded, and cut through Pelmen's bonds. The two animals were harnessed back to back to a pair of large wooden blocks. Each block was five feet high and six feet long, and a pair of chains dangled from each end. At the end of each chain hung an ankle clamp, and now Dolna snapped the ankle chains from the blocks around Pelmen's legs. "You'll have to lie on your back now!" he yelled into Pelmen's ear, and the Prophet nodded and sat down where he was.

"This is a fine pair of animals!" Pelmen said.

"What?" Dolna yelled back.

"These tugoliths!" Pelmen yelled. "They're both beautiful animals!"

"Oh!" Dolna nodded, pleased by the comment, too deafened to consider the incongruity of it. After all, these fine animals were about to tear the Prophet in half.

"Dolna?" Chimolitha called.

"Wait here!" the keeper yelled. He went around to face Chimolitha. "What is it now?"

"Was that man talking about me?" the beast asked.

"Yes—he said you were nice-looking. Now leave me alone!"

"Dolna?" Chimolitha called, stopping the keeper before he even got around the tugolith's forequarters.

"What?" he bellowed, finally losing his patience.

"I like him."

Dolna waved the beast's comment off, and went back to Pelmen's side. The crowd roared in anticipation as Dolna stooped to fix the wrist irons in place, and now

Pelmen gazed up into the blue sky. He alone saw the blue flyer whoosh by overhead, bound for the palace beyond.

Suddenly, Pezi the merchant was standing over him, dressed outlandishly in the robes of the High Priest, and Pelmen had to chuckle. Pezi frowned at him, and looked around to see if any of the crowd had noticed. They hadn't. He carefully got down onto his knees, and spoke into Pelmen's face.

"Have you any last words, Prophet?"

"Why are you dressed like that, Pezi? Where's the High Priest?"

"He sent me in his place. Are those your last words?"

"I suppose they are as good as any."

"Very well. But before I give the order that will kill you, I want a little information."

"What?" Pelmen yelled, for the crowd was delirious with excitement.

"I need some information about where you hid the girl!"

Shock danced across Pelmen's visage, then he smiled. "You don't know?"

"Of course I don't know! Why would I ask you if I knew?"

"Pezi, you don't know how much that pleases me. I certainly don't intend to tell you where she is."

"Be reasonable, Pelmen! In another minute these beasts will pull you apart! What difference should it make to you whether I find the girl or not?"

"What do you want with Bronwynn? You already have your war. Isn't that what Flayh was after?"

"I know little of what my uncle plans, but I know it would please him if I could bring the girl back. Come now, Pelmen, cooperate with me! If you'll tell me, I promise that the house of Ognadzu will build you the finest tomb in Lamath." Pezi said this so seriously that Pelmen laughed aloud.

This caused the headsman to mutter to the warder. "What are they doing? Telling jokes?"

"What?" the warder shouted.

A new group of soldiers suddenly broke from the gate of the dungeon, and they made no pretense of courtesy. They clubbed people out of the way and wedged themselves into the back of the crowd, all shouting as loudly as they could for the warder. He neither heard them nor saw them.

The headsman saw them, however, for his eyes were trained to look for that. "Oh, no!" he murmured bitterly. "Not again!" Then he rushed to Dolna and grabbed the handler's shoulder. "Give the order!" he shouted.

"The man is still with the Priest!"

"This is my responsibility and I said to give the order!"

"Very well then. Thuganlitha? Chimolitha?"

"Yes, Dolna?" the beasts roared back in chorus.

"Pull!"

"Dolna?"

"Yes, Thuganlitha?"

"Is that man being unkind to you?"

"What man?"

"That man I don't like!"

"No, Thuganlitha, he's not. Now pull!"

"Dolna?"

"Yes, Chimolitha?" Dolna ran across the platform to get in front of the other animal.

"Why am I here?"

"To obey my orders, and my orders are to pull—now pull!"

"But one thing."

"What, Chimolitha?" Dolna groaned.

"If I pull this way, and Thuganlitha pulls the other, won't it hurt that man I like?"

Dolna was amazed. Chimolitha had never uttered such a long sentence before. "How did you figure that out?"

"I don't know," Chimolitha said honestly. "It just popped into my mind."

"But things don't just pop into a tugolith's mind," Dolna said, gazing curiously into Chimolitha's saucer-sized eyes. Had he been looking into Pelmen's eyes instead, he might have understood a little better. Pelmen was smiling.

"Are these beasts going to pull or aren't they?" the

headsman shouted. Though the warder still had not noticed them, the soldiers were almost to the platform.

"Dolna, I'm going to horn that man!" Thuganlitha bellowed, and he gave a tug on the block as he tried to turn to his left to reach the headsman. That one jerk pulled Pelmen's arms rigid, and he gritted his teeth against the sudden pain.

"Not until after we've finished!" Dolna yelled, running around the blocks to get in front of Thuganlitha—then he stopped. He stared in amazement as he watched Chimolitha step backward, nudging his block back with his massive hindquarters. Pelmen fell back onto the platform, gasping for breath as he thanked the Power for this respite.

"Stop them! Stop them now!" the warder began shouting, but Thuganlitha would not be stopped. As he jerked around to get at the headsman, Pelmen was spread-eagled again, but Chimolitha answered with a relieving nudge. "Can't you stop them?" the warder screamed at Dolna, who stood transfixed, watching Chimolitha rescue Pelmen from Thuganlitha's rampage.

"I can't stop Thuganlitha now," Dolna shrugged. "He won't be satisfied until he's buried his horn in that fellow."

The headsman leapt into the crowd and tried to push his way through, but as people bolted outward in panic, a solid wall of bodies formed across his path, penning him in.

"Take that man!" the warder shouted, and six soldiers jumped down into the crowd in pursuit. As they seized the headsman and buried him under their weight, Thuganlitha trumpeted and lurched forward. Pelmen screamed as he felt himself being drawn in two.

The guards hustled the headsman around to stand face to face with Thuganlitha, then scattered.

"Nice beastie! Nice beastie!" The frightened man smiled in horror as that monster's eyes lidded menacingly in anticipation of the thrust. Dolna wrestled with Pelmen's chains, attempting to unclasp them even as the warder read the message that the blue flyer had carried all the way from Dragonsgate. Through his pain Pelmen still noticed when Pezi scampered from the platform, holding the Hood on with both hands. Then the pressure suddenly came off of his arm, as the lock clicked open in Dolna's hands. Free at last, his mind clouded. In the few seconds before he passed out, Pelmen was dimly aware of the warder's words. *"The Prophet is right,"* the warder read. *"Spare him, or I'll draw you. Asher."* Then there was nothing.

The day Asher wrote that message had dawned brightly on the General's marching army. There had been a quiet promise of light, then suddenly the sun had broken free from the mountains to the east, and the fabled Dragonsgate became visible in all its awesome splendor.

Asher held up a hand to stop the column and sat there for a moment, marveling. "Here is truly the center of the world," he whispered. The rocky heights rising beyond the pass looked like the citadel of a race of giants, but in Asher's mind the place was far more. Here was the home of Lord Dragon. At last he'd been privileged to view the dwelling place of his god.

Asher had selected an honor corps from among his most favored warriors. Now they rode behind him up the sharp incline, lances and swords held in readiness, heads held high with pride. The northern mouth was the steepest of the climbs, but it was a short approach, and soon they turned the corner into the heart of the pass. There Asher jerked his steed to a halt, and his heart sprang into his throat. The dragon was immense—and he was real.

The beast stood at the far end of the pass, and suddenly Asher realized why. There in the southern mouth stood a host of golden-clad warriors, and the dragon appeared to be speaking with them! Abruptly the beast fluttered into the air, and settled to earth a scant ten feet away from the General. Asher jumped from his horse and prostrated himself on the ground, listening as he did to the honor guard following his lead. Then he snapped upright onto his knees and slammed both arms across his chest in the age-old salute of the dragon.

"See?" Vicia chortled. "See? I told you they would come, that my people would come!"

"We have come, Lord Dragon, to honor you, and to defend you against infidels who exalt gold above the spirit!" Asher closed his eyes in sincere devotion, awaiting the Lord Dragon's reply.

"I told you, I told you," Vicia sang out childishly.

"Close it up, you stupid lizard," Heinox snapped, and Asher's eyes popped open. "There are thirty of them. I have an army of thousands."

Had he imagined it? Or had Asher actually heard one head call the other head a lizard?

"How many are you?" Vicia asked.

Asher blurted out, "Twenty thousand! But—"

"There, you see?" Vicia screamed. "Now I have an army of thousands, too!"

"But Lord Dragon—"

Heinox swooped down into Asher's face. "Call me that again and I'll swallow you."

"Don't you dare," Vicia seethed, "or I'll chew up every general you have, armor and all!"

"You just do that, 'Lord Dragon,'" Heinox mocked, "and watch what I do in return!"

"But Lord Dragon, we are your army!" Asher cried.

"The Chaons are my army!" Heinox roared. "You belong to this disgusting lizard I share a body with!"

Asher felt faint. He stumbled to his feet and leaned against his horse. "Then—the dragon is no longer one . . . the dragon is divided?"

"Yes, and will be as long as this ball of meat on a neck continues to call himself a god!"

"I am a god!" Vicia roared. "You heard him say so!"

"I've heard you say so again and again. That doesn't make it any less a pile of—"

"My army will prove that I am a god! Won't you, whatever your name is."

Asher blinked. "The Lord Dragon does not know my name?"

"How should I? What do you think I am, all-knowing or something?"

"I . . . am Asher."

"There. This Asher will go against your Talith, and you'll see who is a god!"

"Talith is here?" Asher asked.

"Yes, Talith is here," Heinox sneered, "and you had better prepare yourself to meet him, for he's about to destroy you and your nation!"

"Not here he isn't," sniffed Vicia.

"Of course not here. The battle will take place in Lamath."

"Think again, my scaly-eyed friend!" Vicia snorted. "It will take place in Chaomonous! You don't expect me to allow my fields to be ravaged by your barbarians, do you?"

"I certainly don't plan to let Chaomonous be despoiled by your warriors, either!" growled Heinox.

"All right," Vicia said. "Let's do as that merchant fellow suggested. Send both armies into Ngandib-Mar to fight one another. Then the victor can go find that Pelmen person for us."

Heinox snorted, and cocked his head. "That's the best idea you've had since the Pelmen first passed this way!" Suddenly, much to Vicia's surprise, the dragon was in the air again. Heinox happened to be controlling their bodily functions that day, and he wanted to speak with Talith. "We'll send his army through the pass first," Heinox said. "After all, they've been waiting for days."

"Agreed." Vicia was trying to steer his head into the wind to keep from feeling so pulled about. He was already plotting the best way to get Asher through to Chaomonous instead, to pillage throughout the Chaon homeland and teach Heinox a lesson.

Talith had bristled at the first appearance of Asher across the pass, but now he was cowering again. If only the dragon didn't whiz around so fast! It took his breath away each time he saw the monster hurtling toward him.

"We've decided what you're going to do," Heinox began, and Vicia immediately interrupted him.

"Yes, we've decided to send you to Ngandib-Mar."

"I was going to tell him!" Heinox roared.

Vicia sneered, "But I beat you to it."

As the heads berated one another, Talith sought to clear his mind and to consider his options. Tahli-Damen had suggested the possibility of moving into Ngandib-Mar, but the small group of warriors across the pass had inflamed him, and he surprised even himself by breaking into the dragon's argument. "And what if I say no? What if I decide I want to attack that pitiful troop of Lamathians yonder?"

The dragon looked at him with four eyes; then the two heads chorused, "We'll eat you."

In moments, Talith was saddled and his army ready to march. The long, golden column began again to wind its way westward through the pass. Vicia-Heinox took to the air again, planning to explain the situation to Asher.

"Where is he?" Vicia asked. Then he demanded, angrily, "Where is he?"

"Perhaps he grew frightened and ran home." Heinox laughed and dropped his head close to their body to escape Vicia's snapping teeth. Vicia knew better than to bite his twin, but in his rage he wasn't thinking straight. His army, the army of Lamath, was nowhere to be seen.

The warriors of Lamath waited at the foot of the mountain for some signal. When they saw their General and his small troop break into view from the bowels of the pass, all of Lamath drew their swords, and commanders began forming that blue line that had proved such an invincible defensive barrier in the northland campaigns. Tension mounted as they waited for the enemy to gallop into sight—but no enemy appeared. Nor did Asher give any sign to charge. Instead he came right through the ranks, shouting loudly for his falconer as he rode to the signal wagon. Once there, he leapt from his horse and grabbed the stylus and parchment his signaler offered. His chief of wings sprinted toward them with a bird cupped in his hands.

"My best, General Asher."

"It had better be so," Asher snapped back, and the General held the bird skillfully as the falconer affixed the message to its leg. Asher shut his eyes and imagined the square of the capital, and the dungeon, and the office of the warder. When the picture was clear in his mind he tossed the bird skyward with a shout, and the blue flyer made swiftly for the north, carrying the words that would save Pelmen's life.

Serphimera did not watch the execution. She waited it out on the dining plaza of one of those small mansions that overlooked the square. It was the home of a staunch supporter—one who could not quite bring himself to give his body to the dragon and who sought to assuage his guilt by giving his home to the Priestess. He, along with his family, watched and cheered from a balcony high above her. But Serphimera could only pace and mourn, already missing this one who had held so much promise, but who had failed so completely.

Though she wasn't watching, Serphimera was in touch with all that happened beyond the wall through the cries of the crowd. When the laughter and cheers turned sour, she cupped her hands to her mouth and called out, "What's happening? Tell me!"

"It is incredible, Priestess!" her outraged supporter yelled back. "The King has stopped the execution!"

A moment before, she had been mourning Pelmen. Now, abruptly, she hated him again. "This sorcerer has witched even the King!" Before anyone could stop her she dashed out the garden gate and into the street. The crowd parted before her, giving her free passage to the dungeon.

The warder listened silently to her protests, then shrugged. "Priestess, I can only do as I am ordered. I cannot explain the reasons why some sentences are commuted and others carried out. It is the will of the dragon."

"It is *not* the will of Lord Dragon!" Serphimera stamped, and the warder looked away, embarrassed. "I thought that the King understood the need for this man's execution! It was my understanding that Asher had ordered this death, and that the King had agreed! Why would the King overrule his Chieftain's order!"

"The King did not overrule Asher."

"Then who?" Serphimera snarled.

"It was Asher himself who stopped the drawing of this Prophet. He seems to believe the Prophet is right."

Serphimera stood rigid, her body frozen as her mind

wrestled to make some sense of this new information. "Asher?" she said at length. "The Prophet has convinced even Asher?"

The warder nodded curtly and turned away, hoping the woman would take the hint and leave. He hated to get involved in religious politics. Give him the dirt and blood of true crime any day. At least then, the killing made some sense.

Serphimera gave him his wish. She went out the door of the dungeon with her mind aswirl. She gazed downward, and the cobblestones seemed a million miles away. She kept walking, putting one foot before the other, fearing that if she stopped she would plunge to her death on those distant rocks below. She walked no more in Lamath, but in a world of dreams too suddenly shattered. Serphimera felt hopelessly lost amid a universe of yelling people. It was only her reputation and her characteristic dress that saved her from the riot begun by the rampaging tugolith. Fighting crowds would clear out of the way for the dazed Priestess to pass, then would fall back to fighting. Her supporters finally found her, and guided her through the flood of angry citizens to the safety of the secluded garden.

"Pelmen, are you awake?"

"Yes . . ." He really wasn't, but he was getting there. Pelmen's eyes opened, and he gazed up into Bronwynn's face.

She beamed back at him, and shouted, "Rosha! He's awake!"

Rosha came and knelt down in the straw by Pelmen's side as Pelmen struggled to sit up. The Prophet yelped in pain as his weight shifted onto his left arm, and he would have fallen back had Bronwynn not supported his head.

"Why don't you just lie there a while?" the girl asked sensibly, and he smiled.

"Where am I?"

"In the dungeon."

"They didn't kill me?"

"You really need me to answer that?"

"No," he murmured. He thought for a moment. "Do you know why they didn't?"

"We've no idea," Bronwynn answered.

"B-but the warder was m-m-most gentle with you when he carried you in. He s-said something about Asher wanting you whole."

Then Pelmen remembered. He nodded, and forced himself to sit up without using his left arm. Then he moved across the floor to lean against the damp wall.

"Does that make any sense?" Bronwynn asked.

"I think so, yes. Somehow Asher discovered that I was only telling the truth about the dragon. That means he has probably been into Dragonsgate."

"Then Asher is marching on Chaomonous?" Bronwynn worried aloud, a bit surprised at herself for even caring.

"He's probably been in Dragonsgate. Through Dragonsgate, and into Chaomonous? I doubt it. Vicia-Heinox has never before allowed an army to pass Dragonsgate—never in his history. Why should he do so now?"

"B-but if he has?" Rosha wondered.

Pelmen raised an eyebrow. "If he has, I would truly like to know what's happening now. For if any army has passed Dragonsgate, into any other land, then the world has just witnessed the gravest battle since the time before the dragon—the grandest clash since the parting of the One Land."

"It is clear now," Serphimera murmured much later, after the sun had left the sky and the garden's torches had been lit. "I see my responsibility clearly."

"And what is it, my Priestess?" begged one disciple. "What can we do, now that this charlatan is again free to roam the streets?"

"Too long I've wandered these delightful fields of Lamath, sending others to make the ultimate devotion in my place."

"No, Priestess—" one began, and another follower wept aloud in anticipation of her words.

"It is time for the Priestess herself to journey to Dragonsgate."

"No, Priestess, you cannot! Asher's warriors line every section of road from here to the Lord Dragon's nest! You'll not be allowed to pass. Please, stay and reconsider!"

"It's time, I tell you!" All the protestors saw the fire in her eyes. They sat quietly then, watching. When she spoke again, Serphimera was once more in control of herself.

"He has slipped away today. But I have seen this Prophet's doom! A time will come when this one clad in sky blue will be pulled into that sky by the mouths of Lord Dragon, and the Lord will tear him in two!" She glanced around at the circle of faces, her jaw set, her expression carved of stone. "Perhaps," she said, "my own sacrifice can somehow hasten that day."

"Yet there is still the hazard of the journey! How will you come to Dragonsgate, if Asher's warriors hold the road?"

Serphimera's eyelids flickered, and her gaze burned the speaker's cheeks pink. "Am I not able to plan my own passing?" she asked.

"Forgive me, Priestess," he mumbled.

"There is a man of hideous countenance who proved a fearsome enforcer in the cleansing of the Prophet's own monastery. Find me that man!"

"Yes, Priestess," someone replied.

In moments runners were in the streets, searching for word about an ugly man whose name no one knew, but whose face no one could forget.

Serphimera climbed the stairs to the balcony, and gazed to the south. Humbly she saluted the dragon with crossed arms, and curtseyed. "I come, Lord Dragon," she murmured quietly, then slipped back into the lighted interior of the mansion.

❧ Chapter Fourteen ❧

"THERE THEY ARE!" Dorlyth said ominously, and he pointed with his sword. Through the pass below rode warriors armed from head to toe in plates and mail of gold. The afternoon sun reflected brightly off that highly polished metal, wrought by the finest artisans in the world—the craftsmen of Chaomonous. The line continued to come, clearly visible to Dorlyth and his companions, who watched unobserved from the mountaintop above. "You see them, Pahd? Pahd? Pahd, are you sleeping again?"

"Hunh?" Pahd awakened with a start. He sniffed, and glanced around him. "Where are we?"

"We're preparing to go into battle!"

"Oh, yes." Pahd smiled drowsily. "I was just getting a little rest before the excitement starts. Not easy to do on horseback." He leaned over his mount's neck to watch the column a moment, and his eyes brightened. "Ohh. Lots of them, aren't there?"

"Aren't you glad you chose to get up this morning?" Dorlyth mocked. "You might have missed it."

"Come now, Dorlyth. You aren't still angry at me for not arriving in time to break Tohn's siege. Had we arrived sooner, I may well have killed the old gray merchant. Then he never would have had the chance to warn us of all this."

"True enough, Pahd. But as I recall, you were more angry than I."

"And understandably so!" Pahd complained. "To get out of bed and ride all that way just to watch two Lords make peace is not my idea of an exciting outing. You might at least have staged a duel of champions."

The west mouth of Dragonsgate opened onto a large

plain. Far below them, on a slight rise in that expanse of green meadow, stood the castle of Tohn mod Neelis. Its gates were tightly shut, and Tohn and his people had gathered within to wait out the battle that would decide the future of the Mar. They had been waiting this way for weeks, for Tohn had expected Talith's army long before this. His young cousins chafed under his restrictions and mocked him behind his back. But Tohn would not change his mind. He had informed Dorlyth that he would open his gates for no one, either to enter or to exit. His keep would remain an island of calm in the midst of a stormy ocean of battling armies.

Though they could not use Tohn's castle as a fortress, Dorlyth had decided to use it in a ruse to draw Talith into an initial charge. As the old warrior explained his strategy, Pahd just nodded. Strategy made little difference to Pahd, so long as he had an opportunity to exercise his greatsword.

"We'll all have that opportunity, my Lord," Dorlyth said. "More, I'll wage, than even you might wish."

"I doubt that's possible." Pahd smiled, drawing his weapon. "What is the signal for our attack?"

"When Talith charges westward toward the three thousand on the plain and you hear screams from the pass as our archers move into position, then charge, Pahd mod Pahd-el. And may the powers favor you with great strength!"

"I'd prefer that the powers favor me with great foes," Pahd chuckled. "I'll furnish the strength myself." Pahd rode down the mountain to rejoin his cavalry, which was hidden in the forest at its base.

Dorlyth gazed across the pass to the mountains on the northern side and searched the woods atop those cliffs for some sign of Venad mod Narkis and his army of archers. He saw no movement at all—nothing that would betray to Talith that his grand column marched into an ambush.

With Pahd's indifferent blessing, Dorlyth had divided the army of assembled Mari chieftains into three units. The smallest force was composed of Dorlyth's own veteran fighting men, supported by the most powerful warriors from every other fief in the land. This group, only three thousand strong, waited on the plain between Tohn's castle and the pass. The other sixteen thousand Mari warriors had been divided equally, half waiting in the foothills on the northern edge of the pass and the other half waiting in the southern hills. Dorlyth had assembled a group of powerful archers out of each of these divisions, and the two units of archers faced each other across the valley. Each archer carried a plentiful supply of arrows; if the confederation of Mari lords were to win, it would have to win in the pass. Battle-hardened though they were, Dorlyth knew his Mari brethren would never defeat twice as many Chaons in a direct confrontation on the field. He hoped to deplete and demoralize Talith's army before it ever reached the plain.

Dorlyth glanced around at the men who waited with him in the shelter of a small clump of trees. "Remember—our task is to fill the air with a shower of arrows, not to shoot individual Chaons. Fire quickly—the powers will make our bow-shots accurate."

From the pass below came the echo of a great shout, and Dorlyth walked out to the edge of the cliffs to take a look. He turned and nodded, shouting, "Talith has taken the bait!" Hundreds of archers sprang from cover and launched a deadly flock of feather-tipped missiles. An answering volley filled the sky on the far side of the pass, and the first screams of shock and terror began issuing up from the valley. Dorlyth smiled coldly, and arched his own first arrow into the sky. It joined a thousand of its fellows in flight.

Talith and Rolan-Keshi rode through the pass side by side. Talith's heart pounded furiously. A few moments before, the dragon itself had given him leave to conquer Ngandib-Mar. Now, for the first time, he beheld that beautiful mountainous land, and knew at once that he had to possess it.

"Look at this! Look at it! It shall be mine, Rolan-Keshi—this land shall be mine!"

"We must conquer it first, my Lord. And it appears there will be some resistance. Look." They had ridden far enough through the gap to see the small Mari contingent on the field, and Tohn's castle beyond them.

"A tiny force, not to be compared to my army!" Talith laughed, his excitement building. His mount began to trot, as did Rolan-Keshi's, and the riders behind them picked up speed as well.

"Why are they here?" Rolan-Keshi wondered suspiciously. "No one in this land should know of our coming!"

"They are defenders of that fortress yonder!" Talith shouted. "We must take them before they reach its shelter!" Talith kicked his horse and jerked his sword free from its scabbard. He raised it high above him and shouted at the top of his lungs; the answering shout from the warriors charging behind him drowned Rolan-Keshi's protests. The army of Chaomonous streamed out of the pass, pursuing its King into battle, as the three thousand Maris on the open plain below broke and ran for Tohn's castle.

Talith rode the proudest mount in all his many stables, and it was a far stronger horse than any of those who followed him. Soon he was twenty yards in advance of the charge, shouting. "They're running! They're running!" The General rode hard to catch him. It was a foolish charge, and Rolan-Keshi knew it, but it was certainly far more thrilling than the night raids and border skirmishes that had been his only previous battle experience. But Talith was much too far in advance of the main line of thundering riders. If the King should be the first man cut down, it would have a brutal impact on the morale of his army. Rolan-Keshi screamed at his horse and drove his heels violently into the animal's flanks, even as the General saw a few hundred Mari warriors wheel around to face them.

Talith saw them too, when he was but thirty yards away. He almost dropped his sword as he jerked back suddenly on the reins of his war-horse. His charging warriors faltered when their King faltered, and the first blows exchanged between Maris and Chaons went badly for the golden warriors. Talith stood where he was, frozen by the cold metal of those drawn greatswords, suddenly so very near, and he surely would have been hacked from his saddle had not his supporters swarmed around him. Little blood was drawn in this initial impact, but the clashing and clanging and shouting that filled the air kept Talith from hearing the screams of falling warriors in the pass. He found the handle of his sword again and waved it in the air, shouting encouragement to the soldiers who fought to defend him. His courage soared once more when he saw the Maris break off the fight and ride on to join the rest of the Mari force.

The lead riders of Dorlyth's field brigade had by this time reached the walls of Tohn's keep. Watchers on the walls stared openmouthed as these riders parted to either side of the keep, then turned to face the golden charge once again. Tohn's children thrilled at the color and glory. His young men ached to fire a few arrows in one direction or the other. Tohn himself gripped the battlements and stared down at the regrouping Mari line, his face fixed in a frozen frown as stony as the rock walls he clung to. The Mari line extended to the right and left of his keep, the far ends bowed to prevent Talith's force from flanking them. In the shadow of Tohn's wall they waited for Talith to extend his army farther onto the plain, opening his flanks to mounted Maris on the north and south. It would not be many minutes before Pahd's attack struck the Chaon's southern flank.

In the early minutes of the battle, Venad mod Narkis' archers on the northern face of the pass proved coldly efficient. More than two thousand Chaons died or were wounded in the first arrow attacks, but most of these were on the northern side. Dorlyth's archers were less successful, though they poured as many arrows into the air, and this was to have some bearing on the course of the battle. When the shower of arrows began, most of the Chaon warriors panicked; suddenly the whole column no longer marched out of the pass—it pushed and shoved its way onto the field in terror. Dead horses and riders clogged the pass, and the panic combined with the litter of death to slow the line further. There was nowhere to run but forward, for Dragonsgate itself was still filling with more orderly columns, and there, too, waited the dragon. Men who could see an open plain and safety below them would certainly not run uphill into the presence of that threatening beast. As Dorlyth had hoped, the column continued to come—and the arrows continued falling, taking a shockingly high toll.

Vicia-Heinox vaulted into the air, and watched curiously from above.

"It appears," sneered Vicia, "that your army has found someone to fight after all—not any too well, I might add."

"Who are all these warriors? Where did they all come from?"

"From Ngandib-Mar, I would suppose. How did they get onto our hills without us noticing?"

"Because you've been so busy playing god, we haven't had time to protect ourselves! An army that size could do us great harm, yet we didn't even see it!"

"We've seen it now, though. Why get so excited?"

"Let's drop down and burn them off our hills!" Heinox roared.

"Why? Because they are so effectively slaughtering your precious King Talith's warriors?"

"Vicia, try to be reasonable! An army that close is potentially harmful to us! We must deal with the threat!"

"Sorry, Heinox, but I have no wish to aid Talith's army. Though my Lamathians proved to be unfaithful, these from Ngandib-Mar seem quite brave."

"We have never allowed such a battle to take place so close to our nest!" Heinox screamed. "Suppose we should become involved somehow in this fighting?"

"That's simple, Heinox," Vicia replied. "We'll burn both armies to ashes."

Pahd laughed aloud as his mounted forces exploded into Talith's exposed southern flank. Three—no, four—no, five Chaons made the mistake of engaging him, and Pahd efficiently disposed of each. Some may have thought Pahd bloodthirsty as he twisted in his saddle, hacking right and left, laughing more loudly with

every stroke. But it was no thirst for blood that drove
him forward. It was his genuine enjoyment of the sounds
and smells of battle, and the blood-pushing excitement
of personal combat. He dealt with a seventh, an eighth,
then a ninth Chaon, before the golden warriors became
aware of his seeming invincibility and began avoiding
him.

Unfortunately, Pahd's brethren-at-arms were not far-
ing well at all. Since Dorlyth's archers had not killed as
many Chaons in the pass as had Venad's, more fleeing
soldiers joined the southern flank than joined the battle
on the northern side of the field. The Mari attack in the
north proved so powerful that already frightened
Chaons grew more so, and many more Chaons than
Maris died on that flank. But despite Pahd's flickering
sword, which snuffed Chaon life wherever it pointed,
far more Maris died in the south. The full force of the
Chaon attack shifted toward Pahd and his supporters,
and they were driven back against the base of the
mountainside.

After his initial hesitation, Talith's courage flamed up
more brightly than before. Once again he led the charge
against the small force of Maris that flanked Tohn's
castle. Talith still believed his entire army followed him,
and that the battle was confined to his engagement with
these few who were ranged before him. But only seven
thousand of his warriors had chased him all the way
across the field; and as the two forces clashed together,
the experience of the tough old Mari fighters proved the
margin of victory. These waiting warriors had fought
often in field campaigns, for at no time in the history of
the Confederation of Ngandib-Mar had that great land
been truly at peace. The Chaons they mêléed had never
fought in any battle involving more than a hundred men
on a side. The noise was distracting—more so was the
sight of blood-spattered saddles and dying men.

Talith led one force to the left of Tohn's wall, while
Rolan-Keshi led another to the right. Talith shouted encouragement to his young General as he disappeared
around the curve of the battlements.

The charge broke down into thousands of individual

contests. Talíth found himself engaged in a hand-to-hand struggle with a gray-haired veteran in a dirty jerkin. The man looked to be sixty or older, yet he fought with the energy of a teenager. Talith summoned all his experience from years of dueling in his own armory and tried every trick he could remember against this aged opponent. But the real struggle took place in Talith's heart. Was he truly capable of killing another swordsman? It was not the other man's life that concerned him. Hundreds, perhaps thousands of people had met death by Talith's order. It was the thought of himself. Was he really skillful enough to win? Or would he prove himself a failure, and die in his discovery?

It was perhaps Talith's inability to conceive of his own death that saved him. That, and the old warrior's age. The gray fighter had watched too many friends drop in battle to believe that death could not touch him. When his energy flagged, he could no longer resist the raw expression of Talith's fear. With a desperate thrust, the King cut him from his saddle, and the man slept at last, joined with that host of fallen comrades who had acquainted him so well with death.

Talith shouted in exultation, even as his warriors were being beaten back. He broke off, shouting, "To me! To me!" His golden warriors were only too happy to obey. The Maris did not pursue. They regrouped to the west of Tohn's castle, and waited to see what Talith would do.

On the north side of Tohn's keep five hundred Chaon warriors were cut down. Among them was a promising young General who had been denied the chance to lead. Rolan-Keshi had been killed early, and his body now lay under a pile of golden-clad dead.

When Talith broke to the left and Rolan-Keshi to the right, the riders that followed them also broke off to one side or the other. All save one man. Down out of the mountain pass came Tahli-Damen, riding as straight and as sure as one of Venad mod Narkis' arrows to the very door of Tohn's keep. There he leapt from his saddle and ran to pound on the gate.

"Let me in!" Tahli-Damen cried out, straining his

voice to make himself heard above the din. "Let me in! I'm a merchant, can't you see? Let me in, I'm begging you! Look at my clothes, I'm a merchant!" He pounded and kept on pounding until finally he heard a reply shouted from above, and he craned his neck to look up into the face of a wild-haired old man robed in the colors of Ognadzu. "Please let me in!" he called.

"No!" replied Tohn mod Neelis, and the old man started to go away.

"Please! Listen! If you are Tohn, I have important words from Jagd! I'm of the house of Uda, can't you see that?"

"Go away!" Tohn shouted, and once again he started to leave the wall, but Tahli-Damen looked so horrified Tohn felt obligated to give some explanation. "I can't let you in! You're surrounded by battling warriors!"

"I know! I know!" Tahli-Damen screamed.

"If I open my gates, the battle will move in here!"

"Open them just a crack. I'm small! Can't you see I'm a merchant?"

"I can see you wear the colors of a merchant, of a house that rivals my own! No, I will not jeopardize my family and my keep for a merchant from the house of Uda!"

"But what of Jagd? Your alliance? The changes the Council of Elders have sought to institute—"

"It's all destroyed, and you may tell that to Jagd for me when you see him!"

"*If* I see him!" Tahli-Damen yelled. "If I survive, I'll tell him that you are no ally!"

"Good!" Tohn called back over the battle's roar, "because I *am* no longer his ally."

"Please!" Tahli-Damen tried one last time. "I am a merchant!"

"A merchant of Uda! I am of Ognadzu! The house of Uda in Ngandib-Mar is two miles north! I wish you luck in finding it, but I will not let you in here!"

"This bodes ill for the future relations of Uda and Ognadzu!" Tahli-Damen shouted, but Tohn's head already had disappeared from view. The young merchant heard horses charging around the curve of the wall toward him, and he threw himself against the gate as the thundering hooves passed close behind him. Then he slumped slowly down, until at last he sat in the dust at Tohn's front gate, scratching at it with his fingernails as if to find a soft place to dig his way into the keep.

More than five thousand Chaons lay in the pass, either dead or too badly wounded to flee. Another eight thousand warriors slogged their way forward through the rising tide of bodies, still rushing to avoid the deadly hail of arrows that filled the sky above. Dorlyth's arms were beyond being tired. He had fired his bow until his fingers bled from being rubbed and snapped by the gut of its string. He paused to gasp for breath, and looked to his left, down to the valley below where Pahd led the defense—for it had become a defense. Pahd's depleted cavalry was being driven up the mountain, and more and more Chaons shifted to the southern flank, away from that deadly northern wall.

Across the plain, Dorlyth could see the standard of the King of Chaomonous moving to the center of the field. The golden riders that had battled before Tohn's gates now regrouped around their ruler, and Dorlyth watched as Talith led them to join the battle against Pahd.

"He's in trouble," Dorlyth muttered, and he glanced back down into the pass. The arrows continued in a poisonous rain from Venad and his fellows; but Dorlyth could see that, in spite of all those killed in the pass, a huge force of Chaons had gained the field. The Mari northern flank was holding fast, as powerful a barrier as Tohn's castle walls. Dorlyth decided the best place now for himself and his archers was at the side of the Mari King. Not even Pahd mod Pahd-el could defeat fifteen to twenty thousand Chaons by himself—much as Pahd might think so.

Pahd's cavalry, four thousand strong when the day began, had shrunk to four hundred by the time Dorlyth and his reinforcements arrived to help. Yet the King still was laughing. When he saw Dorlyth he shouted. "Never in my lifetime have I enjoyed a day more!"

"Then there's more fun on the way!" Dorlyth shouted back gravely, as he ran his greatsword through a slow-moving Chaon pikeman. "King Talith rides to meet us, with all of Chaomonous at his back!"

"Bring him on!" Pahd shouted back merrily as his blade sliced cleanly through an enemy's shoulder. "I've yet to meet any Chaon who would be a match even for you."

At least there seemed little chance of Pahd falling asleep again, Dorlyth thought to himself. Then he cleared his mind of everything save swordwork. Dorlyth loved life dearly, and he intended to survive.

Talith's standard came streaking toward them up the hillside, just as they were driven back into a small meadow dotted with apple trees. Here Pelmen had first introduced himself to Bronwynn, and from this little meadow Bronwynn had fallen in love with the land of Ngandib-Mar. Here, too, Bronwynn's father and Dorlyth came face to face for the first and only time.

It was by accident that they met, for Pahd had cried out that Talith was his and had ridden for Talith's flag, while Dorlyth, remembering the saucy Princess that had so delighted his son, did his best to rein his horse away. He turned his back on the standard as Pahd rode past him toward it. But Talith had been separated from his standard-bearer almost the entire day; when Dorlyth left the golden flag, he rode abreast of the Golden King. He knew immediately this was Talith by the wealth of the engraving that adorned the man's armor and the splendid workmanship of his helmet.

"You are Talith—the King!" Dorlyth cried.

"I am! Stand and fight!"

"There are others who would choose to battle you, Talith! I choose to leave you to them!"

Talith's sword whistled over the head of his warhorse, and Dorlyth had to respond quickly to block it. "Your fear will not save you from my blade, Mari," Talith shouted grandly, "for I have chosen you!" Once again Talith slashed at Dorlyth, and again the bearded old warrior was forced to react swiftly to keep himself alive.

"Will you hold off, man?" Dorlyth shouted, frowning

fiercely. "I know your daughter! I won't rob Bronwynn of her father, nor will I let you rob my Rosha of his!"

"You know my daughter?" Talith shouted.

"I know her well," Dorlyth began, "and am glad—"

"You are the man who holds her!" Talith screamed, trading his battle bravado for a father's rage. Dorlyth met the first thrust, and the second, but Talith attacked him like a madman, wounding him inside the left arm.

"I hate this," Dorlyth said quietly, and he applied himself again to the task of survival. Talith shouted until he was hoarse, calling Dorlyth every name that came to mind. Soon it became apparent that Talith was no swordsman. Dorlyth slackened his attack, withholding maiming strokes in hopes that Talith would give up, and go to seek his death elsewhere in the apple orchard. But Talith continued to come, wearing himself out on Dorlyth's tireless defense. At last he grew so impatient that he recklessly threw himself forward, his thrust calculated to run the Mari through. Dorlyth jerked away, struggling to maintain his saddle as Talith fell against him. Dorlyth's sword was caught on something, and he pulled up on it, hard, to free it for the Golden King's next attack.

But Talith was attacking no longer, and Dorlyth's sword would not come free. The King had dived onto its point, and already his glazed eyes gazed upon the meadows of some other world. Dorlyth let the dead King's weight carry his sword tip downward, and Talith's body slipped from the saddle and crumpled into the grass.

"It appears I always arrive too late to help you!" Pahd shouted as he rode near. "But you always seem to manage so well without me."

"Would that you had come sooner, Pahd. I already feel a weight from this killing like no killing has birthed in me before."

"Don't think on it overlong," Pahd shouted, slashing a nearby Chaon's face open. "We seem to be facing a limitless supply of these gold warriors."

But the heart had been cut out of the Chaon army when their King had fallen. They were leaderless now.

As Pahd and Dorlyth waded shoulder to shoulder into the crowds surrounding them, the Chaon attack on the southern flank crumbled and reeled backward down the mountainside.

Those three thousand warriors who had baited the trap now linked up with the Mari barrier on the northern side of the field. The Chaons were encircled on the north and west. As Dorlyth and Pahd labored down the mountain, the southern flank was also closing. There was but one outlet—the pass itself—and it was knee deep in bodies, with Mari archers still waiting along its northern face. Perhaps, had Joss been there, the outcome of the battle of the west mouth might have been different. But Joss was not there. The army of Chaomonous was destroyed.

"They have certainly littered our nest," sniffed Heinox as he gazed at the stacks of bodies in Dragonsgate.

"And here they come again," said Vicia. There was alarm in Vicia's tone, and Heinox popped immediately up to eye level with Vicia and gazed into the pass for himself. A mob of howling warriors ran up the short incline from the plain. There were thousands of them. The dragon had been just as uncomfortable as the Chaon warriors during the golden column's march through Dragonsgate. Now, Vicia-Heinox became very tense.

"They are not attacking us," Heinox reminded his companion.

"Yet," Vicia snorted.

The fiery rain fell from heaven—arrows, everywhere the fleeing warriors stepped. No wonder they screamed for mercy, and charged desperately at the dragon. They now believed even Vicia-Heinox was preferable to the powerful Mari swordsmen on the field and those hidden demons who dropped darts on them from above. When those first trembling Chaons dashed into the heart of Dragonsgate, they only waved their swords and pike staves to try to force the beast aside. But when Vicia-Heinox refused to budge, they made the tragic error of thrusting those swords into the dragon's scaly hide.

The dragon—suddenly, incredibly under attack—

immediately put all interpersonal animosity aside, and dealt with the problem. Vicia and Heinox focused their combined fury on the tightly jammed mass of screaming humanity that fouled their ancient nesting place and unleashed anew that dreaded power that had altered the landscape of the entire world so many hundreds of years before. When the sound of the blast died away, eight thousand Chaons were missing, and the pass was clear of everything save ashes.

So began the second great period of burning. Vicia-Heinox was angry. The two heads could never again ignore their duality—they were no longer one, and there was no changing the fact. But that day they realized that, though they hated one another, they hated people even more. Mankind needed a new education in the power of the dragon, and they vowed to be harsh teachers.

Many of Venad's archers were also burned away by the dragon's blast. Those who survived dropped their weapons and ran from the hillsides, but few survived to reach the plain, for the dragon now leapt high into the air and belatedly scorched the mountainsides of Dragonsgate free of forests.

Pahd was no longer laughing. He and Dorlyth were just reaching the plain when the first flash jolted them. They looked at each other in shock, for that flash could only mean one thing. The Maris had no use for history, true, but they knew all of the ancient tales—especially tales of the dragon. Now all the stories had been proved true by the brilliance of that terrible blast. Without another clash of swords, the great host that had been locked in mortal combat throughout the day suddenly dispersed in every direction save east. Chaon and Mari rode side by side, shouting encouragement to each other as they fled the field of battle.

"By the powers," said Tohn in dismay. "Somehow they woke the beast!" Tohn gripped the battlements of his castle and stared. He had been surveying the wreckage done to his beautiful green fields by the battle when the flash from the pass caused him to look up. He watched as the dragon rose screaming from behind the rocks; he shuddered at the sight of those bizarre heads as they scorched away trees and shrubs. The dragon's double-throated scream was audible all the way across the valley and it shocked Tohn into action. He raced down the outer staircase as fast as his old legs would carry him, calling what names of his children, cousins, nephews, and aunts he could remember, calling out other names that he couldn't put with faces, in the hope that someone would answer.

"Get inside! Get inside!" he called. From the battlements ran others who had witnessed the catastrophe, and these echoed his warnings to scramble for cover. Tohn tried to run across the courtyard, but his breath was gone, and he paused to regain it, coughing amid the flying dust. Then he remembered. "That merchant lad," he said aloud, to no one but himself, and he grabbed a lungful of dirty air and dashed back to the main gate of the keep.

"Grandfather! What are you doing?" a young matron screeched, but he either did not hear her, or chose to pay her no mind. He slipped the heavy bolt and threw his weight behind the door to push it open.

There was only time for a quick glance around, for escaping Maris and Chaons alike saw that crack in the castle gate and turned to ride frantically toward it. Tohn leapt back inside and heaved the gate shut behind him. He slipped the bolt back in place even as the frightened soldiers jumped from their horses and ran to bang on the door's heavy planks. The young merchant had been nowhere in sight.

"I cannot," Tohn sighed, more to himself than to the shouting warriors beyond the barrier. "For my family's sake, I cannot."

Powerful arms gripped him on either side, and he was carried across the courtyard by teenage youths whose names he could not remember.

"His mind is a little addled by the battle, I think," said the young mother who preceded them toward the inner keep. "The dragon is loose, Grandfather!" she yelled in his ear. "We need to get inside or he might harm us!"

Tohn said nothing as these, his offspring, patronized

him. Let them think him a senile fool, he told himself.
Perhaps they'd put him to bed. Tohn's heart was breaking at the tragedy beyond his walls. Though he could
not get enough air into his lungs, his chest seemed to be
trying to explode. He needed sleep. Oh! Tohn thought,
how I need sleep!

❧ Chapter Fifteen ❧

WHEN ASHER RETURNED to the capital, he encamped
his forces on a field west of the city. It was here that he
received Pelmen and his party.

"I hope the dungeon was not too uncomfortable," he
said, greeting Pelmen. "I felt you would be safest there
until my return. Who are these with you?"

Pelmen introduced Bronwynn and Rosha, then introduced Erri. The little sailor had met them that morning
at the dungeon gate, holding Minaliss' reins in one
hand, and the white pony's reins in the other.

"You've become a loyal follower very quickly,"
Asher observed as he acknowledged the short seaman's
bow.

"Once you've discovered the truth, it's senseless not
to be loyal to it." Erri shrugged, and Asher gazed back
at Pelmen.

"My feelings exactly. I apologize, Prophet, for nearly
having you killed on such a false charge. Is the arm the
only ill effect you suffered?"

Pelmen's dislocated shoulder had been reset and
bandaged, and his left arm hung now in a sling. "Only
my arm, Asher. And please, don't hold yourself responsible. You were acting sincerely."

"Yes," Asher said grimly. "Sincerely wrong. The
monster—" Asher paused. "How quickly we change.

I've never called the dragon that before." He shook his head, then went on. "The dragon is a-burning."

Pelmen frowned. "I was afraid of that. I saw several charred sections as we made our way through the city."

"And not the city alone. The beast has ruined crops, destroyed villages, and consumed large quantities of our population. Truly, this is no god." Asher spat the words out in disgust. "I've spoken with him and discovered it for myself. The dragon is divided."

"I'm thankful you discovered it when you did, Asher." Pelmen smiled, rubbing his arm. Then his smile faded. "So. The dragon is a-burning. And he can't do that unless both heads cooperate. It appears that Vicia-Heinox has reunited himself in order to punish the rest of the world."

"What can we do? Is there any way to restrain the monster?"

"One way," Pelmen said. "By killing him. And the method of doing that has yet to be discovered."

Asher frowned. "As a boy, I was taught that the dragon is uncreated and immortal. But you say he can be killed—and you've proved yourself a Prophet. If he must be killed—who could discover such a way but you?" Asher's gaze was earnest.

Pelmen sighed. He was thinking of Serphimera's vision. "Who but me?" he said softly. Then he looked around at Bronwynn. "You have the book?"

"Right here."

"I'll study it, Asher. I'll look. This book told us of the beast's creation—perhaps it will yield some clue to its destruction as well. But it may take time—"

"Take what time you need, Prophet. You realize already the urgency of the situation."

The situation was urgent indeed . . . and not just for Lamath. Vicia-Heinox appeared everywhere. Peasants in regions far removed from Dragonsgate, peasants who disbelieved the dragon tales because they had never met a man who had seen the beast, now saw and feared. For Vicia-Heinox did not visit an area without giving it a sampling of dragon-burn.

It was not true that the dragon was systematic in his

devastation—but had the beast reasoned out some pattern, it could not have been more crippling to the mental state of mankind. He struck arbitrarily, burning one man's field while leaving the field next to it to ripen. Witnesses babbled incoherent accounts to their disbelieving neighbors, then hours later those neighbors would chatter their own tales of horror. Villages collapsed into smouldering cinders as the inhabitants watched and wept. Elsewhere, entire populations disappeared, leaving silent, lifeless dwellings as a mute testimony to the dragon's voracious appetite. Vicia-Heinox distributed his misery generously. His path of destruction could be traced through all three lands. While he was certainly not just or fair in his punishment, at least he vented his anger impartially. If there was a soul in any of the lands who did not know the dragon was a-burning, it was because he had cut himself off from the rest of the race and had hidden under the ground. The cry was everywhere the same. "Who will deliver us from the two-headed beast?"

Everyone in Lamath had a different explanation for the cataclysmic events of the last weeks. Many blamed the dragon's rampage on the Prophet, saying that this punishment was Lord Dragon's retribution for Asher's stopping the execution. These would have followed diligently any new command their Priestess might have given, even to storming Asher's compound and murdering Pelmen on the spot. But Serphimera was giving no new commands. Serphimera had disappeared.

Others praised the Prophet for revealing the twi-beast as a sham, and claimed that this destruction was the dragon's attempt at revenge. This new party united behind Pelmen, and the group grew larger daily as it was joined by soldiers freshly returned from the front. They had heard from their leaders the dialogue of Asher's meeting with the beast, and had seen the flash of light in Dragonsgate just prior to this eruption of chaos. "The dragon is divided!" they declared to loud cheers. "The Prophet is right!" These words swiftly formed the foundation of a new litany. Everywhere, the final chorus was the same. "All bless the Prophet! The Prophet will deliver us!"

Serphimera's loyals, prowling the street corners and searching the alleys, clenched their teeth against these new heresies and continued to search for their leader. "Remember," they reminded one another in whispers, "the Priestess has seen his doom!" But where was Serphimera? The inner circle seemed to know, but they said nothing. Most of them wore their gloom wrapped about them like winter capes. The others zealously kept on searching. Where was she?

The double-headed dragon singled out the cities for special punishment. Each of the major metropolitan areas felt the dragon-burn in widely scattered locations. But perhaps the hardest hit was the High City of Ngandib. Lamath and Chaomonous both stood astride giant waterways, but Ngandib sat on a great plateau. All water had to be pumped up from the valley below, and the liquid was always in short supply. Once the twi-beast set his fire upon a section of city, the blaze was nearly impossible to quench. By the time Pahd mod Pahd-el arrived home at the head of his victorious army, the flying monster had burned away half of his capital. Later that same day, Dorlyth mod Karis received a summons by blue flyer, demanding his immediate presence in the court of the King. Weary though he was, Dorlyth mounted his horse and rode west, wondering what Pahd required of him. When he saw the billowing black smoke while still miles away from the base of the plateau, he realized why he had been called.

Pahd's mother ushered Dorlyth into the King's chamber with grim silence. The King reclined, as usual, but Dorlyth noted a distinctive difference. Pahd mod Pahd-el was wide awake.

"You saw?" Pahd asked.

Dorlyth nodded. "Sickening. Worse than I had imagined."

Pahd looked away. Then he exploded. "And I can't do anything about it!" He suddenly reached out and gripped Dorlyth by the wrist. "I need help!"

"Whatever I can do, my Lord, I will—"

"Pelmen the powershaper. Where is he?"

Dorlyth shook his head. "To my great regret, I have no idea."

"None whatever?"

"Only that he left for Lamath some weeks ago with my son. I have heard nothing since."

"Why would he go to Lamath?" Pahd demanded. "I need him here!" The King jumped up, paced the room, then sat on the footstool before his throne and hid his face in his hands. Finally he looked up. "I've never faced anything like this before, Dorlyth. Nothing prepared me for this!"

"No, my Lord," the bearded warrior replied. He laid a hand on the King's shoulder, and the younger man gazed up into his face. Pahd's eyes were wet.

"I have lost half of my kingdom to this burning beast! In only a week! Can't someone help me control this monster?"

Dorlyth patted the King's shoulder, trying to impart some hope and strength even he himself didn't feel. "Perhaps Pelmen will—" he began, but his voice trailed off. It was such an unlikely idea. Why even mention it, and raise the young King's hopes?

Ligne paced the opulently furnished apartments that until lately had belonged to King Talith. They were hers now, but today the gigantic canopied bed brought no smile to her lips. Today the gilt-edged mirrors that ringed the walls reflected an angry pout back at their new mistress. Ligne was now indisputably Queen of Lamath. The bones of her former lover lay charred on some Mari hillside, if Jagd's information were correct. But of what value was a kingdom burned into ruin? Ligne had not opened the shutters for days, for it pained her to see so much of her golden city smouldering. The people were crying out to the crown for help against the monster, but what could she do? She no longer had an army—Vicia-Heinox had scattered what remained of that giant golden column all the way across Ngandib-Mar. The small remnant that had made it home through the forest and the mountains had been organized into a brigade of rebels by that meddlesome General Joss, and her pitiful little palace guard was kept busy guarding her outposts against Joss' harassment. Nor did she have a navy any longer—without coming into bow-shot of a Lamathian vessel, the Admiral of Chaomonous had managed to lose the greatest flotilla anyone could ever remember seeing. The man rotted, now, in Ligne's dungeon, but the damage was done. The mightiest nation in the world suddenly tottered on the brink of military and economic collapse.

Ligne sighed. Ruling wasn't much fun anymore. "Kherda!" she screamed, just as she did a hundred times a day, and the new prime minister of Lamath scrambled from his offices down the hall to appear at her door.

"Yes, my Lady?"

"What are we going to do?"

"Do, my Lady?" Kherda replied timidly. "What— what *can* we do?"

"That's what I'm asking you!" Ligne bellowed, her face turning crimson. "You're supposed to be my advisor! Now start advising or I'll find someone else!"

Kherda winced, and reflected briefly on the irony of it all. He had toppled Talith's government, only to find himself in a worse position in Ligne's. "There—is perhaps one idea that might be helpful."

"Then get it out!"

"I've learned from our contacts that a certain— subject of yours has become somewhat prominent in the government of Lamath."

"One of my subjects? Who?"

"I hesitate to mention his name—"

"Get to the point!" the woman screamed.

"It's Pelmen the player, my Lady!"

Ligne stared. Then she laughed. "In Lamath, is he? And alive?"

"Apparently, my Lady."

"Then Admon Faye has failed me. But go on! What's Pelmen got to do with the dragon burning up my kingdom?"

"It seems, my Queen, that it was Pelmen who started the dragon's current erratic behavior."

"I'm not surprised. That idiot actor is incredibly skilled at getting under one's skin."

"Perhaps Pelmen could calm the beast as well."

Ligne laughed so hard that she choked. "Pelmen? A dragon-tamer? Kherda, you're getting senile!"

"You forget, my Lady, that Pelmen is said to be powerful outside the land. Perhaps he—perhaps he has some power that might be—"

"Ridiculous!" Ligne cackled. Then she licked her lips and thought a minute. "Still, it's worth a try. Where can we get in touch with this fool?"

"Through General Asher, the Chieftain of Defense and Expansion of the Kingdom of Lamath."

"I suppose you know where this General may be contacted?"

"I could have a bird directed to the palace, if that is what you wish—"

"Not *a* bird, Kherda. A hundred birds. A thousand! We will fill the sky of Lamath with blue flyers!" For the first time in days, Ligne flung open a shutter and gazed out. "Pelmen shall know his presence is required at Dragonsgate—by order of his Queen!"

Pelmen and his three initiates had read and re-read the book to one another for days, but they still hadn't wrested any solution from its pages.

"We're n-not going to find anything!" Rosha burst out, his frustration getting the better of his patience.

"We will too!" Bronwynn snarled back at him. She was just as frustrated as he, but was unwilling to relinquish the idea that somewhere in the book they would find some key. "It's got to be here!"

"I'm thinking the lad's right," Erri muttered softly, and the young couple turned to look at him. "Seems to me if the writers of that book knew how to control the twi-beast, they would have done it themselves." The little man's eyes flickered over to Pelmen, who had been sitting in morose silence throughout the morning. "I think perhaps the Prophet is agreeing with me."

But Pelmen said nothing, preferring to keep his own sullen counsel. They all knew what he was contemplating. Try as they might, their words hadn't pierced his gloom. He was reviewing the doom Serphimera had pronounced on him.

"You shouldn't worry about it, Pelmen!" Bronwynn pleaded. "She's just a crazy woman who gets a thrill out of getting others swallowed! Forget her!"

"Oh, she's far more than that," Pelmen murmured, and he rose to stroll around the hot tent for the twentieth time.

"But she's robbing you of your—your creativity!" the girl continued. "If Erri's right, if the writers of the book expected you to find a solution, you need to concentrate! You need to—"

The flap of the fish-satin shelter was thrown open, and Asher strode in. "Still struggling, I see. No results?"

"How can we make any plans when he won't take his mind off that imposter Priestess?" Bronwynn snapped.

Asher's reply was uncharacteristically gentle. He touched the girl's cheek lightly, and said, "Don't be too harsh with your master. When it comes to Serphimera, I have the same disease." Bronwynn's eyes widened, and Asher, embarrassed, abruptly dismissed the subject. "But I didn't come to discuss that woman; I came to tell you news of another. I think, dear Princess, that this will be of particular importance to you. Rather, I should say, my Queen."

"Queen?" Bronwynn asked.

Rosha echoed her. "Q-queen?"

Even Pelmen snapped out of his reverie to listen to this news.

"Yes, my Lady, you appear to be a Queen without a kingdom. At any rate, that is what my foreign-policy advisors have concluded. It seems a woman named Ligne has usurped your father's throne."

"Ligne!" Bronwynn spat.

Pelmen leapt over to grasp Asher's arm. "How did she accomplish that!"

"Through guile, I would wager, having heard a bit about this Ligne from the local merchant houses. But I really don't know. All I can say is that the skies of Lamath are filled with blue flyers this morning, and they all bear the same message. It's to you, Prophet." Asher extended the note to Pelmen, who grabbed it and read it aloud:

"*Pelmen, the so-called Prophet. They tell me you are*

*powerful. Report at once to Dragonsgate and dispose of
the dragon. By order of your Queen. Ligne.*"

"That woman is no Queen!" Bronwynn cried, her
hands forming into claws unconsciously.

"Oh, but it appears she is," Asher observed. "For the
moment, at least."

"But what about my father?"

"I saw your father in Dragonsgate over a week ago."
Asher's face grew very grave, and he spoke more softly.
"There is a strong possibility that your father is dead."

Bronwynn's mouth opened slightly, and her breathing
turned shallow. Then she spun on her heel and faced
Pelmen. "We have got to get rid of this beast!" Her
eyes were flashing fiercely—they were also filling with
tears.

"Bronwynn, that's what we've been trying to do for
days."

"We haven't been doing anything! We've just sat
here talking, while you've moped around!" A tear
streaked down the girl's face, and she frowned the more
savagely as she felt it drop. "It's time for us to move!"

"I'm with h-h-her," Rosha said proudly, and Erri had
to hide his smile behind his new blue tunic.

"But Bronwynn," Pelmen soothed, "you are the one
who has been so insistent that we plan well before we
begin! Rosha, what's your father's favorite saying about
battle?"

Rosha turned away from Pelmen's searching eyes,
and muttered, " 'If you plan it well, you can capture
hell—' "

"And it's true," Asher broke in. He put his hand on
Bronwynn's shoulder and spoke with a fatherly tone.
"The Prophet is right. We really cannot go toward Dragonsgate unprepared. We will never win the battle
against this hideous monster unless we—"

The sound of clattering hoofbeats beyond the tent's
thin walls caught the attention of everyone within. A
messenger burst suddenly through the flaps.

"What is it?" Asher demanded, for no messenger
would dare enter his tent unbidden unless he heralded
some major crisis.

"The Priestess, my Lord Asher!" the messenger

cried out breathlessly. "She and the ugly southerner who carries her have broken through our southern watch! They ride even now to Dragonsgate!"

Asher and Pelmen gaped at each other, thunderstruck. "She's going for ultimate devotion!" Asher shouted.

"Then let's get on the road!" Pelmen blurted back, and both men exited the tent at a dead run.

Rosha, sensing freedom at last from this life of books and talk, grinned broadly. "That was fast! I wonder what made the difference?" He added this last to tease Bronwynn, who was visibly fuming. She whipped around and shoved her pretty nose into his face.

"Don't you mean *who* made the difference?" She flung the book into a corner, setting the walls of the tent a-quiver, and stamped out to get ready to travel. Erri fetched the book tenderly from the corner, and patted it free of dust.

"Do me a favor, lad," he said. "Don't anger her while she's handling the book. The next time, she'll likely aim for your head, and I'd hate to see either of you damaged."

The keeper of Flayh's dungeon knocked respectfully on his master's door. He felt very out of place, and was sure his uneasiness showed. He had dwelt so many years below the surface of the earth that this height made him feel dizzy.

"Get in!" came a muffled shout, and the keeper anxiously entered the room.

Flayh stood by a window, gazing to the south. "My nephew Pezi will be arriving at the gate in a few moments—"

"From the south?" the keeper exclaimed. "How did he avoid the drag—" He stopped. Flayh had turned to look at him, and the old merchant's facial expression had silenced him as forcefully as a scream of command.

"Did I say that he was arriving from the south?" Flayh asked.

"No, my Lord, but you were looking south—I just thought—"

"Have I ever asked you what you were thinking?"

"Ah, no—"

"Then what makes you think I want to know your thoughts now?"

"Nothing, my Lord."

"You stink of a flower bed! Why?"

"Ah, you told me to clean up, master, sir. You told me I stink, and that other soldiers would not want to stand beside me in battle—"

"Other soldiers still won't stand beside you in battle! Get to the far side of the room!"

The keeper hustled to obey Flayh's order, and the old merchant turned back to his window and breathed deeply. "Pezi arrives even now at the gate. He's come from the north with news of a most critical nature." Flayh turned to spear the keeper on a cold stare. "Greet him, and bring him to me immediately."

"Yes, my Lord." The keeper moved swiftly to the door.

"And, keeper."

"Yes, my Lord."

Flayh smiled. "Pezi has grown accustomed to preferential treatment in the court of the High Priest of Lamath. He needs to be reminded what home is like. Treat him none too gently, do you hear?"

The keeper grinned. Here was the old master at last! "Yes, my Lord!" he gloated; then he disappeared into the stairwell.

A few minutes later Pezi came hurtling into his uncle's hideaway, landing in a blubbery pile at Flayh's feet. There he cowered, expecting to be slapped or booted—or at the very least, spat on.

"Welcome, nephew."

Pezi cleared his throat. "Hello, uncle."

"You may rise. Unless you like it down there."

Pezi mumbled, "Thank you." He pushed himself to his feet.

Flayh waited until his cringing nephew looked him in the face; then he smiled again. His smile, as always, made Pezi wince. "How did you find the capital of our fair land?" Flayh asked gently.

"It was still there when I left—"

Flayh chuckled. "A sensible reply, in light of present

developments. Sit down, sit down, tell me of your journey." Flayh sat at his triangular table, and Pezi felt behind him for a stool and sat uneasily. Something was very wrong with Flayh, he decided. "Perhaps something *is* wrong with me," Flayh agreed out loud, and Pezi fell off the stool. Flayh cackled.

"How did you—"

"Read your thoughts?" Flayh laughed. "I don't know!" The old merchant laughed until tears came. Pezi retrieved the stool in the interval, and pinned it to the floor with his bottom. Flayh's chuckles subsided at one point, but began again when he caught sight of Pezi's puzzled expression. At last the old merchant grew calm. "I don't know," he repeated. "The power just comes and goes. Some days I hear nothing, I see nothing. Other days, events a hundred miles away unfold here, in this room. Where are your cousins?"

The abrupt change of subject caught Pezi off guard, and as he began to stammer out some spur-of-the-moment lies, Flayh's cackling began afresh.

"You cannot lie to me, nephew," he said merrily. "I saw the dungeon where you left them, when you left your thoughts unconcealed. Oh, yes!" he went on, "I know that you had the power to free them, but chose to leave them there!" Pezi shrank away from Flayh's bright smile. Flayh's voice softened. "It's all right, nephew. They were fools and hangers-on, and we're well rid of them."

"You're not angry?"

"Angry, nephew? Of course not. I'm positively pleased. I had a vision of you one day, Pezi—lying and scheming with the High Priest of Lamath—and I thought to myself, There's a chance, just a chance, that Pezi could pull this off." Flayh chuckled, and pulled his chair closer to Pezi. "Now then. The news. What's become of this Prophet fellow?"

"I don't know," Pezi replied honestly. "After Asher halted his execution, they took him off to the dungeon. The city was in an uproar, and that's when I left."

"Asher stayed his execution? I wonder why."

"I really didn't wait around to find out, uncle. But it

seems now that it must have had something to do with the dragon!"

"The dragon, yes—" Flayh said to himself, and he walked to the southern window again and gazed up at Dragonsgate. "I've seen the twi-beast in the air a dozen times in the last week, but he has yet to touch this place."

"The rest of Lamath should be so lucky!"

"Why? What did you see?"

"Blackened fields—whole gardens of vegetables burned beyond—"

"Enough about vegetables," Flayh said curtly, waving his hand as if to knock the thought away. He continued to gaze southward. "I had worried that this Prophet might be some threat to our security until the dragon went on this rampage. But since we dwell in the shadow of Dragonsgate, I doubt a soul in northern Lamath will concern himself with our little villa now."

"I wish I felt so secure," Pezi muttered. "Pelmen has been an enemy for so long—"

"Pelmen!" Flayh was staring at Pezi, hard. "Who said anything about Pelmen!" The old Flayh was visible in the merchant's scowl, and Pezi began to tremble.

"Why, you. I mean, didn't you? I thought, I assumed, that—"

"Speak up!" Flayh screamed, and Pezi spoke rapidly.

"I assumed you knew the Prophet was Pelmen! Oh, please, Uncle Flayh, I didn't realize—"

"Silence!" Flayh screamed again, and a hush settled over the tower chamber. Flayh jerked around and looked once more to the south, and Pezi heard him breathe again, "Pelmen."

Pezi marveled at Flayh's tone. Was it envy he heard? Why would Flayh envy anyone, especially this dangerous vagabond? Or was that a tone of respect? Ridiculous. Flayh honored nothing and no one. Fear, then? Well they might fear Pelmen, Pezi thought, for the powershaper-turned-Prophet had built enormous influence among the populace of this sizable nation, even if he had stirred the wrath of the majority. But it really wasn't fear he had heard in Flayh's voice. Flayh seemed to have some sense of longing, as if—

"Not yet," Flayh suddenly announced, and Pezi stared at him in bewilderment. "I am not ready—yet. I'd sooner face the dragon."

"Pardon me, uncle, but I don't know what you are talking about."

"Don't unpack your things, Pezi. I want you to be ready to leave at a moment's summons."

"But where—"

"Should Pelmen pursue you here, he will not find you or me. I'll watch the northern mouth. When the dragon ventures out of his lair again, we start."

Pezi blanched. "To—to try to pass Dragonsgate? While the dragon is a-burning?"

"At the present, nephew, I would rather face this dragon than Pelmen. Get out! I need to think this through."

"We'll try to pass Dragonsgate while the beast is gone?"

"Did I not tell you to get out?" Flayh asked.

"But what if he returns while we're crossing?" Pezi asked. His round face had turned the color of an eggshell. "What then?"

Flayh stared out at the mountains, painted now in stark silhouette by the fading light of the sunset. "Leave the dragon to me, nephew. That day may be one when I have my abilities about me—and I'll show Vicia-Heinox some illusions that will set his two heads spinning!"

Pezi left the room, his hands trembling and his knees weak. He didn't know what chilled him most—the thought of meeting Vicia-Heinox again, or Flayh's parting smirk. The old man was definitely crazy.

❧ Chapter Sixteen ❧

THE WIND whistled around them, and Serphimera had to shout to make herself heard above the noise. "Why aren't we turning south?"

"Leave the navigation to me, Lady," Admon Faye yelled back as he urged their pony on with a boot to its flanks. "I got you past the soldiers, didn't I?"

"I don't question your cunning, Admon Faye, but neither do I trust it. I chose you to bring me to Lord Dragon because of your efficiency in dealing with enemies, but you have given me cause to doubt the sincerity of your devotion!"

"When we get to Dragonsgate, you'll see who I'm devoted to!" Admon Faye yelled back. He was being honest, if unpleasantly so.

Serphimera had good reason to question Admon Faye's motivation in making this trip. They had been within sight of the pass for days, but the slaver had chosen to take them through the dry hills at its base in a zigzagging path that seemed to lead them no closer to it. A dozen times she had felt that they were clearly aiming for the pass, but then, in the name of avoiding Asher's soldiers, the ugly slaver would backtrack away again.

"And when will we get to Dragonsgate?" she demanded.

"When the soldiers aren't blocking the road," Admon Faye growled. That was a lie. They would get to the pass just moments before Pelmen arrived there, if he had his way. Days before, he had purposely revealed himself and his celebrated passenger to a small troop of Lamathian warriors, then had easily given them the slip—all merely to draw Pelmen to Dragonsgate. Admon Faye had uncovered something in Serphimera she hadn't realized was there, and he wagered that Pelmen felt the same.

"Love the Prophet? Me? Ridiculous!" the woman snorted whenever he brought it up. But there was something there. Admon Faye could sense it, just as he could sense the whereabouts of fools in the forest at night. "You're badly mistaken!" Serphimera would scream. "Ride on! Faster!"

"Just why do we ride at all, my Lady?" he often smirked. "Is it to the dragon we're racing? Or just away from Pelmen?"

"The pass is just above us!" she pleaded now in his ear. "Take us into it!"

"Tomorrow, my Lady," Admon Faye told her, and this time he really meant it. In their weavings and wanderings that day, he had spotted Pelmen and his entourage far below them. "Tomorrow you'll meet your lover—whoever he may be."

They sat encamped on the north-mouth field, at the foot of Dragonsgate. Serphimera had not been apprehended, but she and Admon Faye had been spotted that very morning in the foothills above them. Pelmen sat on a rock, talking to the Power.

"I'm assuming there is some reason for all of this," he said, and a breeze came up and blew tangles in his hair. "The girl is a Queen now, of course. She needs someone to win her back her throne." Still the breeze blew. "But I suppose Rosha will do that for her."

The night was passing by quickly. Soon the rocky teeth of the Spinal Range would be visible against the sun's first glow. "The boy needs more teaching. Who else is capable of taking him in hand?" The breeze died away, fading slowly into stillness. "Yet he's already a hero. A bear's-bane—battled Admon Faye and survived—what further need has he of me?"

More time passed. "What about Serphimera? Someone has to protect her from her own zealous nature!" There was a stillness in the air—the kind of stillness possible only on the desert. "But Asher would willingly accept that assignment. And she'll certainly never listen to me."

The sky turned purple, and then pale blue, before Pelmen spoke again. "All right," he said. He held in his mind a picture of the dragon tearing him in two, and gave assent to it. "All right."

"I thought I might find you here."

Pelmen jerked up. It was Asher, come to join him in his sleepless deliberations. "You should be in bed," Pelmen said, unconsciously rubbing his injured shoulder.

"I couldn't sleep, any more than you could. I've tossed and turned all night, thinking of dragons and death. I could wait for you no longer. Prophet, please— do you have any plan?"

Pelmen licked his lips. "I think so." Then he looked at Asher. "But I don't think you're going to like it any more than I do."

The sun came on up before the two men left the field. They were welcomed back to camp by silent, anxious faces. They planned throughout the early morning. Then, by noon, they were ready to march on the hell of an occupied Dragonsgate.

"What if he's here? What if he's here?"

"Whine that once more, nephew, and I'll have you barbecued when we reach Tohn's keep!"

"If I'm not barbecued before we reach Tohn's keep." Pezi shuddered.

They were climbing the last incline into Dragonsgate itself. In a moment they would turn the corner, and they would know at last if Vicia-Heinox were at home.

He was.

"He's here!" Pezi moaned, very near tears.

"Don't you think I can see that?" Flayh snapped.

The dragon, exhausted by his constant travel, had been sleeping. Now one long neck uncurled from the gigantic, scaly ball of his body and craned down to look at these two tiny intruders. "Wake up, Vicia," said Heinox.

The other head did not open its eyes, but answered, "I would think, after all this time, that you would know that when you wake up, I have to wake up too."

"Then get up and come look. We have visitors."

"Human visitors?"

"That's right."

"Ridiculous. No human has come near us in days." Vicia snuggled down into the curve of their tail. "You've been dreaming. Come on, let's go back to sleep."

Heinox leaned down and nipped the exposed end of their tail, feeling that the shock of pain was well worth the aggravation it would cause his other half.

"Why did you do that?" Vicia roared, suddenly wide awake and thirty feet in the air.

"Look," Heinox said calmly, and Vicia saw Flayh and Pezi cowering next to the rocky wall of the canyon.

"There really are humans in the pass!"

"I don't lie."

"It's just difficult to imagine any human being that stupid. Should we burn them, or do you need a light snack? You could have the fat one—"

"The fat one is Pezi, isn't it?"

"Pezi?" Vicia bent down to investigate, stopping two feet from the shaking merchant's face. Then he lifted back up to speak with Heinox. "It *is* Pezi. Do you want to eat him or shall I?"

"Uncle Flayh?" Pezi stammered. "Ah—were there some—ah—tricks you were going to use?"

"I'm trying to remember how they go—"

Pezi groaned loudly.

"What did you say?" Heinox asked, coming down out of the heavens to look at Flayh.

"I said, 'Let us pass!' I am a merchant, as is my nephew! I am a member of the Council of Elders of the merchant families! Our organization has a long-established tradition of service to your Dragonship, which it would not be in your best interests to end."

Vicia looked at Heinox. "He talks like a merchant. Let's see how he tastes."

Flayh stumbled backward in shock.

"What my other head is trying to say," Heinox explained, "is that we no longer wish to maintain any relationship with humankind, except that relationship dictated by our stomach." He was moving closer and closer to Flayh, who suddenly waved his hands in the air and shouted some gibberish.

The heads looked at one another, then both slid in closer to the two merchants, pinning them against the cliff face.

"Was that one of your tricks?" Pezi whimpered, his disappointment very much in evidence in his voice.

"I'm afraid so."

"Did it work?"

"Does it look like it worked?"

Pezi stared up into those approaching jaws and was saying his good-byes to life, when Flayh finally lost his temper. He threw his hands into the air and screamed a series of curses so foul they would have curled the toenails of a troll. Then a most spectacular event took place. A gigantic ball of very white-hot light exploded in the dragon's two faces, and suddenly Vicia-Heinox was blind. So was Pezi.

"What was that? What happened? Where's the light? Am I dead?"

"Come on, you fool!" Flayh shouted, and he grabbed the reins of Pezi's pony from the fat man's hands and led his nephew's mount into Ngandib-Mar at a gallop.

No one was more surprised than Flayh himself—he had worked on that trick in his study for weeks, with little sign of success. But there would be plenty of time to give a logical explanation of his achievement once they were safe. What was needed now was a place to hide, for the flash would not blind the beast forever. All of the woods had been burned off the mountains. They broke out onto the plain and turned sharply to the north. As they rode for their lives, they heard Vicia-Heinox scream behind them in frustration.

Admon Faye heard that chilling scream above them, and for the first time in many years his courage faltered. He stopped the pony.

"Go on!" wailed Serphimera. "What kind of a devotee are you? Go on! We're almost there, can't you see?" The Priestess was pounding on his back and pointing past his ear to the summit. She had worked herself into a frenzy of fear and excitement, and her voice was raspy from her constant screaming.

At last Admon Faye kicked the pony and urged it upward, but not from any sense of devotion. He could hear Pelmen coming in the pass below them.

As he guided the pony over the top of the climb and into the heart of the pass, Admon Faye was analyzing options. His hunch had proved right. He had lured Pelmen to Dragonsgate, and with him the Princess Bronwynn. That he had succeeded in killing them both thereby was a foregone conclusion. What wasn't so clear was how he was to survive, himself, to enjoy the rewards Ligne would heap upon him. His eyes were open wide to every possibility as they entered the presence of the dragon. How pleased Admon Faye was to find that the dragon's eyes weren't open at all!

"You fool!" Vicia trumpeted. "You bumbling, scaly fool! Why do you continue to crash into me!"

"For the same reason, apparently, that you keep ramming me!" Heinox roared back. "Because I can't see a thing!"

Serphimera was trembling with anticipation as she fought to free herself from the saddle. Admon Faye caught her under her arm and ungently assisted her dismount—he flung her into the dust. There she crawled toward the arguing beast on hands and knees as Admon Faye spurred his horse past the dragon and rode hard into the steep southern mouth of the pass.

"Who's there! Someone's there! Show yourself to me, or I'll burn you away!"

It was Vicia who shouted this, and therefore it was to Vicia that the quivering Priestess addressed her pleas. "Oh Lord Dragon, please accept my ultimate devotion! I've labored long and diligently for you! Now I ask that you receive me to your bosom as a pure and final sacrifice!"

"What?" Vicia asked, waving his head from side to side as if that would restore his sight. "Who are you?"

"She's obviously one of your silly followers! Can't you tell that by her syrupy drivel?" Heinox was shaking his long neck. It seemed the bright spot in the center of his vision was fading.

Serphimera looked up at Vicia-Heinox in confusion. This was Lord Dragon, burner of cities, shatterer of lies, the god of her girlhood! This awesome master was all powerful, and yet—blind? Arguing? Divided? It couldn't be! "Lord Dragon is testing me!" she cried out, and she threw her hands up across her face and began to chant the creed. It was in this position Pelmen found her when, a moment later, he and his followers came clattering into the pass.

"Serphimera!" he called, and he swung himself down from Minaliss with his good hand and ran to grab her around the waist.

"What—what are you doing?" she gasped as he dragged her back and away.

"I'm trying to save you from being eaten!"

"But I want to be eaten! Let me go!" Serphimera jerked his hand to her mouth and bit down on it, hard.

"Who's there?" Heinox roared. His head whipped around the dragon's body, a clear indication of his panic. Was he surrounded by humans whom he couldn't see? "Who's there?" he screamed again.

Pelmen sucked on his wounded hand for a moment, but swiftly shot it out to jerk Serphimera back again when she tried to run for the beast. "What's wrong with the dragon?"

"He's pretending to be blind to test me!" Serphimera snarled as she struggled to free herself from his grip. "Let go! I must make the ultimate devotion!"

"You're going to stay right here!" Without considering the impropriety of his action, Pelmen tripped Serphimera back into the dust and sat on her. Then he motioned Rosha toward Ngandib-Mar. "Do it! Do it now!"

"Your Dragonship!" Rosha shouted as he ran to get behind Vicia-Heinox. "Your Dragonship!" he repeated when the beast seemed not to hear. One head slipped up and over the dragon's back to try to peer into Rosha's face. Suddenly, the boy was shaken by the enormity of it all. His memorized speech stuck in his throat, as he stared up at those gigantic jaws.

Pelmen bit his lip and struggled to keep his perch on Serphimera's back. He ached for the boy, as a director sweats and stews when his star actor is in trouble. Pelmen had originally intended Rosha's part for himself, but Asher and the others had refused to allow him to play it. Someone would have to do some very careful swordwork for the plan to succeed, and they argued that Pelmen's dislocated shoulder eliminated him from consideration. Outvoted by all involved, the Prophet had finally, unwillingly, acquiesced. Now he devoutly wished that he had stood firm in his resolve to do it himself.

"Who is it?" Heinox bellowed. Then abruptly the beast's voice softened, and he shouted gleefully, "It's a lad! I can see him, it's a lad!" Then Heinox remembered—he was surrounded by humans. "What are you doing here, boy?" he growled.

"I'm n-not a boy, your D-d-dragonship—"

"Then what are you?" asked Heinox. "Before being killed and eaten, of course."

Pelmen had prepared him for such threats, and the young warrior's courage was returning. He found his ever-hesitant tongue. "Do I have the honor of addressing Vicia or Heinox?"

"I'm Heinox—"

"That is indeed splendid, for it is you, Heinox, that I have come to serve!"

The dragon blinked. "What?"

Rosha launched into his memorized speech: "What lad of the Mar has not heard of the powerful Heinox, who sensibly regards himself as first and foremost a dragon, and never stoops to believe himself a god? What lad of the Mar, having heard that Heinox needed a champion, would turn his back on so wondrous a vocation? I have come, your Dragonship, in answer to your call, to accept that challenge to serve you. I will be your representative in battle against the odious Vicia!"

"The what?" asked another voice menacingly, and Rosha turned around to see that Vicia was behind him—and that Vicia, too, could see.

"The odious Vicia!" Rosha replied, hoping that the dragon would not ask him to explain. Odious was Pelmen's word, not his. He didn't know its meaning—just that it was bad.

Vicia evidently knew the meaning, for he howled angrily, and darted down to swallow Rosha whole. Heinox knocked him aside.

"You shall not swallow my champion."

Vicia stared at Heinox, startled. Then he groaned. "Heinox! We agreed days ago that we would never again side with men against one another!"

"I've changed my mind."

"We have already been made into fools by one man today! Will you make us fools again?"

"I will not allow you to eat this lad! He's my champion. If anyone eats him, I will."

Pelmen was nodding vigorously now at Asher. It was his cue. Asher strutted forward, cutting a splendid figure in a cherry-red robe, a startling change from his usual uniform of dark blue. Only Pelmen wore blue today . . . though Bronwynn and Asher and Erri had all pleaded with him to change his mind. "Vicia!" Asher called. "I must speak to the head named Vicia!"

"I am Vicia!"

"Perhaps you do not remember me, for when we met I was otherwise attired. But you sought that day for a champion, wishing to set my army against Talith's."

"You!" Vicia fumed. "You abandoned me!"

"My army abandoned you, but not I! I have returned, my Lord Dragon, to defend you against this impostor head who refuses to acknowledge your divinity!"

"My divinity?" Vicia snorted softly, and once again the dragon's vanity took control.

"The dragon is not divine, as the sensible Heinox kn-kn-kn—" Rosha's face froze into an expression of panic. Pelmen jerked at the sound of that unfaithful tongue's betrayal, and Serphimera used the distraction to roll him off and claw her way to her feet.

"What?" Heinox suddenly bellowed, looking closely at his stammering champion.

Asher rushed into his next line, attempting to cover Rosha's stumble. "Not divine? Not divine? Who is this that blasphemes the Lord Dragon?" He played his part to the hilt. He had been too long in politics not to have a bit of the actor in him.

But Heinox had noticed. "It's a stuttering, spluttering

boy who speaks, that's who! And *you* would fight for me? You can't even talk for me!"

Rosha's temper exploded. He jerked his greatsword from its scabbard and charged at the dragon, swinging wildly. Only one thing could save him.

That was Pelmen's voice. It lifted above the din, so golden, so commanding, that it couldn't help but claim the absolute attention of all the host gathered in Dragonsgate.

"Of course he can't, and wise of you to realize it! Only the quicker of the two heads would be capable of seeing through my little ruse! Please excuse our tasteless joke, noble Heinox—I am your true champion!"

Vicia turned to look at Heinox, and Heinox at Vicia, and both bent back again to peer down at Pelmen. They knew this voice. Oh, how well they knew it!

"You are the Pelmen!" Vicia snarled.

"You are the cursed Player who caused us all our troubles!" Heinox screeched.

"Of course I am! I'm Pelmen the player, come to finish the job I started! For Heinox, surely you cannot believe that it was better when you were nothing but half of a dragon?"

"I will chop *you* in half!" Vicia rasped, and he darted down at Pelmen with the speed of a comet.

Heinox, however, was faster. They cracked their heads five feet above Pelmen's scalp.

"Oh!" Vicia groaned, enraged. "Why do you do that to me? Why do you always do that?"

Heinox snorted. "He was starting to make sense."

"Don't listen to him, Lord Dragon!" Serphimera raced to clasp her arms around a single talon of the dragon's vast foot. As she clung to her god, she cried out in despair, "It's a trap! A trap designed to destroy you!"

Pelmen's brow creased in concern. A flick of his claw, and Vicia-Heinox could halve Serphimera. He raised his voice in raucous laughter. "Obviously, Heinox, this woman is nothing but another of Vicia's religious dupes!"

Asher sprang forward, ad-libbing earnestly to keep the plan alive. "You blaspheme the dragon!"

"I blaspheme him, if so you wish to call it!" Pelmen shot back, picking up the cue. "I will not believe the dragon is a god! The dragon is and shall ever be a dragon!" The two men began trading insults. As they shouted, Bronwynn and Erri raced to the dragon's feet and dragged a kicking, cursing priestess back out of danger.

Throughout this exchange, Vicia-Heinox sat back on his hind legs and watched in amazement. Old tensions reawoke in the beast, old insults were remembered. Pride and selfishness resurfaced in each mind, until once again the two heads hated one another, and these puny men in the dirt below became living symbols of their rivalry. And these two symbols were mortal.

"Fight!" screamed Vicia.

"Kill him!" roared Heinox. Asher grabbed for his scabbard, and Pelmen seized Rosha's greatsword. The blades flashed into the sunlight.

Serphimera broke loose from her captors long enough to shout, "I've seen your end, Pelmen! I know your doom!" Then they caught her again, and Erri clapped his hands over her mouth. But it was enough.

How will it come? Pelmen wondered to himself. Then he wondered no more. There was only time to fight, and a greatsword was not a one-handed weapon.

The two antagonists exchanged a flurry of blows, and Vicia-Heinox was frothing with excitement. It appeared that the dragon was trying to pull himself apart, for Heinox craned all the way around behind Pelmen and Vicia lined up behind Asher. Both heads cheered and hollered until the canyon rang with the clamor. Suddenly Pelmen jumped back, and held up his sword.

"A word with Heinox!" he cried, and Heinox immediately swept in front of him. Pelmen's heart pounded as he spoke his final lines. "My liege, this will not do. We wrestle in the dust as two lads. Champions must be mounted!"

"Then mount your steeds! Mount your steeds!" Heinox shouted.

"My liege, the champions of Kings ride horses. For a champion of the dragon, that is simply not enough."

"Then what? What would you ride?"

"*You,* my liege."

The idea struck Vicia-Heinox with the thunder of destiny. In both of his personalities the dragon saw in this the ultimate answer he had been seeking for weeks. "Done!" Heinox trumpeted aloud, and Vicia chorused, "Done!"

If Heinox had a chin, it was buried in the dirt as Pelmen climbed aboard the head. There were ridges along both sides of the huge skull, and he gripped these with his knees as the giant neck whooshed him into the air. Pelmen grabbed hold for his life, and stared in shock at the tiny figures of Rosha and Bronwynn forty feet below him. His head was spinning, but he closed his eyes and fought to relax. When he opened them again, it was to watch Asher ascending into the sky on Vicia's back.

But something was different about Asher now. Pelmen's mouth fell open as he realized what it was. Asher had torn his brilliant red robe from his body. Visible now was the garment he had worn beneath it all the way from Lamath—a flowing robe of vivid sky blue.

"No!" Pelmen shouted, but the shout was torn away by the whistling wind, for Heinox was hurtling him toward Asher much faster than he had ever traveled before.

"Fight!" Heinox roared as the two champions whisked past each other without crossing swords, and Vicia echoed, "Fight!"

Pelmen saw Asher's face as it flashed by—the man seemed frozen to his perch. He had replaced his sword in its scabbard, and now clung with both hands to the ridges along Vicia's head.

"Fight for me!" Heinox screamed again as they made another pass.

Pelmen called out, "Draw your sword, Lamathian coward!" But this time Pelmen saw Asher's eyes as well as his face. There was nothing there but death.

Asher rode astride Lord Dragon. He rode a beast he had worshipped throughout his life. He wore a gown Pelmen had believed would doom him—and his mission was to kill the most frightening beast known to man.

Asher had conquered whole nations for his King. He

had killed hundreds on the battlefields. He had directed the movements of thousands of men, while his resolve and courage never wavered.

But this was no mere army to be conquered, no mere nation to be defeated. This was Vicia-Heinox. He rode Lord Dragon. And Asher acknowledged again a simple basic truth. One cannot slough off a lifetime of conviction without any trace of guilt. It just wasn't that easy. The residue of fear remained.

"Fight me, Asher! You have to fight me!" Pelmen was yelling himself hoarse. The dragon would soon grow weary of waving its necks without seeing any action. They had to cross swords at the very least. "Asher, please! Fight me!" he yelled again, and the General seemed to wake. The blue-clad warrior at last pulled his weapon free, and the next time they passed the two swords clashed together. Vicia-Heinox was excited beyond measure.

Again they clashed, as the dragon's necks laced in and out. Pelmen was forced to grip the ridges with his good hand to keep from being tossed a hundred feet into the air. His knees were being rubbed raw, and his thighs were cramping.

"Now, Pelmen!" Bronwynn screamed. "Now!"

Now it must be, Pelmen thought to himself. He shifted his position to get a firmer leg-lock on Heinox' head, and painfully gripped his sword in both hands. Then he leaned down and spoke to Heinox. "Come in very close. Hold me close, and we will end this battle in a stroke!"

Heinox swooped down and back up, then jerked in beside Vicia and hung there. Tightly gripping the haft of his greatsword, Pelmen rammed the point home. But not in Asher. He slammed his sword deep into Vicia's right eye.

Heinox jerked back with an agonized scream, and Pelmen clung to his sword to pull it free. As long as he lived, he would never forget the look he saw on Asher's face. It was a crazy smile, a lost smile, a smile of victory and a smile of good-bye. In anguish beyond anything he had ever known, Vicia tossed Asher high into the air and caught him by the leg, as if he were but a diamond from a long-forgotten game.

Heinox screamed too, for the pain was torture to him as well as to Vicia. "You have killed us!" Heinox roared, and he tried to toss Pelmen as Asher had been tossed. The Prophet-player clamped his blood-soaked blade between his teeth and clung desperately to the dragon's head. He stayed on.

Serphimera screamed and Pelmen wept as both watched the fulfillment of the Priestess' vision. Heinox gripped Asher's free leg between his giant jaws, and Vicia-Heinox tore the General apart. Shreds of blue cloth fluttered to the ground, and Asher was gone.

Pelmen's palms were wet with sweat, and the knobby ridges along the dragon's skull were getting slippery. He would never withstand another attempted tossing. As Heinox screamed out a lament for his own lost life, Pelmen let go and jerked his sword from his mouth. He reversed its blade to stab downward, took a deep breath, and plunged it home, this time in Heinox' eye. Then he clung to its pommel with both hands, as the new spasm of pain rocketed through the monster. Vicia-Heinox shivered from his heads to his tail, and Pelmen was thrown from his seat.

It seemed then that everyone was screaming, except him. He was tossed from side to side and up and down, but the blade stayed fixed in the dragon's eye and his hands stayed closed on the handle. Suddenly the wind around him increased to such a roar that he knew he must be blown off, but he clenched his eyes shut and held on. When he opened them again, he was hundreds of feet above the ground. The dragon had taken to the air.

The pass filled with swirling dust as the beating wings launched the dragon skyward. Bronwynn fell to her knees, trembling. The dragon cleared the top of the cliffs and disappeared from view, and she buried her face in her hands, fearing that if she watched she would see her master tumble to his death.

Vicia-Heinox twisted onto its back, and Pelmen shouted in anguish as he felt himself fly loose and begin to fall. Though his left shoulder still burned with pain, he ignored the feeling as he threw his arms wide apart and began to chant.

Whether he was in that moment the powershaper summoning the wind, or the anointed Prophet of the Power and beneficiary of its grace, not even Pelmen knew. But something wondrous happened. As the pass filled with screams, there was a sudden, deafening roll of thunder that threw everyone to the dirt. Those who managed to peer up through the choking dust saw a sight they would never forget. Pelmen's swiftly falling figure suddenly floated upward—like a feather caught in a draft.

"Pelmen?"

Pelmen chuckled. "Not again. You mean I'm still alive?" His eyes fluttered open. There was Bronwynn, looking anxiously down at him. "How?"

"Don't you remember?" she asked, puzzled. "You did it!"

"Did I?" he said. His head was clearing, and he sat up. "The dragon?"

Bronwynn waved her hand, and Pelmen rolled over to look in that direction. Fifty feet away lay a lifeless mountain of scales. Vicia-Heinox was dead. Pelmen could hear someone weeping. When the lady shouted, he recognized her voice. It was Serphimera.

"You killed him, you murderer!" Serphimera sobbed as she knelt beside one of the twisted necks and stroked the dragon's hide. Pelmen got slowly to his feet.

"Yes, Serphimera—I killed him. He was never a god, my Lady. Can't you see that now? He was always just an idol that stood between the people and the Power."

"Yet we believed him—" she wailed.

"A religion, Serphimera—that's all the Dragonfaith was. A religion—never a living faith." Pelmen stood, and surveyed the pile of flesh, once so fearsome, grown so docile in death. "I didn't kill this religion, Serphimera. The Power did."

"I want nothing of your Power!" the priestess screamed at him. She gathered up her skirts and began to run. She ran to the northern mouth, toward Lamath, and disappeared down the defile.

"Shall I chase her, Prophet?" It was Erri, and Pelmen put his arm out to pat him on the shoulder.

"She won't run far. But I fear you *will* be chasing her, for many years to come. She'll not stop saying what she thinks, just because the beast has been silenced."

"But—how would I deal with her? You're the Proph—"

"Deal with her in love, Erri. Nothing else will pierce that cloud around her. Bronwynn?"

"Yes, Pelmen?"

"Bring me the book—I have some things I need to tell Erri before he goes."

Bronwynn jumped up obediently and trotted over with the volume. Pelmen took it and handled it fondly, feeling its cover and thumbing its pages. Then he thrust it out to Erri.

"Prophet," he said. "Here is your book."

Erri was shocked. "But—you are the only real Prophet! That is your book, not mine—"

Pelmen pushed the volume into Erri's hands and closed the little man's fingers over its edges. "Erri— you've found your calling. I'm still searching for mine." Erri gulped hard. "Come, friend," Pelmen continued. "Don't deny your vocation."

"But what about you? Lamath needs your—"

"Lamath fares better today than the other two lands, Erri. Especially since it has you to restore it. I'll be around, don't worry. But this task is yours. And the book."

"Yes, Prophet," Erri said humbly.

"And Erri—"

"Yes, Prophet?"

"Call me Pelmen."

Erri smiled, and they embraced. Then the little Prophet began trudging down the hill. He had donned once again his sky-blue robe, and it flapped around his sandals as he walked.

Pelmen rejoined Bronwynn, and smiled at Rosha. The boy's face was dark and hard with frustration.

"You think you failed, don't you?" Pelmen said. The young warrior would not reply. "You didn't fail. You tried. In fact, given a sword big enough, you would have split the beast in half by sheer savagery alone. Will you let a trip of the tongue rob you of your achievement?"

Rosha looked up, still surly. "What achievement."

"The winning of a name—Rosha, bear's-bane. And of a woman." Pelmen's eyes flicked down to Rosha's hand, twined in that of the young Princess of Lamath. Both Bronwynn and Rosha blushed, but Pelmen marked well that they didn't unclasp their hands.

There were unexpected hoofbeats in the southern pass, and all three of them jumped in surprise. It was a small troop of golden-mailed warriors—led by General Joss. Rosha felt for his greatsword, then remembered. It was still embedded in the dragon's eye. He felt naked.

Joss stopped his horse and dismounted. "When I spotted Admon Faye bolting from the pass below, I felt obliged to investigate. I'm glad I did." He walked to Bronwynn, who stood frozen in place—and dropped to one knee. "My Queen," he said, and the other golden warriors followed his example.

"Me?" Bronwynn replied quietly. "What of my father? My mother?"

"Ligne murdered your mother, my Lady. As for your father—I'm sorry—but he was slain on the west-mouth plain two weeks ago."

Bronwynn's face stiffened. "By the dragon."

"No," Joss said evenly, and her eyes shot open.

"Then by whom?"

The answer was so shocking the young couple had to lean on each other for support. "Dorlyth mod Karis."

"My—father?" Rosha gasped, stunned.

"If your father is Dorlyth mod Karis," Joss said, eyeing the young warrior as if intending to cut him down in reprisal.

"By Dorlyth," Bronwynn sighed, and she pulled free of Rosha's arms and smoothed down her golden garments. "Well then, General. What is—your next move?"

"I'd like to take you back to claim your rightful throne. An impostor sits in Chaomonous now—a lady you know well."

"Ligne," Bronwynn said, her thoughts far away.

"The same."

Bronwynn bit her lip. Then she looked up at Pelmen. "Where were we going to go next?"

"I never made any plans beyond today, Bronwynn," Pelmen said. "I didn't really expect to need them." He gazed at her face, his eyes serious. "You are free, must be free, to go wherever you choose. You are, after all, the Queen of Chaomonous. And a Queen waits on no man's decision."

Bronwynn looked over at Rosha. He had backed away a step and had been waiting for her to notice him again. He felt sorrow that it had been Dorlyth who had slain her father, but she could hardly blame him for that.

"Where are you going?" she asked him.

"I'm—I'm riding home to see my father. He told me to come home when I'd become a hero." Rosha smiled slightly. "It appears I—I have."

Bronwynn looked back at Joss and sighed. "Then I'll go with you." She didn't see Rosha's smile die as she walked to take up the reins of her little white pony.

"You spoke of Admon Faye," Pelmen said forcefully. "Where is he now?"

Joss looked at the meddlesome player contemptuously—for so Pelmen was, to him. "Riding for his hideouts in the Great South Fir, being pursued by a contingent of my men. Oh, we'll catch him eventually, Pelmen. You needn't worry yourself over that."

Bronwynn rode to join the Chaon party, and Pelmen noticed now that Rosha had retrieved his greatsword from the dragon's eye and was mounting up as well. The youthful bear's-bane patted his horse's flanks, and they trotted over to join the group. Bronwynn looked up at Rosha's face. His expression echoed a look she remembered Dorlyth's face wearing—stony, unflinching, unfeeling where women were concerned. She pointed a finger at him.

"Listen. Just because I have to go claim my throne doesn't mean you're free. I'll see you again, Rosha mod Bronwynn!"

Rosha's eyes widened. Gone was that rock-hewn expression, replaced by a boyish blush. Pelmen stifled a laugh.

"My—my Lady," he stammered, this time with reason. "A Mari woman does not call a man her treasure unless she intends to marry him!"

"I know that!" Bronwynn snapped. "I'm not stupid, you know! Joss, away!" She was gone then, riding south at the head of a troop of golden warriors, and Rosha thought as he watched her go that he had never known anyone so fit to be a regent.

At length he sighed, and looked at Pelmen. "Ready to g-go home?" he asked.

Pelmen's eyes dropped. "No, Rosha. Not just yet. Tell your father I may be there in a few days, or weeks." Then Pelmen shrugged. "Or maybe years. He knows me."

"Indeed he does." Rosha smiled. Then the young warrior cleared his throat. "I remember what you c-called the old Elder at the m-monastery. For you and for him, it seemed—fitting. Somehow—it does to m-me as well. Fare you well, my father."

Pelmen nodded, smiling. "And you, my brother." Then the horse wheeled at Rosha's command, and galloped swiftly down and out, onto the west-mouth plain.

Pelmen folded his blue robe carefully and put it on the ground. By now, the sun had set on Dragonsgate, and Pelmen had spent several hours in quiet conversation with the dead beast that had given the place its name—and with the Power. Now he grinned, and held out his hand. For the first time in what seemed like ages, a little ball of blue flame blazed in the air at his command. Pelmen pointed to the robe, and the ball dropped down onto it and quickly consumed it. Pelmen glanced at the sky, and spoke. "I hope you don't mind, but there's so much to do yet. And I don't think I'll be able to move freely as a holy man—"

A sense of peace stole over him, a warm blanket of good feeling. The Power, he realized again, was real—and it was pleased. It really didn't matter where or how he traveled now. The Power would meet him there, wherever it was.

He sighed, stood, and looked around at the darkness. "Where to go, who to be," he said aloud, then leaned back and looked up again. "Will there be a time, ever, when I can be all my selves at once?"

Not, he answered himself, while the world remained in such confusion. There was still so much to do. Pelmen mounted Minaliss, picked a direction, and began his long ride out of Dragonsgate.

About the Author

Robert Don Hughes was born in Ventura, California, the son of a Baptist pastor. He grew up in Long Beach, and was educated in Redlands, Riverside, and Mill Valley, gaining degrees in theater arts and divinity. That education continues as he finishes a Ph.D. in Missions, Religions and Philosophy in Louisville, Kentucky.

He has been a pastor, a playwright, a teacher, a filmmaker, and a missionary, and considers all those roles fulfilling. He has published several short plays, and presently teaches drama. He is currently the pastor of a rural Kentucky church. He spent two years in Zambia, and while there was bitten by the Africa bug; he hopes to return to live and work on that continent soon. His two passions are writing and football—not necessarily in that order, especially in October. He is married to Gail, a beautiful South Alabama woman who loves rainbows, and fills his life with them.

Most of all, Bob likes people. The infinite variety of personalities and opinions makes life interesting. The sharing of self makes it worthwhile.

LEIGH
BRACKETT

You'll find all that is possible and more...in the fantasy of Evangeline Walton and Katherine Kurtz.

Available at your bookstore or use this coupon.